Praise for *FLED*

"Captivating . . . A tragedy of epic proportions . . . The reader can't help feeling implicated as a spectator of unimaginable hardship."
—*The New York Times Book Review*

"A sweeping, heart-wrenching account of one woman's life-long search for freedom . . . based on the true story of Mary Bryant, an iconic figure in the foundation lore of Australia as Great Britain's penal colony."
—*Fantastic Fiction*

"The pages fly by. Keneally's tale of this fierce, passionate, unstoppable woman will leave you breathless—and wanting more. An epic story of love and liberty."
—Elizabeth Cobbs, bestselling author of *The Hamilton Affair* and *The Tubman Command*

"Grabs you by the collar and yanks you through a riveting story of unexpected twists and turns that will leave you breathless. Jenny Trelawney Gwynn is fierce, brash, and independent. She may be an eighteen-century convict, but she's a heroine worthy of our twenty-first century #MeToo moment."
—Stephanie Storey, author of *Oil and Marble: A Novel of Leonardo and Michelangelo*

"A real page-turner, this breathtaking yarn will keep you on the edge of your seat."
—Dr. Jonathan King, author of *Mary Bryant: Her Life and Escape from Botany Bay*

"An irresistible feast of history, adventure, intrigue and tragedy. Epic yet tender. Authentic yet inspired."
—Clare Wright, author of *You Daughters of Freedom*

FLED

FLED

A NOVEL

MEG KENEALLY

ARCADE PUBLISHING · NEW YORK

First North American Paperback Edition 2021

First published in Australia by Echo, a division of Bonnier Zaffre.

This is a work of fiction. Names, characters, places, and incidents are either the products of the author's imagination or used fictitiously.

Arcade Publishing books may be purchased in bulk at special discounts for sales promotion, corporate gifts, fund-raising, or educational purposes. Special editions can also be created to specifications. For details, contact the Special Sales Department, Arcade Publishing, 307 West 36th Street, 11th Floor, New York, NY 10018 or arcade@skyhorsepublishing.com.

Arcade Publishing® is a registered trademark of Skyhorse Publishing, Inc.®, a Delaware corporation.

Visit our website at www.arcadepub.com.

10 9 8 7 6 5 4 3 2 1

Library of Congress Cataloging-in-Publication Data
Names: Keneally, Meg, author.
Title: Fled : a novel / Meg Keneally.
Description: First North American Edition. | New York : Arcade Publishing, 2019. | First published in Australia by Echo, a division of Bonnier Zaffre in 2018.
Identifiers: LCCN 2019001630 (print) | LCCN 2019004906 (ebook) | ISBN 9781948924283 (ebook) | 9781951627843 (paperback)
Subjects: | BISAC: FICTION / Biographical. | FICTION / Literary. | FICTION / Contemporary Women. | FICTION / Historical. | FICTION / Romance / Historical. | GSAFD: Love stories.
Classification: LCC PR9619.4.K464 (ebook) | LCC PR9619.4.K464 F64 2019 (print) | DDC 823/.92—dc23
LC record available at https://lccn.loc.gov/2019001630

Cover design by Erin Seaward Hiatt
Cover illustration: © Vectorios2016/Getty Images (silhouette); © Howard Oates/ Getty Images (ship); © kentarcajuan/Getty Images (texture)

Printed in the United States of America

For Tommy

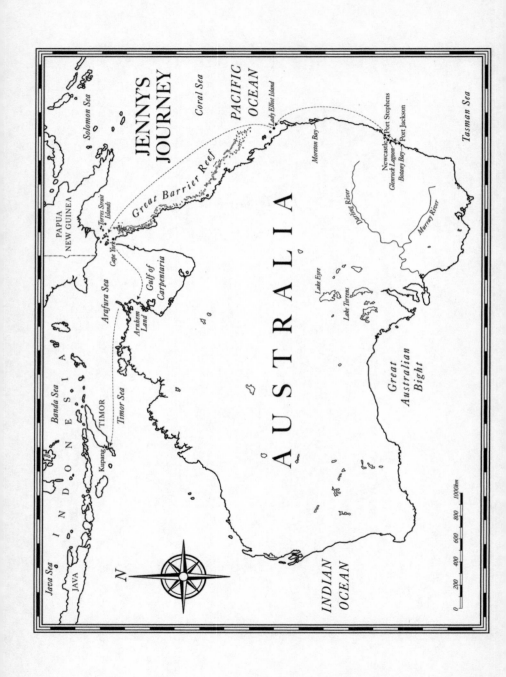

*F*LED

Somewhere in the Tasman Sea, off New South Wales,
April 1791

She never slept deeply, not here. Even if she had, this wave would have woken her, elongating up to the sky and then bending its force down onto their small boat.

She gripped the children before her eyes were fully open. She lived now with the humming fear of one of the ropes she had used to tie them breaking, of waking to find a child gone, of realising they had probably already travelled halfway through the blackness to the sea floor.

They were both there. If Emanuel was making any sound, she couldn't hear it, not above the wind. She couldn't hear Charlotte either, but the little girl's mouth was open, and stretched by terror. She was probably crying, but it was impossible to tell as the constant spray claimed all tears.

Her husband gripped the tiller in the fading light, sitting in water that stopped only a few inches from the gunwales. He was grinding his teeth, trying to keep the boat pointed into the waves, probably worrying that the sun would betray him by setting, and that the boat would suddenly find itself side-on to a salt monster.

Jenny had been dreaming of Penmor. Its stillness; its muted,

1

deadening light. Of her family's narrow, crammed house. Now, though, its door was splintered, its remnants hanging open on one of the hinges as though somebody had enjoyed pulling it out of its frame and destroying it.

She had called, or tried to, but it was a whisper. She inhaled, tried again, but no matter how much breath she added to it, the sound would not increase. In any case, there was no answer.

But someone was there. Her father was lying in front of the fire where they had put him after the wreck, still pale and swollen from the sea. Her mother sat in the same chair as always. Had she moved? Had she spent, in that chair, the years which had propelled her daughter over impossible seas to an implausible country?

Her mother started to speak, but her cheeks cracked from the side of her mouth to her ears, and instead of speech she ejected a blast of wind that sent Jenny back down the hill, into the dream sea, from which she surfaced into consciousness and the chaos of the waves.

It must've gathered quickly, this storm. There had been some chop when she'd gone to sleep in the late afternoon, and since then the winds had been pummelling the water into a new substance altogether, a landscape of moving mountains where no boat had any business existing.

And it wouldn't, not for long, not if they didn't start bailing. Carney was at the sail, trying to get it down before the wind punched a hole in it. But Harrigan was no use. He had retained enough consciousness to lift himself from the bottom of the boat when the wave hit, sitting up so that he looked like a duchess in a bath. But he still had that stare, still looked as though he was viewing a different world from the rest of them, one far more horrific.

Bruton, meanwhile, just sat there, hanging on to his bench, his eyes flicking from Jenny to her children. No doubt he was resenting them, useless passengers who contributed nothing to his survival. She rolled her lips together. Why in God's name did she always have to harangue the men? Why couldn't they see what needed doing and just do it? She kicked at the privy bucket, its edges sticking up from the water inside the boat. 'Bail, for God's sake! We'll founder, and soon! You have to bail!'

Bruton kept staring. Not the type to take orders from a woman who'd tied herself to a bench.

The boat was slowly grinding up a wave, which disappeared underneath them, sending them crashing down. The impact dislodged some of the water, but then added more, and when Jenny wiped her eyes she saw Bruton, stubborn but not stupid, frantically bailing with the privy bucket.

Somewhere beyond these waves was a place where their choices extended beyond drowning or starvation; where she wouldn't have to clench her arms around the children and tell the sea it couldn't have them. But they hadn't reached it yet. Sometimes, when the sea was at its worst, she wondered if they ever would.

PART ONE

CHAPTER 1
Southern Cornwall, 1783

The sea had killed him, they said. Jenny did not blame the sea. Jenny blamed the King: the man who taxed salt and windows and wigs to pay for a war in a place where people had decided they'd had enough of taxes.

So there was nothing left when the pilchards stopped coming, when the shards of silver that had swarmed around the boat every other summer vanished. Their disappearance had forced her father onto the night-time sea. It was hungrier than its daylight counterpart. It had consumed others in their village, sometimes vomiting them up onto the shore, sometimes simply removing them from the world of earth and sunlight.

Her mother was fussing, that morning. Dolly, serving at the big house on the hill now, always knew how to calm her. Jenny seemed only able to make her more anxious. Constance licked her fingers to remove an imaginary smudge from Jenny's face, although there were plenty of real smudges to be dealt with. Adjusting her shawl, sweeping non-existent dust out the door. Going to the window, where the extinguished stub of a tallow candle stood.

Will Trelawney had never been out all night. Constance would have heard the wind, as Jenny had, attempting to tear away the shutters and push open the door. Anyone on the ocean during that moonless night would have needed to be a lifelong mariner to survive.

Will was a lifelong mariner, with a thin, etched face that hinted at more than his forty summers. His father had taken him on the ocean before he could walk properly, Will once told Jenny, and he'd begun fishing when his age was still a single digit.

Perhaps Constance was rolling the thought of Will's competence over in her mind, looking for flaws. Jenny certainly was. She had sometimes seen sailors asleep in their small boats, too tired or drunk to head home. Perhaps her father was beginning to stretch, cursing the morning cold and the scolding he would get when he walked through the door.

When he did come through the door, though, it was clear he'd been floating in the sea for some time. His skin was white with a tinge of purple, particularly around his mouth, as though he'd tried to colour his lips with crushed flowers as girls sometimes did.

There was a gash on his forehead, and Jenny wondered if he'd been killed by a deliberate blow rather than by hitting his head as the ocean tipped him from his boat, the victim of a deal gone wrong. For smugglers, events could take a dangerous turn in the darkness of a Cornish cove. Harold Tippett and his son Stephen, men who had shared the ocean with Will, laid his body in front of the fire, with Harold cradling his head so it didn't flop back and hit the floor. Jenny wasn't sure what the point of the gesture was, but she was strangely glad of it.

Her mother sat, after Harold and his son left, her eyes flicking between Will and the fire.

'Ma,' Jenny said a few times. 'Ma, he can't stay here.'

'This is his home,' Constance said, and said no more.

Jenny knelt and kissed her father's forehead, felt the lack of intention behind it, saw nothing reflected in the half-lidded eyes. She felt the approach of abandoned grief, muted for the moment. It couldn't fully exist as long as Jenny told herself that this piece of flotsam which had taken her mother's voice was not her father.

The grief would come as soon as she admitted that the water-logged hands which lay on his chest had hauled nets with hers, had shown her how to tie ropes. She was not ready, yet, to concede that fact. There was no space for it next to her rising anger. She wanted to pound at the thing by the fire, ask it why it had taken her father's mind out to sea and hadn't carried it home. She wanted to take an axe to the boat, to burn it. She wanted to punish anyone who had profited from the penury that had sent her father to the night-time sea.

A small boy had once lived at the Trelawney house on the hill above Penmor Harbour, a narrow building like its neighbours, mean-windowed and crammed between other buildings which were distinguished only by their occupants. They were confronted in their cramped condition by the vastness of the ocean, and by the bravery of the little boats that punched through the estuary waves to reach it.

The boy in the Trelawney house, Nathaniel, had shared quarters with his parents while Jenny and Dolly gossiped and occasionally fought in the darkness of the next room.

Nathaniel stopped living there around three months after his birth, when a vicious winter drew his soul out of his body, leaving a meaningless amalgamation of flesh in the cot.

It was, perhaps, Jenny's fault. She did wonder. She'd been doing the work of a boy, even an infant who would not be up to it for some years. Perhaps he had slipped away because he felt he wasn't needed.

Jenny and her father were often driven onto the November sea by the revenue men, who sat like great toads, their mouths open, ready to gulp down whatever came in their direction.

After one blustery day, Jenny dumped out the contents of her creel for her mother's inspection.

'They're not as big as they were, are they?' Constance had said, turning each pilchard over, smelling it, running her fingers over the scales.

'Checking if one of them is a revenue man in disguise?' asked Will, coming in with an armful of firewood.

'Perhaps,' said Constance. 'How about this one?' She flung a fish across the wooden table on which the catch was laid out.

The pilchard struck Will in the chest, and he caught it before it fell to the ground. He tossed it back on the pile. 'Late in the season,' he said. 'Perhaps that's why.'

'You can tell these fish, then, that it's their fault your daughters wear old dresses.'

'Everyone does anyway,' said Dolly, guiding Jenny to the stool by the fire. 'I know it's fun to blame Pa – I enjoy faulting him for just about anything,' She smiled at her father, who winked. 'But mother, really, Jenny and I don't need new dresses.'

Dolly started trying, as gently as she could, to undo a knot that the wind had tied in Jenny's hair. A soft girl, Dolly, with well-behaved honey hair that refused to allow the wind to tangle it and concentrated instead on framing her delicate face to best effect.

Jenny shared Dolly's impish chin, her upturned nose and grey eyes, but her brown-red mop insisted on mimicking seaweed as often as possible. The matted, salt-crusted thicket was resisting even her patient sister's best attempts. Jenny was glad it was taking a while; she didn't want to move from the stool by the fire, even as it baked the salt into her clothes and hair.

'Jenny's dress wouldn't last, anyway,' said Constance. She walked over to the fire and lifted the snarl at the back of Jenny's head. 'How hard do you have to try to get it like this?' she asked, kissing her daughter's forehead.

'The wind does all the work,' Jenny said.

'Hm. Will, do you truly need her on the boat?'

He nodded. 'Half the deckhands have been press-ganged, and the rest are in the mines. She is good at it, too.'

Jenny knew she was. A girl of torn skirts and wet feet, a creature of the sea as her sister was a product of the hearth.

It was the hearth her father sat down in front of each night to remove his salt-soaked boots, while her mother wrinkled her nose and declared she preferred the smell of Nathaniel's worst emissions to that of her husband's feet.

One night, when her mother padded towards the back of the cottage, she did not return with the baby boy ready to settle at the fire and give up her milk. Constance's moan started softly. Jenny thought it was the wind, until the sound rose to a shriek as her mother carried the small, still bundle to the hearth.

It alarmed Jenny, later, that she could not remember Nathaniel's face. The thought that her parents might not be able to either alarmed her even more – it seemed cruel to her that he should exist, that his smiles should be answered and his cries attended to, and then vanish and become faceless thanks to the poor memories of those sworn to love him.

But she always remembered his absence, which swelled to occupy far more space than his presence ever had. It pushed her mother to the window, there to stand for half an hour, an hour, more. Putting all of her effort into staring; she must've done, for clearly she had no energy left to power her ears, which didn't seem to admit the entreaties of her daughters.

Before Nathaniel died, Jenny would often go out on the boat with her father. He would sit in the bow and tell her it was her job to watch the clouds, to let him know if any of them might become dragons, so he could bring the boat in.

For a time, the absence of his son pushed her father out alone, onto the estuary and past the two squat towers that guarded its entrance into the sea. He would even take his small boat out after a good catch, when he didn't need to, whenever he could find a deckhand to help with the ropes in the nets and sometimes even when he couldn't.

But with one son dead and no prospect of another being born, and a great many of the village's young men off fighting against the freedom they didn't understand, Will again brought his daughter out with him. This time, though, her responsibility extended beyond keeping an eye out for dragon clouds. This time, she needed to know how to mend a net on a heaving sea, how to reef a sail against a storm, how to set a net and haul it so that more fish ended up back in the boat than they did in the ocean. It helped that Jenny felt no fear at the sight of a saltwater hill bearing down on the boat, and that she didn't scream when they were caught side-on by a wave that threatened to return them to the sea.

Whenever wind began plucking at the ocean, she enjoyed standing or crouching in the bow. Her father would yell at her to sit down, but she could feel the ocean through her feet better than she could through her backside. She could know it.

When the village men came to take Jenny's father and put him in the earth, her mother seemed not to notice. Her eyes stayed fixed on the place where he had lain, and she made no attempt to draw her shawl around her when Dolly, given special leave from the scullery, placed it on her shoulders.

Constance stayed like that after nightfall, well after the house had been set to rights and the laundry done and delivered to those expecting it.

Then Jenny sat on the floor and hugged Constance's calves as though trying to prevent her from fleeing to the place where Will had gone. She rested her head on her mother's lap and wept silently into the rough folds of her skirt, allowing her mind to blur until she became insensible of her mother's hand creeping from her side and slowly stroking her hair.

CHAPTER 2

'It's ready, then?' Constance asked. 'We can sell it?'

There was no need for a boat in the Trelawney household, now. At least, not as far as anyone apart from Jenny was concerned. So she had decided to repair it before selling it, had spent the past few weeks making it right. A few timbers had been staved in by rocks where the sea had pushed the boat ashore, and some of the seams needed attention. It was easy work for a girl who'd held a pot of pitch while watching her father make winter repairs.

'Try not to let anyone see you,' her mother would say. A girl with a reputation for doing men's work might have difficulty finding a husband, particularly when that girl was already known as something of an odd one.

Jenny took her time, telling herself and her mother it was because she wanted to do the job right, get as good a price as possible. But she knew, as did her mother, that she was using the time to say goodbye.

Then the boat was fixed. Then the boat was sold. It brought in enough money to push away immediate penury, and Dolly took a position as a cook in one of the grand houses of a family who made gold from tin. But even with the wages she sent home, they would soon be in trouble again.

There was no work to be had, at least not in Penmor. Jenny was known everywhere as an unpredictable girl with an unladylike mouth.

Her mother didn't scold her for being such an unsuitable prospect. A dressing down would have required an interest in the outcome, and Constance seemed to believe that she no longer had a stake in anything, including her own survival. She continued taking in laundry but didn't give it the care she once had, so it was often returned late and in a poor state. Before long, she had only her own washing and a few items brought in by customers who wanted to show support, who believed her malaise was temporary.

Jenny had no such belief. Not on the days when she went out to pry limpets from the rocks and returned to find the fire unfed and her mother sitting, shivering and immobile, in the fading light.

'I'll go into Plymouth, shall I?' Jenny said to her one night, mainly to throw a stone in the silent pool between them. 'Might have better luck there, when it comes to work.'

'No one will know you there,' said Constance, keeping her eyes on the section of floor where Will had briefly lain on his journey from the ocean to the cemetery.

'That is probably all to the good, Ma.'

By lunchtime the next day, Jenny was further from Penmor than she'd ever been on land, although not nearly as far as her father had sometimes taken her out on the boat. She was not concerned about being robbed by a highwayman, who were said to be common in these woods; it would be plain to anyone hiding in the closely packed, crackle-branched trees that they weren't likely to get much of a bounty from this girl in her rough skirts, which might once have been blue and were perhaps not quite heavy enough for the advancing cold of autumn.

Still, when she heard hoofbeats and felt their vibration becoming stronger, she forced herself into an echoing trot, eyes on the road where forest creatures had excavated holes, perhaps for the pure delight of seeing travellers trip. As Jenny looked a bit too far ahead, she didn't notice a particularly narrow rut at her feet until it had snatched her toes out from under her.

The horse pulled up beside her. It was a sturdy animal, not the kind a lord would ride but better than most she'd seen. The rider – perhaps not richly dressed, but warmly so, in the kind of well-made clothes merchants favoured – dismounted and walked over to her. He didn't reach out to help her up. He put his hands on his hips and stood there, bent over and staring, as though trying to decide how best to use the grimy girl that providence had thrown into his path.

He is appraising me like he'd appraise a coat or a hog, she thought. *He is deciding whether I have any value, and I will not get any say in it.* She tried to stop her body from tensing, from betraying her intention to jump and swing and run.

But now the undergrowth was shifting and crunching, leaves being disturbed. When the merchant saw her glance over his shoulder, he half turned towards the sound. Another man, taller and broader, in shirtsleeves that would offer no protection from the oncoming winter, had stepped into the road behind the merchant. The second man, his features concealed by a broad-brimmed black hat, had grabbed the reins of the horse between one of Jenny's breaths and the next.

He smiled at the merchant, inclining his head slightly. 'I prefer not to stave anyone's head in, particularly this early in the day,' he said, and Jenny noticed a club in his belt coated with dark stains, likely the result of past stavings.

His mark clearly knew this dance. He swore and spat on the ground, narrowly missing Jenny. Then he started forward and reached into his jacket, drawing out a short, pitted blade.

Jenny doubted he could overwhelm the thief, not with a knife that would have trouble cutting an apple in half. But she hadn't liked the way he'd been examining her before they were interrupted. So she reached out, grabbed his ankle, and pulled.

The man was not quite quick enough to put his hands out as he fell, winding himself so that he lay face down, head to the side, gulping lungfuls of highway dirt.

The thief moved smoothly towards them both, fluidly drawing the club out of his belt. In a few seconds, he had one foot planted on either side of his victim. When the merchant rolled over, he found the club inches from his nose. The thief said nothing, and didn't have to. His victim inched backwards, trying to get far enough from between the man's legs to sit, stand and run.

'Your jacket,' the thief said.

The smaller man, still wriggling backwards, allowed his momentum to draw his arms out of the jacket. His shirt, which had been hidden, was covered in brownish and yellowish stains. He left the jacket on the ground and stood, the tip of the club tracking his nose.

The thief bent to pick up the jacket, running his arm through the loop of the horse's reins as he did so. 'Thank you,' he said, and the smaller man turned and ran in the direction he'd come from.

The thief didn't seem to notice Jenny. He walked to the saddlebags and drew out a purse, hanging the jacket over the pommel and mounting the horse in a smooth, practised arc.

Jenny got to her feet, thinking to step to the side of the road among the bushes, but the thief turned in the saddle and threw something in her direction. She flinched, and he laughed and inclined his head to where the object lay on the road. It was a silver coin.

'For your assistance,' the man said.

She bent over, keeping her eyes on him so that she couldn't see exactly where the coin was, having to scrabble in the dirt with her fingers to find it.

He laughed, almost indulgently. 'I don't intend to hurt you – you've nothing to steal, and if you have any charms that might interest me, they're far too well hidden under those dreadful clothes.' He urged the horse on, coaxing it to walk a few paces before suddenly pulling back on the reins. 'Tell me,' he said, 'would you like more of that?'

Jenny didn't answer. She had no idea what he would expect in exchange.

'I would pay handsomely for you to fall in the road again, the next time a horse is approaching,' he said. 'Far easier to stop them that way than by jumping out and trying to grab the reins. Had my foot trampled once, would rather not have it happen twice.'

Jenny stared at this creature who discussed theft so casually, as though it was legitimate enterprise, as though he was musing on how to make a farm more productive.

He was clearly tired, though, of waiting for a response. 'I'm at the Plymstock Inn most nights,' he said. 'Don't suppose you know it, but most will when you get to Plymouth. I'll pay you well, as I already have.' He turned, kicked the horse's flanks and rode on.

Jenny turned too, in the other direction, clutching her coin hard enough to leaving an imprint on her palm. She began to run, heedless of the ruts in the road, back to Penmor. She was anxious to be near houses and people, and away from stands of trees that might hold men far less polite than the one she'd encountered. Anxious, too, to bring home the silver trophy, to see if it was valuable enough to buy a smile from her mother.

CHAPTER 3

She had seen enough highway robbers slowly losing their flesh at the Four Turnings to know the risks.

The noose, though, was not what prevented Jenny from going to the Plymstock and taking the thief up on his offer. He could hardly, she thought, be worse than the state-sanctioned thieves in government offices and on estates around the country. But he would be no better, and she had no intention of exchanging one type of servitude for another.

If she could operate in freedom, according to her own wishes, and at the same time dent those who enclosed lands or grew bloated on the proceeds of rotten boroughs ... the idea, really, was alluring. And the threat of the noose was no more disturbing than the threat of drowning when at sea – a possibility that was always there, and easier to ignore because of it.

Despite her excitement Jenny had decided, on the way home, not to show the coin to Constance. To return with such a prize might rouse her mother to ask questions. Jenny, more than most, was vulnerable to whispers. She told Constance she'd found work in an inn between Penmor and Polkerris, close enough for her to come home each day. Nothing fancy, without uniforms like

Dolly wore, unfortunately. Washing, scrubbing floors. Not the kind of work to give rise to questions when she came home. Intimately acquainted with washing and scrubbing floors, Constance didn't need to have those tasks described to her by her daughter.

There was no urgency – the silver coin would last some time after she had made a few purchases in other villages, to break it down into coins of the type that wouldn't raise suspicion. She listened to the highway's heartbeat, watched the ebb and flow, determined who was likely to be travelling at what time of day, and whether anyone else was likely to be watching from the side of the road. But sometimes she found it hard to convince herself that she wasn't about to take a step that could not be untaken, one on a road which could lead to her murder at the King's hands.

Jenny had never liked approaching the forest from the Penmor side. The Four Turnings had to be traversed to gain the trees, hardy specimens that had resisted the axes used to clear their cousins to make way for fields and mines all around.

The crossroads was where they displayed the bodies.

Occasionally someone from Penmor would find themselves at the end of a rope after being convicted of theft, poaching, smuggling, or any other act designed to transfer resources from the powerful to the powerless. They weren't hanged in Penmor, of course; the village was too small to boast a gallows. Usually the job was done in Plymouth or Portsmouth or Exeter. But that didn't mean the village which had spawned such sin should be spared the sight of what the King's justice left behind. So every now and then, the justices at the assizes would suspend a strangled son or daughter of Penmor at the Four Turnings, to rot while serving as an example should anyone else be thinking of transgression.

Many travellers crossed themselves or made less sanctified signs when they passed a carcass dangling there. Jenny would force herself to stare at the bodies, despite the inevitable creeping fear. She felt she owed them that much, that an averted gaze would be an insult; she imagined shadows climbing to the ground and dogging her steps.

But the dead weren't always there. Perhaps it was their absence that led Jenny to do what she did on the last day of June.

She risked a trip into Polkerris, buying some cheese and bread. She would just, she told herself, walk in a little way, so she could eat in the shade and the peace. The woods, surely, would not take that as a promise, a sign of commitment. She found a flat rock a little off the road, and sat and ate. She stayed there for hours, taking pleasure in surrounding herself with an element that belonged to no one – despite what the lords thought – and would not submit to the excise men.

There were others here, she could tell. She knew by the rustles, by the regular footfalls betrayed by leaves, and an occasional distant exhalation. They did not molest her, and she came to trust that they wouldn't. Perhaps they felt she was one of them.

She was, though, so intent on listening for footfalls from the forest that she nearly missed the ones coming from the road.

It was a man, she saw as she crept towards the edge of the trees. A young man, thin and with an unlined face. He had a decent coat on: well made, a nice thick wool, with a handkerchief in the breast pocket. She knew such garments easily sank into the river of clothing sold second-hand. This was the best kind – good quality, but not distinctive. No one could point to it and say, with absolute certainty, yes, that's mine, everyone has seen me wearing it.

He was young and thin, true, but still likely stronger than her. However, she needed more money, and a coat, after all, was hardly a purse.

She customarily carried a small knife in a leather pouch hidden in the folds of her skirts. It was far too blunt to be of any real use, and festooned with rust spots, but she fancied she could brandish it more threateningly than that merchant had wielded his.

It came out of her pocket now. She looked at the spotted blade and asked herself whether she would really use it to threaten a spotted youth.

Before she could consciously answer the question, she found herself stepping into the road.

The young fellow stared, probably trying to make sense of the fact that a girl around his age was suddenly here, in the middle of the forest. As he did, Jenny realised she had no idea what to do next. She did nothing, then, but stare back: a frank gaze most boys hadn't seen from most girls, at least not the kind their mothers would want them associating with.

This boy's eyebrows stayed clenched in a frown, but a tentative smile emerged. Jenny took a few steps towards him, and he didn't move. He seemed to be wondering if an offer was being made, not suspecting a threat was coming instead. She quickly pounded out the few remaining steps that separated them, raised the knife and rested its rusted tip just beneath the lad's ridiculously prominent Adam's apple.

'I'll be taking that coat from you, my lover,' she said, mimicking the greeting she heard older women give to returning sailors and market stall customers, an intimate word rendered meaningless by its liberal use.

His smile disappeared, and she saw his fist beginning to clench. A nice boy, probably, but it could only be moments before he realised that he was the stronger of the two, and that the knife resting at his throat was impossibly blunt.

She pressed it hard enough to hurt, hoping this would confuse his perception of its sharpness.

'Now I wouldn't want to be ruining the day by drawing blood,' she said. 'You simply need to take off that lovely coat – gently now, where you stand – and leave it on the ground, and away you go. Else I might have to call my brother out.'

Oddly, this invocation of a long-dead boy made her feel far worse than stealing a coat at knifepoint. The young man didn't know that Jenny's brother had never walked. His eyes raked the trees, looking for a hulking enforcer who could come crashing out.

'It's all right, Nathaniel,' Jenny said loudly, and already the lick of guilt was diminishing. 'This one looks like he'll be reasonable, so you can stow the club.'

The lad did as he was told, then, shrugging the coat off and letting it fall.

'Thank you,' said Jenny, still smiling. 'Can I ask, where are you from and where are you going?'

'Home to Polkerris,' the boy said. 'Where I have brothers of my own I can bring back.'

She would sell the coat in Menabilly, then.

'Best get about it,' she said, lowering the knife. 'Off you run, before Nathaniel joins us.'

The boy did.

She had made him do it, she realised. She had scared him so badly that he was probably still panting his way through the woods. He'd probably decided to turn Jenny into a strong man in the retelling of the story. She was not, among these trees, weak or poor. She was not a strange girl to be mocked but a shadow to be feared.

Jenny picked up the coat. Well made, as she had thought.

Nothing in the pockets, unfortunately, except the handkerchief. But it should fetch enough, for now. A garment like that, it wouldn't last long in the marketplace, and Jenny wondered if she would have the opportunity to steal it again from its new owner.

Often a week, even a fortnight would go by before a suitable candidate came down the road. Jenny had very specific criteria. They needed to be young, or small, or in some other way vulnerable. They needed to look as though they could afford to part with their coat or their bonnets or their purse – she had no intention of sending an impoverished girl or a starving boy further towards the grave.

Then, suddenly, they'd be walking past. Usually boys only just grown to manhood, their muscles not yet having fulfilled their promise. More rarely a woman, forced by circumstance to tread the road alone, no doubt fearing an encounter with someone like Jenny. There were more of them, now winter was beginning to fade and the increased ration of daylight emboldened travellers to risk the forest road.

So Jenny would smile a nasty smile, and call forth her dead brother, and take enough to make sure that Constance had more than limpets to eat.

Until the day Jenny felt a hand on her shoulder and heard a rasping voice. 'How discourteous. I invited you in the front door, but you've chosen to sneak around the back.'

CHAPTER 4

The highwayman was wearing the coat she'd seen him take. But he wasn't wearing the broad-brimmed black hat that had shaded his features, and she could see bare patches of scalp showing through uneven hair, black threaded with grey.

He smiled, then, and the odour of his ruined teeth assaulted her before he had a chance to. 'What am I to make of this? Such an insult, to have my offer rejected in such a way. I thought, so I did, that I was dealing with a woman of principle. She'd rather starve in honest labour, I thought, than eat well dishonestly, and good luck to her. I can admire someone like that. But this – this is simply wrong.'

A small thought emerged through Jenny's sudden, brutal fear. *This is someone who sets store by courtesy. Someone who would be expecting an apology.*

'I'm sorry,' she said. 'I didn't mean to wrong you. It came upon me, sudden, a boy who was all but begging for it, and when I saw the food I could get for my mother, I kept doing it. I meant no offence.'

The man laughed. 'You didn't mean it, and you are only doing it to feed your mother. Are the prisons not full of people who have

said exactly that? Do the tongues which spoke those words now lie
still in the mouths of those who dangle at the crossroads? No, the
law does not accept that as an excuse, and neither do I. Amends
will have to be made.'

'But how am I …?'

'You will continue as you have been – picking up the easy targets,
getting what you can. You will bring me your catch, and I will tell
you where best to dispose of it. You will bring me everything you
earn for, say, a half a year. You can keep enough for food. After
that you can keep half.'

'I'm sorry, I shouldn't have, I know. I'll stop, yes? I'll stop picking
off the easier travellers, leave them to you. I'll find other work, and
you'll not see me again.'

'That is not how I do business,' the man said, stern suddenly,
speaking like a disappointed reverend. 'You have started on this
path now, and you cannot leave it. Should you try – should you
decide to wait, say, more than a week between catches, I may
find myself arriving at the Trelawney house, talking to your
mother. You are not the only footpad in these woods, Jenny.
Some of them are from Penmor, and recognise an unusual girl
like you.'

'You're no better than an excise man,' she said, and then gasped
at her own words. Goading someone like this might be fatal.

He laughed, though. 'Yes, I am. I'm only taking some of your
earnings – I'm not asking the baker for some of his too, so he
has to charge you more. It is the best bargain you will get, Jenny.
Especially when the alternative is, well … I know where to hide
things.'

'Where are you hiding your name?' she said. 'How am I to
find you? I fancy you wouldn't like it if I came into the Plymstock
asking for Mr Thief.'

'No, I wouldn't. Confusing, too, as there are many who would answer to it. I have not gone by the name I was born with for some years. You may call me Mr Black. Best not to use that name to anyone else, though. When you come to the Plymstock with your takings, you'll see me easily enough, or I'll see you. Please, do not let more than seven days go by before you find your way there.'

Jenny had enough left – just enough – to replicate the wages she would have earned at an inn. She told her mother, as the days lengthened, that she might have to start staying overnight at the inn. Would Constance be all right? Constance nodded – she required little in terms of company, conversation, now.

Her mother did reanimate, a little, when Dolly came home for a visit. Constance seemed to enjoy hearing about her elder daughter's work, the pretensions of the house and its owners, and the clothes of the women who lived there and who visited; they wore more money on their backs than Constance would see in a lifetime.

Afterwards, Dolly and Jenny went down to the water and sobbed into each other's shoulders. Dolly shed quiet, restrained tears. Jenny snorted and gulped.

'You mustn't let people see you like this, you know,' Dolly said. 'Bad for your reputation.'

'Mother would be delighted with that,' said Jenny. 'Anything to prove I'm not a boy.'

'Is she still ... well, *there*?' asked Dolly. 'Every time I visit she seems to have faded a little. Unless I caught her in a particularly glum mood.'

'No, no, you haven't. She's more there for you than she usually is. She does what is required to keep herself alive, and I worry that she'll decide even that is too much of an effort.'

'The laundry looked in good order, though.'

'I do it, Dolly,' Jenny said. 'She would lose the business, otherwise. And I won't have all the neighbours gossiping about how Constance Trelawney is a ghost who never raises a hand anymore.'

Dolly nodded, then wordlessly hugged her sister.

'But Doll ... there might be a problem. I might need to spend more time at the inn. Don't know whether I'll be able to keep it all up.'

'Jenny, you know I can't come back more often. I'd love to ...'

'I know, I know. I'm not asking you to. But could you talk to her? I'll go outside, so she won't feel she has both of us to contend with. Maybe she'll listen to it, coming from you. Realise there are things she needs to do if she wants to keep living.'

'I'll try, of course,' said Dolly. 'Although there are times when it's unwise to push through to a choice between living and dying. Which inn is it, by the way?'

'Oh, a small one between here and Polkerris. Not easily seen from the road.'

'Why on earth would anyone build an inn where it's not easily seen?'

Jenny shrugged. 'It is known, this place. To those who know such things. I wouldn't be surprised if the owners pay some of their well-connected customers to talk up the place.'

After Dolly spoke to Constance, she shook off enough of her despondency to pay more attention to the laundry. But she still gave no sign that she might fret at Jenny's absences. Whenever Jenny said goodbye, Constance simply nodded, her eyes fixed on the dying fire, making no move to replenish the wood. Jenny wondered if her mother would simply sit there until she died, if she had no one to raise her from her chair and make sure she ate.

Jenny's money was dwindling; she needed to get out from under Mr Black long before a half year was up. She'd started to spend nights away from Penmor, but not on straw on the floor of a pub – she found hollows, ledges, small caves where she could shelter. The one part of her haul she kept back from Mr Black, when she went to see him in Plymouth, was a flint she could use to kindle fires. She took care to keep them small enough to avoid attracting attention; she was reasonably sure she wasn't the only person who spent nights in the woods.

She would get up with the sun to rob early morning travellers, occasionally coming upon other forest-dwelling bandits, snoring and drooling into the dirt, while on her way to take up her roadside vigil. She would always station herself as far as she could towards the start of the road so she could pick off travellers before anyone else got to them.

But she was still nowhere near paying back Mr Black.

He came and found her, every now and then. He'd be waiting when she woke up, stiff and cold and with dirt rubbed into the creases of her face. He was too large for the leather jacket he had stolen, ramming his thick arms into its sleeves, but he seemed quite attached to it, even as the seams began to complain and come apart.

Whenever Jenny had money, she gave it to him. More often than not, these transactions took place at the Plymstock, where he was well known.

'That your ponce?' the innkeeper asked her once, seeing her look around and fixate on Mr Black.

'My ponce?'

The keeper laughed. 'Never mind, you've answered my question.'

She wasn't the only thief Mr Black was running, far from it. She'd seen them come into the inn: men and women, mostly young but with the occasional respectable-looking matron. They would walk in and blink away the sunlight, turning their heads in the vain hope that no one would notice, stopping when their eyes came on Mr Black.

But he still liked paying the forest visits. He told Jenny that it kept people honest, made sure nothing was being held back.

'I can't get enough money,' she said to him one morning. 'I won't be able to pay you three pounds before my family's money runs out, and I'm no good to you dead of hunger.'

He looked at her thoughtfully. 'A better road is what's needed,' he said. 'A better road and a sharper knife, and some company. Oh, and some breeches.'

Jenny had still been spending the occasional night at home. She would wash when she could find the water after rain, getting rid of the smell of the forest and the pervasive dirt that hid beneath its fallen leaves.

Her mother seemed to be improving. The coughing sickness that visited Penmor most years had taken Mary Tippett with it, and Constance had been spending some time with Howard, helping to console him and seeing to his domestic duties.

Jenny told her mother that she'd found another position, with better money but further away. She would visit when she could, but it might not be for weeks. Constance nodded, embraced her daughter and told her to be good. She didn't weep as she'd done when Dolly's departure had created a hole in their now permanently ruined family.

A better road, Mr Black had told Jenny. It was a fair distance from Penmor, the road that delivered passengers from the ferry into Plymouth.

'You mentioned company,' she said to him.

'I did,' he said. 'I also mentioned breeches.' He handed them to her, the type a farm boy might wear, slightly too big. 'Easier to leg it in these, should the need arise. Cover your head, too – no need for anyone to know you're a girl, at least from a distance.'

He led her out to the Plymstock Inn's stables. As they approached, Jenny noticed two stablehands. One was standing and pacing, while the other sat on a stump and idly whittled with a knife nearly as blunt as hers. The lad looked up. The skin was clear of stubble but pitted by a childhood bout of the pox. The hair, unevenly hacked – quite likely with that blunt knife – fell to the shoulders. The eyes were round and brown.

This was a woman, Jenny realised. Her loose shirt hid her breasts, but she sat with her knees together, not spread wide the way a stableboy would. Keeping her legs together was probably the only injunction from her mother that this woman still followed.

Jenny turned her attention to the other stableboy, seeing that this was also no boy. Shorter than Jenny by a hand and a half at the least, the second woman had smooth skin and matted hair tied back in one of its own tendrils.

Mr Black addressed himself to the woman on the stump. 'It was help you wanted, Elenor, and here is help … It *is* Elenor this week?'

'Elenor will do,' said the woman. 'And she will be no help to me in skirts.'

'That can easily be changed, and will be.' To Jenny, he said, 'Go in there and get those breeches on.'

'It's a stable,' she said. 'There's a horse in it.'

'He won't mind.'

'If she's scared of horses,' Elenor said, 'what will we do when a cart comes by?'

'You can stop whining and all. Haven't I got what you keep asking for?'

'If it's two of the same, they'll be turning me off and showing me at the crossroads before the week's out.'

Jenny listened through the stable wall as she shed her skirts next to a whickering dray. *Two of the same.* The other girl must not be to Elenor's liking any more than Jenny.

She came out, holding her skirts in a bundle. 'I have no fear of horses,' she said. 'I have fear of starving, and of lippy women.'

Elenor smiled, and her breath whistled through a missing front tooth. The contraction of her mouth produced an effect more sinister by far than Jenny's well-practised mean smile, and Jenny was reasonably sure this was Elenor's intent.

The other girl smiled too, welcoming and hopeful and perhaps slightly nervous.

'This is Beatrice,' said Mr Black to Jenny.

'Bea, if you like,' she said.

'Bea's only done a few,' Mr Black told Elenor. 'You have to be patient.'

'I'll need the patience of the Blessed Virgin herself,' said Elenor. 'You know she tripped, last time? Just lay there. The cart drove around, but the driver could easily have stopped, tried to arrest us both. If there'd been more than one of him, I think he would have.'

'Harder to apprehend three than two,' Mr Black said, 'and this one, I can tell you, generally only trips when she needs to.' He gave

Elenor a bundle wrapped in oilcloth. 'Dinner,' he said. 'Off with you now, all of you.'

'Are we not staying here?' asked Jenny.

Elenor's vulpine grin appeared again. Mr Black ignored the question and stalked back into the inn, the transaction complete.

'Slept in the woods before?' Elenor asked Jenny.

'Yes. Lots.'

'Better than this one,' Elenor said, inclining her head towards Bea. She handed the bundle to Jenny and started walking out of the yard. 'Quick as you can, come on now. Harder to find the place in the dark.'

The place, after an hour's walk, turned out to be a small clearing in the forest, with the remains of a fire at its centre, ringed by trees and small piles of human shit.

Elenor handed out the bread Mr Black had given her, tearing it into three parts in a way that seemed very inexact and ended with her getting the largest chunk. This was something, Jenny thought, which would need to be addressed. But not tonight.

'What's your village?' she asked Bea.

'We've no village, none of us,' Elenor said, before Bea could do more than open her mouth to answer. 'We are of the forest. We are no one.'

CHAPTER 5

Jenny was getting used to waking much colder than when she'd gone to sleep, and to moving her limbs as quickly as possible, before she was fully conscious, to get the blood flowing.

Her hair, matted as it was, tended to snag leaves and small twigs. She would run her hands over it, on waking, to see what she had managed to snare in the night, what offerings needed to be returned to the forest floor. The dirt, the blackness which got ground into the invisible creases of the face – well, that could be seen as an advantage. From a distance, she might look like a boy desperate for his beard to grow as a way to impress the local lasses.

There was no bread left this morning. There had been some, before Jenny had gone to sleep. She had wrapped it in her skirts and used them as a pillow, breathing in the scent of sweat and salt, the ghosts of past catches. But the bread wasn't there now, although her skirt was still rolled under her head when she woke up, exactly as it had been when she went to sleep. She looked at Elenor, raising her eyebrows.

Elenor grinned, not spitefully but like someone trying to convince a friend that the joke they'd just made was indeed amusing.

'Fairies in these woods, like as not,' she said. 'Bound to be. They can burrow their way in anywhere, and they do like bread.'

'Yes, I'd heard,' said Jenny. 'Yes, it must've been the fairies.'

Elenor looked back at her for another moment, then nodded. She went over to Bea, who was miraculously still snoring on a pillow she'd fashioned from a clump of moss, soft but wet so that when Elenor kicked her awake – gently, but still a kick – and she sat up, her face was covered in flecks of green and glistened from last week's rain.

They sat on small stones around the dead fire, Elenor occasionally poking it with a stick as though expecting it to flare back into life. 'Foot travellers are beneath us now,' she said. 'I'd like to pay off Mr Black in one go.'

'Me too – I owe him a little over two pounds,' Bea volunteered. 'I borrowed money, you see. Just to tide us over until my father got work. Only he didn't.'

Elenor stood, went over to Bea and cracked her across the face with the back of her hand. Bea didn't retaliate, just sat with her palm pressed to her cheek, silently crying. Jenny wasn't sure what made her angrier: Elenor's violence, or Bea's meek acceptance. But after the disappearing bread, Jenny wasn't inclined to let Elenor take any further liberties, to slap the rest of them into submission. Jenny got up and walked over to Elenor until they were close enough to feel each other's breath. 'If you hit Bea again, you will find yourself waking up tomorrow without one of your ears,' she said.

It was bluster, of course, and Elenor knew it. 'If Bea won't keep her mouth shut here, she might open it in other places. Then we are all of us in danger. I'll hit her as many times as I like until she learns that.'

'That will work very well, of course – taking part in a perilous venture like this, with someone who hates you because you won't stop whacking them.'

'A few boats and I'm rid of you both,' Elenor said with a scowl.

'Boats?' said Jenny. 'Not many of them on the Plymouth road.'

Elenor snorted. 'We want someone rich, but not mounted or in a coach,' she said. 'There is only one place to find that. The ferry.'

The ferry passengers tended to stay together on the road, in the hope of avoiding attack. They usually had plenty of company. The port of Plymouth seemed to attract ships from everywhere and nowhere. Carts brought goods down to the docks, to be loaded and sent wherever a ship could travel, or to receive the odd cargo that arrived from places like Spain, Italy, Virginia in the New World – tobacco or spices or strange, bright fabrics.

A large group of foot travellers, mostly male, was just as difficult a quarry as a coach. Still, the three women went every day. They waited at the point where the trees began to cut off the sunlight, where the road could no longer be seen from the port. Day after day, well-shod bands of travellers marched past, some with pocket watches, some with expensively topped canes. All huddled into one another, brought to intimacy by the threat of the roadside.

Now here came another batch, walking almost shoulder to shoulder with their demoralising solidarity. Prissy women, who clearly hadn't come within shouting distance of a man before, now seemed happy to be wedged between male strangers. In their wake, as always, the passengers left three girls who were poorer than they'd been the day before.

Elenor spat on the ground, as she always did, for its failure to give them an isolated target.

Jenny cuffed her ear.

'Didn't think you objected to spitting,' said Elenor.

'I don't, idiot. Look.'

Rounding the corner, scurrying in an attempt to catch up with the other passengers, was a woman. Her skirts were clean and had been drawn slightly too tight to allow her a full range of movement. Jenny saw the edges of white petticoats beneath pale rose fabric, and a bodice of the same material. A reasonable amount of material was needed: this woman had a stout frame, and stoutness was a rarity. She wore a small bonnet – well made, beautifully decorated, distinctive. Expensive.

Elenor looked at Jenny and Bea and nodded, holding up her hand, ready to chop it downwards in their signal to begin. The hand stayed where it was as the woman scuttled closer. Jenny heard the heavy breathing brought on by her attempt to catch up with the group. The woman clutched a shawl around her shoulders – thicker, softer and more expensive-looking than any Jenny had yet seen. As she moved, the shawl moved with her, offering glimpses of something that shone around her throat.

Most ferry passengers would glance at the side of the road every minute or so, hoping by their vigilance to ward off threats. This woman was doing no such thing. She was looking at the rutted, uneven surface in front of her, her fine leather shoes unused to such insults.

When she passed by, Elenor's hand went down.

The three of them stepped into the road behind the woman. Jenny was the tallest, probably the strongest. The others seemed to assume she should be the one to take physical risks. Elenor stared at her and flicked her head in the direction of the woman, who was advancing slowly away from them. Jenny closed the distance in a few paces, put her hand on the woman's shoulder, and pulled.

The woman wasn't as old as Jenny had imagined. For some reason, she always presumed that wealth was acquired through age, despite the many ageing paupers she had known. But this woman's face was unlined, her eyes a clear brown, and the little hair that could be seen under her bonnet did not show any obvious grey.

The woman screamed.

'Now, my lovely, there's no need for that,' said Jenny. 'We'll be having that bonnet, now, your shawl and,' she felt around the woman's waist, 'oh, yes, and that lovely fat purse you have there. The necklace too, of course, and that's a handsome ring. So you will be giving them over to us, now, and be on your way.'

The woman was trembling but hadn't looked away from her attackers. She inhaled sharply, and breathed out a soft, shaking word. 'No.'

'You don't mean that, we know you don't, my dear. There's three of us, and my friend here, you see she has a blade.'

Elenor extracted her knife and turned it around, examining it as though looking for nicks.

'Here, I'll help you,' said Jenny. 'We'll start with the bonnet, shall we?' She reached out and pulled on the black silk ribbons that held the bonnet fast to the woman's head.

The woman, though, had found her voice. 'No!' she screeched, and the toe of a very expensive leather shoe connected with Jenny's shin.

Jenny grabbed the woman's shoulders. 'Don't do that again, my lovely. There's a great difference between walking this road with fewer belongings, and never walking again.'

Of course she had no intention of carrying through on the threat, did not consider herself a murderer. But the woman didn't know that, and began to flail, scratching at Jenny's face.

This woman, thought Jenny, *has never had to eat limpets. Has never had to experience the kind of cold that kills a baby. Has never had to worry that an absent school of pilchards will destroy her.* Perhaps her father had paid for the necklace, the bonnet, the shawl. Perhaps he yet lived, and had no need to choose between starving and placing himself in the hands of the midnight sea.

Jenny drew back a hand and cracked the woman across the face. She fell to the ground, sobbing now, and shaking. There was blood at her mouth, and a strange gurgling sound merged with the word, 'Please.'

Jenny bent down and jerked the bonnet roughly from the woman's head. She tried to tear the necklace away, but it was too well made. 'Hold her!' she hissed at Elenor and Bea, who looked almost as shocked as the woman. With the two of them pinning the woman to the ground, Jenny removed the necklace and the shawl, and snatched the purse from the woman's belt. 'We'll leave you the ring. Least we can do, in thanks for your generosity.'

Jenny, Bea and Elenor backed away from the shuddering creature in the dirt, watching to see if she would spring up and offer a fight.

She didn't. She sat there, watching the road as carefully as she had when walking, sobbing and sniffling and shivering from shock, and perhaps from cold as her shawl was now bundled on Jenny's arm.

The three highwaywomen looked at each other, nodded, and began to run. Not towards the protection of the trees, but into Plymouth, where they would hide among hundreds of others with goods to sell.

CHAPTER 6

Elenor spilled the coins onto the table in front of Mr Black. 'Twelve pounds,' she said. 'For the money Bea and I owe you, and for Jenny – surely enough to buy her way out from your arrangement.'

'There's only nine pounds here,' he said.

'We kept back a pound each. Now we've repaid you.'

They'd had no trouble selling the necklace, and the shawl and bonnet had already found new owners. Elenor had conducted all the transactions and was handling the money, an arrangement Jenny wasn't sure she liked.

Mr Black moved the coins around the table with his finger, picking them up one after the other, squinting at them, even licking one or two. He put them down and looked up at the girls. 'Good enough. I'll do right by you girls – you're too valuable to me to have you running off because you think I've cheated you.'

Elenor nodded as though she often made this kind of transaction, as though it was only to be expected. For all Jenny knew, it was.

'I'll show faith by getting you some rum,' Mr Black said, whistling at a barmaid who'd clearly received similar requests from him before and knew what was required.

Jenny watched Elenor throw back her head, open her mouth and pour as much rum into it as she could manage. Jenny did likewise. Bea sipped at hers slowly, not enjoying it any more than Jenny was. Mr Black ignored her, while Elenor took a moment from her attempts to impress him and shot Bea a disdainful glance.

'Stay clear of the ferry for a while,' Mr Black was saying. 'Be cautious, after that. You didn't kill her, did you?'

'Not sure,' said Elenor.

'No, we didn't,' said Jenny. 'She might have a split lip, and she ended up on the ground, but that's all. We were a bit – well, a bit rougher than I wanted to be.'

Jenny had beaten a woman. She was shocked at how her voice sounded. But something in her was stretching and stirring, and deciding she also rather liked the way she sounded. Hard, unemotional. Unassailable.

Jenny tipped a second rum down her throat. While she could leave the taste alone, she did rather like the way it sat, warm and coiled, in her stomach. She was thinking of ordering another, but for the first time in months she had coins in her pocket, and she didn't want to be careless enough to lose them or have someone relieve her of their burden. The rum, and the coins, were making her feel invulnerable.

Until the door at the end of the room was pushed inwards, and three men entered abreast. This was rare in the Plymstock, where most tried to pass in and out as unobtrusively as possible. Of course, those who wore constables' clothes weren't interested in entering any inn unobtrusively. Jenny had been told that they usually left this one alone – it wasn't the worst of them, not a place where stolen goods were openly exchanged for money. But someone must have attracted the attention of the constables, and when the regulars found out who it was they would not be welcomed back.

Everyone stayed in the position they'd been in when the doors opened. Some had cups raised halfway to their lips, held up by their elbows. Nobody wanted to be the first to move.

It didn't take long for the constables to stride to the highwaywomen's table. No one made any attempt to impede their progress. A hand closed around Jenny's arm, far more forcefully than it needed to. Then she was on her feet, dragged and held there so that even if she'd given her legs permission to stop working, she would still have been suspended by her arm.

The other two constables took Elenor and Bea. Elenor tried to shrug her right arm out of the man's grip, and he responded by taking both her arms and bringing them together painfully behind her at the elbow.

The one who held Jenny looked at Mr Black. 'You know these?'

'Not till tonight, I don't,' he said, and Jenny noticed the coins were no longer on the table.

The constable nodded, turned and propelled Jenny in front of him to the door, followed by the man holding Elenor, who was spitting and cursing, and the one holding Bea, who was beginning to sob. Before they were out the door, Jenny noticed that those who had retained their freedom were already going back to their drinks.

Some passengers had stayed at the dock for a little while, chatting, after the ferry arrived that day. It had been some time before they followed the rest, and they had come upon a bloodied and weeping woman, still lying in the dirt, with no bonnet or shawl but quite a story.

It was known, among those who knew such things, that three girls were operating together, occasionally with items for sale. No one asked where they acquired them, but no one expected they had done so honestly.

This, at least, was what Jenny was able to discover once her case went to trial.

The women were taken to gaol, after being called briefly before a magistrate with unnaturally pink cheeks. He had committed them to stand trial at the Exeter Assizes.

'Highway robbery, was it?' said the guard. 'They hang robbers.'

As he closed the door to the women's cell, Bea began to scream. Elenor, though, sat down, legs apart with her arms resting on them, as though about to dispense judgement herself. Elenor, thought Jenny, had already known.

If Jenny was to be turned off, what then? Would she still look like herself when they displayed her at the Four Turnings? Constance had never been one for leaving the village and was unlikely to start. But Dolly might pass the crossroads, or one of the Tippetts, or anyone among the dozens of villagers who had known Jenny from birth. They might bring back word of the felon hanging there, her clothes loose as her flesh rotted away. Before it did, someone, surely, would see something familiar in the thing that had been Jenny.

But she didn't believe, not really, that she would be hanged. Not when horse thieves and poachers retained their necks – at least sometimes, or so she had heard. It was far easier for her to believe she would die of old age in this gaol.

In Penmor, though, sat a woman who might think her daughter was dead. Jenny had not sent word to Constance for a while. What would she say? 'I'm alive'? It had seemed a message not worth the price. Now, Jenny would have paid anything to send it, together with a warning that it may not be the truth much longer, that her mother and sister should avoid the Four Turnings.

Jenny didn't know how many weeks had passed in the dark cell, with its damp, sticky floor that was supposed to be covered in straw but never was, excrement piling up in the corners. The high, barred windows only admitted small amounts of air and light, and the cell's perpetual dusk made it hard to keep track of the passage of days. Lice dripped from Jenny's head by the time a month had passed. She'd stopped hearing Bea's wails, stopped attending to Elenor's railings as she belched spite into the air, was insensible to the moans of the cell's lags.

It was Jenny's fault, Elenor said, often and loudly. 'The constables don't go hunting at the Plymstock. Not unless they have a good reason to. Not unless you leave someone bleeding in the dirt, you stupid bitch.'

The first time they came to blows was over Bea, who hadn't uttered a complete sentence in weeks that didn't centre around her family, her desperation that they would think her dead, her fear that they might find out she wasn't. It was never clear what set her off when she began to keen, but usually she wouldn't stop for some hours. Elenor would stalk over to her, threaten her, yell to drown out the miserable sound. She would slap her before returning to her own corner of the cell. Bea would hold her cheek, stare after Elenor, rub a little more skin from the abraded mess around her eyes, and go silent for a time.

Bea did not defend herself, any more than she had in the forest. She was used, perhaps, to taking beatings in silence for fear of making them worse. The misery she wrapped herself in was so stifling that a slap added hardly any weight to it. After one such slap, on one such day, she kept up her noise and seemed hardly to notice the pain. So Elenor struck her again. Balled her fists and struck a third and a fourth time. Shifted her shoulder backwards to add weight to the next blow. Jenny barrelled into her, knocking her onto her back, scratching her cheek and creating a gouge that would suppurate if she wasn't careful, the rot starting even before she was hanged.

In three months, there was an end to it. When it came, Jenny was grateful. Terror, she thought, was preferable to monotony.

The three of them were shackled together and loaded into a cart. With more access to daylight, Jenny could better see the changes in Bea and Elenor. Both were thinner, much too thin, and their yellowing skin stretched like a drum over their cheekbones. There were sores here and there, from where flesh had rubbed too long against the stone walls, or where moisture had treacherously softened skin until it fell away. Jenny had no doubt she looked just as awful; she had the same sores on her forearms, and a rasp in her voice that hadn't been there during the forest's coldest nights.

'Where are we being taken?' Elenor asked one of the guards imperiously.

'Exeter Assizes,' he said. 'From there, hell, probably.'

In Exeter the men and the women were separated. Jenny didn't know what the men's cell was like. She couldn't imagine it would be worse than the women's, though, with over a dozen of them sharing rotting straw bedding strewn on a damp floor, and squatting over a bucket in the corner that was rarely emptied. After a few days guards would come to the prisoners, one by one, when it was their turn before the bench. Mostly, they didn't come back.

Elenor was taken, and then Bea. Neither of them returned to the cell.

Then Jenny was before the bench in the Assizes Hall, wincing at the light from the large arched window behind the judge, while the woman she had last seen on the Plymouth ferry road pointed at her with a hand that trembled perhaps a little too artfully, and said, 'Yes, yes, she's the one, the unnatural one who struck me like a man, and was dressed like one too.'

'I was forced into men's clothes, and onto the highway,' Jenny called out.

'Oh?' said the judge, without looking up from the black marks he was gouging into the paper in front of him. 'Who forced you?'

'His Majesty the King.'

The judge chuckled, glancing at her briefly with indifferent eyes that sat on top of a tiny upturned nose. Of course.'

'The taxes. The land enclosures. It's impossible to survive.'

'Yet people do, and they do so without beating women senseless on the King's Highway.'

'Sir, you can't expect –'

'Your Honour, if you please.'

'Your Honour, then, although I can't see what honour there is in this whole business. If you stop us from feeding ourselves honestly, you have to expect us to do it dishonestly. We will not simply lie down and obligingly die to save you some trouble!'

'Will you not?' He reached into a small box on the bench, extracting a black cap. Little more than a square scrap of fabric, really. It didn't need to sit securely on top of the judge's curled wig; it simply needed to rest there while he said words he had surely said before this day and would again, words apparently rendered meaningless to him through repetition, as he delivered them with all the emotion of a cook ordering vegetables at the market.

Jenny didn't really hear those words. She'd known what he was going to say as soon as she saw that black scrap emerge.

'Jane Trelawney, for the crime of feloniously assaulting Agnes Lakeman on the King's Highway, putting her in corporeal fear for her life on this said highway, and violently taking from her person and against her will on the said highway one silk bonnet valued at twelve shillings and other goods to the value of eleven pounds eleven shillings, you will be taken from this place back to your prison, and thence to a place of execution where you will be hanged by the neck until dead, and may God have mercy on your soul.'

The judge's gavel struck the bench, and he rolled the piece of paper that had been in front of him into a tight tube, handed it to an associate, and received the next one as Jenny half walked and was half dragged by a guard out of the courtroom.

The condemned cells were not the place of wailing and lamentation Jenny had expected. The one she shared with Bea and Elenor and the other condemned women was cleaner than the others had been, and the vibrating current of desperation with which Jenny had become so familiar was oddly not present here. Jenny would not, she vowed, pass the time by sleeping or allow herself to fall into a stupor as some of the other women had. There would soon be plenty of government-enforced eternal sleep.

Bea was quiet now, staring. Elenor wasn't quiet, far from it. But her words were making less and less sense. She walked up to Jenny, grasped her shoulders and wetly hissed in her ear. 'We will jump on the guard, so we will, when he comes in with food. Or, no, Bea can pretend to be dead – she's almost there anyway – and then we can attack when they come to take the body out.'

Jenny nodded, saying it all sounded wonderful, knowing escape from here was impossible. She lay on the ground, staring at the oozing stone. What was it about gaols that made their stones so slick, so wet?

As the afternoon wore on, the cell slowly filled with women. Some of them sounded almost cheerful, chattering away, asking one another for details of their offences. But Jenny was left alone. There seemed to be an understanding that those who were silent wished to remain so.

She had almost fallen asleep, despite her promise to herself. She was brought back to full consciousness by the cell door opening and a guard walking in with a candle.

Night had fallen and the cell was lit by dim moonlight. Their dinner had been brought, and the assizes were over, so Jenny had expected there to be no more company for them. Perhaps the guard wanted to see if any of the condemned women were keen for a last taste of the carnal – or perhaps he just fancied picking a woman and trying her regardless of what she wanted.

That fear, though, lasted as long as it took for a second man to walk through the door behind the guard. He was plainly but neatly dressed, standing as erect as she'd ever seen anyone stand.

He unrolled a piece of paper, held it up, and then glared at the guard, who held up his candle.

The stiff-backed man looked around the cell and cleared his throat. 'At the assizes and general delivery of the gaol of our Lord the King, Holden at the Castle of Exeter before Sir James Eyre, Knight, Baron of the Court of Exchequer, Sir Beaumont Hotham, and others, their fellow justices. Whereas certain prisoners were, at this assizes, convicted of felony for which they were excluded benefit of Clergy, his Majesty hath been graciously pleased to extend the Royal Mercy to them, on condition of their being transported beyond the seas for and during the term of seven years, each, and such intention of mercy hath been signified by the Right Honourable Thomas, Lord Sydney – one of His Majesty's Principal Secretaries of State. It is therefore ordered and adjudged by the court that those named here be transported beyond the seas accordingly, as soon as conveniently may be, for and during the term of seven years respectively.'

He then read a list of names. Bea Ormond was one of them. So was Elenor Watkins.

The last was Jane Trelawney.

CHAPTER 7

The women hadn't been told exactly where the cart was taking them. They were cargo, now. Toxic, requiring careful handling, but also important enough not to be broken.

A light rain fell, unworthy of the name, almost mist. Enough moisture, though, to get underneath the irons at Jenny's wrists and ankles, to soften up the skin and make it more vulnerable to the brutality of the metal. She hoped the constant presence of pain would make it easier, after a time, to ignore.

She had hoped to see fishing boats on Devonport Harbour, but her view was obscured by the ships which travelled across the seas as a matter of course, not as the endpoint of a life of criminal ingenuity.

Even these, though, looked tiny in comparison to a ship moored close in, which appeared to be serviced by its own dock. *It might not, actually, be a ship*, she thought. It had no mast, for a start. Therefore no sails. She couldn't see spindly oars poking out of its sides, and in any case all of the hatches were closed. Its only ship-like attributes were its shape – broad and bloated but still with the delicate curve which ran downwards until one side of the hull met the other – and the fact that it was floating.

The cart pulled up at the docks and the prisoners were unloaded, still shackled together. Jenny had a moment of divine relief when the irons were removed, trying not to look at the deep, wet furrows they had excavated in her skin. She was hurriedly bundled into a small boat with Bea and Elenor and some others, and rowed the short distance to the monstrosity.

Rampant across the ship's flank was a green blight, which – judging by the smell – was either decaying or forcing itself into the grains of the timbers to rot them.

Up on the deck was a man not nearly as well turned out as the one from the court. Either he lacked the means or the interest to dress himself neatly. He did, though, have a piece of paper from which he glanced up from time to time as he spoke to the convicts. Jenny had become used to being harangued and words from past tirades clogged her ears, forcing her to concentrate on what her latest captor said. Knowledge was all she had.

She did, vaguely, hear him inform them they were aboard the hulk *Dunkirk*, and she most certainly heard him when he said escapees would be shot, but his words began to bleed into each other when he started talking about the men being taken ashore to work each day. His clothes seemed to have been selected to match the splotched brown of the deck. Apart from the crimson wounds at the wrists and ankles of the convicts, the brightest colours that mankind had contributed to the scene belonged to the red coats of the marines. Several of them stood in a line off to the side – although some had a liberal interpretation of what it meant to stand, leaning against the walls of the huts that had been jumbled onto the deck, looking up from under their eyebrows at the convicts.

Two marines were having a loud and unashamedly carnal conversation, assessing the attributes of the new women. One of them was staring at Bea, who was looking at the deck. Jenny stared at them: boys, really, not much older than her. Without their rank and the weaponry that went with it, she would be equal to them on the highway, and far more than equal in a small boat on a lumpen sea. She did not look away until she was certain they had seen her looking, certain that they knew she had heard them. It didn't take long – clearly, they too felt the uncomfortable tightening, the slight ripple she always felt when being stared at. They looked up, almost in unison, and went silent. Until one leaned into the other, whispering something with his eyes still on Jenny, and the two laughed with a snorting abrasiveness.

But another pair of eyes was on them now, belonging to a slightly older man who shared with them the red coat and little else. He stood straight but not self-consciously so. He didn't seem to be following orders; it was as though he simply didn't know any other way to stand. He could glare, though, and the two younger marines' sniggers trailed off and fell silent.

The older marine turned to Jenny, then, who gave him a small smile that she had calculated to hide her rotting teeth. He nodded briefly: a perfunctory courtesy, but courtesy nonetheless in a place not overburdened with such gestures.

'You'll be given canvas slops, and I don't care what you do with the clothes you're wearing now,' the dull-clothed man was saying to the convicts, in a voice so dreary that even Bea seemed to be struggling to pay attention, while Elenor was openly looking around. 'When you're not working, you're below.'

'What about women?' Jenny was surprised the rasping voice was hers. 'What's happening to us, and where are our clothes?'

'Your clothes are on your back, and you're going below until they decide where you're going from here, or until the Lord makes the decision for them.' As the marines started to move forward, the man held up a hand. 'Don't know whether you've heard of the riot on the hulk at Portsmouth,' he said to the convicts.

Jenny hadn't, but she suspected some of the others had. They straightened their spines for the first time in days. Stories of riots, of insurrection, were frequently embellished beyond recognition, so that the participants achieved glorious escape or ignominious execution. Surely, some of them must just end with bread and water. It was a rare opportunity to hear of such things from a man in an official position, even if she wasn't sure what that position was.

'It came to nothing,' he said. 'Those involved were flogged. I think they might hang the next lot, if anyone is stupid enough to give it a try.'

Then he nodded to the marines, who herded the convicts towards holes in the deck through which some would emerge for work, and some would never emerge again.

There was the salt, and the air. At least there was that.

Jenny had stared at the sky for as long as she could before they went below. This sky, the one she had once scanned with her father for dragons, might be lost to her soon, and she didn't know what her new sky would be like.

The hold was split into two cells, one for men and one for women, with holes through which the marines could fire at need, and bars through which the two groups of prisoners could keen at each other.

The seaward shutters were kept open during the day. They allowed a small ration of daylight and air into the hold, but for all its salted heaviness the air could not compete with the thick reek of confined humanity. Nor was any breeze able to carry the stench out of the hatches on the other side, as these were kept closed to avoid offending the olfactory sensibilities of people onshore.

Some of the female convicts had been in there for months, some longer. Some had nearly served out their sentence. True to the word of the overseer on the deck, there were no canvas slops for any of them, so that those who had sat in their own ordure for any length of time wore ragged shadows of the clothes they had stood in to hear the sentence of the court.

Each day two marines – usually the spotted idiots who had sized up Jenny and the other women on deck – would come below and, turning their backs to the female enclosure, choose half a dozen men to go and work on shore that day. Jenny caught the name of one marine, Lieutenant Farrow. She would press her face to the bars, so that they scoured her cheeks with their rusted strength, and watch as the men were ironed and taken above; she yearned more for the touch of their rough canvas slops than she could ever imagine doing for any of those who wore it.

Sometimes when that day's labourers rattled past, Jenny would be the only one whose face was framed by the bars. But that depended on who'd been chosen: certain men drew quite a crowd among the women, who would elbow each other aside for a look. The more popular boys would be shown glimpses of filthy skin as some of the women drew down ragged necklines to expose their breasts, yowling propositions they knew they wouldn't have to make good on. Those who had been there the longest needed to make little effort to show themselves, their clothing falling open with small, well-judged movements. It did not take long before Elenor joined them, relying on her status as a newcomer to attract some attention.

Some of the men – those walking past, and those watching

from the opposite enclosure – would simply leer; others would call out counter propositions. Occasionally, one or two of them would try to start a conversation.

'Why do you never show me anything of yourself?' a man said to Jenny one day. He was one of the more popular ones, one of those who had probably been shown more flesh in the past month than a Penmor boy would see in a lifetime.

Jenny didn't answer. She didn't know what to say, and in any case the man wasn't given time to stand and talk, his words hurled from the side of his mouth as he passed by. His face was hardly that of an angel, and bore the start of the creases which Jenny had seen the sun gouge, over time, in her father's skin. But this man had clear blue eyes, and he had not given up.

Others had. Some women, those who had been there longest, barely moved, not even drawn to the bars by the passage of men. They lay on one of the sleeping platforms, some with their faces turned away from the open hatches.

The loudest despair came from women who had struck up relationships with marines or crew and then been cast back into the hold.

'Might be an opportunity for you,' an old woman, Dorothy, croaked at Jenny when one sobbing woman was cast down from an officer's cot, wearing clean clothes that wouldn't remain so for long.

'Plenty in here exposing themselves,' Jenny said.

'Yes, they are, aren't they?' said Dorothy. She seemed amused, her tone that of a mother grudgingly impressed with a prank played by her children. 'Why would a man be interested in gazing on any of them, when he has seen their sagging reality?'

Dorothy was eighty-one, by far the oldest person Jenny had ever met, and certainly the oldest prisoner. She had been in the hold for six months, but the manacle wounds in her wrists and

ankles hadn't suppurated and her lungs had not collapsed under
the weight of phlegm. She spoke, sometimes, of looking forward
to being on the sea, the journey started.

But her assumption she would survive until they got to their
destination seemed arrogant in this place. The past week had seen
a young woman sewn into a shroud and dumped overboard after
a lung complaint stopped her breathing.

Jenny felt a strangling desperation at the thought of her mother.
She called out, sometimes, as the marines and turnkeys passed
the bars. 'I need a letter sent. My mother should know what has
become of me. I can pay.'

Mostly she was ignored, but sometimes men seemed happy to
admit that they'd heard; sometimes they laughed. 'Pay with what?'
they would say. Or, perhaps, 'We can arrange a price.' But no one
had proposed one to her.

She knew there was a currency she might be able to trade in,
a coin she hadn't yet spent. Better to spend it and get something
in return, than to have it stolen. And once she was above decks,
she could look around – check the beam of this not-ship, assess
whether the distance between rail and water might kill her. Perhaps
get a sense of whether there might be lapses in vigilance, lulls when
the marines were distracted.

So one morning she pressed herself to the bars with the other
women, though she still didn't open her shirt like the flaps of a
tent or rub herself up and down. She waited for the vile Farrow to
pass by, so she could waylay him as she would love to have done
on the highway.

But when he came to select that day's workers, Farrow was

accompanied not by his equally puerile friend, but by Captain Corbett, a slightly older marine. One of the most senior officers aboard apart from the captain himself, he was lean and lanky, with a hawk-like nose in the middle of a face that bore the rosy skin of a child. When they walked past the women, Farrow's head stayed bent, and as the warders unlocked the bars of the male cell, he only betrayed emotion in the roughness with which he hauled the workers out into the corridor.

It might have been Corbett's presence. Perhaps he wasn't the kind to approve of liaisons with convicts. Perhaps he thought such behaviour was beneath a brother marine.

After the male convicts had been returned from their work, locked back into the cell from which they shouted possibilities to the women, Corbett paused by the female cell.

Jenny was again sitting near the bars. She had discovered, quickly, that to move from such a prime position was to relinquish it. There were those who would have gladly dragged her away and forced her into a far corner. But Jenny was a highwaywoman, while most of the others were country girls arrested for stealing bread or a ribbon. That earned her a certain amount of latitude. Even more so than Elenor and Bea, as she was the one who had drawn blood.

Mr Corbett stopped beside her, then dropped down onto his haunches until their faces were level. 'I saw you, this morning,' he said.

Jenny didn't speak. Was this a prelude? A gentlemanly way to make the same offer the men in the cells had been shouting? A polite start to a transaction that would end very impolitely?

'Will I find you exposing yourself, next time?' he asked.

'I don't think so,' Jenny said. 'There's enough to do that already, and with the same thought they'd give to taking their hat off.'

He smiled, then. 'Yes, I suppose it has become something of a ... convention,' he said. 'Nevertheless, I should be disappointed to see you engaging in the same behaviour. I always am, when the hulk swallows what's left of a woman. That sort of thing is – well, it's inadvisable.'

She was still staring at the ladder long after Mr Corbett had climbed up to the deck.

'He may not be seeking a woman,' said a male voice close by, 'but I am.'

Jenny straightened, then dragged herself hand over hand up a bar until she could see who had spoken. It was one of the warders, Prentice, a far less appealing figure than a marine in a red coat. His clothes were the colour of wet sand, and he wore a neckerchief like many of the men he guarded. But he had keys, and clothes not stiff with grime.

He wasn't a handsome man, as far as she could tell in the dim light. His nose was small and upturned, with the delicacy of a noblewoman's. And he was balding, with small fringes of hair hanging down over his collar. He looked about the same age as her father. The seams of his skin hadn't taken on the same amount of dirt as those of the convicts, but it was impossible for anyone on the *Dunkirk* to avoid attracting a measure of grime – even Mr Corbett's fingernails had dirt under them.

'And if I go with you ...?' Jenny asked.

'You'll get food – more of it than now, anyway. A wash every now and then. A night on a mattress here and there, and I heard you say something about wanting a letter sent.'

'So,' Jenny said to Prentice, later that night, 'shall I tell you what I want to say?'

'About what?' he asked. He was lacing his breeches up, while Jenny smoothed down her skirts. She was sitting on the mattress in his small hut, one of the hastily built structures on the hulk's deck. The whole business had been blessedly brief, a little painful at first but no worse than she'd feared. Afterwards, she had put her hand between her thighs to investigate the moisture there, withdrawing it to see a faint smear of blood; she doubted Prentice had noticed, or cared. He'd handed her a small oilcloth bundle, which turned out to contain some salt pork. Jenny had eaten it immediately, as she doubted it would last long in the hold.

'What I want to say to my mother,' she explained to Prentice. 'You said you would get a message to her for me.'

'Did I? Can't think why. Don't have any letters.'

She frowned, wondering why his lack of other letters would prevent him sending one for her, before she realised what he was saying. 'You can't write.'

'Not needed, for this work.'

Then she was up from the mattress and clawing at him, or trying to. He quickly put out a hand and held her away, sending her back onto the mattress with a shove. 'You might want more salt pork. Have a care.'

'I've no objection to salt pork, but that isn't the bargain we made,' she said. 'My ma is in Penmor wondering whether I'm dead or worse.'

'It's worse, then.'

'Yes, it is,' she said, and started to cry.

Along with the muck, tears were one of the most plentiful commodities on the *Dunkirk*, cutting trails through the grime on the women's faces, and some of the men's too. Plenty from the young girls who had lifted a cabbage, and the older ones who had been torn from their children. But this was the first time Prentice, or anyone on board, had seen tears from Jenny. In the forest and at the inns, a wet face signalled vulnerability and was an open invitation.

It would not now, Jenny suspected, carry much weight with Prentice.

So she inhaled deeply, taking the opportunity to fill her lungs with air that was slightly less rank than that in the cells. She wiped her eyes with her sleeve. She said, 'Where did the pork come from?'

'From a pig,' he said, and chuckled softly at his own wit.

'And one that died around the time I was born, by the taste,' she said. 'How did this pig come to be in my belly? From the stores?'

'They don't swim around the hulk, you know. We don't dangle a line over the rail to catch them.'

'You would, of course, have gotten permission from the quartermaster to use the pork in payment for a tumble.'

He paused, looked at her. Said nothing.

'Mr Corbett, he seems like an upright man,' she said. 'Probably goes to church. Reads us our prayers on Sunday. Pious people can be a bit inconvenient, I find.'

Prentice smiled in spite of himself; stopped smiling as she continued.

'Particularly when they're made aware of theft,' she said, standing and walking over to him until their faces were inches apart 'Theft of food, especially. Theft of the means to pay for another sin. I imagine Mr Corbett might think that having someone who could do such a thing around the likes of us convicts, who've already sunk almost as low as it's possible to sink, so we are told, would be … inadvisable.'

'You'll keep your mouth shut about it, of course, if you want more.'

'Even if this is the last ten-year-old salt pork I get to eat, I still know you'll give me enough food to keep me alive. If they wanted me dead, they would have turned me off after the assizes. So I have no objection to ancient pork, but I don't want it as badly as I want to get a message to my mother.'

He nodded slowly. 'Thing about the pious,' he said, 'a lot of them tend to be educated.'

'I suppose that's so.'

'If I were to ask Mr Corbett, as a favour to me, to write and send a letter for you – would you then be seeing any need to talk about people who may have taken pork from the stores?'

'No, I don't think so. I believe the relief would wipe any such thoughts from my mind.'

He nodded again, gave her his hand and hauled her up from the mattress. Then he shoved her – not hard enough to make her stumble, but enough to make a point – towards the door.

'I may be by again, next couple of nights,' he said. 'I think you can expect to see Corbett before that.'

Mr Corbett knew, of course he did. He would know Prentice well enough to realise that the man wouldn't have asked him for a kindness without some sort of inducement. Corbett didn't mention it to Jenny, though, and did not seem to be judging her. But he did say, 'I would have done this for you anyway. Why did you not ask?'

He had brought a stool with him, and some writing implements, and sat himself down by the bars where Jenny had wormed her way through the other bodies.

Though he was here to do her a kindness, she suddenly felt angry. 'Have you not heard me? Every time someone comes for the men, I call out that I need help with a letter. Oftentimes, it was when you were down here. So don't blame me for not asking. You did not answer.'

He nodded, looking towards the opposite wall. 'You hear so much, that sometimes you stop hearing it all … Never mind, I will write this letter for you, and I will make sure it is sent. What would you like to say?'

Jenny had spent so long trying to get somebody to send this message, she had forgotten precisely what message she wanted to send.

After she'd been silent for a few moments, trying to find a way to wrap her current situation in words that might make it seem less desperate, he said, 'You can start by telling her you're alive.'

Jenny snorted. 'Won't she know that when she gets a letter from me?'

He smiled. 'It's my habit, you see, to send the good news in before the bad. You could perhaps say you're being well fed.'

She glared at him.

'Very well,' he said, 'not well fed. Fed, though. You have to give us that.'

'Yes, fed. I am in Plymouth where I'm being fed by no less a soul than His Majesty.'

'As am I,' said Corbett, beginning to make marks on the paper. 'So you are being fed, but you are very remorseful because you committed a crime for which you were caught.'

'What am I remorseful for, do you think?' she asked. 'The crime, or the catching?'

He laughed. 'The latter, of course. But we will let her take whatever meaning she likes from it, shall we?'

'Very well. Then perhaps we can tell her that the King has extended his most generous mercy towards me.'

'Does that sound like something you would say? Would she believe the letter was from you, if it came from someone talking about generous mercy?'

'Yes, all right. Through the King's mercy I'm not to be hanged, but to be sent … where? No one tells us, Mr Corbett.'

'I promise I will tell you as soon as I have certain knowledge of it. You're to be sent across the seas, where you shall serve your sentence and make good.'

'Then I'll return? I'll return to help her.'

'Seven years is a long time, Jenny. I would not be making any promises about returning. You may, in truth, decide that where we are going is better for you than where we have been.'

'No talk of returning then. But could you put down that I love her. Tell her to eat, and tell her to get into Howard Tippett's bed so she has the means of eating.'

'I'll do all but the last,' Corbett said. He read the letter back to her, and then spoke the words he'd written at the bottom of the page. 'Your loving daughter, Jenny.' She nodded, and he asked, 'Would you like to sign it? Here, take this.' He handed her the pen and held the page up to the bars with one hand. With the other, he took her wrist and moved it so that it made a shape on the page that meant no more to her than any of the other scratch marks. 'You see, you're making a J,' he said, as he moved her hand down and then into a curve. 'Now the T,' he said, drawing her hand across and then down. 'JT, you see?'

'JT – what does that mean?'

'Remember those letters, Jenny, and remember how to write them, if you can, but please remember what they sound like. Remember what they mean. Those letters are your initials, Jenny Trelawney. They are who you are.'

'Will we be seeing you with a silk bonnet and pretty little shoes soon?'

The call came from across the way, from one of the boys, and despite its questionable wit it drew waves of laughter from the other men.

Mr Corbett had gone a few minutes before, promising to send the letter at the earliest opportunity, and Jenny had stayed slumped against the bars, thinking.

The speaker, as far as she could tell, was one of the better-looking boys. One of those who kept getting picked for work because of his strong shoulders. She glared at him, looked away.

'A warder and an officer,' he said. 'Perhaps you will try the captain next.'

'Perhaps I will,' she called out. 'You're all busy with each other.'

Howls, this time, outrage which she knew was hollow – she had heard grunts at night from across the small space between the cells.

'Oh, but what about the vast sea we have to cross together, my lover?'

She didn't know the faces that went with most of the voices. But this new voice, this one she knew. It was Cornish. It was soft, belonging to someone who was not in the habit of raising his voice to be heard. The blue-eyed man, Dan Gwyn by name.

'Perhaps you'll find a little time for me on the ocean,' he said. 'Perhaps you'll be in need of a little comfort when the weather gets rough. Perhaps you'll be scared.'

'Perhaps not,' she said.

'Oh, but this sea – the one we're going on – you've never been on it, have you? It's vicious. That it is, not polite like our English waters.'

'I know nothing of English waters. Cornish ones, though, nothing polite about them. I have seen them in their worst tempers, and they have never scared me.'

'I've been on Cornish seas all my life,' he said. 'If they don't scare you from time to time, you're either a fool or the bravest woman alive.'

Jenny could, probably, swim better than most of the marines. Certainly better than Farrow, she liked to think. Absolutely better than Prentice, if he could swim at all; he sweated too much to be good at cutting through the water.

Escape from the hulk, though, looked like a bad bet. She could probably make the jump and survive it. But the water below was murky, green, studded with rotting things – not a substance with which she wanted to douse the wounds on her wrists and ankles. And the marines, with their slender weapons, often looked overboard. There was always one on duty, and she would make quite a splash even if she kept her legs straight.

It might be better, she thought, to wait until they were underway. Untie a cutter and make for an isolated shore.

The wait was interminable. They had entertainment from the physically impossible suggestions of the men, and the fights among the women, when dirty, cracked nails gouged marks in grime-filmed cheeks. Jenny, at least, had the occasional meal of antiquated pork, when Prentice – whose first name she still didn't know, nor did she care to – took her up to his hut and pounded at her for a few minutes, handing her that oilcloth bundle afterwards which she always ate there and then.

The hulk occasionally rocked if the weather was bad, a feeble pitch or two. But it was enough to make some of the girls squeal, those who had never sat in a boat even if they had grown up around them. Bea was one of them, always gripping Jenny's hand if they were near enough when the hulk began to pitch. Jenny didn't know how Elenor felt about it: she had blown herself out like a storm, expended her anger in the gaol. She had joined those who lay and stared at the bulkhead. She would hit whoever came near her, or anyone who tried to take her food. Otherwise, though, she was an absence.

Two months passed, or three. Jenny hadn't counted in a while. There was not so much need to sacrifice warmth for fresh air, and the arguments that had often broken out during the colder months over opening the hatches began to abate.

People died, here and there. The impossibly aged Dorothy was still sitting in her corner and offering blunt nuggets of advice: 'You could have done better than Prentice,' she told Jenny, 'had you waited. I'd take an officer over a warder any day – fewer fleas.' But several younger women succumbed to chest complaints or fevers, and more than once Jenny woke to become aware of a cold stiffness at her back.

Mr Corbett seemed to have decided that the spiritual welfare of the depraved was his responsibility. He came down every Sunday to read them their prayers. He made his voice rise and fall with the words, imbuing them with life.

One Sunday, he brought more than prayers.

'I said I would tell you our destination when I knew it. We will be travelling to Botany Bay.'

'Is it closer than America?' Jenny asked.

'Much further, I'm afraid. Further still than Africa. I expect we will be at sea for some months.'

The women nearby heard him and groaned at the prospect, and a few began to weep – the ones who seemed to have an unending supply of tears.

Jenny smiled, and after Corbett left she traced the initials into the grime on the cell floor. JT – that was who she was. She had repeated the sounds to herself every night, before sleep, whether lying on a board in the cell or on the thin mattress in Prentice's cabin. She feared if she forgot them, she would slip away from herself.

There was no risk of that now, though, not with the prospect of months in a moving boat before her. JT was who she was. She was going back to the ocean, and she told it, silently, to try to drown her and see how far it got.

PART TWO

CHAPTER 8

Jenny's months in the hulk had been dreamless, sleep simply an absence of consciousness, of understanding, of knowing what and where she was. Since they'd been at sea, though, the dreams had happened every night. Often they were of her father failing to save her from drowning, doing so and thinking better of it, or simply deciding to push her in. Or her mother, walking down the shore, gathering pieces of kelp in a basket, the waves visible through her translucent body as Jenny called and called with no response.

When her head was slammed into the bulkhead by the lurch of the boat, she understood why the dreams had come back. They came with the ocean, and were not possible without it.

The *Charlotte* had been sailing with the fleet for a few weeks now, and there had been rough seas which turned it almost on its side, which drew screams from the women and from some of the men in the cell nearby.

Their confinement arrangements mirrored those in the hulk. But here, with waves hurling themselves at the hull, the hatches weren't open. Here, with only inches of wood separating Jenny from the sea, she could not smell it. She fell, as they all did, into a boredom that slowly changed its shape, became torpor and then trance. She existed in her guts and resented anyone who spoke to her, who broke the deadening progress, forced her back into full consciousness and the realisation that time was passing, that she had used up another breath and another beat, and had nothing to show for it. Bea was the only person she responded to. Elenor refused to talk to her anyway.

When she was brought above decks for exercise, after the fleet moved out of swimming range of Portsmouth it was the first time she had seen full sunlight in four months.

What she saw on the faces around her nearly made her want to go below again.

Some of the women had been with her since they were loaded onto the *Dunkirk*, and she remembered feeling envy at the smoothness of their skin, not scratched and creased from sleeping on a forest floor and exposure to wind. They were the faces of girls brought up on green expanses rather than blue ones, girls who had drunk milk straight from the cow or regularly tasted its meat.

These girls, now, were unrecognisable. They wore the clothes they'd been sentenced in, some tattered almost beyond utility, flapping in the breeze on frames far smaller than those the garments had been made for. The chests of many showed skin stretched tight over ridges of bone. Their hair was stiff and matted, but their faces were the worst of it: cracked and bleeding lips, the sag at the jowls after the fat of the cheeks had been used up. And the colours – some were white, and some, an alarming number, were yellow. Old Dorothy's skin sagged down from her body as though she was a child in a woman's clothes.

When Jenny glanced at her own wrist, she saw yellow as well.

The men, with more rations, were looking slightly better, but they too showed signs of their confinement, and many mouths had more gaps between the teeth than when the *Charlotte* had sailed from Plymouth to meet the rest of the fleet.

Jenny grew used to the yellowed horrors who shambled around the deck with her, used to the idea that she was a yellowed horror too.

She studied every inch of the *Charlotte*. She ran her fingers along knots, committing them to memory. She looked between the planks of the deck to see how much pitch was used to bind them together, how many nails studded the expanse of wood. She counted the sails: thirteen separate sheets of cloth, each bigger by several times than the small sail on her childhood boat. She ran her eye along each of the ropes that held the ship together like a spiderweb, trying to tell where they ran to and what their purpose was. She looked at the sailors, what they were doing, what sails were being trimmed and why. She tested the wind, using a trick her father had taught her, licking her finger and holding it in the air to gauge the breeze's direction.

The men seemed undeterred by the change in the state of the women, their suggestions increasingly depraved. Of course, they could do no more than on the *Dunkirk*, but now they had a destination, and many of their suggestions started with, 'When we get there ...'

Blue-eyed Dan Gwyn was on the *Charlotte* too – as rough as the rest of them, and as profane. But the other men loved him, every bit as much as some of the women seemed to. He boasted as much as or more than anyone else, spending one of the few currencies available to him: stories of evaded revenue men and keen negotiations over a bolt of silk.

But Dan was alone in encouraging the others to boast too, and never calling their tales into question. 'John,' he would say, 'tell us again how you hid in the tree while the constables walked right underneath looking for you.'

John Carney, an Antrim thief, would smile and talk, and say, 'I didn't hide well enough, though, did I?'

'Neither did none of us. No shame in that, or we're all shamed.'

The lads, as most referred to the strange collection of men in the opposite cell, respected Dan. Quieted down, sometimes, when he told them to, with his habit of using such requests to coalesce them around a common cause. 'Best shut your mouths, boys,' Jenny had heard him say. 'No need to give them any more proof that we're animals.'

Because he had the trust of the men, he got the trust of the marines too. At Mr Corbett's suggestion, Dan was put in charge of distributing the rations. He would measure out all of the food in full view of the others so that everyone could see he was being even-handed and taking his own share last.

One of the lads, Joseph Clancy, had a high reedy voice that he used mostly to complain. He would daily grumble that Dan had been uneven with the rations, had given him less than John Carney and some of the others. Joseph was largely ignored by the men, most of whom viewed Dan as a bridge between them and the marines. Such a man, one who could win the trust of both the lags and their gaolers, might have his uses.

Still, Dan was one of the most enthusiastic and imaginative of the men, judging by his stated intentions with regard to the women.

He saw Jenny licking her finger, on a day when the wind was refusing to behave, refusing to decide on a direction, and he said, 'I have something you can lick.'

She glanced at him briefly and looked away, held her finger up and stared at the clouds.

'Where is it from, do you think?' His voice was closer, and when she looked back she saw he was near enough to touch. He wasn't leering now, or mocking. Nothing in his stance was suggestive. He was looking at her finger, at the sails, at the sky. He was frowning.

'Hard to tell,' she said. 'It seems to not be able to make up its mind. It was from the north earlier – did you see the sails? They were stiff as boards, or looked it. Now, though – it's turning around. It's getting, I think, stronger.'

'They think so too,' he said. 'Look.' She did, and saw sailors climbing the rigging, nimble on the ropes for the most part, as those without agility did not tend to survive long. The sailors were untying the sails, reefing them in, tying them to the mast.

She looked again at the sky. The clouds were being smeared across the blue, and they were pendulous now, bruised.

'I remember you saying you've been on the ocean,' Dan said.

'A lot, when I was younger. My father fished.'

'Poor bastard,' he said. 'Precious little fishing in Cornwall, now.'

'You're from the sea too,' she guessed. Those convicts without childhood training on the waves were showing no interest in what was happening with the sails, no inclination to ask why the sailors were urgently crawling over the ropes.

He nodded.

'Was it the ocean that brought you here?' she asked.

She rolled the question around in her head after she'd spoken it, realising how ridiculous it sounded, how badly she had mangled the meaning behind it. She cared, oddly, that he think well of her, or at least not think her simple. He was tall – taller than her, not always the case with men. He seemed to have retained some of the muscle he had earned on the work gangs, and some of the curiosity that had probably been with him for much longer.

He took her meaning, though. Did not say: *Of course the ocean brought me here, brought all of us here.*

'Yes, in a way,' he said. 'Fair trading – and an excise man who was less dim than most of them.'

A smuggler, then. A crime that had killed her father. A crime most didn't consider criminal.

'You took some bread, or a cabbage,' he guessed. 'Or some clothes from a line.'

'No. No, highway robbery.'

He laughed, a rasping chuckle that had rusted from lack of use. 'Had you a horse? And a pistol?'

'No. My feet, and a knife. Sometimes a staff.'

He frowned, then, looking at her from under drawn brows, seeming to search her face for any sign she was lying – that she was perhaps hoping to find a gullible creature from whom she could get some amusement. She would be damned, she thought, if she tried to convince him; if she wasted breath on laying claim to her crime. Anyway, she'd received no better or worse treatment for stealing jewellery on the Kings Highway than she would have had she lifted a cabbage from a garden.

'They hang the highway robbers,' Dan said.

'Sometimes. Why hang livestock, though?'

'We're not livestock.'

'We are nothing but. You're the bullock who drags the plough along, I'm the cow. They'll be wanting me to produce more bullocks, otherwise they'll have to do the work themselves.'

She licked her finger again, held it up. She didn't need to this time, though. The wind had finally made up its mind, had turned to the south, and was gathering a roar in its throat. Whitecaps were scabbing over the crests of waves, and sailors were scuttling back down the rigging as fast as they could.

Farrow was walking towards them, planting his feet on the deck as though trying to punish it.

'No more fresh air, then?' Jenny said to him.

'Too much of it about to be flung at us,' he said. 'You're going below now, all of you. If you complain about it, I'll do you a great disservice – I'll let you stay up here.'

It was, by a long way, the worst storm they had sailed through.

The ship lurched like a drunk to one side and then the other, so that in the space of a minute Jenny would be forced against the hull, and then scrambling to hang on to the board on which she lay. The nose would tilt up, and up, and the longer it spent in the air the worse the landing would be, as the waves that had forced the ship skywards suddenly disappeared and it smashed back down onto the jagged water.

The worst of it, thought Jenny, was the noise. The wind was loud and angry, screaming like a madman of the wrongs done to it. There were answering screams from some of the women, which earned them thumps from the more hardened lags.

Jenny did what she could for the panicking women. She sat with them and rubbed their backs, her murmurs snatched by the rattling timbers. She told them to scream at the storm as much as they liked, as long as they didn't expect it to listen.

After the screams came the vomit, as one woman after another evacuated her stomach contents. It was carried on the ship's movement until it splattered against the deck or the hull or someone's cheek.

The storm lasted almost until morning. It must, Jenny thought, have sent gallons of water spilling across the deck during its fiercest hours, for quite a bit of it had made its way down into the hold. It now sat, ankle-deep and refusing to drain, soaking hems and stinging open wounds.

By sunrise, the worst of the storm was over, and Jenny was grateful the sun couldn't penetrate here with any great strength, for she knew what she would see: a murky salt pool, a soup of vomit and excrement, as the buckets in which they relieved themselves had been sent spinning across the cell.

Some of that vomit was her own. But not from seasickness – a malady she didn't suffer from, something she was profoundly grateful for when she saw the misery even the calmest of days inflicted on others, whose roughest journeys before this had been in a cart on a rutted road.

It was perfectly calm by the time the contents of Jenny's stomach flavoured the salt pool. She found it impossible not to draw attention to herself, impossible to keep down the animal noise she could hardly believe her throat was making. She continued to make it long after there was nothing left in her stomach.

She feared it would take some of the shine off her in the eyes of the others. The grudging respect she had become used to on the hulk, the intermingled fear and fascination towards her status as a highwaywoman, wasn't as much of a shield here in any case. In the hold of the *Charlotte* were London women, she-lags who boasted that their criminal pedigree went back centuries, forgers and prostitutes and murderers and batterers. They saw highwaywomen as dabbling amateurs, bored girls playing at crime.

Susannah Waybright was one of the worst. She had been trained from the age of five to lift items from the pockets of gentlemen as they strode through London's streets. She'd been good at it, too, particularly in her own retelling. 'They never knew my hand been in their pocket,' she would say. Most of the other women would listen with great attention, as inattention tended to attract a blow. For all her self-proclaimed dexterity, Susannah was a big woman, with a flat face and flat hands like small porcelain plates.

Jenny had disliked her immediately. She seemed only to fully exist when surrounded by adoring – and slightly scared – women, who would exclaim over her cleverness and thank her for striking out on behalf of the poor.

Jenny had always refused to sit with the women who gathered around Susannah as she outrageously embroidered her adventures on London's night-time streets. There was one adventure, though, that she never spoke about: the night her legerdemain had failed her. The night she felt a hand encircling her wrist while it was in a gentleman's pocket, trying to work free a watch caught between folds of fabric. Jenny heard – for such things were whispered about during strolls around the deck, when women linked arms and pretended they were in Kew Gardens – that Susannah had responded by biting the man's hand, forcing him to release her wrist while she ran. But the crowded streets that served as a pickpocket's camouflage were not kind to Susannah that night. She couldn't move fast enough through the press of bodies until the same hand, smeared with a little blood from the bite wound, came down on her shoulder.

After hearing that story, Jenny was unable to resist baiting Susannah at every opportunity. She would call out from where she lay on her plank: 'Do you want help with your food, Suse? Your fingers might not be up to it,' or, 'When we arrive, I hope you bite the captain as you get off the ship.' For the most part, Susannah ignored her, giving her brief glances that consigned her to the status of an irritation.

But when one of the women spoke as though Susannah was a class hero, Jenny would say, 'How much of the money did you give away, Suse? Feed any children, did you?' The woman would push herself up from where she'd been squatting, wade through her acolytes and stomp over to Jenny, raising a hand. Jenny would stand, too, almost taller – they were the two tallest women in the hold – and say, 'I can bite too, and I have more teeth to work with.'

Susannah's concern for the poor clearly did not extend to the matter of food. She and Elenor had formed a devil's alliance, the pair of them standing over the weaker ones, extracting rations by any means they could. They had tried to talk Mr Corbett into giving them the same job among the women as Dan had with the men, but he'd refused.

At mealtimes, Suse didn't care who put some of their own share onto her huge outstretched palm, but knew someone would. Bea tried to, once or twice, but Jenny held her back.

'We're locked away in here for now,' Suse would say to some of the younger girls, 'but what happens when we step ashore? What happens when we're in a place of monsters and savages, a place which hasn't heard of English law, and there's nothing between us and the men? What do you think they'll do, them who have been locked down here with us, able to hear and smell and rant, but not touch? You will need a protector, then, little thing like you. I can't protect everyone, but I'll remember who was generous.'

It was a tactic she had tried on Jenny early in the voyage. Jenny had replied, 'And while you're protecting us from the men, who's protecting us from you?

Suse and Elenor had targeted old Dorothy, too. 'The depravity of these men, mother, you've no idea,' Elenor said to her. 'You hear what they suggest, day and night. It's all they're thinking about, and they won't hesitate as soon as they're in a position to do it. Starved as they are, they won't see age as a barrier.'

'Half my luck,' said Dorothy. 'My only chance of surviving long enough to have a bit of a tumble is to keep all my rations to myself.'

Susannah had been the first to lose her stomach contents to the storm, had been one of the screechers whose terror was expressed through the jangled scream.

Now, as Jenny lay with her head over the side of her plank, Susannah laughed. 'The rest of us are better now, the boat's hardly rocking,' she said. 'It takes a special one to still be losing her food hours after a storm has passed.'

Jenny rolled over, too weakened to get up. She did her best to glare before retching again.

'There she is, girls,' said Susannah, 'the queen of the seas. As long as she is on a mill pond, she'll be fine.'

A few – perhaps those most frightened of Suse – sniggered.

The next day, when Jenny was on the deck, she looked over the gunwales. The sea was all tiny smooth peaks and troughs, with no trace of foam. A wonderful northerly wind was pushing the fleet forward. Jenny loved – when she was able to see it – watching the sailors throw a knotted rope over the ship's side, counting how many knots were forced to the surface by the ship's movement.

'Five knots,' one of the men called out. It was a more-than-respectable speed, even for a boat with no waves to impede it.

Her stomach again contracted to push out whatever it contained, and a small helping of porridge hit the water. Rations weren't so plentiful that Jenny could see them disappear into the ocean with equanimity, even if they had already been partly digested. Yet she was, uniquely among the women, getting fatter.

She knew why. But she did not want to. For a start, the weakness her condition brought made any thought of escape impossible, at least for the next few months. And it would make her more vulnerable to Susannah, even though there would, hopefully, be increased rations for a pregnant woman.

The baby would probably be pushed into the world in a different hemisphere to that in which its father dwelt. It was possible, even likely, that father and child would never look at the same sky.

CHAPTER 9

Charlotte Prentice came screaming into the world with another storm, roaring in sympathy with the wind as it forced the ship sideways and folded waves over the deck.

Jenny had hoped to spend some time on deck before the business got underway. But the authorities clearly believed that allowing the convicts the merest glimpse of a landmass would induce them to hurl themselves overboard and strike out for shore. The lags were tamped down in the hold whenever the ship put into a port, so that places with musical names, Tenerife and Rio, slid past without Jenny having seen them, and therefore might as well not have existed. Any of them, though, might have provided an opportunity for escape under different circumstances, and Jenny wasn't the only one bent on it. A male convict from another ship, they were told, had scaled down the side of his transport at Tenerife, taken a cutter and sailed around the island. He had found a beach there, looking hospitable enough with its unmarked sand, and pulled the cutter ashore. He may have exhaled, relaxed, started looking for food – before the fleet rounded the island's corner and saw him.

But Jenny had been anchored to the *Charlotte* by her growing stomach.

Bea attended the birth, wiping Jenny's forehead and checking
between her legs, and yelling at the men who whooped and
catcalled every time Jenny let out a particularly guttural moan.
They only stopped when Dan told them he'd throttle the next
one who opened his mouth. Bea, Dorothy and a few of the other
women, who had lost any squeamishness long ago, helped pull
Charlotte out into the miasma of salt and sweat.

A glistening mound of purple tissue followed Charlotte, a
nurturing presence that had outlived its purpose, attached to
the baby by a fleshy cable which the ship's surgeon came and
cut in the calm that followed. He picked up the little girl,
gingerly holding her while protecting his sleeves with a cloth,
and examined each part of her minutely without taking her in as
a whole person. Charlotte quieted, staring back at him through
the protective moons of his spectacles, clenching and unclenching
her fists. 'A fine girl,' he said to Jenny, and handed her daughter
back.

'Here's one whose ration Suse won't be able to steal,' said
Dorothy. 'Best get her on the teat, my love, straightaway now.
She'll have a hunger, after all that.'

Charlotte clamped on to Jenny, still flexing her fists as though
to warn off Susannah or Elenor or anyone else who might make
a claim on her portion of the world's nourishment.

Jenny hadn't noticed Susannah sidling over, her arm snaking
out towards some hard bread: part of Jenny's ration that remained
uneaten as she'd been otherwise occupied. Jenny would have looked
for it later. Found it missing. Suspected it resided in Susannah's
stomach, but been unable to prove it.

She was saved the trouble by a kick aimed at the back of
Susannah's knee, buckling her leg long enough for another hand
to reach out and grab the bread.

The hand, and the kick, were Elenor's.

Elenor gave the bread to Jenny. 'Leave her alone, Suse. You can't make milk out of thin air. If her baby dies, we will all have to put up with the wailing.'

Susannah was too startled to object.

Later, with a glutted sleeping Charlotte being rocked by Bea, Jenny went over to Elenor.

'You didn't have to do that,' she said.

'Suse needed teaching.'

'Thank you.'

'I'll be expecting repayment,' Elenor said, in a low, insistent whisper. 'An opportunity will come.'

'I have nothing to pay you with.'

'Maybe you will.' Elenor looked over at Charlotte. 'Can I hold her?'

A clench of fear, of the kind the sea couldn't call forth, rose in Jenny. She did not want her daughter held by this woman, this creature of obscure motives.

'She's sleeping,' Jenny said. 'If it's wails you fear, I wouldn't wake her.'

Elenor shrugged. 'Good though, is it? To have someone belong to you?'

'She doesn't ... well, in a way I suppose she does.'

'Course she does, and you to her. That makes you lucky. No one here belongs to anyone now. 'Cept the Crown, maybe.'

'El ... who did you belong to?'

Elenor winced and turned her head, and Jenny began to move away. Then she realised Elenor was speaking, very softly, as though to see how badly Jenny wanted to hear.

'A man ... a man with debts,' she said. 'Cards, mostly. In danger, great danger, from those he owed money to. I borrowed from

Black, you see, to pay them off. And then he went … somewhere, I'm not sure. Just wasn't there one day. Mr Black needed repaying. I thought my man might find me, come for me. No chance of that now, unless he has wings.'

Jenny wondered what her daughter – out of her mother's belly but still in the belly of her second mother, the ship after which she was named – would make of their destination. Charlotte would be carried ashore to a land that didn't know her, and that likely hadn't seen a baby of such pale skin and blue eyes since the mountains first rose from the sea.

Before Charlotte's birth, Jenny had made the most of her time on deck. It was where she and Bea, and a couple of the other girls, had played a game of quietly mocking their guards. The knot of women would choose a marine, a sailor, an official; they particularly liked the ones who strutted around as though at court. In unison, the women would run their eyes over the man and lean their heads together, whispering, while timing their laughter to emerge at the same instant, peppering the man with derisive grapeshot. Sometimes men had glared back, and Jenny had thought, *I will jump into the ocean before I let you tell me where to look.*

Now she was consumed with tracing Charlotte's soft eyebrows, to holding out a finger to be grasped, to memorising the precise shape of her baby's nose, to trying to find meaning in the impossibly black hair on her head. She did not know if Prentice's hair, before it started to grey and fall out, had been black. She still didn't know, had never bothered to find out, his first name.

Occasionally, she wondered whether some more refined creature had come into the cells at night, when Jenny was sleeping as well as anyone could on a bare board, and given Charlotte to her, as it seemed impossible that Prentice could be the author of such a being, that the child could have resulted from a physical transaction involving antiquated salt pork.

'Can I have a hold of her?' asked a male voice.

Jenny pulled the baby into her and hunched her shoulders as though they were wings that she could close around her child. 'No! Why would you want to? What would you do?'

Dan Gwyn. Such a man, with his muscles that refused to waste despite extreme deprivation, and with eyes that still held something more than hunger. She didn't know why he wanted to hold her baby, and she was certainly not going to allow it. He might dance away, perhaps in jest, while holding the little girl, or dangle her over the edge of the ship. No, he would not be given the opportunity, despite his threat to the other men as they'd matched her birthing moans with their catcalls.

'I only want to look at her,' Dan said.

'Look, then,' she said, easing one shoulder back slightly but keeping her arms clamped around the child.

'I thought … I thought it might do good, you see. To look at something – someone – uncorrupted.'

Jenny smiled without intending to. 'Look at the sky, then. Look at the ocean. Look at how we cut it open and it closes behind us as though we were never there. Where we're going – I've heard there will be savages, but there will be no roads or sewers, no buildings, no gaols. It will be pure too.'

'Yes, maybe,' he said. 'Maybe, until we get our hands on it.'

Mr Corbett still enjoyed reading prayers on a Sunday, although Jenny wasn't sure how he knew which day it was. She had taken to counting the days between readings – sometimes, yes, seven would pass, but more frequently five or six.

Corbett had a pleasant voice, soft but deep, rumbling sometimes in his throat. He would do his readings on deck when the weather was fine enough, but he seemed to have no objection to descending into the hold, where the wood was surrounded by water. Effluvium from the seamen's quarters would occasionally drip through, and anyone who spent any time there would find their hair slick with substances best not named.

Really, it was the captain's job to make sure the convicts' bodies were in a sufficient state to survive the voyage, and their souls equally healthy should they need to make another journey. But Captain Archer was a dry man who rarely addressed the convicts, even to bark threats; he preferred to leave that to Lieutenant Farrow and the others who took such pleasure in it. Archer would sometimes read the prayers, say amen, and walk away.

Then out would come Mr Corbett. He no longer restricted himself just to psalms or homilies; he occasionally read poetry – fairly boring, in Jenny's view, going on about flowers or clouds. Most of his audience was similarly unengaged in distant and dead men and their views on the wonders of nature. They would wander off while Corbett was reading, if he was doing so on deck, or turn away and gossip with each other if he was below.

'Do you not mind when so few listen?' Jenny asked him, as Suse herded some of the women into a corner of the cell, possibly to talk them out of their most recent ration. The food was less of a prize than it had been at the start: the rice contained more living things than all the convicts in the Empire.

'Not really,' Corbett said. 'It passes the time, whether they listen or not.'

'Why aren't you reading to the officers, then?'

'I don't think they'd show any more interest than most of the convicts do.'

'Don't let them hear you,' Jenny said. 'Comparing them with us – Farrow would probably push you overboard.'

Corbett laughed. 'Very possibly, and I wish him all the luck in the world trying it.'

Jenny had noticed that Corbett never held a handkerchief to his nose when he passed a convict, never yelled when speaking would do just as well.

'You don't seem to mind it down here,' Jenny said, as rainwater from about half an hour ago worked its way between the boards and dripped onto them both.

'I daresay I'd mind it if I couldn't get up and leave.'

She frowned, turning away slightly. It was time he went, anyway. Charlotte, in her arms, had been lulled to sleep by the sound of his voice reading, but was beginning to stir and would want feeding shortly.

'I'm sorry,' he said gently, 'but I do remember, you see, what it is not to be able to get up and leave. I do recall, as much as I don't wish to, what prison is like.'

'You were never in prison!'

'I was, actually.'

'What did you do?'

'I wore a red coat, and I sailed with lots of other men in red coats to America, where I helped fire cannons at people who wanted the right to govern themselves.'

Jenny nodded, drawing her brows together in what she hoped

was an understanding expression. 'You sound like my father. He spoke of independence too. Loved a fellow called Paine, who said monarchy was against the word of God, or some such.'

Corbett raised his eyebrows, leaning closer so she felt his breath through the bars. 'Be careful whom you talk to of Paine and his ilk. Very few appreciate his views as much as we do.'

'Oh, so you know –'

'Yes, and I'm familiar with his argument that government by kings is against scripture – although he doesn't think much of scripture either, to be honest. But such views are treason, of course, and I'm not sure how much tolerance the governor has for freethinking. We will hold Paine close to ourselves, shall we? Guard him.'

Did ideas, then, have a value, that they needed to be guarded? Did they, she wondered, grow in pungency like mould when under lock and key?

'Why are you a marine,' she said, 'if you want to guard Paine?'

'My father was a dancing master, successful enough to afford a commission. This is the best way for me to rise, anyway. And, I do believe, there's something to be said for having men of conviction inside the castle walls, and in the garrison rather than the gaol.'

'Will they put *us* in gaols, when we get there?' she asked. 'Will the men build us proper gaols with stone walls?'

'God, I hope not. We don't need to remake Newgate on the other side of the world. Well, I imagine there will be a guard house, or something like it. I'm sure that not everybody has left their criminal disposition back in England. But the entire place is intended as a prison. We'll have no need of walls for the most part, it is to be hoped. We'll have the ocean.'

'But we already have the ocean, and we're still locked away.'

'Oh, yes. You see, the fear – or one of them – is that you'd mutiny, dooming us all, as I doubt there are many on-board with the skill to sail this ship.'

'Not many. But a few.'

'Not a vessel like this. You know, these cells were supposed to be crowded with stonemasons and farmers and fishermen, people who could build the settlement. But I think there is only one fisherman, Gwyn. A few others have some seamanship, including Carney and Langham. Only a handful who can manage a boat, and only one who knows one end of a seine net from the other.'

'I can fish,' said Jenny. 'I can fish, especially if better rations come from it.'

Corbett looked at her, one eyebrow working upwards. 'I doubt they'll put you in fishing boat, Jenny,' he said. 'But you've mended a net in the past, I presume.'

'Mended them, and made them so they don't need mending,' she said. 'I have good eyes, can see a shoal from a distance. I know how to use the tides and listen to what the wind is telling me, and stitch a sail –'

He smiled, holding up a hand. 'You've a baby to be caring for, as well.'

A question had settled at the bottom of Jenny's mind some months previously. She had kept it there, forcing it into the space also inhabited by worries about her mother. The space for concerns that could have no resolution, could only sap her. This question had been growing, though, exerting pressure as it pushed upwards, magnified by each league they travelled.

She needed to ask it now. Corbett's visits were sporadic; she didn't know when she would see him again, or when he'd have time and inclination to talk. As the fleet grew closer to landing on an unseen beach, she thought the calls on his time would probably increase while the visits would decrease.

'Will Charlotte be safe?' she said. 'Will she be looked after? Will I have what I need for her?'

Corbett exhaled sharply through his nose, a sound that unsettled her. A sound that usually meant someone was about to say something they regretted.

'I will do everything I can for you, and for her, but I cannot say whether any of us will have what we need,' he said. 'I cannot say anything of the sort. Only one group of ours has been there before, and it was there for a week. So we don't know if the land will take crops, or if there's anything worth hunting.'

Jenny drew Charlotte closer to her, the unknown threats to come suddenly infecting the cell.

'I will tell you this,' said Corbett. 'The governor – yes, he's been given that title, even though he has no idea what he will be governing – will make sure that those who have the greatest utility are well treated. The good reverend, now ... he's interested in less corporeal concerns. Your best hope lies in convincing one man that your body is worth saving, and the other that your soul still has a chance.'

CHAPTER 10

The ocean was all the world they had after so many months: the blue and the grey, the white flecks of foam and the sun-induced glints. Jenny wondered, sometimes, whether all the land had sunk, whether all that was left were these ships, sailing to a promised destination that no longer existed.

Then one morning, when the convicts were exercising on deck, the green appeared. Hard to recognise at first, even for those like Jenny who were used to viewing land through the prism of sea mist and distance. It sat on the horizon, perhaps a dark cloud coloured by hopeful imaginations. It grew, though, slowly, and took on shape from the air around it, until even the city lags who had never been on the ocean before this voyage could see what it was. By this time, the lookout's cry of 'land!' was being echoed in the hoarse and rusted-in throats of the sailors who hadn't used the word for an age, and who were now crawling all over the ship like cockroaches.

Bea came up alongside Jenny and clutched her arm almost painfully. 'Is this it?' she said. 'Is this where we're going? Will we be able to get off the ship soon?'

'Maybe, duck,' Jenny said.

Then the winds rose, pinching the water's surface into peaks, piling wave upon wave. Soon the convicts, herded and tamped down, were again being flung into walls and staying out of the way of the privy buckets.

Bea began to cry. 'I thought it might be over,' she said to Jenny. The two of them sat in a corner, and Jenny was holding Charlotte in the crook of her arm nearest to Bea, so the little girl had the padding of their bodies on either side.

'I know,' Jenny said. 'But it won't be long, I'm sure of it. This storm isn't going to send us back into the blank ocean. We'll be ashore within days, I promise.' She hummed to Charlotte until both the baby and Bea were asleep.

The storm abated as all the others had, and when it did all of the ships in the fleet were still in the world of air and sunlight. The scene returned to blue innocence, making the grey boiling horror seem like a grotesque, half-glimpsed nightmare. It wasn't, everyone agreed later, the worst storm the fleet had encountered since leaving England. But it was the cruellest, because it had snatched the land away from them.

When the land had seemed so close, a promise, everyone – bonded and free – was anxious to see it, to step on it. They would make their accommodations with their own situation later, but for now they hungered for the strangeness. When they were blown back, though, everyone in the hold was desolate. Some of the men muttered about a curse, or about a living land that could sense the garbage it would be asked to ingest and had rejected it outright. A few said the only way for them to see land again was to sail the ship there themselves.

'Have you sailed a brig, Vincent?' Dan shouted. 'You, Jim? Me, I could take a fishing boat anywhere. But a ship this size? Wouldn't have a clue, and neither would any of you. You'd just bring them down harder on us.'

The lads were quiet then, apart from the occasional mutter.

'Don't know about sailing,' said Vincent Langham, a merchant seaman convicted after a tavern brawl. 'But I could navigate anywhere.'

'You can navigate while you swim, then,' Dan said.

Neither Mr Corbett nor any of the other officers knew what was being said below. But Jenny could see that Corbett, at least, had enough sense to know the disappointment afflicting those on the deck and in the cabins would be magnified in the hold. He couldn't make the land reappear, but he could distract them. He told them stories of men who made wax wings that melted close to the sun, or who had to carry the entire world on their backs; of gods of sun and lightning, and of a two-faced god called Janus whose name was associated with betrayal and deceit.

Dorothy felt this was unfair. 'Hardly his fault, is it?' she said. 'You can't help how you're born.'

Then Corbett brought down a book and read them the story of a woman called Katherine. Jenny liked her a lot, at first: she refused to do as she was asked, simply because she was asked it. Jenny stopped liking the story, though, when the woman changed into an obedient bride after many attempts by her betrothed to influence her.

'Are you trying to tell us to be good, Mr Corbett?' Jenny asked.

'I would always advise you to be good, Jenny. Particularly here. The governor, he understands that everyone in the belly of these ships will be needed to build the settlement, and I'm confident that anyone who behaves well will be rewarded for it.'

'She can't have been happy, though,' Jenny said. 'Not afterwards, not when he took her away from herself. He can't have loved her, not to do that.'

'Pity your husband, then,' called Dan from the men's cell.

Corbett had a deep voice but was a natural mimic and, to much hilarity, fluted away when reading the female parts. In doing so he had got the attention of the men, who were always happy to see an officer making an ass of himself.

'You'll be doing well to get a crone with no teeth left in her head, Dan Gwyn,' Jenny yelled back.

'As luck would have it, I'm unmarried and free,' Dorothy called.

Corbett's story, though, had served its purpose. It had given those who were mourning the land something to latch on to, a world to step into where clothes weren't routinely salt-soaked, abrading the skin almost as much as the irons had done.

It would be days, as it turned out, before those in the hold would have any other evidence that land still existed; before the rocking of the *Charlotte* subsided, and they heard the scrape of the anchor chain and the feet of the crew jumping around above their heads.

Everyone in the hold was sitting upright, and even Elenor and Suse had smoothed down their skirts and neatly folded their hands in their laps when the booted feet made their way down the ladder. Mr Corbett, together with Farrow and a few others, unlocked the men's cell. They chose the strongest ones by the look, Dan Gwyn among them. The others stayed where they were, for now. Dan would be one of the very first of their kind to see this place, and Jenny wondered if she could forgive him for it.

'We'll have a special welcome ready for you ladies,' he called over his shoulder.

'They're probably taking you to feed to the savages,' Jenny yelled. 'They'll be picking bits of your beard out from between their teeth by tonight.' This earned her a bark from Dan that sounded like laughter.

Charlotte began to sputter and then to cry, a baby of sensibility who objected to her mother's cruder pronouncements. Jenny replaced the rocking of the ship with her own, to comfort this child who had never been without movement.

The strong fellows, she knew, had been taken ashore to construct shelter for the rest of them. It was generally agreed that it would be a matter of hours – a day at most – before the women were landed.

They were still in the ship the next day, though, and the day after that.

'Do you think you could have been right about feeding the savages?' Bea said to Jenny nervously at one point, but nobody came to unlock the rest of them.

A horrible thought began to grow in Jenny's mind – and in the minds of others, for it was soon all the way around the cell. Perhaps they were never to be brought ashore. Perhaps these ships would become hulks, have their masts excised and be left at anchor in this impossibly distant bay that the inmates would never see. There were certainly none of the sounds Jenny had expected: no livestock being unloaded, no heavy boots continually crossing the deck.

When the thump of the boots did come again, it was accompanied by voices saying words the lags hadn't expected to hear: 'A sail! A sail!' That, of course, started a fresh round of speculation in the hold. Had their government sent fresh shiploads of convicts out a few days behind them, or more soldiers? Perhaps even more provisions.

No one had expected the sails to be French. That was what Corbett told everyone when he came down, finding himself in the middle of a storm of questions. The French ships, he explained, were there on a mission of exploration.

A rumour quickly spread. A French convict, so it went, had appealed to the patriotism of some countrymen and been concealed on board one of their vessels. Rumours, of course, were as contagious as any disease down in the darkness, fed by boredom until they grew grotesque.

But the possibility bothered Jenny. Had a man grasped the freedom that she'd intended to be among the first to take? She worried that she would grow complacent; that she would wait for the right opportunity until every opportunity had passed. That her daughter would grow alongside her bonded mother, believing such servitude was normal and right.

The group of able-bodied men was brought back, already darker from their time in the sun, blinking in the low light of the hold. Dan briefly knelt at the bars of the female cell, reaching in to offer Charlotte his finger to grasp, smiling at her.

After the soldiers had gone back up, the returned men soon let everyone know what they'd overheard. The officers had been expecting a robust stream near this landing place, but it had turned out to be a trickle without a hope of supplying water for all of those on board. The ground was sandy and looked wholly unsuited for growing anything. So discouraged was Governor Lockhart that he had set out that morning to investigate another bay, further north.

The *Charlotte* shuddered again as the anchor rose and feet stamped on the deck. Then the rocking resumed, quieting little Charlotte who had been irritable during their calm stay.

'We will be out, soon,' Bea whispered. 'We'll be on land.'

'Maybe,' said Jenny. 'Maybe … We will have to see, won't we, duck?'

It was the purest form of frustration when the rocking quieted, the ship stilled, the anchor fell and the marines came – but only for the men. All of them were released this time, and herded towards the ladder that would take them into the air and onto the unaccustomed ground. All of them, without exception, leered at the women as they passed. They made promises about the kind of welcome that would be waiting ashore.

The women weren't the only ones to hear the men's promises. A few hours later, Mr Corbett came back down. He pulled the stool to the bars near where Jenny was sitting, rocking Charlotte to give the little girl comfort that her world hadn't changed irrevocably, that there was still swaying to be had.

'It will be a few days more,' Corbett said. 'A few days, and then you'll be landed.'

'After the other livestock,' said Jenny. They had heard the thumps on the side, the squeals as farm animals were lowered one by one in harnesses to waiting boats, to be rowed ashore to a place that had never seen anything like them.

'You should know,' he said, 'I don't think much can be done to keep the men from you all. I don't think there's any intention to prevent such a thing. The ones on the *Charlotte* are bad enough. Some men on the other ships have not laid eyes on a woman for over a year.'

There was always, for Jenny, a creeping fear that lay just under the surface of her mind. It surged forward now, accompanied as it often was by frustration.

'Why are you bothering to tell me, if nothing can be done to prevent it?'

'Because there are some, I think, coming out of the ships now, who would toss aside a baby to get to its mother.'

Jenny drew her arms around Charlotte, squeezing a gurgle out of her. She had known, she supposed, that the men would take every woman they could. She hadn't thought, though, that the life of a baby who had never touched ground might be viewed by some as a small price to pay – or that the responsibility of the government to protect the convicts stopped short of preventing ravishment.

'You may be interested to know,' said Mr Corbett, 'that Reverend Gibson does not approve of licentiousness. I doubt he's ever seen anything vaguely resembling what's likely to occur when you're all brought ashore. But he knows, as well as anyone, what men of a criminal bent who have been denied female company for so long are likely to do.'

'He'll pray for us, then. That'll be nice. Prayers always work.'

'No doubt he will, Jenny – and something else, as well. He has seen the governor, talked to him, and he'll be taking names of convicts willing to marry. As I've told you there is one, only one, fisherman out of those on board.'

'Dan Gwyn.'

Corbett nodded. 'It would certainly make sense if he were to marry someone with skill in that area herself. Someone who can mend nets, or make ones which don't need mending.'

Dan Gwyn, not the least handsome man Jenny had ever met, and had shown kindness to Charlotte in a world unkind to children.

'Does Gwyn know of the reverend's intentions?' she asked.

'Yes. I've made certain of it. I did mention that marriage would show a steady temperament, and that if such a convict brought in fish, the governor might be persuaded to allow him to keep a portion of the catch.'

Bea, who had been sleeping, stirred now and drifted over to the bars. 'Mr Corbett, are there savages?' she asked. Perhaps she had been entertained by lurid dreams of tribesmen.

'After a fashion, Beatrice,' he said, smiling. 'There are Indians, certainly. They don't, however, seem to be savage. They are well armed, as far as spears go, but they are cautious and have made no attempt to drive us off. Expect them to show interest in your baby, Jenny, as they seem very delighted with children. I took the son of the *Lady Penrhyn*'s quartermaster – Anthony, lad of about seven – for a walk the other day. He'd been getting under his father's feet, you see. And we came upon a group of them. They were fascinated with the boy, and one of the old men put his hand on Anthony's hair, but they seemed very gentle.'

'So they're not going to eat anyone?' Bea asked.

'They have certainly shown no inclination to do so yet.'

She nodded, looking relieved. 'What do they wear? Do they have big, beautiful, colourful feathers? Jewelled silks?'

'No feathers, and no silks. They are – to a man, woman and child – naked.'

The mention of savages had drawn the attention of other women, and their speculation reverberated around the hold long after Corbett had left.

No one, though, had heard what he had told Jenny about marriage.

She didn't want Dan surrounded by women the second they landed. He was still a bit of a favourite, and over the months of the voyage Susannah had made several suggestions to him through the bars, proposals that Jenny wasn't sure were physically possible.

She whispered to Bea that night, as they lay on a board. 'Duck, first thing we get ashore, you should find yourself a husband.'

'But I don't know any of them, not really.'

'Take the hand of the first man you like the look of, tell the fellow he will have better rations if he marries you, and march him up to the reverend. Don't wait a day. Because names don't matter when it comes to marriage. When they find themselves with no bars between them and us for the first time, they won't bother to ask our names.'

CHAPTER 11

Jenny's father would have liked the small cutter in which the women were being rowed ashore. She sat, with Charlotte in her arms, towards the rear of it, in the place where her father used to sit in his boat. This one was bigger, though. There were several women in it, and several dozen trips ahead of it before the ships were emptied.

She had known, of course, that there would be no streets, no taverns, no carts or roads or buildings here. She had known their shelter would have to be built, fashioned out of whatever supplies had survived the many storms of the crossing, and whatever they could find on the land. It was still odd, somehow, to be rowing towards a shore where there was no stone seawall, no pier or dock, no hands outstretched to receive a barrel of pilchards. Instead, there were honeyed platforms of rock, indecently yellow sand, and pale blotched trees with bark like drowned skin gathering near the shore.

Until now, she had played a game with herself. Tried to pretend they had not really left, that they had been sailing all these months just out of sight of Plymouth, and that when they had been taught their lesson they would disembark to the familiar smells and shouting and stone buildings and boarded windows. This was a fantasy, but in the unguarded moments before sleep she had almost believed it. She found it impossible, even in hallucinatory half-consciousness, to believe it now – not with the trees shouting evidence to the contrary.

Some of the women needed to be helped out of the boat. Jenny moved before help was offered. She held Charlotte forward, facing outwards, so that the little girl could have a good view of her new home. Then Jenny started to cry, because Constance didn't know she was a grandmother, Dolly didn't know she was an aunt.

There were tents up, and smoke from a few cooking fires round about – the flames certainly weren't needed for heat. Everywhere, there were men: felling trees and hauling cargo, managing the too-thin livestock, digging holes for unknown purposes.

When the women had landed and were walking past, they leant on their shovels or put down their axes. They contorted their faces and openly discussed the relative attractions of the women before them. One of them, leering along with the rest, was Dan. Jenny stepped away from the small column of women being herded towards the main section of the camp; tents would, for now, serve as a women's barracks.

'Mr Corbett spoken to you?' Jenny asked Dan.

He turned towards her. She was still holding her daughter facing forwards, her arms crossed over the baby's middle. Charlotte's fists were pumping up and down, her nose detecting smoke for the first time: an odd smoke, such as her mother had never smelt in England.

Dan looked at Charlotte, smiled and stroked her forearm. 'You can throw a punch better than most of them here,' he said to her, smiling. 'I think your mam could too.' He looked up, looked at Jenny, making no attempt to disguise his eyes as they ran over her face and down to her body. 'Corbett has spoken to me,' he said.

'What did you think of what he had to say?'

Dan now gazed towards the woods at the back of the bay, towards the narrow, ghostly trees. 'I remained unsaddled in England. Why would I come all this way and then accept a bridle?'

'Because it will get better rations, maybe a hut,' Jenny said.

'Perhaps I don't want a hut.'

'It will get you someone who knows fishing, knows the sea,' said Jenny.

'I know the sea well enough myself.'

'It will get you a woman.'

'Which I can get without the need for marriage,' Dan said. 'Without taking on a child.' He glanced down again, smiling apologetically at Charlotte.

'You'll likely be able to fish,' Jenny said, 'and get to keep some of them.'

'So Corbett says. Haven't heard anyone else say it, certainly not the governor.'

'And … and Charlotte needs protection,' Jenny said, thrusting the little girl towards him. 'Mr Corbett thinks she might be tossed aside, in what's to come.'

This was the closest, Jenny told herself, that she would come to begging this man – who would not have met with her parents' approval – to marry her, to shield her with the threat of violence contained in his broad shoulders.

'I'll think on it, Jenny. I'll think on it.'

'Don't think too long. There may be nothing left of me by tomorrow.'

The women were assembled and told to be silent for the governor.

Edward Lockhart. Ruler of the odd collection of people he had been given, he was more powerful than the King here. Seeking orders from England would take, once the ship left and then returned, more than a year.

Lockhart was a tall man who seemed oddly immune to the sweat that coated every other face, even though he wore a uniform every bit as thick as theirs. She had the sense that any perspiration that tried to colonise his brow would be dealt with severely. His breeches were still white, and bore no salt stains or marks of the earth that was being torn up.

The man next to him stood equally erect, but not quite as tall: a short-legged and bull-shouldered officer who was scowling at the convicts in open hostility. His breeches had one or two brown smears, and his face had a sheen of moisture that looked as though it would soak his sleeve were he to wipe it away.

The governor stood in front of the women, hands behind his back, looking at them one by one. There was no menace in it, unlike in the gaze of his companion. He looked at each convict in turn, not rushing and not bothering to conceal the fact he was assessing them.

'You will find,' he said, 'that those who are regular and behave well will have in me a friend. I will cherish them, I will raise them up. Those, however, who transgress, who continue in the behaviour which saw them transported here, will feel the full weight of my displeasure. It is my fervent hope that I shall never have to order a hanging – however, I will not hesitate to do so should a capital offence be committed. As we have not yet farmed the soil, and we have not yet assessed the ability of this land to provide us with sustenance, I remind you that theft of food is one of the offences that will be met with immediate execution.'

The air seemed unusually still after Lockhart finished speaking; even the convicts working nearby had stopped. Jenny thought they had probably received a very similar welcome when they were first brought up the boats – but it would not do, she supposed, to interrupt the governor's pronouncements with a badly timed whack of an axe on a tree.

One of those who paused in his labours was Dan, barely visible at the edge of the forest that only stopped when the soil gave way to sand. So as the women dispersed, heading towards their canvas roof, Jenny stayed where she was.

'Sir,' she said to the governor. He turned around but did not approach, so she clutched Charlotte a little more tightly and scurried up to him as fast as she could, dropping in what she hoped was his idea of a curtsy.

'You will address the governor as "Your Excellency",' said the shorter man next to him. 'Insubordination is one of the crimes we intend to deal with harshly here.'

'Major Rowe …' said the governor, in what sounded like a warning.

'I'm sorry. Your Excellency,' she said. Bobbing again, but carefully so as not to overbalance and send Charlotte plummeting to the ground. 'I had heard, Your Excellency, that convicts who marry might be given positions of trust.'

'Oh, you've heard? Where might you have heard this?'

'I'm not sure, now, Your Excellency. But rumours, they spread quickly among us.'

'They have grown wings, clearly, if they were able to reach you in the hold of the …' Major Rowe said.

'The *Charlotte*, Your Excellency,' she said to him.

'You do not address *me* as "Your Excellency", only the governor,' the man snapped. 'You may call me "sir".'

'I was on the *Charlotte*, sir.'

'Your child …?' asked the governor. 'Was her father also aboard the *Charlotte*?'

'No, sir. Your Excellency. Her father is in England.'

'And are you free to marry?'

'Yes, Your Excellency. I have never been wed.'

Rowe grunted. 'It's as I told you, sir. They're whores. All of them.'

The governor glanced sharply at the shorter man, before looking back to Jenny. 'We are, as you have heard, encouraging of marriages between the convicts here. I take it, from your inquiry, that you have a prospect in mind?'

'Yes, sir. A very useful man he is, too – a fisherman. He will be able to haul in net upon net of whatever fish swim in these oceans.'

'What would you know of the fish that swim in these oceans, if there are any?' Rowe said.

'I was brought up in that line of work myself, sir. I know how to salt fish so that they will keep through winter. I know how to make nets and sails. I can handle a boat.'

'You won't be required to do so,' said the governor. 'As for making nets and sails … there are possibilities there, I suppose. This remarkable fisherman of yours, where might I find him?'

'He's over there, sir,' she said, pointing towards Dan who had resumed digging a seemingly pointless hole. 'This is Dan Gwyn, the man who has agreed to marry me,' she added loudly, as they approached.

Dan's head whipped towards her, his eyes widening, before his face drew itself into a scowl.

'He's a steady man, as I told you, Your Excellency. Not the type to fail in keeping his promises, of course. You can rely on him.'

Dan's face quickly rearranged itself, smoothing over, although he did risk a sharp glance in her direction.

He understands me well enough, she thought.

'I see,' said the governor. 'Off the *Charlotte* as well, I presume. You have agreed to marry this woman?'

'Of course, sir. I wish to serve the colony.'

'He is … to be addressed … as "Your Excellency"!' Rowe barked.

'Your Excellency,' said Dan. 'Well, if it will serve the purpose of helping us all survive, you may rely on me.'

'Yes, well, survival is very much on my mind at present,' said the governor, 'and I am wondering why you are digging there – what are you digging, exactly?'

'A latrine, sir. Sorry, Your Excellency.'

'I see. One assumes you would rather be on the sea.'

'Very much so, Your Excellency. It's what I was born to, you see. I can say with all honesty, I am the best fisherman in the land. This land, of course.'

Lockhart chuckled, and Rowe opened his mouth and closed it again, possibly about to upbraid Dan for insubordination until he saw his superior's amusement.

'Very well, Gwyn,' the governor said, turning away. 'You should return to work for now, but we may be able to find more suitable labours for you. I shall let Reverend Gibson know of your desire to marry.'

'Thank you, Your Excellency.' He hesitated for a moment, inhaling deeply. 'As I'm to take on a child which isn't mine, and her mother, may I have your permission to build a hut? Barracks living, it's … well, no place for a young one.'

'Oh … well, you'll have to find your own building materials. Very well then. On the western shore, mind. Near the rocks.'

Lockhart walked off, his aide trailing behind him. Rowe was a man clearly used to walking on ships or paved streets, not to a path where exposed tree roots could snag a toe – and he stumbled on one. Jenny giggled, and Dan was unable to suppress a snort. Both of them immediately regretted it.

Rowe turned around, strode back to them. 'Do not, Gwyn, think that an escape might be in prospect. If you are allowed on a boat at all, I will ensure it is under the strictest guard.'

'Escape is the furthest thing from my mind, sir, with my impending wedding and all,' Dan said. 'Where would I escape to? We barely got here in those fine ships in the bay, so I would certainly not try to return in a little cutter. I might as well save a lot of trouble and pitch myself into the ocean straightaway.'

'I may assist you in that endeavour,' said Rowe, turning and striding off again.

This time, Dan and Jenny waited until he was out of earshot before smiling, laughing. She guffawed in a most unladylike way.

'Jesus, you even laugh like a fisherman,' said Dan.

'It's for the best, you know,' she said.

He stopped laughing, looked at her oddly. 'Best for who? You tricked me into this.'

'Yes, I know.'

'You don't seem sorry.'

'Not in the slightest. You've already profited from this, and were happy to do so. It will be good to have a hut.'

'Why the rush, though? We're neither of us leaving this place, not soon.'

'I was afraid old Dorothy might get to you first,' she said.

'I'd have accepted. Nothing like a bit of wisdom.'

'I've the wisdom for both of us, as you'll find.'

He grinned. 'Will I? What if I've no time for anything you might call wisdom?'

'You will,' she said. 'Providing, of course, you keep your end of things going.'

'My end of things?'

'Yes. It begins with defending your family against whatever the rest of them plan to do, now there's all this space, and no one's managed to build any cells yet.'

He looked down at Charlotte, his smile softening. 'Perhaps you'll grow into a more honest woman than your mother.'

'Dan, if she is to grow into any kind of woman, I won't have her trampled in whatever is to come. I can tell there's very little holding the lads back now. The soldiers with their muskets are just about managing it, but when night falls …'

'Yes, not a safe place for a baby, and likely to be more of them made tonight.'

'You'll shield us, then, Charlotte and me.'

'Yes, I'll protect you from the men. All but one of them.'

The moisture that had been hanging in the air all day found its expression that night, in a sudden rain which was as strange to Jenny as everything else on that shore. It didn't start slowly, build itself up, let itself be known with a tap on the nose and a drop or two on the forearm. It was dry, and then it was drenched, and there was very little warning that things were about to move from one state to the other. It was loud, hurling itself against the canvas, beating the hulls of the ships out in

the harbour, gouging divots into the earth and filling the holes
the men had dug.

Not that the men cared, Jenny knew. They had been waiting
for the dark, and didn't particularly mind that it had brought a
rainstorm with it. They came into the women's tents, which was
unguarded; as yet, no one had formulated even the most outlandish
escape plans. Who would brave the frenetic sea or the unknown
woods? And the savages within them, who had already become the
scaffold on which uninformed legends were being built.

Jenny later learned that some women were willing when the
men stormed in, some were not. Very few, in any case, could clearly
see the faces of those they were engaged with in frantic congress,
and nobody asked for names.

Jenny and Charlotte were not in the women's tents, or against
the trees where some of the women were taken or dragged. Dan
had found for them a little clearing a few paces beyond the tree
line, likely further than any of their kind had gone thus far into
the land's uncharted interior. He had managed to take a piece of
sailcloth, folded and wadded up, for Charlotte to lie on underneath
the branches. They shielded her from the worst of the rain, while
Dan kept his promise and protected Jenny from the men. All but
one of them.

Jenny waited until the sun was up before she took Charlotte back
to the tent barracks.

Bea had not taken her advice – had not taken the hand of a
man and marched him up to the governor, insisting he marry her.
She was sitting, now, against a tree, looking at the ships as they
swung on their anchors out in the bay.

Jenny sat down beside her, Charlotte in her lap.

'Can I hold her?' asked Bea.

Jenny handed the baby over, and Bea squeezed her so tightly that the little girl began to grizzle. 'Ease off,' said Jenny, putting her hand on Bea's arm and noticing a graze there, one which Jenny was certain had not been there the day before. 'Last night?' she asked.

'Two of them, I think,' said Bea. 'Maybe the same one twice. It was dark.'

'Did they hurt your arm?'

'I don't think so. I think I stumbled at one point, afterwards. Looking for somewhere to sleep that didn't stink. They got Dorothy too.'

'But she is over eighty!'

'I don't think it mattered.'

'And the officers. They did nothing, of course.' A lot had changed on this journey, but not an English soldier's reluctance to defend a prisoner.

'They probably thought it'd keep the men quiet. Easier to manage. Whatever the truth of it, they just left us to each other.'

There were no flowers or new muslin dresses at Jenny's wedding. The event occurred on her first Sunday on this shore. Nor was the day hers alone: she and Dan were one of five couples lined up in front of Reverend Gibson. He stood before each pair and said the words required to invoke whatever magic resided in the ritual, before moving on to the next.

Jenny also had to share the day with the colony itself, brought into being by the planting of a flag, a speech from the governor, and a percussive gun salute that made Charlotte cry.

There was deep suspicion, especially among some of the more prudish marines, that the marriages may not be valid: that they may have been prompted by the possibility of a hut, and the removal of the need for men to storm the women's tents to gain release.

A marine from the *Friendship*, Lieutenant Reid, quizzed a few of the couples beforehand, asking them several times whether there was a spouse in England, holding his nose up as though scared of breathing in their criminality. Protestations to the contrary seemed to have no effect on him, as he clearly held the suspicion that at least a few wives and husbands resided over the seas and still had beating hearts. John Carney, Dan's friend from the *Charlotte*, had been denied permission to marry due to an inconveniently alive and impossibly remote spouse.

'They might as well be dead, even if they're not,' Jenny said to Dan. 'No one will ever go back across the seas – no one who came here in the hold, unless they can buy a passage.'

'If those marriages don't exist here, these ones surely won't back there,' said Dan. 'This one, for instance. Doesn't count, except here.'

To the lack of dress, flowers and family, Jenny added a husband who didn't believe he really was one. She had never been given to fantasies about marriage. But she had certainly never imagined her first conversation with her husband would be a complete repudiation of the vows they had just undertaken.

She felt a tickle at the bottom of her eyes and bit the inside of her cheek to keep the tears from forming. She would, very much, have liked a lover. But she needed an ally and did not want to give him an excuse to abandon a union he didn't believe existed.

'Here is what we have, now,' she said. 'Here is all there is.'

'For you, and for the beautiful girl here,' he said, smiling as he always did at Charlotte, running a finger over her cheek. 'I have only two years left, though.'

There was, at least, that. Few men would show kindness to someone else's by-blow. Jenny had seen Dan playing around and joking with some young lads, children of convicts or sailors, who'd been chasing each other and found they suddenly had a larger playmate. 'They make no demands of you except time,' he'd said to her. 'Time is one of the only things we have in abundance here.'

'How would you even pay for a passage back?' Jenny asked now.

'Won't have to. There will be ships making the journey, ones that might have lost crew on the way over, need replacements.'

The hut they had been promised would be theirs, but of course it would need to be built. It was to be constructed on the rocky western shore, across the water from where the governor's house was to rise as soon as materials could be made to build it.

When Dan brought Jenny to look at the land they'd been given, she noticed a hole already dug there, wet and empty, with other holes containing four posts already filled in.

'Mud,' he said. 'Can't build a hut without mud. Get some twigs.'

'What about wood?' she asked.

'They say it's hardly worth the effort of cutting it down, here. Very poor, not up to much.'

'Will it not wash away?'

'You've built houses before, have you?'

So twigs were fetched and mixed with mud and woven through the posts. The heat did a decent job of baking it, even though parts began to flake off, prevented from binding properly by the sand in the soil.

One wall was nearly done when the next storm came.

Not as violent, quite, as the night-time storm that had greeted the arrival of the women. But here, rain couldn't be trusted to fall directly to earth, not all the time, not when the southerly winds blew, driving it horizontally into whatever flat surface impeded its path.

The next morning, the wall was diminished, soft, and unlikely to survive another drenching.

Jenny stood, flicking her eyes between the wall and her husband.

'You'd be delighted about this, I suppose,' he said.

'No. Why would I?'

He scowled at her, and trudged back towards the main settlement, still a collection of tents as the convicts wrestled with the knotty wood from the strange trees. He did not turn to check if she was following.

So bark from the worthless trees – which made excellent firewood but not much of anything else – would have to do.

The wounds to Dan's pride over the hut's construction closed over quickly. It helped that he lived under a roof, even a crude one, while the governor was still in a tent. It helped that his workmates on the gangs openly envied his home, and the fact that it contained a woman who was, by all accounts, practical and calm and not above gutting a fish.

But it helped most of all when Dan got what he believed he deserved and became one of the most important convicts in the colony – because it was thanks to him that a great many of them ate.

Whether it was because the government hadn't had the foresight to sentence many skilled farmers to transportation, nobody knew. Even they may not have been able to convince anything to grow well in the sandy soil, which choked the life out of the seeds, little packets of potential brought all the way from England that refused to develop in the unknown earth.

While the sheep ate the riotous long grass that grew here, they were still thin, and too valuable alive to be slain for food in any great numbers. The cows, showing a bovine prescience that the convicts lacked, had escaped. Then there were the beasts already here, although nothing resembled native cattle or sheep: small possums, not much good for meat; larger creatures who propelled themselves on their hind legs, able to easily outrun the governor's hounds, and the newly appointed gamekeeper had no better luck.

Fish, though, was another matter, and Dan was put in charge of procuring it. He was allowed to select his crew and go into the bay with a seine net. The ocean was not yet sure about them, not yet willing to provide a good catch all the time, and sometimes there was little to show for a night's work. But on occasion they would bring back hauls of bream and snapper, and strange creatures: large blue fish the length of a man's arm, or mottled white and red fish with long trailing spines.

At a time they were assured was early evening, but which had enough light for any early afternoon in England, Beatrice would walk down to the water with Jenny and Charlotte. Bea would care for the little girl while Jenny and other convicts appointed to the task waded into the water, holding the edge of the net and waiting for the call from Dan to haul, haul, haul.

On more than one occasion, as Jenny's feet splashed into the bay's surface and the sand closed over her toes, she found Mr Corbett next to her.

'Oddly enough, the governor has not yet gotten around to building a theatre, or any other place of entertainment,' he said once. 'A man must fill the time somehow.'

He would stand near her throughout the night, together with the other convicts – many of whom had to be compelled, as they trusted neither the ocean nor the fish – and seemed to have no quarrel with taking orders from Dan when he boomed out the command to haul.

Corbett, Jenny discovered, was equally happy to be heard praising a convict as taking orders from one. He would mention Dan at every meal where the fish was served.

So nights spent holding the net became, for some, a tempting route towards the approval of those whose decisions could make their lives easier or harder, despite their mistrust of the ocean. Above the water were strange creatures, beasts which offended the natural order, which moved as they didn't at home, or which had been cobbled together out of other creatures. If the land could generate these oddities, what did the sea hold?

Shells were collected along the shore too, to be burned by some of the more unfortunate men, the weak ones. The resulting lime, which would ultimately be used as mortar, unbound their skin as it bound everything else that it touched, leaving their eyes a staring red.

Many of the women were bored. There had been talk of spinning and weaving, and a lucky few helped the surgeon. All the women did laundry: officers' clothes, and convicts', draping the garments over one rock and pounding them with another. Jenny wondered why nobody bothered to ask whether such a practice was cleaning the fabric, as it was certainly destroying it. Beyond that, the women swore and they ranted or they huddled and sobbed, and some of them looked for the kind of distraction they couldn't find with the men.

Meanwhile, many of the men who had received their rations from Dan's hand aboard the *Charlotte* did not wish to be reminded that they still relied on him for sustenance. There were enough orders, too, given by those who wore uniforms, and many convicts felt they didn't wish to receive them from the hoarse throat of a smuggler as well.

But others had noticed the runtishness of the crops, those which managed to grow at all. They had seen the inability of the governor's hounds to catch the large birds with the ridiculously small wings. While the dogs sometimes had better luck with those hopping mammals, bringing one down couldn't be relied on; in any case, the meat tended to end up on the table of the governor and his officers, and few convicts tasted it.

Governor Lockhart had quickly dispatched an officer – one of his favourites, Mr Corbett said – with some convicts to Norfolk Island, where there was supposed to be good land and enough flax to make all the sails they could want. Even if this officer had better luck than those in the main colony, though, it would be a year or more before they could rely on him for food.

When most people managed to eat something that had once had a heartbeat, the chances were it had been brought in by Dan and his crew. Some saw an advantage in aligning themselves with the man who mined the sea, at least in the eyes of those who had what passed for power here. The number of volunteers for the task increased after muster one morning when the governor, passing Dan, gave him a casual clap on the shoulder, almost as though they were comrades. 'Here he is,' Lockhart said, 'the man who keeps us fed. Stay well, Gwyn.'

The Gwyns did stay well. Allowed to keep a portion of the catch, they were flexible in their understanding of the share which would bypass the stores and find its way to the hut on the western bank. The storekeeper didn't know. Others, however, did.

Shortly after the governor praised Dan, Elenor appeared at the shore. She walked past Beatrice, who was making faces at little Charlotte, without acknowledging her. She glared at Jenny on the way past, and made straight for Dan. 'Me and Joseph want to help,' she told him.

Jenny turned. Just behind her, approaching, was Joseph Clancy: the man whose whining voice had scratched at her ears on the *Charlotte*, complaining that Dan was being uneven with the rations. Bea had told her that Joseph and Elenor were close.

After that first profane night, men were told they would be punished if they tried to go into the women's tents. They did try, of course, and a group of men were dressed in women's clothes and marched through the settlement as penance. It didn't stop the incursions, though, so flogging was now the penalty for breaching the canvas wall. Elenor and Joe must have found a way to get around the restrictions, as had a great many others.

'We can both hold the net,' Joseph told Dan. 'We will haul when you say, and will take one or two of the smallest for the shovel.'

'We've enough workers already,' said Dan. 'Don't want to scare the fish off. We're all fed from the same pot, here. No one who holds the net gets extra rations.'

'You do, though, don't you?' said Joseph. 'You've got a hut and a share of the catch, don't think I don't know. You can spare one.'

'Joe, we don't need the extra help, and I'm not giving away fish. Not allowed to, anyway. You know what they're like about food.'

'Wonderful at sharing things out, aren't you, when they're not yours.' As Joseph spoke, he gradually advanced towards Dan, until he was looking up into a bearded face that was browner than it had been a few months ago. 'Some might take a view that things need to be more even. Some might take certain steps in that direction.' Spittle came out with the words.

Dan, slowly and deliberately, bent his head until his nose was touching Joseph's. 'Some people,' he said, 'should take steps back towards camp. The ocean, it's unpredictable, even on a calm day like this. You wouldn't want to find yourself in deeper than you thought.' He placed the flat of his palm against Joseph's right shoulder and pushed.

Joseph stumbled backwards and fell, landing with a splash on his backside in the few inches of water they had been standing in.

The other workers laughed. They had seen out the night with Dan and Jenny many times; they knew when to haul and never asked for fish.

Joseph stood, turned and – with a slow walk that he might have intended to be stately – made his way back up the shore. He spat on the ground near Charlotte and Bea as he passed, with Elenor stalking after him.

CHAPTER 12
Sydney Cove, May 1790

The shack hospital was not a place Jenny would choose to visit. Not without a good reason. But staying in the good graces of Surgeon Drummond, or anyone with any authority, was reason enough. If you went to them when they asked, they didn't come to you – and would be less likely to notice that more fish were in the Gwyn hut than there should be, or the hole in the floor where salted fish lay wrapped in canvas.

The fish themselves concealed a small leather purse. Dan had been able to take a small sum – honestly acquired, he swore – with him on the journey. It had been left in care of the captain of the *Charlotte*, and returned to him when they'd landed. A common arrangement, and no one begrudged the convicts their funds – what, here, would they spend it on? But money was money was money, and would likely disappear if anyone came to know of it.

Jenny no longer had to carry her daughter everywhere. The little girl was able to make a halting progress along the rutted path towards the surgeon's makeshift hospital. There were now two streets in the colony, meaner than any Jenny had known, which became churned with mud in the rains. There was little, in fact, to distinguish them as streets, apart from the huts that lined them, poorly built and with twig lattices as windows. They barely held together, far less substantial than the colony's other buildings that had sprung up like pox around the landscape. The governor's house, the stores, then the thatched houses of the officers. Only when these were built had the convicts been given the task of constructing their own lodgings.

Charlotte still did not view walking these paths as a necessity; it was an amusement she engaged in when it suited her. When she tired of it, or when she felt the ground wasn't cooperating, the small arms would be thrust towards the sky, and the grey eyes would look up at her mother with their silent command. The command was always obeyed – the little girl always found hands beneath her arms as she was lifted and hoisted and slotted into her accustomed position on her mother's hip.

There was less, though, of her mother's hip than there had been, and Charlotte had to stretch her legs a little further in order to maintain her position there. Jenny was one of the very few people in the colony whose bellies were growing.

Now, nearing the hospital, Jenny shifted her daughter towards the front of her body, so that the girl's bottom was perched on the top of her mother's stomach. Jenny expected she might have to wait for Drummond. These days the surgeon was very busy.

The crops had not shown any more liking for the winters here than they had the summers, and the livestock kept dying. The stores brought from England were long gone. There was word, too, that more ships were coming, not with food but with those who needed to be fed: a second phalanx of officers and convicts who would be disappointed if they expected better rations on their arrival than those they'd had aboard ship.

The most devastating news, though, concerned two ships that would never arrive. The *Guardian* and the *Sirius* had been wrecked oceans apart but within months of each other. Each had been carrying food, and hope with it. The little *Supply* – the only one of the ships in the first fleet to have not yet trickled out of the harbour – had been sent for food, but she was a woefully insubstantial vessel on which to rest their hopes.

Rations had been halved, and the stroke of Lockhart's pen on the order had produced ranks of shambling creatures with protruding eyes and distended bellies, lacking the energy to work, speak and, eventually, breathe. Scurvy had become rampant and did not discriminate between the convicts and the free. People's teeth dropped out, and Surgeon Drummond was also dealing daily with swollen limbs, fever, and the type of noxious substances that only a navy doctor or a convict could be entirely familiar with.

The scurvy and the hunger picked off the weak first. Half a year ago, Dorothy had succumbed and was buried just outside the settlement, in a short and flatly delivered ceremony from Reverend Gibson. Jenny had stayed at her grave for a while, weeping for a woman buried in soil that was not her own, and had overheard Gibson say to Mr Corbett, 'We're all being buried alive, here. No one is coming save more mouths.'

The malaise had since made some inroads into the stronger convicts, and several younger women and men lay with Dorothy, ushered into the afterlife by a similarly perfunctory rite.

Jenny, who'd shed tears for all of them, could not help but feel she was rehearsing for the time when she stood there burying a small, too-thin body. That if she didn't find the means of removing Charlotte from this place, her daughter would be planted in the earth that had failed to nourish her.

Escaping into the dark bush was an increasingly tempting prospect. Others went in every few weeks. One convict from

Madagascar, an inveterate escapee, seemed to be surviving with the help of occasional raids on whatever crops had managed to defy the conditions. For the most part, though, escape inland wasn't a good bet. Some who had taken the risk were found later, sinking into the ground. Some staggered out after a few weeks, thinner even than those who had stayed in the settlement.

Their salvation would have to come from the sea. When the transport ships had left, some had played host to convicts who had secreted themselves along their wooden spines. This, Jenny knew, would be impossible with a young child who could cry out at any moment.

Every day, Charlotte's cries were getting weaker. She was not, though, caught in the staring lethargy that so often preceded a trip to the plot where Dorothy lay. And Charlotte's survival was partly thanks to the leaves Jenny now carried wrapped in a piece of cloth.

As she pushed through the rickety door of the hospital, Drummond looked up and held one finger in the air to ask her to wait. The fingers of his other hand were coated in a salve that he was daubing on the wounded leg of a young convict, a boy who had helped Dan remove stumps when they had first arrived. The lad now had an unfocused stare and didn't flinch when Drummond vigorously rubbed in the paste.

The surgeon rubbed his hands on a cloth, which looked as though it had absorbed the aftermath of many past treatments, before he walked up to her. 'You have them?'

'Yes. I know where they grow – I can get as many as you like.'

He unwrapped the bundle, picked up one of the leaves and rubbed it between his fingers, sniffing it. The leaf looked like ground ivy but gave off a sharp scent that no plant in England possessed.

'I must say, they seem to have some nutritional properties. Did you try them dried, in the end?' he asked.

'Yes. Hard to know whether they're better or worse, but the tea didn't smell as much.'

'Hm. We will stay with what we know, then. Brew them, if you please.'

'Yes. But, my daughter ...'

'Of course. She shouldn't stay here longer than necessary. Leave her with one of the other women and return straightaway if you please, Mrs Gwyn.'

Jenny had taken to visiting the hospital a few times a week and brewing an astringent tea out of the strange leaves. This drink seemed to help those stricken with scurvy, if they weren't too far gone. The ones dying of hunger could be helped by nothing but more food, which refused to grow with the same enthusiasm as the leaves.

She didn't know if she was the first to learn of the plant's effects, and certainly nothing was stopping anyone else from collecting its leaves in great quantities. When she told Drummond she knew where they grew, she didn't mention that many others knew it too. If he thought she was the best source of the leaves, she was also happy to let him believe that she had, through her own experimentation, discovered their properties.

She did not, and never would, tell him about Mawberry, the native woman.

Jenny had first seen the Darug shortly after her wedding day, when she was walking up from the shore one morning, Dan's share of the night's catch under her arm. She was getting used to the patterns that the slanted morning light threw onto the sand, the shifting shadows of the unchanging trees. That morning, though, there were other shadows.

They watched her from the edge of the forest – a few men, holding spears. But their grip on the weapons was casual, as though they had simply been holding them for so long they had forgotten about them. The men offered her no violence as she walked up, made no greeting, but turned their heads slowly as she passed.

She felt, strangely, as though she owed them some courtesy, these watchers in the woods who seemed to lack the predatory intent that she felt when at the edge of a faraway forest.

She turned towards them, put her bundle of fish on the ground, and curtsied.

One of them smiled in response, showing a mouth with a single precise gap made by the absence of one front tooth. When the others laughed, she saw the same gap in their mouths. It was made more obvious by a whiteness in their other teeth, a shade seldom seen among convicts.

Keeping her eyes on them, she bent over, picked up her bundle, nodded and went on.

She continued this game – as she suspected they viewed it as such – whenever she saw them. She would put down whatever she was carrying, unless it was Charlotte, and curtsy to the men, earning laughs from them – laughs that got louder when Charlotte was old enough to be taught to do likewise.

Jenny had seen the watchers mutter to each other: indistinct words, if words they were. A language it must be, for they seemed to convey meaning to one another, but the syllables were unlike any she had heard, and the cadence was more of a slow meander than an artificial singsong lilt or the natural music of her Cornish speech.

The only words she knew in their language had been taught to her by Mr Corbett, after the *Charlotte* had first come in sight of the coastline near Botany Bay. She and the others had been sent back down into the hold, but Corbett had told her later that some tribesmen had been seen on the cliffs, shaking spears and yelling, 'Warra, warra.' Of course, she had no means of exactly translating the words, but their intent was easily guessed.

She would never use those words to these men, though. She did not want them to go away.

Neither did Governor Lockhart. He had tried – very hard, according to Corbett – to build some sort of accord with the natives. The natives had offered the settlers no violence, at least en masse, which in itself seemed odd to Jenny when they had been subjected to unprovoked attacks and dwindling, siphoned resources. Eventually there was retaliation: occasional clubbings, or convicts wandering into the woods and never wandering out again. Their loss was blamed by most of the colonists on the natives rather than the terrain that yielded far more in the way of treacherous gullies than it did food. Sometimes, much later, bones were found, once with the skull missing. Soon afterwards Lieutenant Reid had brought back a skull, which Drummond proclaimed had belonged to a convict; Reid had reunited it with the rest of the remains and buried them under a tree.

But there had been no attack on the camp, and no attempt to harm or capture convicts as they walked close to the woods. So Jenny continued to curtsy in safety, met with good-natured guffaws.

She hadn't a hope of discerning names from the stream of syllables that came from them. But there were some names that she knew.

Wangal, Gamaragal, Gadigal – an officer was cobbling together a dictionary of the native language, and he had said these were the names of some of the local tribes. That information, imparted by Corbett one night when they were holding on to adjacent sections of seine net, made Jenny oddly sad. If she had been asked, by one of them, what the name of her tribe was – not the Cornish, but this odd collection with whom she had come here – she would not have known what to say.

She had also learned the names of two tribesmen: Yarramundi and Ballooderry.

Ballooderry had been captured by the governor in Gamaragal country, when all other means of establishing a dialogue between the settlers and the natives had failed.

'Tell me, Mr Corbett, do you think the governor is stupid?' Jenny had asked after he told her of the capture.

Corbett remained her best-placed source of information on the upper echelons of what passed for society. You couldn't stand in the water next to a man, holding different parts of one skein of rough rope, without remembering he held significant influence here.

He had spoken to her with uncharacteristic sharpness that night. 'Mind your tongue with regard to the governor, Jenny. Do not forget who has ultimate authority here, and do not put me in a difficult position.'

'Of course, Mr Corbett. But it doesn't, to my mind, make any sense.'

'I see,' said Corbett, still stern. 'Your mind is trained in the ways of statecraft, is it?'

She should, she knew, be quiet. Although Corbett was one of the kinder officers, he was still an officer with the power to have her hanged if he put his mind to it.

She was still musing on the wisdom of remaining silent when she heard her own voice.

'No, it's not,' she said, 'but it is trained to see what's in front of my eyes, and no person I've ever met would see being captured as a friendly gesture.'

Corbett rolled his lips in on each other. He was standing before her in the dying light, his breeches soaked up to the knees in the black water from the incoming tide. For a moment she thought he would take her to task again. She feared that she might lose his friendship, the ease with which they spoke, the fact that their delivery of the syllables – in a clipped accent or a Cornish one – didn't matter to either of them, only the content of their conversation.

He didn't berate her, though. His arms went slack, and she thought he might drop his segment of net, so she tensed to be ready to take up the slack.

'The same thought had occurred to me, actually,' he said. 'That abduction is not the way to build the bridge. But what else is to be attempted? Everything we have tried has failed. The natives have shown an inclination towards befriending a few individuals – Drew, for instance, who's writing down their words when he can – but one of those individuals does not happen to be the governor, and there is the problem.'

Ballooderry was from north of the harbour. The settlers dressed him in English clothing and taught him how to shape his mouth into English words. He had been overjoyed, at first, with the manacle placed on him, believing it to be an adornment, but flew into a rage when he realised it was there to detain rather than decorate him.

Amicable captivity didn't suit him. He pined for his tribesmen, and tried to escape several times, once nearly drowning after he jumped off the *Supply*.

His escape, when it came, was horrific.

One afternoon Jenny had come out of the woods, where she had been collecting sweet tea leaves. She wandered down to the shore as she often did, looking for wheeling seabirds so she could tell Dan where to send one of the small fishing boats they sometimes used in place of a seine net.

She saw, from a distance, something near the shore being rolled back and forth by a small wave. Driftwood, maybe. Any wood was useful, and all the better when you didn't have to go to the trouble of cutting it.

But wood wasn't covered in small white blisters. Wood didn't have puckering skin and a swelling stomach and the blank eyes of a young boy who would never grow.

Jenny ran to Drummond and found she wasn't the first to alert him. A woodcutting party had found some bodies in the forest, and several other corpses had choked the stream and been seen floating further out in the bay.

The convicts started looking at each other, watching for the start of the pustules, the small blemishes that would consume one person, and then the next, and then the settlement. Many of them knew what to expect. More than a few, like Elenor and Suse, had skin pitted by their last encounter with this disease.

But it never arrived in the colony. It went through the natives, though; it broke over them and left far fewer when it receded.

Ballooderry appeared at Drummond's hospital tent shortly after the outbreak started. He sang to those who had been brought there for treatment, or he talked to them, or stroked them. Then he joined them, after the disease jumped into him from one of the many he had tried to comfort.

But still, no one in the settlement sickened. There were murmurs of divine judgement, or of curses gone wrong.

'They have reason enough to curse us,' Jenny had said to Dan. 'Doesn't seem to be in their nature, though.'

'How else do you explain it, then?' He was sitting on a stone outside their hut, picking chunks of fish off the freshly caught carcass he had cooked on his shovel blade.

'Maybe it's the same as us not getting sick on the ocean – us who are accustomed to it. Those who aren't, they retch at the smallest wave. Maybe we're used to the pox, and the natives are not.'

'Our little bird isn't used to it,' Dan said. He often used that name for Charlotte, who knew no other father and was more than happy to accept this one. Dan could be relied on for sea dragon rides: taking the girl into the ocean on hot mornings, holding her hands around his neck, and bobbing her up and down in the water as she sat on his back and giggled.

'I'm keeping her away from the hospital tent, of course,' said Jenny.

'Good. I need someone free around, to remind me what it looks like.'

'Are you not concerned for me?' Jenny asked, without any real annoyance. She wasn't concerned for herself, and did not expect him to be.

'I suppose I would be a little put out if you died ... Wait, though, can Bea mend nets?'

Jenny picked up the innards of a fish she had been gutting and threw them at him, whooping when they landed on his face.

'A kiss then, I think,' he said, standing and letting the guts fall to the ground. He chased her as she ran laughing into the hut at a deliberately slow pace.

Shortly after Ballooderry's death, the governor tried to acquire another forced ambassador, and this time he caught Yarramundi in his net: tall and strong where Ballooderry had been slight, gregarious where Ballooderry had been melancholy. Yarramundi laughed and danced and smiled at children. Judging by the greetings he received from his tribesmen, whenever he saw them at the fringes of the camp, he was something of a leader of their people.

He stayed in the home of Lockhart, the first house built in the colony. He soon spoke English far better than any of the settlers spoke his language, for all their protestations of interest. He was successful at everything he did – including his escape.

He did not stay away, though. He took to visiting the settlement, and he and Lockhart would sometimes chat away like two washerwomen. Yarramundi became friendly with some of the convicts as well. Dan had spoken to him several times; he delighted in children as much as Dan did, and hurled himself into the chasing games Dan played with the young lads, uninvited but welcome nonetheless. Yarramundi kept a little more distance from the settlement's women. But when he saw a need for intervention, he intervened.

He had stepped in front of Jenny one morning as she was carrying Charlotte towards the main settlement. 'You are Dan Gwyn's woman,' he said. He had been taught English by Lockhart and some of the officers, so he sounded like them. She found it odd, though, hearing a voice like that of the judge who sentenced her to death in the mouth of this man.

She nodded, looking straight at him. Some of the women still averted their eyes from the unapologetic nakedness of the native men; for them, nudity came from punishment or poverty. Jenny made a point never to look away.

'Not as many fish now,' he said.

It was not an accusation, though he had every right to accuse. The fish had never been plentiful, had never shown the same inclination as Penmor's pilchards to sacrifice themselves. Now, though, fewer were coming in with each haul. Sometimes, a night of fishing would produce nothing.

'Tell Gwyn, he will not listen to me,' Yarramundi said. 'Tell him to mind the currents. He ignores them. Tell him they are not so ... so polite as your currents across the seas.'

She nodded. 'I will. Thank you.'

He looked at Charlotte then, and Charlotte looked back. She had shown no surprise at his appearance. Sudden comings and goings were commonplace to her, a girl who had never lived in a fishing town where one saw the same few people from birth to death.

Yarramundi smiled at her, reached out and tickled her face, and she giggled. Then he looked back at Jenny, frowning. 'She is not, I think, as well as she should be.'

'None of us are,' Jenny said.

He nodded. 'I will send someone.'

'Send ...?'

'Someone, yes.' He nodded, as though confirming to himself he had used the proper word.

Jenny looked closely at Charlotte's face, examining it for a spot or a pallor or a rash that could explain Yarramundi's concern. When she looked up again, he was gone.

✦

The fringes of the main settlement were not the only places populated by shadows. The Gwyns' hut was within sight of the settlement but in a small clearing of its own. For the most part it was too small and prone to fire for Jenny to cook in, so she'd built a small fire pit where vegetables were boiled in a battered pot and fish were cooked on the blade of a shovel.

Her fire pit sat on the only piece of land which, Jenny felt, was entirely hers, although she knew both the King and the Gadigal would disagree. While she peeled potatoes or gutted fish, she would often crouch on her haunches, as she had on the prow of her father's boat, and watch Charlotte lurching around like a drunk.

When Charlotte learned to walk, she glared at her mother as though asking why Jenny had not informed her of this wondrous activity. Whenever she could, the little girl was on her feet, racing and tripping and swaying, and not particularly caring about grace or finesse as long as she was moving forward, always forward.

But when Charlotte did stop, did halt in her wheeling, Jenny knew she had seen one of them.

Some were quite tall, taller than a man. Covered in a course grey fur, they had a long snout that terminated in a hare-like mouth. Jenny thought that their designer had something of a sense of humour to give them such small forelegs and such large hind legs; if the same proportions were applied to a man, his arms would finish at the elbow and his legs would be six feet long. Those forelegs, though, had far sharper nails than even Elenor possessed.

The beasts never tried to hurt Charlotte or Jenny, but whenever the girl would pause and then start running towards one of them, Jenny would call her back. The beasts would hop off anyway, but she'd heard stories that the claws on their back legs were sharper than those on the front, and could be used with precision for the purposes of disembowelment.

When Charlotte stopped careening around one afternoon, Jenny casually glanced up to make sure that the creature wasn't one of the larger ones, the seven footers, and that it was hopping away into the undergrowth.

There was no beast, though. There was a woman. She was entirely naked and seemed unashamed of the fact, standing there and staring at Jenny with a curious, open look.

Jenny stared back, as she would have at anybody who had looked at her too long in the Plymstock Inn. There was nothing mocking in the other woman's gaze, though, nothing artful. It was mere curiosity, the same gaze that Jenny had directed at the kangaroos when they'd started visiting her little clearing.

Jenny noticed a small child peering from behind the woman's legs, wide-eyed and a few years older than Charlotte. After standing from her hunched position by the pot, Jenny put the fish she'd been scaling on a small stone nearby. She glanced at Charlotte, who was still staring. Jenny whistled, as she did sometimes to get the girl's attention, and beckoned her over. Then, after staring at the woman for a moment more, Jenny beckoned her over too.

The woman seemed – and it was easy to tell, without clothes – to be pregnant, but early on. Jenny was too. Her usually strong stomach now decided, from time to time, that it couldn't countenance fish or potato or the wilted leaf from a cauliflower.

The woman walked towards the edge of the fire. The natives must, Jenny thought, have fires of their own, or how did they get anything cooked? How did they manage in the winter nights? Those nights did not descend with the vicious and suffocating cold that had taken her baby brother's life, but they were cold enough. So a ring of stones with a fire in the middle was not, Jenny thought, an unknown concept to this woman.

The woman walked forward a bit further, looked at the fish on

the stone, then pursed her lips and cocked her head to the side as
though she was assessing the job Jenny had done on the scales and
finding it adequate but lacking in finesse.

She looked at the pot, filled with hot water to receive the
potatoes Jenny hoped Dan would be able to acquire.

She walked to the edge of the clearing, confidently leaving her
little boy standing by the fire, where he gaped at the small pink
girl who was hugging her mother's leg.

Charlotte found herself scooped up and clamped onto Jenny's
hip within a few seconds, as the woman beckoned Jenny over to
the bush that grew at the side of the hut. She plucked a broad leaf
and crushed it between her fingers. While looking at Jenny, she very
slowly held the leaf up to her nose, loudly inhaling before handing
it to Jenny, who sniffled at it: a sharp smell, not wholly unpleasant.
The woman nodded, smiled and picked more leaves. She had all of
her teeth, did not share the male characteristic of missing one. But
Jenny noticed – as the woman's hands flew over the bush, quickly
removing leaves and placing them into her other waiting palm – that
the little finger of one hand was gone below the knuckle.

When she had finished she showed Jenny the leaves in her
hands, twenty or thirty of them, which she crushed together. She
walked towards the fire, nodded at the pot and raised one eyebrow.

Jenny shrugged, before thinking that perhaps shrugs had no
meaning here. Nods clearly did, though, so she nodded, and the
woman opened her palms and let the leaves fall into the hot water.
Jenny fetched two earthenware cups, dipped them in and handed
one to the woman. The resulting brew tasted as sharp as the leaves
had smelled, but oddly sweet.

After the woman had drunk, she stood, nodded again, and
pointed over at the bush while nodding several times. She put her
arm on her little boy's shoulder, turned and left.

In the late afternoon Dan returned after Charlotte had drowsed away, with no potatoes or anything else. 'The vegetables are not to be had,' he said. 'If you were a better gardener –'

'How am I to coax a carrot along, when the best farmers we have can't do it?' Jenny asked. 'Fish and carrots and potatoes together would be nice, but out of the lot I'd rather have fish.'

'You're right, I suppose. And you can haul with the best of them. I'd think you were a man if I didn't have firm evidence to the contrary.'

Jenny smiled and cuffed him on the ear, and he smiled back, grabbed her wrist and dragged her, with no need for dragging, into the hut.

Later, she showed him the brew that the native woman had made. For a moment she expected him to reject it, to say that it wasn't to be known what was in that pot, it could be poison, it could be a ploy.

'Yarramundi sent her, I think,' Jenny said.

He sniffed at it. 'None of them seem to be showing any signs of lack of food, those that survived the pox,' he said. 'Would you not think that the governor would ask the natives how they feed themselves? Would you not think that would be the first question anyone would ask? They've shown a willingness to help us – far more than I would, in their situation, I'll be perfectly honest with you about that.'

Dan held out his cup to Charlotte, then stroked her hair while he dribbled tea into her mouth. She grimaced but let him feed her a few drops, before he hauled her onto his lap and fed her morsels of his fish.

'They know about fishing, too,' said Jenny. 'The woman, she

came while I was scaling this one. She looked at it as though she knew how to tell a good job from a bad one. Yarramundi, by the way, says you're ignoring the currents, and you're to stop it.'

Dan grunted, nodding.

'Perhaps he can tell us more about the fish, or she can,' Jenny said. 'Perhaps they can tell us about the tides and the currents in places where there are more to be had.'

Dan nodded again thoughtfully. 'That, actually, is a good idea.'

When Dan asked Yarramundi, he was told to go further out.

'But how are we to get further with the tiny boats we have?' Dan said to Jenny. 'The officers don't like me using the cutter, particularly not Major Rowe. He said he might never see me again if he lets me loose with it.'

'Yes, he might never see that belly of his again if he doesn't let you use it.'

The vegetable crops continued to fail, and the settlers' teeth continued to drop out, and the hospital continued to fill and then empty as people died. And Jenny, Dan and Charlotte continued to eat fish, and continued to stay well.

CHAPTER 13

Jenny didn't know whether the woman would come back. Really, what difference would it make? She had Charlotte for company, and of course Bea, who was seen as one of the better-behaved convicts. Whoever was on watch always let her by on the way to Jenny's hut without the slightest hesitation. If Elenor had so much as looked beyond the camp to the edge of the settlement, she would have been back in irons.

How, though, had the woman known what the Gwyns' needed, what the danger was? What might she know still, that Jenny did not?

Jenny did feel a certain sisterhood. It went beyond the fact that they each had children, one outside and one in. The woman had watched from the margins, and then stepped forward. It was an act that Jenny admired. But now, the woman stayed away.

Dan was shy, too. Shy, at least, of approaching the governor. Of asking for the use of the cutter.

'Why won't you do it?' Jenny asked. 'You know – better than I do, you saw it first – that our value here, any importance we have, turns on our ability to get fish. The catch isn't what it was. And there are fewer salt fish in our hut than there were. You need to go out further, Yarramundi said so.'

Dan looked at her, and then turned back to the shovel he was holding over the fire, a few very thin strips of white flesh roasting on it. 'We've a hut, 'cause I asked for it,' he said. 'We've a share of the catch, 'cause I asked for it. I would ask for the cutter, too, if it would do any good, but it won't.'

'Of course it will! Go out further, get more fish. Keep our hut, keep our share of the catch. If you won't go and ask him, I will.'

'No, you won't,' said Dan. 'You will not shame me, not if you want to stay pretty.'

Jenny stepped back, for a moment, into the shadows. The threat was delivered in a flat voice, and all the more frightening for it. He was a rarity among husbands, had never hit her, and she had grown used to it. Perhaps, though, the violence had been collecting under his skin, waiting. The thought that he might do something to her face, something that would punish her while preserving their unborn child, terrified her.

But not as much as starvation did.

Even Elenor had stopped her requests for an extra fish, aware they wouldn't be granted, and that anyone caught in possession of extra food would be assumed to have stolen it and punished accordingly. Such punishments had been meted out already. One woman had been tied to the end of the cart, walked through the settlement and then flogged. Another had been hanged, along with a few male convicts. Six marines had made a copy of the key to the stores and taken food in small quantities; they were hanged in a row, dispatched together for their collegial crime. A gallows had been built near the storehouse they had robbed, and Jenny and the rest of the settlement had watched as they fell away through its floor.

'Even if I did, I'd need to know where to fish,' Dan told her as he removed the shovel from the fire and set it down to cool. 'It's a big ocean and the man just pointed outwards, so he could have meant anywhere between here and England – they will be watching me on the cutter. You've seen to that, with your talk.'

Again? thought Jenny. Who had overheard this time, and who had she been talking to? She had to keep track, try to remember whom she said what to, and where.

With the catch dwindling, she didn't know how long they would be allowed to keep their share, and their hut. She had started asking around about boats, and stores, and maps, and tides. Oblique questions, certainly. Conversational, bearing no relationship to anything in particular. Jenny had no thoughts on how to use the information. She stored it as she had once stored salt fish against the winter.

She tried, too, to press a morsel of that fish on Bea, who had bruises on her face and had recently lost a tooth to scurvy – the same one that the native men deliberately knocked out. Most of Bea's afflictions came from injuries delivered by Elenor, while the other women who shared their hut backed against its periphery, all turning their heads.

Jenny kept looking for the native woman, not only in the trees ringing the small patch at the back of her hut, but also in those at the edge of the beach, where she'd never seen her before. The woman clearly felt no inclination to leave the mothering hinterland and again step into the world of the invader.

Those watchers on the beach might know her, Jenny thought. The woman may have mentioned to them that she had visited one of the strange new people.

It had been a month, so the woman's belly must be more prominent. When Jenny next saw the watchers in their customary spot between the trees, she pointed at them and used her hands to carve out an imaginary pregnant belly in the air, larger than her own real one.

They frowned at her. Had she offended them somehow? Where was the genial mocking, the laughter that contained both genuine amity and a small amount of contempt for these creatures who stumbled through the same bush the natives moved in so assuredly? Then they turned and walked into the shadows.

'They think you're asking them to impregnate you,' said Mr Corbett from beside her. He had been helping Jenny and the convict workers on the net that night, although the catch was getting so light that extra muscle was barely needed.

Jenny couldn't stop herself blushing, and was immediately angry. Corbett would assume, no doubt, that her rising colour was due to feminine scruples. But the red flush was put there by embarrassment at her stupidity: she had been miming every bit as lyrically as some of the women had, up against the bars in the hulk. She hadn't thought properly beforehand about how to get her message across. She must not allow that to happen again.

'They would have a difficult time of it,' she said to Mr Corbett. 'Someone is already in there.'

He smiled, reached out and squeezed her shoulder. 'I thought as much. It's the only reason here for someone's girth increasing. Congratulations to you, and to Dan.'

'Thank you,' she said. She meant it. She had heard other officers discussing pregnancies in the colony, and the conversation usually started with speculation on the identity of the father, whether the woman in question was married or not. There were a great many here – the pinch-faced, sniffy Lieutenant Reid among them – who thought that all convict women were whores. So Jenny was grateful for Corbett's unquestioning belief in her child's paternity.

'There was a native woman,' Jenny told him, 'who came to my hut, a month or so ago. Showed me those leaves, the ones the surgeon is now using on those with the scurvy.'

'She did you a great service, then.'

'She may well have. Charlotte doesn't much like the taste, but I'll wager she likes the idea of keeping those new teeth in her head.'

Corbett gave a closed-mouth chuckle and knelt down to where the little girl stood next to her mother, her arms around Jenny's leg. While Jenny had been miming to the watchers in the trees, Charlotte had curtsied as usual and was dismayed by the lack of laughter. She was now, Jenny thought, close to tears, and when tears visited Charlotte they didn't manifest as a misty dew on her cheeks but as a torrent every bit as violent as the storms here.

Still kneeling in front of the little girl, Corbett bowed his head, lifted up her hand and said, 'Good morning, Princess Charlotte. May I request the pleasure of your company on a walk through the palace gardens later?'

Charlotte had no way of knowing what a princess was – or a palace, for that matter. But she knew when she was being treated with the deference she felt was her due, and paid Mr Corbett for it with a gap-toothed smile.

'I want the woman to visit again,' Jenny said. 'That's what I was trying to tell those men – she is pregnant, you see. She told us about the leaves, and I would thank her.'

'Very good of you to go to that much trouble just to thank her,' said Corbett.

'And find out what else she knows, what else may be of use.'

'Oh. Yes, well, as long as it's in the spirit of acquiring knowledge that might assist the settlement —'

'Whether it will or won't, I'm not to say. But it certainly won't if she never gets a chance to tell me about it.'

'Pregnant, you said. Could be Yarramundi's wife.'

It was widely known that Yarramundi continued to come and go as he pleased, and on his own terms. He continued to receive gifts and enjoy the governor's friendship, so in reality it was a matter of debate who had captured whom.

'Do you think he might ask her to come to me again?' Jenny asked. 'Perhaps I should talk to him.'

'Their women tend to stay back, you know, much as I imagine ours would in a similar situation,' Corbett told her. 'The natives are protective, certainly, of women and children. Yet more reason to view them not as savage but just differently civilised.'

Perhaps Yarramundi felt one favour was enough, was preventing the woman visiting again. But she had seemed forthright, unafraid, matching Jenny's stare with her own, and comfortable enough to bring her child into the clearing where the little hut stood.

'You could ask Yarramundi for me, Mr Corbett. He might listen to you. If I find out anything useful, I promise to tell you.'

'Very well,' said Corbett. 'I shall talk to Yarramundi. Do not hold out much expectation, though. The woman might not be his wife, and if she is, he may not be willing to send her again.'

But the woman did receive the message, and whether on her own or at the direction of Yarramundi, she appeared at the edge of the clearing of the Gwyn hut the next day.

After Jenny beckoned her forward, she and her little boy came into the clearing.

Jenny had been salting fish and was putting aside as much as she could. She took out a salted flathead, its eyes staring at the sky, and pressed so that it lay flat in her palm. She handed it to the woman, who sniffed it and immediately handed it back.

Jenny pointed at her chest. 'Jenny,' she said.

The woman's eyes flicked over her, assessing, as though she was trying to decide if Jenny deserved a name in return. Finally, she said, 'Mawberry.'

Jenny held up the flathead, pointed to it, and shrugged.

'Magura,' Mawberry said. 'Badiwa.'

She doesn't understand me, thought Jenny. *She doesn't know I want to find out where they are.*

So Jenny took Mawberry's elbow, half expecting her to flinch. When the woman didn't, Jenny guided her over to the edge of the clearing, where a gap in the trees afforded a partial view of the bay. Sometimes, in the darkness, Jenny would stand here and watch small fires spring up. Not large enough to be campfires: small red licks of light. Impossible that they were campfires, anyway, for they were in the middle of the bay. They wafted about in the dark, traversing the black absence of the water. One mild night, she decided to stay outside until the lights were extinguished or floated out of view. She sat with her back against a rock, and followed them with her eyes, until she fell asleep.

The bay now lay flat and innocent, for all the world as though it would never be so badly behaved as to rise in foamed peaks and hurl itself against the shore.

Jenny pointed out to the water and then to the fish in her hand, and shrugged again.

Mawberry nodded. 'Maguri,' she said. Jenny thought she had

been understood. But then Mawberry turned, and Jenny could see a narrow, muscled rear which, from behind, did not look like the backside of a pregnant woman. She and her little boy, without glancing back, walked into the trees.

Perhaps I should try to find Yarramundi, Jenny thought, *and speak to him myself.*

Later that day, as the light began to slant across the water and through the trees, Jenny sat outside watching Charlotte tear around the clearing, letting her enjoy the last of the day. The girl was also watched by a large grey kangaroo. She hadn't noticed the beast – would surely have run straight over to it if she had done, probably scaring it off. But Jenny was watching it, alert for any movement towards her daughter, as it bent its head to nibble at a leaf.

Mawberry was there, now. Perhaps she had been for some time, standing at the other side of the clearing. Without her boy this time.

Jenny had seen some of the natives pointing at the English livestock and yelling, 'Kangaroo, kangaroo!' at the top of their voices. Perhaps it was their name for any large animal; perhaps it had a different meaning altogether. But as it was one of the only native words she knew, she used it.

She pointed at the mass of grey fur in the trees and said, 'Kangaroo.'

Mawberry shook her head.

Jenny pointed again. 'Kangaroo?'

Again, the small and dainty shake of the head. 'Patagorang,' Mawberry said.

'Patagorang?'

Mawberry pointed at Jenny, then put her fingers to her lips and said, 'Kangaroo', moving her fingers away from her mouth as she

spoke. *Kangaroo is your word.* Then Mawberry pointed at herself
and repeated the gesture, saying, 'Patagorang.' *Patagorang is mine.*

So the governor, the reverend, the surgeon and all the officers
had it wrong. They had been using the wrong word, and with an
undeserved confidence. Jenny wondered what else they knew with
such certainty was false.

Mawberry came over to her and gently clasped her elbow, as
Jenny had done to her earlier that day, guiding Jenny towards the
opening in the trees. The lights were there again, wafting around
in the void. Mawberry pointed at them, one by one, and then back
to the fish that Jenny had been salting. 'Maguri,' she said again.
Then she held her hand out to the side and swept it in a graceful
arc overhead, following it with her eyes, then looking at Jenny and
pointing to her, and then herself. 'Barrabugu, guwing,' she said.

Jenny thought she understood. Tomorrow night, she hoped,
Mawberry would take her fishing.

CHAPTER 14

'Why would you be bobbing around out there, when I need you on the nets?' Dan asked. 'How could you possibly see anything, catch anything? Do they even have nets? No, you're better on the shore, where you'll catch some fish at least.' He ran his hands over the fish he was scaling as he sat on a rock near the hut.

'I might not, though, Dan,' Jenny said. 'There were no fish last week, were there?'

'Ah, but that was just the winds, wasn't it? Hard to catch anything in that. It's calmed down now. The bottom's all stirred up, that might bring them out a bit. There will be all sorts of tempting little specks floating around in the water that they can't wait to feed on.'

'Perhaps. But Mr Corbett says he will help on the nets tonight. I will go, and see what's to be seen.'

Dan stood and took her by the shoulders. 'No!' he shouted. 'No, you won't.'

Jenny stepped backwards. 'So you're scared that I might be right, Dan?'

'No one would be happier than me if you were. All right then, go and prove me wrong. Go and sit in the darkness on a piece of bark, not knowing where the current will take you, and I hope I see you in the morning.'

Jenny hoped so too. Mr Corbett had arranged for Bea to look after Charlotte in the hut, and that night Jenny squeezed her daughter so tightly that she threatened to cry before a bout of tickling averted the catastrophe.

At the edge of the clearing, as the sun dropped, stood Mawberry. The two of them walked down to the shore and then around the headland, over jutting rocks that prevented those in the main part of the cove from seeing beyond it.

A bark canoe was waiting on the shore, well made as far as it went. It looked like the perfect size for one small person, not two with large bellies.

Mawberry began to kindle a fire in the base of the canoe, and Jenny wondered if the whole thing would be burned through. But she'd often seen the lights out on the water, and presumed the natives didn't build new canoes each morning after swimming ashore with the fish in their teeth.

Looking down the shore Jenny saw more fires being lit, more canoes being launched. Every one of them was being handled by a woman.

With both of them in the little boat, it sat low in the water, and Jenny pushed herself as far as she could from the flames in the middle. They gave off the astringent scent that the tall, ghostly trees always did when burned.

Mawberry sliced her paddle easily from one side of the boat to the other in order to maintain a straight line, following the other boats out towards the middle of the bay. Occasionally she frowned as a turn caused a small amount of water to slop into the bottom of the boat, given the unusual weight it carried. After this happened a few times, she shook her head, looked at Jenny and pointed at the fire, moving her finger up and down emphatically. *We will stay here.*

She showed Jenny a hook made from a type of shell that seemed to have obligingly curved itself in the right direction. Mawberry had obviously, though, honed it and sharpened it, because when Jenny touched it and rubbed her fingers together she felt moisture, and when she held her hand over the fire she saw a small speck of red.

The hook did its work. It attracted the attention of a silver flash, whose lip became impaled as soon as Mawberry quickly pulled the hook upwards. This fish looked a little like a pilchard, but bigger, much bigger. Jenny, Dan and their workers had occasionally hauled in ones like this in their net. Mawberry put it at her feet where it thrashed about violently, attempting to hold on to life far more desperately than any pilchards Jenny had seen.

Soon enough it was joined by a different type of fish with an ugly mouth and a strange black dot on its flank. It looked far less appetising, far less plump than the one they'd just landed, but Mawberry pointed at it, smiled and rubbed her large tummy.

There were four others by the time they turned back. The other canoes were still out there, and Jenny had no way of knowing what their haul was. Did the six fish that now lay still represent a good or very disappointing night? She helped Mawberry haul the canoe up the beach a little way, so the tide that was slowly coming in wouldn't snag it.

Mawberry reached into the canoe, took the second fish they had caught and handed it to Jenny, who didn't feel as though she should accept it. She had done nothing except weigh the canoe down, and she was unused to being in a fishing boat without having a purpose. She would never, she decided, let that happen again. She knew what it was to be a passenger; to have her fate dictated by the decisions of another who may not have as much skill – although Mawberry was clearly far more skilled than her when it came to these waters.

The woman held the fish towards her again, nodding, then pointing to herself and the canoe to show that she would go back out alone. She was probably hoping to have better luck than she'd had with a stranger causing water to lap into the canoe.

So Jenny accepted the fish, taking it carefully to avoid the spined fins, and spoke her thanks in the hope that Mawberry would understand her intent. Without thinking, she reached out and grasped Mawberry's shoulder, pulling her as close as their swollen bellies would allow, leading with her chin across the gap and kissing the woman on the cheek.

Mawberry smiled, nodded, even waved. Then she settled herself into the canoe, where the embers were still glowing, and broke back out into the darkness.

The fish was delicious, sweet and flaky and flat enough to cook evenly through on the blade of a shovel. 'Ugly thing, though,' said Dan.

Jenny had saved the spines from the fins, thinking she'd make needles of them if they hardened up after drying. She was tempted now to use one on Dan.

'Have you ever cared what a fish looks like?' she asked. 'You're eating it, not bedding it.'

He looked up from his dish – one on which the meat wasn't augmented by any vegetable – and grunted before returning to it.

'We weren't out there long at all,' she said, 'and we got six. With a shell hook attached to some sort of vine. We can do better, far better, in the governor's cutter with a net.'

'I'll think about it,' said Dan.

'You can think all you like. If you don't ask him, I will.'

After Jack Starkey died, Dan became even more difficult.

Jack had been among the older convicts. Though he was thin and wiry, in the early days of the settlement he'd been as able with an axe or a shovel as any of the lads, thanks to a lifetime as a farm labourer – which had ended after his master hit him, and he hit back.

Jack's frame, though, did not have any spare meat on it. After rations were cut, he gradually became slower, weaker. He was no longer ordered to do hard physical work, and while the gesture was intended to be humane, it robbed him of the muscles he'd brought with him across the sea. Within a year, he shuffled instead of walked. He no longer met people's eyes, no longer hurled bawdy jokes at the other men. He concentrated on navigating the uneven path to the storehouse, and hiding his rations well enough afterwards.

The storehouse was the last room Jack saw. He had put his cupped hands out to receive some dried peas. He stood staring at them for a moment, perhaps concentrating on keeping his fingers together so that none of the shrivelled green spheres fell to the ground.

'They're not going to get any fresher for you looking at them,' the commissary had called. 'Move now, Starkey. Let the others through.'

Jack had looked up at the commissary, and kept looking as his knees buckled and the peas spilled from his hands. He was carried to the hospital tent but expired on the way. When the commissary went to sweep up the peas, they were gone.

Jack now lay not far from Dorothy, whose grave Jenny visited whenever she had time to find the strange, cloth-like white flowers the old woman had loved.

Jenny felt the pull of those two deaths eddying around her, and knew they would drag her down if she didn't drag herself up. She felt grim now, rather than excited, at the prospect of escape. But it was still an imperative, the only path that led from the graveyard.

Dan saw no salvation in plotting to get away, though. Jack's death, and the ones since, had convinced him that the only hope lay in silence. He became surly whenever Jenny prodded him on the matter of the governor's cutter. 'Why would you wish to remind him of us?' he said. 'And of the bargain we struck, that there are fish which never see the storehouse.'

'It could be her, next,' she said, and nodded towards Charlotte, who was plucking leaves off every plant she could find and throwing them into a pot on top of the dead fire. 'Her,' said Jenny, 'and the one to come. Do you think they'll forget about the fish if we stay low? We need to find more of them, not hope Lockhart forgets there's such a thing as fish.'

He shook his head, turning away. 'There will be no conversations. With the governor, with anyone. We will do what we can for our own, and let them look after the rest, and hope.'

'I don't believe in just hoping,' she said.

Dan would, of course, be angry when he found out. But his anger always followed the same trajectory, flash and noise with no real fire, followed by a sullen day or two during which she refused to acknowledge any problem, while he slowly forgot. She would far rather face his raging than a dead child.

And while the fish that her request brought in would help, she had another reason for making it, one that she had not yet exposed to the sunlight. There would be no harm, none at all, in getting to know the cutter. If people were used to seeing Dan in it and eating the fish it brought back, they would think nothing of seeing him repair it. Make it stronger.

So she approached Governor Lockhart after Sunday prayers. This was a little easier now, as the odious Major Rowe had been sent off to run Norfolk Island a few months ago. The marines had been delighted, Mr Corbett had told Jenny and Dan, and some had consumed a week's grog ration on the night he sailed out of the harbour. 'Should've brought some for us,' Dan had said. Soldiers and convicts had been on the same ration for a while now, the only difference being an allowance of spirits for the free.

But while Lockhart's guard dog was gone – and she had heard many say Lockhart was as overjoyed by this as his officers were – the governor wore a perpetual frown, perhaps put there by the necessity to feed people with crops that wouldn't grow and livestock that kept dying.

He didn't appear to have found comfort in the prayers that Sunday, judging by the look on his face. He stared at the ground as he walked slowly away from the service, wearing a closed, pinched expression that did not invite conversation.

Jenny didn't wait for an invitation. 'Sir,' she said as she approached. She couldn't decide whether a bow or a curtsy would be more likely to succeed with this man; she ended up producing a most unsatisfactory hybrid, which she hoped he didn't take for mockery.

If he did, he gave her no encouragement. Simply raised his head and looked at her.

'Your Excellency, it's Jenny Gwyn. Wife to Dan, who brings in all the fish.'

'Yes, Mrs Gwyn. I know who you are.'

'Sir, my husband is doing his best with what tools he has.'

'Yes, as we all must under these circumstances, in this place.'

'Yes, sir. But the fish – close to shore, sir, you must've noticed, the catch is not what it was.'

'No. It's to be hoped it will recover now the winds have turned.'

'But we don't need to wait for that sir, if you'll pardon me. There are still plenty of fish to be had – just a bit further out. If Dan was able to use the cutter … well, the stores would increase. I'm sure of it.'

'You're sure of it.'

'Yes, sir.'

'Once your husband is in my cutter, what is to prevent him sailing out through the heads?'

'He would not be so foolish, sir. He knows the sea, and he knows that taking a vessel such as that into the open ocean would be death.'

'Hm.'

'Sir, if I could make a proposal.'

'Are you in a position to make a proposal?'

'If you want more fish, sir, yes.'

Jenny sent up a silent prayer of thanks that the repugnant Rowe was no longer there. That was exactly the kind of statement that would have earned her immediate dismissal or worse.

'How would this be, sir?' she continued. 'You let Dan take your cutter out. Night's the best time. Send someone with him.

Mr Corbett, perhaps. With his musket. If Dan tries to sail into nowhere, Mr Corbett can use that musket. If Dan comes back with a boat full of fish, you will know we mean as we say and can be trusted with the boat. You'll have fish for supper a lot more often.'

The governor stared at her.

Social barriers had been breaking down. There were still only 1500 of them, and some had drifted beyond the reach of the law while others had been born into imprisonment. It was not unusual to hear soldiers and convicts conversing like friends. There were limits, though. Perhaps a convict berating the governor. A female one, who had no business talking about fish or anything else.

Lockhart turned and looked behind him, and for a moment she was sure the rest of his body would follow, that she had offended him and that she and Dan would be condemned to the dwindling returns of the shallows.

The governor didn't walk away, though. He saw the man he was looking for, and beckoned him over. Within half a minute, Mr Corbett had answered his summons.

'Corbett, you know this woman.'

'Yes, of course, Your Excellency. Dan Gwyn's wife. I occasionally assist, as you know, in hauling nets with the Gwyns.'

'What is your assessment of her character, and that of her husband?'

Corbett turned to her, his face shadowed from the eyes of the governor, and gave her a lopsided smile. It would have been more comfortable on the face of a young boy about to put a burr under a horse's saddle.

She tightened her jaw and widened her eyes, not wanting to risk a head shake but hoping her expression was warning enough not to joke.

Then Corbett turned to fully face the governor. 'I haven't a complaint in regard to either of them, Your Excellency,' he said. 'They have been temperate and of good behaviour since our arrival here, and before. They were both of them on the *Charlotte*, where Gwyn distinguished himself in helping with the management of the other prisoners. I believe they may be trusted as much as any convict here.'

'Do you feel, Captain, that there might be some merit in exploring Mrs Gwyn's claims of better catches further out?'

'Yes. Certainly, with the new fleet on its way, there can be no harm in investigating.'

This was the final, irrefutable argument, as Jenny knew it would be.

'Very well. You will take the cutter out with Gwyn. He will take you to where he believes fish are to be found, and if he comes back with sufficient numbers, I will consider letting him have use of the cutter.' The governor turned to Jenny, then. 'Of course if your husband comes back with nothing, one might be tempted to ask oneself what his motives were in asking for the vessel.'

'There will be fish, sir,' Jenny said. 'As to how many, I couldn't say. But more than we are hauling these days. My husband is willing to bet his reputation on it.'

When Dan found out he had bet his reputation on it, he drew back his hand to strike Jenny.

'Now before you go doing that,' she said, her calm manner stilling him momentarily, 'I'd like you to think how it would look to Mr Corbett. You know he doesn't hold with that sort of thing, and – well, Corbett's goodwill is useful to both of us. So I wouldn't, if I were you.'

Dan closed his fist in midair as though snatching at an insect, lowered his hands to his sides and swore. 'Why did you pretend you were speaking for me? Why did you speak at all? I've never been to this place where you say the fish are to be found! Wouldn't know where to find it, especially not in the dark. If I come back with an empty boat, Lockhart will see it as proof of a planned escape, and you and I will be watched. They might even move us into the barracks so they can do a better job of watching. You may very well have ruined everything.'

'If I wanted to ruin things, I would leave them as they are, bringing in fewer and fewer fish until there were none, and everyone – including us – starved, and they moved us out of our hut because a fisherman who can't bring in fish isn't worth it.'

She let him sulk for a while, then led him to the gap in the trees and pointed to where Mawberry had brought her on the water.

'I don't think they go out every night – at least, not to this place. They have their own fires, of course, but I don't like your chances of getting the governor to allow you to light one in the cutter.'

Dan stared out, his eyes unfocused and jumping from one side of the bay to the other. 'He was probably reluctant to give us the boat because of you.'

'Me!'

'You talk to people you have no business talking to. Asking about everything from pitch to soap to flax.'

'All useful things.'

'Especially when it comes to repairing boats or making sails. For God's sake, stop it. We do not want them to start counting fish.'

'You will not be watched. They will not believe it can be done in the governor's cutter, with my big belly. And for now, the only thing I'm keen to escape is a move to the women's huts.'

But perhaps after a few good hauls, and months of returning the boat each morning in good condition, Dan might be allowed to take it outside the heads. Jenny could join him. They might see what the coast was like outside the sheltering arms of the harbour. The last time she'd been past the coast's southern reaches, she had been below decks. It would be useful to be out in a boat with no decks at all. As for the northern coast – very few English people, as far as she knew, had seen that.

For now, though, she told Dan everything she could about where Mawberry had found the fish, and showed him a hook she had made out of the shells Mawberry used.

'Well, you'd better come with us,' he said.

Jenny smiled. If she hadn't been invited, she would have insisted, but far better to have her presence asked for.

'Yes,' she said, 'I suppose so. Don't want you and Mr Corbett rowing round in circles out there until dawn.'

The dreams came to her almost every night, with varying degrees of intensity. Sometimes in fragments, sometimes in seemingly endless, circular stories that followed their own logic.

Occasionally Jenny was in a canoe like Mawberry's, rowing out through the heads, trying to turn north before a wall of water silently formed in front of her. Or she was back in Cornwall, walking to the door of her house, opening it, seeing her mother and Dolly at their work by the hearth, embracing them and weeping – only to find they did not notice her presence, did not feel her kisses, continued talking as before.

Dawn would bring the laughter of birds, and sometimes of Charlotte if Dan was in a playful mood and decided to tickle her. Jenny would haul herself up through the water of her dreams to the surface, then set about the daily task of not dying and ensuring that neither of her children – the one without and the one within – did either.

So escape was not immediately possible. But the idea continued to flit around the edges of her vision, an impossibility that refused to be forgotten as all impossible things should be.

John Carney came with them in the end. He was known to Mr Corbett and had earned the gratitude of the marines by not giving them any reason to exert themselves on his behalf. And the cutter had six oars.

Neither Carney nor Mr Corbett showed any surprise when Jenny arrived with Dan, although Corbett fussed over her a little. 'Help her on, man, and be careful with it,' he said to Dan. 'Make sure she doesn't bump herself.'

Dan did as he was told, helping Jenny haul herself in. She scrambled to the front, to what she viewed as her place, and no one stopped her.

'So,' said Dan, 'where are you taking us this evening?'

'Back to Cornwall, I thought,' she said, and everyone in the boat laughed, though the words did not have the ring of a joke.

As night fell, she guided them to the spot that Mawberry had shown her. No canoes were out that night, but there was enough of the moon to light the way.

She sat with her newly crafted hook dangling from a thread she had extracted from her skirt, while the men hauled the net. By midnight there were close to twenty fish in the bottom of the boat.

'Will this do, do you think?' said Dan. 'Will these fish make our case?'

'I imagine they will,' said Corbett. 'As we are out here, though, we might as well give the ocean enough of a chance to prove itself. A few more hours, at least.'

The fish threatened to flop off the piece of canvas and onto the dirt. Dan could have presented them in a barrel, but he wanted to show off. So he held the end of the canvas drawn tight until he could release the catch before the governor's feet.

When Lockhart nodded his approval, Jenny and some of the women took the fish away for gutting and scaling. Dan's theatrical moment was all very well, but leave them there too long and he'd be standing in front of a stinking pile of unusable rot.

The boat was, in all but name, Dan's from then on. He trained a crew – John Carney and Vincent Langham, the former navigator of a merchant vessel – to fish with him, and trained up a few of the lads so he could call on them at need.

News of the better catch spread quickly, and brought with it the renewed attention of Elenor.

She and Joseph had married in a ceremony as sparse as Jenny and Dan's. Perhaps they'd been hoping for a hut of their own, or at least permission to clear land and build one. They were surely disappointed, though, for both remained in the main settlement.

The pair of them enjoyed gossiping; both adored being the first to pass on news of a skirmish with the natives or an attempted escape. If anybody else dared to bring information into the clannish convict society, they were ridiculed, sneered at, told they were lying.

Because Elenor and Joseph wanted to be the sole purveyors of truth, the only ones who could be relied on to say what was what.

One of the truths they had been purveying recently was the story of an affair between Jenny and Mr Corbett.

Jenny had snorted when Bea had told her. They were sitting cross-legged on the ground, each with a fish on a piece of bark in front of them. Jenny had taught her friend to gut and scale fish, but Bea still couldn't match Jenny's speed and accuracy – Jenny had had her hands inside fish bellies since early childhood. But it was good to have the help, and the company.

It was also good, Jenny had to admit, to have someone who could enlighten her on the state of things in the settlement. One of the few disadvantages of the Gwyns' living arrangements was isolation, and in the hole left by Jenny and Dan, darker things might grow. They *were* growing, by the sounds of it.

'Can you imagine anyone less likely to bed a married woman than Corbett?' she said to Bea. 'I wonder if he even knows how.'

'There have been women, from time to time,' said Bea. 'Not often, and not for long. He's discreet, and he takes care of them.'

Oddly Jenny felt jealous, and tried to crush the impulse to find out who these women were.

'Well, my bird,' she said, 'I can tell you for certain that that particular rumour is false.'

'Of course it is,' said Bea. 'Most know it, too. But it doesn't stop them talking about it, does it? They have to entertain themselves somehow.'

'This'll be Elenor's doing, I expect.'

'Her and Suse, yes. They say, particularly Joseph, that you're being given a bigger share of the catch. That you're being given extra rations, too. That you and Dan threatened to withhold the fish if you don't get what you want.'

'Do you believe the governor would allow us to do that?'

'I don't, no. But Joseph, you see, he's clever. He never makes something up out of thin air. He chooses a fact and rolls it around in the mud until it is roughly the same shape but much bigger and uglier. So no, I don't believe it. But there are those that do, those that say you're holding the settlement to ransom, you and Dan. They say action must be taken.'

Jenny was suddenly very, very angry. Had those who said such things actually tried to learn how to fish, or offered to help with the scaling and gutting and pressing?

'Will you tell them, then, that any fish that ends up in their guts was put there by us?'

'They know that already. It's what makes them angry.'

'Angry that we're feeding them?'

'Angry that they have to rely on you.'

'But Dan … You saw how it was on the *Charlotte*. The lads love him.'

'They did. Some of them still do. But not everyone came here on the *Charlotte*.'

'What can we do, Bea?' said Jenny. 'I'm not giving away our share of the catch, that much is certain, although you can have as much as you want.'

'I wouldn't be giving anything away either,' Bea said. 'You earned it. If you start giving fish away, even one, they'll think you have far more than you need. The next day there'll be ten people waiting down at the shore, or twenty. When you can't magically produce fish from under your skirts, they are not likely to be forgiving.'

'So we just go on as we are, then. Catching as much as we can, and keeping as much as we can.'

'Yes, I think so. At least I can't see any other way. But be careful. A great many people would like to see you and Dan brought down to the same level as the rest of us. They're sitting at Joseph's knee like a child hearing a story.'

It didn't take long for the first request to arrive. The next day, as Jenny wasn't occupied with fishing, she was put to work with the other women. Because she was large and ungainly, she wasn't able to do anything except collect shells for burning. Today, she was collecting them with the group of women that included Elenor.

Almost immediately, she saw what Elenor was doing. The woman inserted herself between Jenny and the rest of the group, walking slightly away until the distance widened to the point where a hissed demand would be heard only by Jenny.

'This is your doing, all of it,' Elenor whispered. She flung her arm around Jenny's shoulder in a gesture of seeming amiability, but her nails dug into the flesh of Jenny's upper arm.

Hunger was driving many people to anger, to violence or despair. Now, it had clearly ended the period of relative peace between Jenny and Elenor.

'It isn't, though, Elenor,' Jenny said. 'You were there, you took part, and I don't recall you refusing an equal share.'

'You were the one who bashed her. You were the one who made her bleed, who made her screech and scream and get attention. We would probably be back in Plymouth by now, after maybe a few years in prison. Now we are here, we will always be here.'

'Do you know, Elenor, how boring you are?' said Jenny.

The nails dug in harder. 'Tell me, then, how boring am I?'

'Ask any lag – here or in Newgate or in Plymouth – whether they deserve what they're getting. Ask any of them whether they committed the crime. Most of them will tell you they didn't, and those who own to it will tell you about their starving mother or grandmother or children or aunts. The real cowards, though, will tell you how someone else made them do it.'

Elenor's nails punctured Jenny's skin, leaving half-moon indents. Jenny inhaled sharply but refused to cry out.

'You might remember, I am owed a favour. You will give me one fish a day,' Elenor said. 'I will come to your hut to collect, every morning. No little ones, either. The biggest you have. Actually, you know what? Now I think of it, you'll lay all of your fish out for me, and I'll pick the one I like best. Every morning, starting tomorrow.'

'No, Elenor. If you come to my hut tomorrow, or any other time, I might find the need to practise with my knife.'

'You may use the knife, if you wish. I'd rather them scaled, actually – the scales do stick to your lips a bit, otherwise. So I'll choose the fish, and then you will prepare it for me. I look forward to bringing it back to the settlement and sharing it out as you never do.'

'You'll have nothing to share, then,' said Jenny, 'and those who always suspected you're a lying bitch will know it for certain.'

'If I come back with nothing, I will make sure that everyone knows how many fish you have, and that everyone knows they may come and take some. Take whatever else they like, while they're about it. You might want to start on the scaling before I arrive – I would not want to be late to muster.'

The next morning Elenor came, and blighted Jenny's favourite time of day.

There was always noise from the settlement: the yells and creaks penetrated Jenny's little glade when the wind was right. But at dawn they had not yet reached full voice. Jenny, who had never been much for sleep, would take Charlotte outside in fine weather to watch the sunlight. It washed over the cliff and began to spill onto the surface of the water, and then on to the trees that marched up to their hut.

Dan was still asleep and the light had not yet gained the land when Elenor appeared. 'You have fish for me,' she said.

'I have nothing for you.'

'If you don't, by midday everyone here – everyone who isn't working under an overseer at the time – will have come, will have made their demand.'

'Tell them to watch their footing. The rains have washed away some of the earth around the tree roots. They might trip if they're not careful.'

Elenor looked at her for a moment. Opened her mouth. Closed it again, nodding. Turned and left.

Jenny didn't feel as calm as she hoped she'd sounded. She knew Elenor was not joking – she and Joseph knew how to generate belief, and how to keep generating it.

The next person to step into the clearing wasn't another convict, or a mob of them demanding fish. It was Mr Corbett, closely followed by Lieutenant Farrow.

Dan had woken by this stage, and she had been intending to tell him about Elenor. She'd thought that she still had time.

But Corbett and Farrow marched up to Dan, seized him by the arms and placed his hands in manacles.

'What are you doing?' Jenny shouted, prevented from running to him by Charlotte who was clinging to her legs. 'What in God's name are you doing?'

'Arresting him, you stupid bitch,' said Farrow. 'In the governor's name, not God's.' And he cracked Dan, who was struggling, across the face.

'Lieutenant Farrow, please ensure your actions do you credit,' Corbett snapped.

But he made no effort to free Dan, who was swearing now, and spitting.

They had leg irons with them, but as Farrow bent over to clamp them on, Jenny yelled to Corbett, 'You know the track's too rough! And where would he run with his hands in irons?'

It was, perhaps, not the most stirring plea from a wife for her husband. Some might have expected her to hurl herself on him, weeping and begging for his freedom.

She would have done so, if freedom was a possibility. But it was not, and she had no intention of providing entertainment for the sneering Farrow. The best she could do was to buy Dan a little extra comfort, reduce the chances of him stumbling on a tree root and landing face first on a rock, without hands free to protect himself.

Farrow looked at Corbett. 'You know this track, then,' he said, and showed Corbett a nasty smile. The rumours of the convict barracks often infected the officers' barracks as well.

Corbett turned to Jenny, a crackling anger in his face, before turning away and leading Dan off with Farrow.

CHAPTER 15

When they were newly arrived, when each hill might have hidden fertile pastureland, Governor Lockhart had clearly felt ensuring a steady supply of fish was worth the cost of one or two of them going home with the fisherman. But now, with dead livestock and withered seeds and vegetables a third of their regular size, he was no doubt regretting the bargain.

Then Dan had given a fish to a convict who worked at the government gardens, in exchange for a small cauliflower.

'You were never told,' Lockhart thundered when Dan was dragged into his study, 'that you could trade your fish or sell them. They were for your use, yours alone. What you have done is a form of theft.'

No one had stopped Jenny trailing in after the small group. At the governor's last words, her face began to tingle, and she heard a small whimper from Charlotte. *How does she know*, Jenny wondered, *at such a young age?* But of course the little girl didn't know: her mother had simply squeezed her hand tightly enough to call forth a small yelp.

Jenny knew what the penalty for theft was here, what it had been since they first landed. Some, like the six marines, had already had the penalty brought down upon them, for the governor had to be seen as resolute. If he was willing to hang six free men, a convict would surely not present any problem for him.

Dan was taken to the gaol, and Jenny tried to scurry after Mr Corbett. He rounded on her, though, moving more quickly than she had ever seen him do before. *I must not forget*, she thought, *that he is soldier. He has fought, and he will continue to fight.*

'Please, Mr Corbett,' she said, slowing as she got near him. She was used to seeing his face relaxed, open. But now it was taut, and she had a sense that he was barely restraining himself.

'Mrs Gwyn, return to your hut immediately.' He turned and kept walking.

'Mr Corbett, please! What will happen?'

'I suggest you take that up with the judge advocate.' He did not slow as he said it, did not turn, did not raise his voice, simply cast the words into the air without seeming to mind if Jenny caught them.

'Why are you angry with me? I've done nothing to you, Mr Corbett, truly. Those rumours – no one believes them, and those who do, well, they don't think less of you for it.'

He turned around and slowly walked towards her, forcing words out as he went. 'It's not … about … the blasted rumours!'

'Then what have we done?'

'I spoke for you – for both of you, because half the ideas in Gwyn's head were put there by you. To the governor, the judge advocate, Farrow and his ilk. I told them Dan could be trusted with the cutter, that neither of you would abuse the privilege. The governor will not trust me again. I have lost his ear, and very possibly the ability to moderate the disciplinary excesses of many of those here. For a cauliflower!' He turned and walked away.

Jenny decided she would never eat cauliflower again, if she could help it.

She ran back the way she had come, towards the tent of Anthony Price, the judge advocate. A grand title, but the man who bore it was only around five years older than her.

She'd learned quite a lot about him from Corbett. He had been sent out here to make a mark in a less crowded field than that in London. His father was prominent and felt his son would rise significantly faster if a tour of duty beyond the knowledge of men was undertaken. Price was expected to return as a honed blade, tempered by the colonial fire and far more capable than those who had spent a few years at the Inns of Court. He was equal to anyone in the colony in terms of intelligence, and seemed aware of that fact. While he wasn't a cruel man, he could be arrogant and mercurial. No one ever knew how he would respond to requests.

But Corbett had told Jenny to ask the judge advocate, so ask the judge advocate she would.

She found him at his desk, scratching away at a piece of paper. 'Mr Price, sir ...'

He looked up. 'Mrs Gwyn.'

'Mr Corbett suggested I see you. To find out what happens.'

'What happens?'

'What happens now. To Dan. To me and Charlotte.'

'To you and your child, nothing, as neither of you have committed a crime as far as I'm aware. Dan will stand trial. Evidence will be presented and assessed, and if he is found to have committed the crime of which he is accused, there will be an appropriate punishment.'

Price went back to his document.

'An appropriate punishment?' said Jenny. 'He'll be hanged!'

'Yes. If he's guilty and can be proven to be so, it's highly likely he will be hanged. We cannot, under any circumstances, allow theft, Mrs Gwyn. If you don't wish to see your child die of starvation, you would do well to remember it. This is not a useful conversation, though. Your husband has not yet stood trial, and we are already discussing his execution.'

When witnesses were called, the first to step forward was Joseph Clancy.

When Joseph came forward to give evidence, a murmur began trickling around the room. Jenny followed its progress until she saw Elenor towards the back, smiling.

Joseph said he had seen Dan talking to John Rush, one of those who tended the government gardens. He had seen Rush hand over a cauliflower to Dan in exchange for a parcel. After following Rush at a distance, Joseph saw him unwrap the gift: a fish.

Joseph, as everyone knew, could be trusted. Joseph knew everything that was going on in the settlement.

As Dan was found guilty of theft, preparations began for another execution.

The evening found Jenny on the doorstep of the governor's house. She hadn't wanted to leave Charlotte, who was agitated. The girl didn't know that her father was to be strangled, but she had absorbed her mother's fear and was only slightly mollified by songs from Bea, who had come to the hut.

The governor's house was the first brick structure anyone in this place had seen since leaving England. It sat above the eastern shore of the cove, small and squat and meaner than some Penmor cottages, but the apex of civilisation here. There were lights in its windows against the advancing dusk, more tallow than Jenny would use in a year.

'I must speak to him, and it must be tonight,' she kept saying to the guard.

'I keep telling you, Mrs Gwyn, to go back to your hut.'

Then Lockhart's called out, from a room off the hallway, 'For God's sake, she's not going to give me any peace until I see her.'

She was allowed inside. In his broad-windowed study, the governor was sitting behind what had to be the most ornate desk ever to rest on this soil. Imported, no doubt – the wood here just wasn't up to it.

Jenny had no interest in the desk. She ran into the room, put her hands on its polished surface, and leaned forward as far as her distended stomach would allow. 'My husband will hang.'

'I am sorry, Mrs Gwyn. It is the penalty for theft of food, as you and he know very well.'

'He stole nothing,' she said. 'I heard the bargain you made with him on that first day. You never mentioned anything about cauliflower, simply told him he could keep part of the catch. He made a fair exchange. You may have changed your mind – and it wouldn't surprise me, for I know things are bad. But he was following your rules.'

'No, Mrs Gwyn, he was not. The fish were for his own use – and yours, and your family's. They were not to be sold, for money or cauliflower or any other commodity.'

'After you turn him off, it won't happen as much. The thieving.'

'No. That is my hope.'

'Because there won't be anything to steal. Without Dan, you'll all starve a lot more quickly. How many kangaroos have your dogs managed to bring down? Enough to feed everyone here? Enough to feed those who are coming?'

'There are others who can fish, Mrs Gwyn.'

'Others who can haul a net, maybe. Even sail a boat, in a pinch. But Dan tells them when to pull and where to put the boat. He knows where the fish are, knows whether they're likely to be on one side of the harbour or the other. No point in just throwing a net down there and seeing what happens, Your Excellency.'

'Mrs Gwyn, I don't want to see your husband hang – nice fellow, all things considered, and he was a fine fisherman. But if I spare him the noose, our stores will be picked clean, and there will be nothing left of us.'

'There will be nothing left of us – any of us – a lot sooner, if you hang Dan. Without him, more people will die.'

The governor leaned back behind his desk, exhaling slowly. '*With* him, people will steal,' he said. 'Mrs Gwyn, do you know why the stores haven't been raided every night? People know they will hang if they try it. If your husband goes unpunished, they will try it.'

'Punish him, then. But don't kill him. Punish him and send him back on the water.'

'It may surprise you to learn that I am not in the habit of having policy dictated by convicts.' Lockhart nodded to the soldier at the door, who came forward with his hand outstretched, seeking to take her arm.

She ignored him. 'What will the convicts do when they find you cannot be trusted to keep a bargain?' She turned, glared at the soldier, and stepped around him towards the door.

He followed her out of the study and closed the door behind him. 'You need to mind the way you talk to the governor,' he said.

'There are some who think he's a little too soft on all of you. They might decide stricter treatment is in order.'

'How many fish caught by us have slipped down your gullet? Have a care or you might find yourself coming up against one of the few things that can be relied on in this place – there are more of us than there are of you.'

The notion of a convict uprising had entered her head before, as it had surely presented itself to most of those here. But after an uprising, what was to happen? They would still be trapped in the same landscape, with its stubborn inability to nurture crops. By the time the second fleet arrived they would be easily recaptured.

In any case, those like Joe and Elenor, who thought of themselves as the convict caucus's informal leaders didn't have the courage to carry such a thing off. But Joe and Elenor weren't entirely without wit, or without influence.

The governor had shown no sign of listening to her when she'd stood in front of him, and nor had she expected him to. Perhaps he had, though. Or perhaps others in authority had also drawn the very short, straight line between Dan's death and reduced rations.

Whatever the truth of it was, Lockhart announced that Dan's punishment would not be carried out at the end of the rope. He was to be flogged. One hundred lashes. He was to lose his command over fishing operations, and his cut of the fish that went with it. But eventually he might be allowed to resume fishing under the supervision of other convicts.

Dan and Jenny would lose their hut, would go back into the communal convict barracks – he with the men and she with the women. They would try to make what life they could with his scarred back and a baby born among squabbling lags rather than the unearthly streaks of the trees around the glade that was no longer theirs.

CHAPTER 16

Both calamities happened the next day.

All convicts were required to watch floggings – if they weren't haunted by the sight of a back with no skin and mangled flesh, how could they be trusted to behave?

The soldiers brought the triangle out. It was an ominous symbol, a profane and subverted trinity. Not that Dan showed fear when he was trussed to it. He looked straight ahead, a certain tension in his jaw but no other indication that he was experiencing anything other than boredom.

One hundred lashes was a survivable punishment – as long as your heart didn't stop from the shock, and you avoided growing a rot in the wound, a decay which would turn your blood to poison.

Jenny had felt ill the first time she witnessed a flogging. It had taken place in Plymouth, and she'd been free then although already on the path that would bring her here. She went out of curiosity, and because Elenor had urged her to. 'We may even get to do a little business on the side,' Elenor had said. 'Not as good as a hanging, but even with floggings people tend to be fixated on one thing. It's remarkable what can be removed from a pocket while the owner is gaping at some poor sod in pain.'

Jenny had thought she already knew what to expect; had a vague picture in her mind of a bound man, another man tickling his back. But the scourger had propelled the flail through the air with a precision that terrified her. He wrapped the cords around his victim's back and removed a predetermined amount of flesh with each blow.

Had she a choice, she never would have seen another one. But she had seen many now, and they'd all seemed not quite as horrifying as the first one.

The horror returned when she saw Dan with his shirt off, having his arms tied above his head. This was a creature of the waves, someone with the power to steer a small collection of wooden planks through the worst of storms. It should not have been possible to constrain him like this.

Some of the lags had scars upon scars. The ones who couldn't help themselves, the ones who didn't have a special skill and wouldn't be missed if they were pulled out of their gang. They were the ones who said flogging changed a man. She wondered what would be left of Dan when it was over.

Here, the authorities tended to get convicts to administer floggings. Jenny supposed they didn't like specks of blood on their shirts. But convicts were often hesitant to deliver blows that were too hard; they had to be urged to it, giving their masters the opportunity to deliver two lessons in one.

But the man who walked towards Dan wouldn't need any urging.

Joseph Clancy was flanked by two soldiers, presumably to prevent him evading this duty. They needn't have bothered, thought Jenny. If the King himself arrived in a boat and beckoned Joe aboard, the man wouldn't go. Not until this business was done.

Jenny felt movement beside her, a hand on her arm, and found herself looking into the freshly bruised face of John Carney.

'I tried to stop the bastard from informing, but he rounded on me with a stick,' he whispered. 'I'll make sure you're safe, you and the little one, until Dan's well. You put your face into my shoulder if you have to, no one will blame you.'

'I have to watch,' she said. 'If I look away I'll be deserting him.'

The first crack was loud, louder than it normally was. Dan grunted, which Jenny knew he wouldn't have done if the blow had been delivered with the usual force. He would know, she thought, that his best chance of survival – and hers, and Charlotte's, and that of the baby who would arrive at any moment – lay in maintaining the respect some of the others still had for him. Men who cried during floggings were expendable.

Dan wasn't wailing, but somebody else was. Charlotte stood beside her, no longer able to gain a perch that she considered acceptable on her mother's hip, which had disappeared as her belly grew. The last thing Jenny had wanted to do was to bring Charlotte here. But the whole settlement was forced to attend, so Jenny had no one to leave her with.

Jenny wished, desperately, that Mawberry would come. Perhaps the woman would have consented to take the child into the woods for the day. Perhaps there were other little girls Charlotte's age who might distract her, while the man she knew as her father was being flayed. Such a thing, though, was not possible.

The night before, their last in their hut – and without Dan, who had been locked in the guard house – she'd tried to prepare the girl. 'It's like a play, I suppose,' she had said, before realising that her daughter had neither seen nor heard of plays. Her stories came into the world without the aid of a playwright to write the parts, or actors to inhabit them.

'Is it fun?' Charlotte asked. She was nearly three now, and detested being in the same place looking at the same thing for too long. If she had to stay where she was, she would bring her considerable powers to bear on changing her environment, drawing intricate and meaningless patterns in the dirt with a stick, ripping leaves off trees and sprinkling them where she felt they would sit to best effect.

'Not fun, no,' Jenny told her. 'But ... it may look as though your pa is being hurt. I want you to know, you are not to be upset by it. It's a game. One you should never seek to play, but one you don't need to fear.'

That night, Jenny had cried. Not because of their circumstances, although those were upsetting enough. The tears came because, for the first time, she had lied to her daughter.

Now, when the flail again connected with Dan's back, Charlotte let out a piercing screech. She started forward, and Jenny knew she intended to race up to Joseph, grab his leg, tell him to stop it, now! Jenny knelt quickly and pulled her daughter back, lifting her and hugging her. Her small body was straining to turn around so that she could see what was happening, and her legs, muscular from constant movement, were kicking wildly so that Jenny had to put her down in case she harmed the baby.

'It will be over soon,' she whispered, 'and Pa will be back with us. Listen, can you hear him crying? He's not, is he? He won't want you to, either. You have to show you are as brave as he is, the bravest of sea dragons.'

It was over soon, and Dan was cut down and taken off to the hospital. Apart from the occasional grunt, he had not made a sound.

Jenny and Charlotte went to the huts that housed the female convicts. They were made of wooden slabs and bark, much like Dan and Jenny's, and while the winds were barely impeded by their construction, at least the worst of the rain was denied entry.

Charlotte was still trembling, and on the walk to the huts had encircled her arms around Jenny's knee so that they hobbled along as one ungainly organism. When they entered the hut, a place where Charlotte had never been, her imperiousness reasserted itself. 'We will go home now,' she said.

'You are home, duckling. This is where we will be staying.'

'No, it is not. We will go home.'

Nothing Jenny said could convince her otherwise. Bea sat with Charlotte while Jenny went to find a shared pot in which she could cook their ration. When she returned, the girl was asleep.

But Charlotte was awake when Jenny awoke later. She was looking towards the entrance, waving cheerfully.

Jenny sat up, a process that now required several attempts. Charlotte was smiling. That was good, Jenny thought – perhaps Dan's scourging had not featured as much in the little girl's dreams as it had in Jenny's.

Her relief ended when she saw who Charlotte was waving to. On the other side of the hut, sitting alone, was Elenor. She was returning Charlotte's waves, and sometimes shaping her hand into a duck then having it nibble on her other arm, which made Charlotte giggle.

When Elenor saw Jenny was awake, she stood up and came over. She sat down in front of them, smiling at them both. When her face turned to Jenny the smile elongated on one side, showing a few broad teeth. 'A good day's work by my Joseph,' she said over Charlotte's head.

'More days' work like that, and some may decide he belongs on the other end of it,' said Jenny.

'Ah, they won't decide that. For he has the governor's ear.'

Jenny snorted.

'Well, they think he does,' said Elenor, tilting her head at the centre of the hut. 'Amounts to the same thing.' Then she turned back to Charlotte.

Jenny tensed and drew her arms around her daughter, flicking her eyes over Elenor to see if any of the folds of her skirt might be concealing a knife.

Elenor noticed. 'Don't be ridiculous,' she snapped. 'She's a child.'

It was true that Jenny had never seen or heard of Elenor or Joseph harming a child. They reserved their poison for the fully grown.

Elenor did seem to have a genuine desire to distract Charlotte. She taught her the same clapping game that Jenny had, one both women had learned twenty years ago in different parts of Cornwall. Charlotte clearly already knew the rules, which didn't stop Elenor from teaching them again while she exclaimed at how quickly the girl was picking them up.

Jenny was so tense her body began to hurt. She crouched unsteadily so that she could be ready to move should she need to, ready to intervene should the woman begin to look as though she intended harm.

Elenor did intend harm, naturally. But no amount of vigilance from Charlotte's mother could have prevented the blow landing. By the time Jenny realised that the violence would be verbal instead of physical, it was too late to reach out and block the little girl's ears, or scoop her up and run from the hut.

'Charlotte,' Elenor said, 'where's your pa?'

'Pa's out with the fish,' Charlotte said, because that was what Jenny had told her when she'd asked for Dan.

'Pa's not with the fish, and won't be for some time,' said Elenor. 'He's in the hospital. He might die there.'

'He will not, and nor is he close to it,' said Jenny, pulling Charlotte back into her and moving to block her ears.

But before she could, Elenor landed the blow. 'It's odd that you call him Pa. He is not, did you know that? Your pa is a pig-nosed, lice-ridden gaoler in Plymouth who doesn't know you're alive, and would not care if he did. Over here – and it's a long way, Charlotte, such a long way, you could sail until Christmas and still not get back – over here you have no pa.'

She reached over, smiling and patting the little girl's knee, then aimed another snarl at Jenny before standing and walking out of the building.

CHAPTER 17

Jenny was waiting for Elenor when the woman returned from the shore with armfuls of officers' clothes, wet and perhaps a bit more frayed than they had been.

Bea had been sent off that day to collect oyster shells and had taken Charlotte with her, pretending they would be looking for sea fairies in each shell they picked up.

Jenny was grateful. She had a job to do, and she did not want Charlotte to see it.

She had stood outside the hut, pacing a little around one of the cooking fires, dead now in the middle of the day. She doubted herself, for a moment, when she saw Elenor, Suse and some of the others walking up with the clothes over their arms. Jenny wondered if the clothes Elenor carried belonged to Mr Corbett. Whoever owned them was likely to need to borrow some shortly. Elenor would not be expecting her to act, clearly thought she had Jenny under her control now – with Elenor and Joe the reigning king and queen of the huts, able to tip poison into a little girl's ear with impunity.

Elenor's smile came back as soon as she saw Jenny, a look of vicious narrow-eyed delight. She walked right up, handed over the wet clothes and said, 'Hang these out.'

Jenny took them, looking at the ground. Made to shuffle over towards the lines, reaching into her pocket with her free hand and closing it around the rock she had been hiding there. Mr Black had always told them to hold something heavy if they could, if they had to use their fists. She stretched out her arm, pretending to reach up to drape the white breeches she was holding on the line. They nearly made it to their destination, too, and Jenny could feel the credulous joy of Elenor as she watched the queen of the highway obey her.

Then Jenny dropped the breeches, and pivoted, and the hand holding the rock connected with the side of Elenor's face.

The force of the blow set Elenor on her backside, and blood streamed from her mouth.

I may have knocked out one of the teeth the scurvy hasn't taken, thought Jenny. *I hope I did.*

Elenor didn't remain stunned for long. She reached a hand behind her and pushed upwards, trying to spring into a standing position so she could return the favour. She glanced at Suse for some help, but the larger woman was backing away, turning, perhaps going to fetch someone. There wasn't much time left for Jenny to deliver a warning that would be indelible enough to buy her some peace.

Elenor was halfway up when Jenny reached her, shoving in her shoulder so that she again thudded onto the ground. Jenny knelt down, her knees on top of Elenor's legs, letting her feel the full weight of a mother and an almost-born baby. 'I will kill you, next time,' she said.

Suse was coming back now, puffing hard to move her bulk along at a speed that she felt was appropriate to the situation. She had fetched a soldier. The soldier was Mr Corbett.

'She attacked me!' screeched Elenor, with a slushiness to her voice that Jenny hoped meant Elenor had at least bitten her tongue. 'I was coming back with the laundry and she ran at me. Maybe you were keeping her in that hut because she's too dangerous to have among the decent folk. There's Mr Reid's breeches, trampled into the dirt!'

Corbett stood with his arms crossed, making no move to drag Jenny to her feet. He looked at her, both eyebrows raised.

'She is – and I will never say this again – right,' Jenny said. 'She wanted to upset Charlotte, tried very hard to do it. Will not do it again, if I have a say.'

'Now you are compounding your offence by attempting to grind her into the dirt along with Mr Reid's breeches,' Corbett said. He took her hand, grasped her under the elbow and helped her to her feet, then dusted his hands off before reaching out to Elenor.

'She needs a flogging, so she does,' said Elenor.

'You would be happy to see her flogged in this state?' said Corbett.

'That belly of hers didn't stop her whacking me.'

'Tell me, Elenor. How many times does an argument result in someone getting hit, here?'

Elenor said nothing.

'Quite a common occurrence, I think,' he said. 'Yet I can't recall Susannah being sent to fetch me or anyone else to intervene. Nor can I recall those with bruises on their faces, put there by you, demanding your flogging.'

'Suse was in fear for my life, Mr Corbett!' said Elenor. 'That one, her husband takes from all of our mouths, and she could have killed me. She could be a murderer. You haven't seen her, Mr Corbett.

You didn't see her on the highway, the day we were arrested. We begged her to stop, we had the bonnet and the necklace but she kept going. There is a darkness to her, and the next time Suse fetches you it might be to collect my body.'

'I do have a lot of trouble believing a … an experienced girl such as yourself would have any difficulty surviving an attack by one so encumbered. I will, of course, mention this matter to the judge advocate. Flogging does seem a little extreme in this case, though.'

'Aren't you going to arrest her?'

'And take her where, Elenor? Where do you think she will disappear to, if I don't arrest her? No, I'm sure you can both come to terms with each other. It will go on the list, and if there is any penalty it is out of my hands.'

After he had gone, Elenor grabbed the neck of Jenny's dress and pulled her as close as her belly would allow. 'I was right, I was,' she hissed. 'He's fucking you, he must be. If it was me I'd be in the guard house by now.'

'It would be a great day for you and Joe if one of your rumours was actually proven true,' said Jenny. 'But Mr Corbett's not fucking me, nor I him. He just doesn't enjoy being fetched like a governess when the children are fighting over the toys.'

'There will be more to fight over, soon,' said Elenor. 'Those ships, they can't be far off now. And you without your extra ration. A shame you'll have so many to feed, when you've been used to so much.'

Emanuel was born the same week the second fleet started straggling in. The first to arrive was the *Lady Juliana*.

In other circumstances Jenny might have received attention

at the hospital after the birth, but now the surgeon was overrun. Those landed from the *Lady Juliana*, for the most part, did not have energy for the debauchery that had characterised the landing of the women two and a half years before. Half were ill, and a great many of those scarcely able to move. Naked, lice dripping from them, several drew their last breaths on their first few days in Sydney Cove.

So Emanuel's birth was attended by Bea, as Charlotte's had been, in the women's hut. Without her, he would have been unlikely to survive. The thick blue and purple rope that emerged with him was looped around his neck. Bea lifted it over his head, jiggling him, while Jenny, her legs still open, sat on her elbows and watched the floppy wet creature.

'Breathe!' she yelled at him. 'Breathe, breathe!'

Charlotte, sitting nearby, joined in. 'Breathe, breathe, breathe, breathe, breathe!' she commanded her brother.

He gulped in the air and became pink in an instant, trying out a halting cry that grew in strength. Within a few seconds everyone close by knew that Jenny had had her baby.

Still holding the naked child in the cool air, Bea looked up and beamed at Jenny. 'Aren't you a clever one?'

'For God's sake, wrap him in something,' Jenny said.

Bea frowned, reached out and took a piece of rough cloth she'd set aside for the purpose, swaddling him quickly and handing him to Jenny.

Charlotte waddled over and made to head around to the business end. Perhaps she wanted to see the cavern from which her brother had emerged, for surely he was much too big to have come from her mother.

Jenny snaked an arm around her, drawing her in. 'This is your brother.'

Charlotte studied him. 'He's very ugly,' she said.

'I think he is very handsome,' said Bea, smiling. 'He looks like his father.'

'My father, *mine*,' Charlotte said and began to wail, until Bea offered to take her down to the shore to look for mermaids' necklaces.

Dan was congratulated by officers and convicts alike. Some remembered not to clap him on his still-healing back.

'You'd think you were the one who did all the work,' said Jenny. 'That you lugged him around for nine months and tore yourself open bringing him into the world.'

'I was the one who kept you all fed,' Dan said.

He had smiled when Emanuel was presented to him, picking his son up for a moment and jiggling him the way he thought babies should be jiggled. Then he'd handed him back. There was no word of congratulation, no question as to how Jenny was faring.

'I hope he survives,' was all Dan said.

The scarred men had been right: Dan was diminished.

Their quarrels, now, were hardly worthy of the name. They sank into the river of loud abuse and quiet secrets that flowed through the place.

Jenny was almost grateful for these quarrels, and for any sign at all that Dan still breathed. Because when Joe had taken the skin from his back, he had taken something of Dan with it. Whether it was the flogging that changed him, or the removal of his control over the fishing operations, or the loss of the hut, she didn't know. But quiet sniping was as close as he got to demonstrating any vigour.

When the governor saw the catch diminish precipitously, Dan was put back on the boats. But he was under the direction of John Carney, simply part of the crew and no longer vested with any authority.

The governor was wise enough to reinstate Dan at just the right time, as more fish than ever were needed after the second fleet landed. Its other ships, as they dribbled into the port, disgorged convicts who were in a similar condition to those who had stumbled or been carried off the *Lady Juliana*, while another ship, the *Justinian*, had brought some stores but not enough.

There was a farm, now, up the river to the west where the land was somewhat more cooperative than that to be found around the cove. But after a few years it still wasn't producing anything like the quantity of corn needed.

At least the new convicts and marines brought news from England.

Jenny wished she could get word of her mother and sister. They might be dead. Dolly may have married and had children. They might be staring at Cornwall through the same grey eyes that Charlotte used to examine a kangaroo.

Jenny had also wondered what was happening on a larger scale. London might have burned down again. The King might be dead. England might be at war with France.

None of these events, it transpired, had occurred. Instead of a war breaking out between France and England, France was at war with itself.

Elenor, who had been assisting Surgeon Drummond, had some of the more lurid details from newly arrived patients and did not mind sharing them, even with a group that included Jenny at its fringes. 'The King himself! Down his head plopped, into a basket like it was a cabbage. Then they took the French Queen's head, and those of a great many lords and ladies. And now those running the country are as common as muck, like us. Some of us more than others.' She aimed that last comment over the heads of her listeners towards Jenny.

Many others were far less gleeful at the news about France. As rumour built upon rumour, the soldiers' banter with the convicts began to seem stilted, forced, as one group looked at the other, wondering whether the news would prompt them to a similar rebellion.

One soldier, though, was delighted.

The morning after she'd heard Elenor's tale, Jenny had seen Mr Corbett trudging from his hut to the governor's yard. 'Wondrous news,' he called to Lieutenant Reid. 'I confess I celebrated a little too fulsomely. A brave undertaking, too, and one which will improve the lot of the French people.'

'Don't say that too loudly,' Reid said. 'Anyone would think you want a revolt against our King.'

'No, not at all. He's not a licentious tyrant who spends vast sums on baubles while his people starve.'

It should be me, Jenny thought. *Me to whom he crows about some impossibly distant uprising.*

If he would not give her back her place among the few he spoke to honestly, perhaps she could take it. A surprise attack, a shock to make him forget to pout.

She approached until she was walking quietly alongside him. 'What if some of us were to follow the example of the French?'

Corbett glanced at her, pursed his lips, looked away and kept walking. 'Your freedom was justly taken from you. That does not compare to the freedoms of an entire nation being unfairly curtailed. To escape from lawful imprisonment is a crime, but to risk everything in pursuit of a liberty that belongs to you, and to succeed, that ... well, that is a miracle.'

He paused, stared at her for a moment and stalked away, his stiff back making it clear he would not welcome further conversation.

Dan didn't blame the poor farmland or the new fleet for their circumstances. He blamed Jenny. She had forced him to marry her, he said, although the banns had never been read, for God's sake, and the marriage would not stand. Not at home in England, where he would go after his sentence expired, as soon as he could find a ship that needed a mate.

At first, he mumbled his bitterness to Jenny out of the corner of his mouth, looking away from her as though she wasn't worth the effort of turning his head.

But it grew, over the weeks, so that it could no longer be contained in a mutter. His words became louder, and they began to reach other ears, especially when he was sharing contraband rum with the other convicts, a practice he indulged in more frequently now he was among them. He still carried weight with some of the men, including most of those from the *Charlotte*. So people listened, and people talked.

'It was for you, you know,' Dan hissed at Jenny one night. 'I traded the vegetables for you, for the baby. It was for you I took those lashes – you might as well have been holding the flail yourself.'

She could have pointed out that the source of their troubles slept in one of the men's huts. She knew, though, that no matter what she said, Dan would just throw the same complaints back at her. They became truer in his mind with each repetition, gaining a weight that threatened to drag her down with him.

So she would turn away and silently cry, mourning the half-formed hope that his son would make the marriage real for Dan in a way the reverend's words never could, in a way the austere Christ of their rulers had failed to do.

Dan's sentence, to hear him tell it, would expire within the year. But this was no guarantee he'd be released, as the governor had not been given any records relating to the convicts whose fate he now controlled. It was always possible that someone might take it upon themselves to lop a few years off their sentence in the retelling. Those who had previously brought back tales of mines or pastures that turned out to be groundless now regretted it, as anything they said about the length of their sentences was looked on with suspicion.

If Dan went to England, he would be going alone. Jenny's sentence would not have expired, and while Dan's skills could pay for his passage, a woman and two young children would have to pay with money. It had been a long time since she'd held a coin in her hand.

Dan irritated her constantly, no question. She'd never had much patience with those who moaned. But the colony without *her* Dan would be bleak – not the current mass of scar and self-pity, but the one who could read the ocean, the one who would take Charlotte looking for sea dragons, the one who advised the marines themselves on the behaviour of tides and currents.

Jenny would be left alone with two young children, one a confirmed bastard and the other possibly so, if Dan was right about the marriages here not solidifying and retaining their shape beyond the seas.

She decided that if the two of them were going to aim whispers at each other in the dark, they might as well be whispering about something useful.

One night, he complained to her about the freezing water that had lately been finding its way in to the bottom of the cutter. She listened and nodded and offered to rub his shoulders. He accepted with a grunt, and she moved behind him, clenching and unclenching her fingers over his muscles. She made a fist and screwed it into the knots in his back as he sat there, silent, a king being attended by a servant beneath his notice.

After a few minutes, though, his shoulders lowered somewhat. Perhaps he was just tired, but perhaps he was beginning to relax. If she tried to wait for a sunny mood from him, she thought, she might as well give away her plan. So she leaned forward and whispered, 'There are many here who would not be alive but for you.'

Dan nodded, accepting the praise without offering any in return – without any thought that it was Jenny to whom he owed the knowledge of where to get the best catches.

'Now you're reduced to a deckhand,' she said, 'expected to do the same work for no reward, no share of the catch, your family herded into the convict huts, separated from your wife.' She felt his shoulders tense and redoubled her efforts to loosen them. 'With the right boat, I think you could sail just about anywhere,' she told him.

'So do I,' he said.

'Do it, then. Sail anywhere. With me, and Charlotte and Emanuel. We have something that most of them here don't have. The skill to leave, and the courage to do it.'

CHAPTER 18

Odd that it should be fish that saved Jenny from the convict huts. The very creatures that had abandoned Penmor.

In her own hut she had grown too used to her privacy. To hearing one snore instead of ten. Walking six feet without brushing skin with anyone else. She could ride Dan without the catcalls that accompanied coupling in the convict huts, and she could stand naked alone in the clearing afterwards. During those nights, with the sweat pulled out of her skin by the moist air, she had thought of Mawberry, even fancied them sisters.

But while space was the only blessing this colony provided in abundance, it was one of the many denied to the hut convicts. Jenny now lived in a place of wails and screams and sobs and fights, of stench upon stench, of dangers buried in innocent conversation.

She had lived in this world before, of course, in the gaol and the hulk and the ship. She remembered feeling choked by the heavy presence of so many bodies, so many fractured hearts and damaged minds. Back then, though, she had known she would be leaving – perhaps for somewhere worse, but leaving nonetheless.

Then, too, she had not had a baby who was lighter than an

armful of officers' breeches. A too-small boy who mewled instead of wailed, and then only rarely.

Her walks to the shore were for Emanuel, so she told herself and anyone else who inquired. The sun and fresh air might be able to do what her own milk had not.

Charlotte had a child's understanding that a new baby stopped her mother from holding her back. She would run on ahead if she saw something interesting, although her pace was slowing as the weeks passed. But the figure of a child crouched at the other end of the beach – that was worth galloping for.

By the time Jenny reached them, Charlotte was digging in the sand with a naked boy. They were absorbed, each content with their own company but happy to share their patch of sand with the other.

Mawberry, standing nearby, frowned when she saw Jenny and nodded in the direction of her old hut. Jenny shook her head and pointed up the shore at the convict huts. Mawberry nodded, and Jenny suddenly feared for her, imagining the woman striding up to the main settlement, walking past the male huts – where many of the men knew nothing of beauty, so chose to mock it – or encountering a guard with a musket, made unreasonable by hunger.

Jenny pointed again, then back at Mawberry, and shook her head.

Mawberry shrugged and looked down at the children. They were using their fingers to embellish a small oval mound of sand they had built, giving it scales and placing eyes where they had no business being. Mawberry glanced at this sand fish, then behind her to where a canoe was pulled up onto the beach. Then she raised her eyebrows at Jenny, who smiled.

Mr Corbett looked confused as the fish spilled out of a sack onto a piece of canvas Jenny had laid at his feet. She would have preferred to lay them out like wares at a market, but she was holding Emanuel in one arm. So she had shaken them out of the sack in a tumble: a few silver ones turned grey with death; some of the flattened, sandy creatures with eyes at the top of their heads; two of the delicious green monstrosities with a single black spot on their flank.

Corbett looked up at her, and down again.

'They're fish,' she said.

'Yes. Yes, so I see.'

'Thought you mightn't recognise them, being scarce and all.'

'And they came from?'

'The ocean.'

He frowned at her, and she regretted her answer.

'These haven't been held back from the government catch?' he asked.

'No. I caught them. In a native canoe.'

She didn't tell him about the heads: the sandstone arms that led from the open sea. Today, she and Mawberry had paddled right up to them and dropped their shell-hooked lines. They'd grinned at each other when the whiskered snout of a seal appeared for a moment above the water. Jenny had felt the tug of the current as the ebbing tide forced unimaginable gallons of water between the heads. She had looked up at the scrub that peered over the edge of the cliffs, then down at the half-submerged boulders that had fallen from them.

She'd noticed the lookout officer at his post on the southern headland. He was gazing to the south, the direction from which the fleets had come. He was surely not expecting to see anyone arriving from the north. Or leaving.

Now, as Corbett stared at the jumble of fish, she said, 'These are yours.'

'I'm not at all sure they are,' he said.

'I am paying our debt,' she told him. 'The fish that was traded for the cauliflower – I'm replacing it, with more to spare. Take it to the governor. You will eat well tonight, or better than you have been.'

'I see. And you?'

'We need more than fish,' she said. She held out Emanuel, all sunken cheeks and ribs. 'Look at him. He is the quietest baby I have ever seen. Babies should not be quiet, Mr Corbett.'

Corbett frowned as he looked at Emanuel. He reached out and stroked the boy's cheek with his thumb.

'Whenever anyone starts coughing, so does he,' Jenny said. 'He will not survive the huts, Mr Corbett. Dan has paid, and now so have I. Emanuel has a chance if we have our own place. Please, can you talk to the governor?'

'I doubt he would listen.'

'He might, if you remind him of how the catch has reduced since the flogging. If you say you believe it may increase if Dan is given charge of the boats again. And if you tell him that returning our family to our hut will help Dan heal faster, so he can work harder. Perhaps the governor will not act to save a baby's life, but surely he will act to save his own. Particularly if you tell him this as he is eating one of these fish.'

'I don't know what … Well, I will ask.'

'Ask prettily, for all our sakes,' said Jenny.

Corbett laughed then, the rueful sound of a parent reluctantly amused by a naughty child.

'Whatever else you say, Mr Corbett, you can't say I haven't paid what's due.'

'No, I can't,' he said, shaking his head. 'And Jenny – thank you. I admire you for doing this.'

After muster, Mr Corbett told Jenny that the governor was already well aware of the discrepancy between Carney's catch and Dan's previous numbers. And Lockhart feared that more ships would soon come, with more convicts and marines. 'The governor's not pleased with the condition of the convicts who came off the second fleet,' said Corbett.

'I heard it took over three hundred days for the *Lady Juliana* to get here,' said Jenny. 'No wonder they were in such a state.'

'It's not only that,' said Corbett. 'Those ships, they're not the property of His Majesty. They've been hired from private interests that are chiefly concerned with profit, and so were the men in charge of the vessels. I sincerely doubt most of those on board got their full ration. And I've been in the hold of the *Lady Juliana* – it's putrid, far worse than the *Charlotte* on its worst day after a storm with the privy buckets rolling around. The masters had no incentive to keep anyone alive, either. Quite the reverse: anyone who died, they kept the allowance. His Excellency has written home about it, but who knows if his letter will get there before more ships are sent?'

'In the meantime,' said Jenny, 'you have the colony's best fisherman working as a deckhand and living in with the men. Tools don't last if you don't look after them, Mr Corbett.'

Jenny was delighted to carry Emanuel to their family home, and to be getting away from the noxious games of Elenor and Joe. But she worried that the partial restoration of Dan's status might dull any hunger he had for escape. Still, the marines were to watch him very carefully to make sure that all of his catch wound up in the store. He would not like that.

Dan continued to dismiss the idea of escape, at first. 'We would need pitch, for starters.'

'We can bring it,' Jenny said, 'and food, too.'

'Not enough, not without stealing it. I'm not going to steal food, Jenny. There will be no flogging next time, you must know that.'

'That's one of the reasons why I don't think we have any choice. Your last crime wasn't a crime, we both know it was Joseph talking to the right people – he must have some officers who are friendly to him. And who's to say he won't do it again, and see you at the end of a rope? If you stay here, it will happen. I'm certain of it.'

Neither Dan nor Jenny was able to stay away from the shore. They were both known for seeking it out, separately or together. Now they could take advantage of the privacy afforded by an unoccupied stretch of sand without exciting comment.

Dan nodded out towards the bay. A southerly wind was making small foam-headed peaks, and the governor's cutter rode them as it lay at anchor. 'That's the boat you'd have to take,' Dan said.

'Unless you want to steal one of the brigs,' said Jenny. 'Maybe ask some seamen to join you.'

When Dan smiled, the muscles in his face relaxed so that the pinched and bitter creature was momentarily banished and the man he had replaced came back.

'Don't worry about stealing food,' she said. 'I'm not suggesting that we go tomorrow. You and I, we'll salt a little bit away from our rations. The hole in our floor is still undisturbed. We'll put aside enough rice, enough salt pork. Over a few months, we should be able to get enough for the journey. I'll bring some of the tea leaves that ward off the scurvy.'

Dan kept looking at the governor's cutter, of which he had once been master in all but name. Then he shook his head as though trying to clear it, turning to her. 'I can't see it working, Jenny. You and I, and two small children. Why would you put them in such danger?'

It was a question Jenny had been asking herself. The voyage would certainly be dangerous. She had only the vaguest notion of what they might do once they were out of the harbour: where they would go, how long it would take. But Emanuel was small and sickly, and Charlotte had too soon lost her childhood plumpness. If they stayed, they would be in more danger from starvation and disease than from the ocean.

Children Charlotte's age and younger lay in the graveyard at the end of the settlement. Jenny had seen Amelia, a former London whore, lie on the freshly turned earth that covered the cloth-wrapped body of her young son, refusing to move when night fell as she did not want him to be alone in the dark.

Dan, though, was right that an escape wouldn't work with just the four of them.

'Do you not think others might wish to come?' she asked him. 'Others who can help. What about John Carney?'

'He might like what he's doing now,' Dan said. 'Who's to say he will not do what Joseph did?'

'You know he won't. There are very few people I trust, Dan, and he is one of them. Him and Bea.'

'You didn't mention me.'

'Of course, you,' she said, smiling. She did not mean a word of it – had he not been telling her that their marriage didn't exist, and that he would take the first opportunity to get a berth on the boat back to England? The only way she could trust him was if they were engaged together in a plan that would result in their deaths should it fail.

She had no intention, though, of laying things out for him quite as baldly as that.

'This would be a big undertaking,' she said.

He nodded.

'Not something we should do without thought,' she said.

'No, we shouldn't.'

'That's why, Dan, we should start planning. Keeping our eyes and ears open. If we believe those plans can't succeed, then we abandon them. But if they can succeed, you will never again have to take anyone else's direction on a boat.'

But someone else had a similar idea.

A crew of five men, most of them from the second fleet, sailed by moonlight down the river from the government farm on a punt. They exchanged it for one of Dan's fishing boats and slid unseen between the arms of the harbour entrance. No one in the settlement knew in which direction they had turned, although those who'd worked with the ringleader, Richard Tallow, on a government farm later said he was intending to head for Otaheite.

Very few thought Tallow would get there. The boat the men had taken was not in the best repair, and it was generally assumed they had drowned.

Their departure prompted a renewed vigilance. No one was watched more closely than two convicts with their own hut, and with seafaring skills. Surely, though, there could be no objection to Jenny and Dan entertaining a friend.

While Dan was still unsure about Jenny's idea as a whole, he had at least agreed to think about it. Then, one evening, he brought John Carney to the hut.

Carney was among the least brutish of the men here. He simply wanted to be on the ocean and have enough to eat, and he wanted to marry a girl named Ann who had come on the *Lady Penrhyn*. But he was denied permission as there was a wife at home, and his protestations that she was probably dead by now did not count for anything. He was also never allowed to take a share of the catch, and he lived under constant threat of losing the ocean – of being sent to the saw pits or brick mills, or up to the new government farm.

And, as Carney told Jenny, he was very, very bored. 'I understand you're considering a bit of a journey, missus,' he said.

'Not I, no. I would never consider such a thing.'

'Nor I, of course. But I have met those who would. I've spoken to those who have done it.'

'How might that be?'

'When he first arrived, I slept next to Richard Tallow.'

'I'm sure you would've reported him to the authorities had you any idea what he was about,' said Jenny.

'Of course I would have, straight away. He raved like a madman – I barely listened. Still managed to hear quite a bit, though.'

The details came: how far away Otaheite was, in what direction, how long it might take a crew of convicts – non-existent convicts, of course, because everyone in this hut was far too upstanding to consider such a venture – to reach it, what provisions they would need. Most importantly, where they would find a vessel equal to the voyage.

'Do you know, if anyone was dishonest and foolish enough to consider such a venture,' Carney said, 'they would need a navigator. Vincent Langham – you remember him, from the *Charlotte*? Irritating man, but knows a fair bit about navigating and doesn't seem to be enjoying his life here.'

'I suppose there could be no harm in having a conversation with him,' said Jenny. 'Just to ensure he has no plans of escape.'

'All these conversations are going to get us hanged,' said Dan.

Jenny snorted. 'Joseph and Elenor are going to get us all hanged – most especially you, even if you're more virtuous than the reverend from this point on.'

Scowling at her, Dan muttered about his plan to finish his sentence and get a position on a ship that would bring him home.

Carney frowned. 'Of course, there's no point in having any conversations if not everybody is as upright as we are. If not everybody has the same desire to do what needs to be done.'

Carney didn't come to the hut again or make any further comment when he saw Jenny. Whenever she raised the possibility of escape with Dan, he would say it was too risky.

He said a great many other things as well, to a great many other people. Most especially, he kept making his view clear to all who would listen that Jenny wasn't really his wife, or wouldn't be once he left these shores. People started taking this seriously. Someone – possibly Joseph, possibly another, as there was no shortage of resentment now that the Gwyns were back in their hut – spoke to the judge advocate about it.

Then Anthony Price spoke to Governor Lockhart, who helped Jenny more than anybody had for a long time. He decided to make a new rule: one that prevented men with dependent families from leaving the colony, even after their sentence had expired.

'Your husband has only himself to blame, you know,' said Mr Corbett.

Jenny had been sent to collect laundry from the officers, including Corbett. She could always tell which breeches were his – they had patches of dirt on the knees, a result of his habit of kneeling to examine interesting plants or help children who had fallen over.

'Dan doesn't think that,' she said. 'He blames the governor. You. Even me. But not himself.'

'It was the way he carried on which prompted this rule in the first place. He put the fear of God into His Excellency, who has enough dependents as it is, that he might have to take on the abandoned wives and children of sentence-expired convicts. And now your husband must feel quite desperate.'

He did. Desperate enough, it turned out, to tackle the possibility of escape with a vigour she hadn't seen him devote to anything since before the flogging.

Jenny knew they were being watched. They were a long way from the only convicts suspected of harbouring plans to escape: little knots of people met at twilight under trees, down by the shore or around fires. Their mutterings could not be overheard by their overseers, and therefore immediately made their overseers curious.

But some convicts had seen people walking up the track towards the Gwyn hut, then walking back down later than might be expected. People who had never visited before – people with the skill to aid in an escape attempt. It would only take a word to a marine to ruin everything.

Carney had brought in Vince Langham, the navigator, for starters. Next he brought a rough fellow, James Bruton, who'd been transported for breaking into a house and threatening its occupants with a knife. For that, and for the linens he'd made off with, he had been given seven years – the same sentence as Jenny.

She felt that was a little unfair. But then, she had to remind herself that a lack of consistency in sentencing had saved her from dangling and rotting at the Four Turnings. In a judicial system where pickpockets were frequently hanged, transportation for a highwaywoman seemed a lucky escape. And if she'd made one lucky escape, why not two?

Bruton had little beyond his muscular strength to recommend him, but it was enough. Dan said they would need to cut timber in order to make repairs wherever they landed – or would land if they went through with it.

Jenny soon noticed that Bruton had a habit of clenching and unclenching his fists even when still. He was a watchful one, always listening and never speaking. Dangerous, in Jenny's view. Dan knew him from the men's camp and wore a mask of brittle joviality whenever he visited the hut. The man wouldn't respond when Dan clapped him on the shoulder or laughed far too loudly when he said just about anything.

'You're frightened of him, aren't you?' Jenny asked Dan.

'Not a bit of it. But someone as strong as him – well, the rest of them are a bit slight.'

'Did he overhear you talking about it?'

'Not at all,' Dan protested, 'I'm very careful.'

You aren't, though, Jenny thought. Not stupid enough to talk about their plans openly, but Dan knew that the respect of the strong was valuable, and he wasn't above bragging if he thought it would do him some good. Would Dan hint at a secret in front of a man who intimidated him? Would that man then demand to join the enterprise?

Either way, Bruton had been accepted by Dan and Carney. But he would bear watching by someone trustworthy; he needed a foil, a counterpoint. And, Jenny knew, there was still one skill that none among them possessed.

'So are we to sail for the rest of our lives,' she said, 'or do you think it's a good idea to have somewhere to sail and some way to survive once we get there?'

'There's always fish,' said Dan. 'More than enough skill in this room to feed us.'

'Is there?' she asked. 'When you don't even know where we're going, let alone what fish are there. But wherever we land, there will be just that – land. Do you think, in your wisdom, it might be worth bringing someone who knows how to farm it?'

The man they found, Thomas Harrigan, was from the second fleet and in his fifties – one of the oldest men in the colony. Old, but not slow or weak. His crime in England had been stealing pigs; he'd carried two away, one under each arm. He had lost some of that muscle on the long and malnourished voyage, but it had returned after his frequent woodcutting stints.

The Gwyns had a crew, then. A vessel – or one in mind. That still left provisions, though.

The answer came by sea.

CHAPTER 19
January, 1791

The *Supply* was a nimble little ship often absent from the cove. It flitted around ports where it might acquire supplies for the colony at the best advantage, although it was never able to bring enough food to stave off famine, not with more than two thousand souls needing sustenance. In Batavia the *Supply*'s master made the acquaintance of a Dutch captain, Pietr Vorst. The master knew that Vorst was shrewd, that he had access to all markets run by the Dutch, and that he had the ability to bargain and therefore to acquire supplies at a better rate than a stranger had any hope of doing.

There were two things, however, the master didn't know: that Vorst believed in profit above all else, and that he hated the English. They behaved, Vorst thought, as though the Dutch had no right to their possessions between here and Europe. They believed they were superior, and they spoke loudly and slowly as though he lacked the wit to understand – he, who had learned their language when they seemed incapable of learning his.

It wasn't just that Vorst was Dutch. His mother, a woman of Batavia, had given him dark skin that amplified their sneers.

He took the colony's money and promised to procure the flour,

206

butter and salted meats required. And he did. But when his ship, the *Waaksamheyd*, arrived at Sydney Cove, it bore less of everything than had been paid for.

Carney, unloading the day's catch at the storehouse, had been given a note by the commissary to take to Government House. It wasn't sealed, so Carney saw no harm in peeking at it on his way: a list of those provisions most urgently needed, and in what quantities. The storekeeper clearly hoped that the items he'd listed could be unloaded first and brought immediately to him. But there was less of everything, and none of some things for which Vorst had been paid. And the note had gone undelivered – not because it was superfluous, although it was, but because shouting preceded Vorst out the door of Government House.

'I couldn't understand what Vorst was saying,' Carney told Dan and Jenny. 'But it was fairly unmistakable that if you said it in Holland, you'd find yourself laid out pretty quick.'

The news jumped from one person to the other, as news there did: the rorting, and the powerlessness of the governor to do much about it. Lockhart did insist on an additional ton of butter to make up for the flour and other goods that simply hadn't been loaded. He also refused the price Vorst asked for transporting some soldiers back to Britain, eventually agreeing on something more realistic.

Corbett occasionally drifted down to the shore now to look at the fishing boats, although Jenny didn't know whether this was a sign of increasing forgiveness or increasing scrutiny. He was far less ambiguous in his views on Vorst. On one visit, looking at the *Waaksamheyd* riding at anchor, he spat on the sand. 'The man's a mountebank, a fraud,' he said. 'We are on the brink of famine, and he's using our desperation for profit.'

'I don't think Vorst likes us any better than Corbett likes him,' said Carney after the officer had stalked off.

'I don't think he likes the governor very much,' said Jenny. 'He might look upon us differently.'

A mercenary man, Vorst resented – or so Jenny had heard – what he saw as the unfounded high handedness of the British. Such a man might be open to inquiries from convicts.

When Dan had been sentenced to be flogged, Jenny had taken his purse from the hole in the floor and buried it at the edge of the clearing beneath a distinctive tree. Now Dan dug it up and went to visit Vorst on the *Waaksamheyd* as it rode at anchor, its captain glaring towards the shore and planning how best to defraud the passengers he would take back to England.

'I didn't think I'd have enough money,' Dan told Jenny. 'I truly didn't. From what I've heard of the man, he's not one for dispensing charity.'

But Dan had clearly given Vorst enough, judging by the bundle he'd brought back with him. He and Carney immediately went down to the shore again and landed the rest of his purchases. It was, thank God, a moonless night – detection would have been fatal.

'Vorst was difficult to convince, at first,' said Dan, as he lowered the supplies into the hole in the floor; carefully, as they didn't wish to risk a candle at a time when all convicts should be asleep. 'When I assured him, though, that selling me the goods would ultimately lead to the embarrassment of the governor, Vorst became more cooperative.' Dan turned a sack of rice from side to side, trying to find an angle that would allow it to fit into the hole. 'We agreed on a price for this, for a start,' he added. 'I'm to return tomorrow, to talk further. See if there's anything else he has that we want, and see if we can afford to buy it from him.'

'He's trying to see how desperate you are,' Jenny said.

'I think he knows we're desperate enough.'

'He must be somewhat desperate himself,' she said. 'I think he'll be bobbing up and down there for a while. I can't see the governor inviting him to dinner, but he won't be willing to leave until he's settled on a price for the charter and his passengers are ready to go.'

'Life aboard ship in sight of shore or in the middle of the ocean – what's the difference?'

'Dan, you went ashore straightaway when we arrived. You did not have to sit in the hold, hearing the noise of the ship being unloaded, the splash of the boats as people were taken ashore. I couldn't see where you were going. But I knew something was there, something beyond. He'll be sitting in his ship now, looking at the fires, thinking of the governor and his officers at their dinner, knowing that no invitation will be coming.'

'I doubt he'd accept, even if it did.'

'Possibly not an invitation from the governor. But Lockhart isn't the only one with a roof.'

The next night, the cargo Dan brought ashore was Vorst himself. He was a slight man, far shorter than Dan, with long dark hair lying on the collar of a finely made coat. He had, no doubt, seen homes far grander than the one-room hut, and furniture finer than the rough wooden table that Dan had built and on which Charlotte always tried to stand. But Vorst was a sailor and a mercenary one at that, so he had probably seen worse.

Jenny was standing outside to greet him. She did her best estimation of a curtsy, the one she had used with the tribesmen by the beach. When Charlotte saw her mother make the familiar bobbing movement, she did likewise, which dragged a laugh out of Vorst.

'The governor sits there with so much and will not share it with me, and you have so little and yet here I am,' the captain said. 'I thought all English were cold and superior.'

'We're not English,' Jenny said. 'We're Cornish.'

She told him that the next time Dan came to his ship to purchase something, Vorst should hand his laundry over as well. 'Life on a ship makes it difficult to wash clothes, I know,' she said. 'Frustrating, too, to be in sight of a shore with all the requisites but unable to use them. I will wash your clothes as well as I do the officers', then bring them back to you at night.'

Vorst was obviously a lover of clean clothes, and Dan returned from rowing him back to his vessel with salt-stained breeches and a blotchy shirt.

Jenny was a lot more gentle than she'd ever been with the officers' clothes, even Mr Corbett's breeches. She rinsed Vorst's garments in fresh water and dried them in the sun, then asked Dan to row her out that night so she could present them to Vorst.

'Such fine fabric,' she said, after the captain had opened the door to his cabin. 'The English, you know, they pride themselves on the quality of their cloth – you should hear the ones from Exeter go on, particularly. I have never seen cloth from other parts before now, and it seems to me that are being a little conceited.'

She tried to forget the bolts from France that had taken up space in her family's small cottage in Penmor, waiting to run from merchant to merchant through Will Trelawney's hands.

'Oh, most definitely,' said Vorst, accepting the folded clothes. 'More English conceit.'

'It must get a bit sickening, after a while, having to deal with them as much as you do,' she said, and Dan squeezed her shoulder in warning. She wanted to think he was pulling her back out of fear she was becoming too obviously artful; she tried to dismiss the idea that he simply didn't like her stepping into the role of the talker.

Vorst didn't seem to mind. 'It does, by God. The masters of the sea, they are, and no one else is able to build ships half as well or sail them with any competence. Everyone else is beneath their notice – unless you force them to notice you. They've noticed me now, so they have.' He sat straighter and raised his chin a little; he seemed to be daring anyone to say he was still a nonentity, just an opportunistic sea captain.

'You must've sailed a long way indeed,' Jenny said. 'Holland, Batavia, here – would you show me on a map? I was practically born in a boat, you see. Have been sailing all my life. Dan, too. We would be fascinated to hear of your voyages.'

The three of them sat down in Vorst's cabin, a dark low-ceilinged room with its hatches open to the night breeze. The captain spread a large chart out on the green baize of the table and dragged his finger along the coast, all the way up to the tip of the continent – a far greater distance than Jenny had realised.

'A shame this place is so remote, permits no escape,' she said. 'Of course, that's why we are here. It would be very embarrassing to the governor if some convicts were to escape, but they would need somewhere to escape to.'

Vorst looked up sharply. 'I have no intention of aiding any convicts in an escape attempt.'

Jenny feared he was about to fold up the chart along with any hope of identifying a destination. 'Of course not, and I would never ask such a thing,' she said, trying to sound calm. 'It is simply interesting to think on. The masters of the sea – they take so little account of the waters beyond their own. I am ignorant of anything that does not fall under His Majesty's domain.'

'As you say, any disappearance would be very embarrassing to Mr Lockhart,' said Vorst.

'Oh yes.'

'For intellectual interest, then,' said Vorst, 'if I were a convict, knowing what I know of the sea, I would consider the venture almost hopeless.'

'Almost.'

'Yes. There is a chance, a small one. One that has been taken before. You have heard of the famous mutiny?'

Jenny looked at Dan, who shook his head.

'Not so famous as the English like to suppose, then,' Vorst said. 'It happened on a ship called the *Bounty*. They'd been in Otaheite, and the crew rather liked the climate and the women. They were sorry to leave, even sorrier after a few weeks back under the command of their captain, who was arrogant and unreasonable. So they took the ship.'

'Where?' Dan asked.

'I'm not sure, and neither was their captain. They put him in a small boat, you see, with a few loyal crew members, and set him adrift.' Vorst paused and sat back, unwilling to dole out more of the story without some supplication.

'And,' said Jenny, 'he perished at sea?'

Vorst chuckled. 'You would think so, wouldn't you? No, he made his way by fits and starts to a haven. One provided by the Dutch. One which may interest you – from a theoretical perspective, of course.'

'Of course,' said Jenny. She didn't try to repeat the two unfamiliar words he had used, fearful to reveal any ignorance.

Vorst leaned over the map. 'Anyone attempting such a voyage would need a strong vessel,' he said, 'and significant skill. If a person had both of those things, they could sail close into the coast all the way up here, then across this gulf – the Gulf of Carpentaria – and along to the north-west. If one wanted to get away from English superiority, one could keep going until one reached here.' He tapped the chart twice, driving his dirty, broken fingernail into an archipelago on the delicate paper. 'That,' he said, 'is Coepang. That is where the captain of the *Bounty* ended up. There, one would find no English, no gaolers. Only Dutch. They might be persuaded to help unfortunate victims of a shipwreck. We are generous, you know.'

'How far did the *Bounty*'s captain sail to get there?' Jenny asked.

'Three and a half thousand nautical miles. It would be a little further from here. While the man was a bastard by all accounts, he was highly skilled and had an experienced crew. I would, of course, strongly advise against anyone taking such a journey, let alone a group of felons with far less experience than the captain. But I suppose it could be done.'

Jenny stared at the lines on the map. She couldn't interpret the symbols she knew to be letters, but she could divine Vorst's meaning. With enough supplies, and enough skill, they could leave Sydney Cove behind.

Vorst went through a lot of laundry, and Jenny needed to be stealthy in the washing of it. Early each morning she visited a nearby stream to do this work, before hanging the garments out to dry in the hut. Each evening, Dan rowed her to Vorst's ship.

They would have liked to have brought Vincent Langham with them, as he might have been able to commit Vorst's chart to memory. John Carney would have been welcome too. But it was far too dangerous for Dan and Jenny to bring anyone, and Vorst would probably not welcome the additions. It was one thing to be sharing his knowledge of the sea with two people who had shown him kindness, another to be seen plotting.

On each visit they asked to see the chart, and by the third it was already laid out on the table. Vorst made no further remarks on it. He seemed to pretend not to notice the avidity with which they studied it.

After a week, he announced that he had decided to give them a gift. He was a businessman, though – the gift would be theirs if they would also buy two of his muskets, and powder to load them. When Dan dug up his purse and spilled its contents onto Vorst's chart table, the Dutchman clapped his hands, expressing delight that there was just enough to cover his costs. The muskets may have cost all of their remaining money, but what came with them was worth far more.

Nestled in the wrappings of one of the muskets, they found when they got it back to the hut, was a quadrant. Wrapped around the barrel of the other was the chart.

CHAPTER 20

Jenny desperately needed Dan to keep his nerve, just as he seemed to be losing it again. She had hoped he would be dragged out of his morose fog by their return to the hut and his restored command of the fishing fleet. She missed the blazing, impetuous rogue, but his only animation still came through rum-soaked anger. Rum wasn't new to Dan, but where it used to spur him to boasts and good-natured scrapping, it now called out a dark, seeping resentment.

Having brought a bottle with him from the main settlement, he sat on the ground sucking on it as Jenny swept spiderwebs and droppings out of the hut. She took care not to send any billows of dust towards Emanuel, who lay silently on a square of canvas nearby. Charlotte played on the ground near Dan, casting little glances at him over her shoulder while staying quiet, not drawing his attention to her. But Dan was usually her playmate, and eventually she tottered up to him. 'Will you take me to the water?'

He didn't look at her, swigging from his bottle again. 'No.'

'Maybe there are fish there.'

He snapped his head around to face her and bellowed, 'I said no!'

Charlotte's tears drew Jenny from inside the hut. The girl ran

215

to her, hugging her legs, and Dan found himself roughly prodded with the broom handle. He turned, snarling, grabbed the broom, dragged it out of Jenny's hand and sent it spinning across the clearing.

Keeping her eyes on him, she crouched and took Charlotte by the shoulders. 'Go inside, duckling.'

Her daughter stared for another moment at the monster who had replaced her father, then ran inside, sobbing.

'She has done nothing wrong,' said Jenny. 'She might never trust you again.'

'Perhaps she shouldn't.'

'And should I?'

Dan stood unsteadily and flung the now-empty bottle into the bushes. 'You have no right to trust me!' he yelled. 'No right to expect anything!'

She picked up Emanuel, whose head lolled backwards, and walked slowly towards Dan, half expecting him to lash out at her. Instead, his shoulders slumped and he sat again. She lowered herself onto her haunches in front of him. 'I took risks to get us back here, because I do trust you. To get us away from here before we starve – before your son stops breathing. I trust you to ensure his survival as well as your own.'

'He'll stop breathing if he is tossed from a boat into a heaving sea,' Dan said. 'I know the ocean, I know its greed. And you want to dangle the children over its open mouth.'

'The earth is greedy too. It won't feed us, but its hunger shows no sign of being sated. Emanuel's death at sea is a possibility. His death here is nigh on certain. As it is for all of us.'

He wouldn't look at her, slowly exhaling as his shoulders rounded into the familiar posture of despair. 'And I can't prevent it,' he said.

Slowly, she unwrapped Emanuel's swaddling. She traced her fingers over his ribs, then reached for Dan's hand and placed it on the baby's stomach. 'Perhaps you can, perhaps you can't. If we stay here, though, he will leave us without ever having run or smiled, ever having hit his sister, ever having learned how to fish.' She paused. 'Don't die before you're dead, Dan. Otherwise your son will slip off while you sit here sucking on a bottle.'

Dan would never acknowledge she was right. The next morning, though, he was up at dawn. She woke to see him bending over Emanuel, cupping his sunken cheek, tracing his ribs as Jenny had the day before.

Dan turned when he heard her moving. 'We will go,' he said. 'God help us, if He has any power where we're travelling.'

Jenny stood, went to her husband, took his hand and kissed it. 'You are a brave man.'

'Not brave enough to defy you, I suppose,' he said.

Over the following couple of weeks, they all behaved like model convicts. Jenny began to worry they were taking it too far when Corbett pulled her aside after muster one morning. 'I must say, I'm gratified,' he said. 'You and your husband are among the most upright in the colony.'

But Dan kept finding reasons to delay the journey now that they had everything they needed. The hole in their floor was filled with food and weapons and the tools that would take them to Coepang.

Langham had been exceptionally excited when he saw the chart and quadrant, declaring he had what he required to get them to their destination. He said that no cloudy night could stop them. If they were to put his boast to the test, though, it would need to be soon. February was making everyone's skin slick with its characteristic humidity, and Jenny had been here long enough to know that after the sweat came the storms.

Everyone agreed that they needed to go before the heavy seas and the rain set in. But no one knew what would be waiting for them when they headed north, whether distance from their prison would intensify the winds.

Yet Dan was reluctant to name a day. 'The boat needs to be made ready,' he said. 'That will take time.' He and Carney were working on it whenever they could, caulking seams while Jenny spent her nights weaving sails out of flax. Ostensibly this was to make the cutter more fit for fishing, an enterprise of which the governor approved.

'Every day we wait, every minute, puts us at greater risk,' Jenny said to Dan one night.

'Don't worry about the storms. We can manage those, and we won't leave so late that we will be sailing into a gale.'

'It's not the storms, Dan. Not only the storms, anyway. How well do you know Bruton, really? Harrigan? They all have women, don't they? Do you think they've told them? Some of those women, they'd do anything to keep a man once they've got him. I've lived with them, so I know them well. They might even decide to have a word, give the information in exchange for their own man's safety, while the rest of us hang. Every day we hold back is a day closer to that happening.'

'*You* wouldn't do such a thing, of course, even if you weren't coming,' said Dan.

'Of course not.'

'No, because you don't have to. I'm just about a free man, now, Jenny. Or supposed to be. But because we've been united in a false marriage, I can't leave except in this way. So you don't have to turn me in to keep me – you've shackled me far more effectively than they have.'

The other men were nervous; none believed their luck would hold indefinitely. Bruton, in particular, felt the strain of not drawing attention to himself, the stress of the held-back blow.

Charlotte didn't know they were soon to leave. Every day, Jenny took her down to wade in the harbour and peer into the bushes to see if they could spot the possums to which the girl was so drawn. Without knowing it, Charlotte was saying goodbye.

Everybody seemed to be living on held breath, none of the conspirators daring to visit Dan and Jenny's hut now. They were being watched, they knew, but not as a mass: all convicts were watched as a precautionary measure.

Dan and Carney, at least, had opportunities to speak while at their work, though Jenny wasn't told what passed between them. But she had seen the governor come down to look over their repairs to the cutter and praise them for their industry. Neither betrayed any flicker of shame or guilt when they nodded and grinned and accepted Lockhart's compliments.

A week later Dan and Carney took the cutter out fishing as usual, one of the last such trips they expected to take. They'd done everything they could think of to the boat; they had even installed a sea drogue, a piece of cloth that could be trailed into the water to steady the vessel.

At Yarramundi's request, they'd agreed to take some of his kinswomen out with them: a woman with two sons around Charlotte's age, and a girl who needed to be shown the places where her ancestors had drawn fish from the sea.

Dan and Carney let the boat drift a little further than usual. It came around from the shelter of the point it usually hid behind, and was exposed to the mouth of the open ocean. The harbour entrance was some miles away, but the ocean could still be felt, rolling waves into the bay until they smashed against headlands and reverberated back, sometimes at unexpected angles. Angles that could catch unawares fishermen who had let their boat drift.

Assaults on the cutter by the Tasman's waves over the past few years had weakened its seams, and Dan's repairs hadn't had a chance to cure, to settle in. So the boat did what they could not afford for her to do once they were at sea. It began to leak.

Dan and Carney hurled water out faster than it could get in, stopping the boat from foundering.

The Wangal woman nodded to the girl, who slid beneath the water and surfaced several feet away, swimming strongly but without haste. Then the woman eased into the water too, holding one boy in each arm, kicking as she swam on her back after the girl.

The men kept bailing. But they neglected to keep the nose of the boat into the waves, and the next to hit caught them broadside, tipping the boat over and hauling it towards the rocks. Dan was going to insist that Carney swim for shore anyway. At least, he told Jenny later that that was his intention. No such insistence was necessary: Carney struck out to shore the moment the boat rolled over, no doubt expecting Dan to follow.

But Dan hung on to the precious boat, trying to nudge it out of a current that was bringing it to the sharpest rocks. Trying, and failing.

Then came a splash from the other side of the boat, heavier than water on water. Around the upturned bow Yarramundi's face appeared, grinning. 'These are the currents I warned you about,'

he said cheerfully. He pointed ahead and to the side a little, and
began swimming in that direction, guiding the boat along with
Dan doing the same from the other side.

She still ran aground on a tiny inlet; she was still smashed in
places. But, for the most part, she was whole. Some of Yarramundi's
friends – with whom he'd been fishing from shore while keeping an
eye on his kinswomen – had jumped into the water and collected
the oars. So the cutter was still intact. It was not, however, seaworthy.
Some weeks would pass before it could be set to rights.

Dan became known as the convict who had risked his life to
save the governor's cutter. The officers praised him, clapped him
on the shoulder and raised their cups to him. No one thought to
raise a cup to Yarramundi, without whom the boat would have
been firewood.

Dan was again put in charge of repairing the boat, setting her to
rights, making her as seaworthy as she could possibly be. This time
he made sure every seam was utterly caulked, and he put aside
enough resin and soap to make repairs on the journey, secreting
them with the brooding mass of supplies under the floor. Jenny
could hardly believe visitors didn't feel the weight of it, hear it
begging for release.

She was now the one backing away from the journey. She
had seen escape as a choice between the certain starvation of her
children and peril possibly followed by freedom. Now, though,
each option seemed equally doomed.

Until someone else made a sea voyage: someone who shouldn't
have been alive to do so.

Captain Andrew Harforth had always been among the lustier

marines. It was rumoured he'd participated in the debauchery that first night, while his brother officers had turned away, above such animal behaviour. Harforth had, though, now gone too far even for those experienced in the turning of blind eyes.

He had come upon the daughter of a convict, Julia Morrow, in the forest. Julia's mother had been transported for drunkenness and continued her offence in Sydney Cove, so her daughter was haphazardly raised by other female convicts who pitied her and gave her what attention they could. She was left with hours of leisure when she often wandered into the woods, and some had feared she would be attacked by natives. But the attack, when it came, was from Harforth, and its nature was easy to guess for those who knew of his appetites.

Julia was forced to describe the incident to the judge advocate. She was eight years old.

In a place where theft of food ended lives, it was widely assumed that such an attack on a child would lead to execution. Instead, Harforth was sent to Norfolk Island. The governor tried to forget about him, though Julia would never be able to.

'She cries all the time,' Bea told Jenny. 'She won't play with the other children, and won't let me hug her when before she was always pestering me for cuddles and stories.'

Jenny looked at Charlotte. If she survived, she would soon become prey for those with the same leanings as Harforth. Such men might be emboldened by the fact that apprehension would earn them no worse fate than banishment to a penal satellite, where they could continue satisfying themselves away from the governor's gaze.

Jenny again urged Dan to go faster, to get more work done on the boat each day than he had the day before.

'If I go fast and it saves us a day, we might all drown because I missed something,' he said.

So she paced around her yard when no one was looking, breathing her frustration into the open air. Occasionally she ejected an inarticulate, full-throated scream into the twilight. Otherwise she did as she was told, mending nets and collecting oysters and their shells, and dressing fish and washing clothes. And she waited.

As the weeks passed, Jenny became certain that they would not get away this year. It was growing too late in the season. But while each day they stayed increased the risk of them dying in a storm at sea, it also increased the risk of discovery.

Bruton and Harrigan felt the same way. They had taken to visiting the Gwyn hut again, as the scrutiny on them had slackened off with the boat's incapacity and the distraction of Harforth's offence. They liked the sweet tea that Jenny brewed for them, also liking her uncomplicated nature, her willingness to squeeze an ear or swat a head when she felt it was called for.

'We'll wait, is all,' Bruton said to her. 'We know how to do that, at least.'

'The pork doesn't, or the rice,' said Jenny. 'We've enough rations for the journey if we leave today, tomorrow. By the next sailing season, we'll barely have enough for a picnic.'

'Not the best, I grant you,' said Bruton. 'But unless you intend to swim to Coepang with the victuals on your back, I see little point in complaining of it.'

'I'll complain if I feel like it.'

'The biggest risk,' said Harrigan, 'is Bruton getting into a fight. The last thing we need is for him to be in the guard house once we're ready to sail.'

'Getting into no fights,' Bruton insisted. 'I told you I wouldn't, and I haven't.'

'I saw you, today, you know,' said Harrigan. 'When Darley tripped over your spade, and cursed at you. I saw your shoulder start to go back, don't tell me I didn't. So as for waiting until next season, I don't think you will get there.'

'There will be no risk,' said Bruton. 'I'll practise on you to make sure I'm not tempted.'

'I'd thrash the both of you,' said Jenny, 'if it would get us out to sea any faster.'

No thrashing, however, proved necessary. Dan walked into the hut slowly, shoulders back, a stance that always accompanied good news. 'The boat, it's finished,' he said.

'Are you sure?' Jenny asked.

'Did I not do it myself? Me and Carney.' There was a sharpness there, striking hard against the banter of a few minutes ago. 'And more news beside. The *Supply*'s off again in the morning. I rowed out to see Vorst – he's leaving too, in three days. Something else is happening in three days too.'

'The new moon,' said Jenny.

'The new moon,' Bruton repeated. 'Dark then.'

'And empty,' said Jenny. 'Nothing will be able to catch us, even if we're seen by the lookout at the head. It will be days, perhaps a week before they have any way of pursuing us.'

'By which time we might even be in Coepang,' said Harrigan.

'Not Coepang, not in a few weeks,' said Dan. 'But I can tell you one thing – we won't be here.'

CHAPTER 21

One of Jenny's biggest fears was that Emanuel would cry. Babies' cries were a common sound here, but not one that usually emanated from the dark water.

Bea could always calm him, holding him close and humming a half-remembered song. The sound rose from deep in her chest so that it was as much vibration as music.

Jenny had been in two minds about whether to ask Bea to come on the journey. She had desperately wanted to, knowing that she would very quickly miss female company – Bea's in particular – and knowing that the children would miss her too. But Bea was not a creature of the ocean and might consider the voyage a greater punishment than any that could be delivered on land.

Jenny put it to Dan.

'We can't take anyone else who cannot do anything towards our survival,' he said. 'We are bringing two children already, and that will have to be it.'

So Jenny took what she viewed as the only possible course of action. She brought Bea to the clearing next to the hut, told her about the plan, and invited her to come anyway.

Bea smiled, a little sadly. 'That's what's been filling up the hole in your floor, then. Provisions for the journey.' Jenny scowled, and Bea laughed. 'I've been over that patch of your floor many times, more than enough to hear by the sound of my footsteps how full it is.' She took Jenny's hand. 'Thank you, my bird, thank you. But I shall stop here, I think.'

'Why, though? Bea, please. We don't know when the food will run out. We don't know when the ships will be back, or if they will. And who will fish when Dan and John are gone? You might not survive here.'

'I know even less whether I can survive there, wherever there is,' said Bea, nodding out to the bay. 'Don't frown, duck. I am absolutely certain *you* will survive, but just as certain that I wouldn't. Not on the sea, and not with the fear of it. And there's Jack, now.'

Jack Carrow was one of the convicts on the brick kilns. Not exactly a poetic soul. This life drove the poetry even out of those who possessed it to begin with, and Jack had not been among their number. But he was not a bad man, far from it. Loyal, or seemed to be. Did not use his fists without greater provocation than most. Well regarded, too, by the governor and the judge advocate. When Dan, Jenny and the rest of them went, his calm nature might see him put in a position of leadership. He might even find himself in Jenny and Dan's hut.

Jenny would like it if Bea was with him. She understood the temper of the place, could read it between the shifting shadows in the shafts of sunlight that the trees allowed into the little clearing.

'But what about Elenor?' Jenny asked. 'Who will protect you from her?'

'She is not, you know, as well thought of as she used to be. Those rumours spread by her and Joe – some were right, a lot were wrong. Joe has told some very outlandish stories of late, involving curses by the natives to stop the hens from laying. Fewer people listen to them now, and those who had arrived on the second fleet never listened to them in the first place. I will have no trouble with Elenor, Jenny. You're not to worry on that count.'

'I'll worry less if you take this,' Jenny said, handing Bea a small cloth parcel. Inside was a paring knife, much like the one she had used on the King's Highway, with similar rust spots but a much sharper tip.

'What on earth do you expect me to do with this?' said Bea.

'Hopefully peel potatoes, but if Elenor gets aggressive you can wave it around a bit.'

'Won't you have more need of it?'

Jenny lifted the hem of her skirt, showing Bea a section that was stiff and heavy, weighted down by something sewn into it. 'I've kept the sharper one, sorry.'

Bea laughed, but Jenny noticed a few tears were quietly sliding down her cheek. She felt an answering moisture on her own face.

'I will come to the shore tonight, if I can,' Bea said. 'But don't look for me. If I think I may be seen, I'll stay in the hut.'

Jenny kept watching the trees long after Bea had stepped through them. She had hoped, for the last time, to see a mass of grey fur looking back at her. Instead, as night began to fall, she saw Mawberry stepping towards her, flat bellied now, a contented child dozing in the crook of one arm. The woman looked at the harbour and then back at Jenny, and raised her eyebrows. Jenny nodded.

Mawberry shrugged, holding out her hand to Jenny. It held a small green package: a broad leaf wrapped tightly around a clump of the leaves that had kept many from the grave when the scurvy was at its worst. Jenny took it, smiling.

Leaning forward, Mawberry touched her forehead to Jenny's.

Then she turned and, with the bearing of a princess, carried her baby away into the trees.

The others, Jenny knew, were also saying quiet goodbyes. None of the other men were married, but they had liaisons in various states of permanence. These needed to be shattered, and Jenny still worried that one of the women would decide to inform.

But nobody did. It was perhaps their salvation that Joe and Elenor no longer held the sway that they used to, that those who had been in the habit of bringing them snippets of information – as payment for entry to their circle – no longer bothered. Elenor and Joe would have informed on the conspirators without a second thought.

At midnight, Jenny sat cross-legged on the floor of her hut. She avoided resting her leg on the section of her hem that contained the knife and, now, that small bunch of leaves, for which she'd found some oil cloth.

One breast was bare as she fed Emanuel, heedless of the men walking in and out, emptying the cache under the floor. She wanted her son drowsy, replete, happily snuggled into his mother with no need to make any noise. Having avoided detection up till this point, to be betrayed by a baby's wail would be too cruel.

Emanuel finished, his head lolling back, with the glaze in his eyes that always appeared when he couldn't ingest any more milk. Jenny shrugged her dress back onto her shoulder, wrapped Emanuel in a cloth, and woke Charlotte. 'We are going to play a game with Pa,' she said. 'We are going out on the boat to look for sea dragons. We might have to go very far to find them – very, very far. But they won't come out if we make any noise at all, so we are going to have to step so, so carefully and make sure we don't say a word until the sun rises.'

Charlotte nodded solemnly. Such a sacred task was to be taken seriously.

They walked out of the hut, passing the now empty hole.

'Ma, shut the door!' said Charlotte in a whisper that seemed as loud as any yell.

'No need, my love. No need for any doors, now. But just remember, sea dragons have very good hearing. If they know we are after them, they will hide, so you must say nothing more.'

The new moon that Jenny hoped would conceal their escape made it difficult to navigate down to the shore, difficult to pick out slightly darker shapes against the night sky. She could hear just as well in the dark, though, and recognised the slap of a small wave against a wooden hull. She also knew the sound of a foot on undergrowth. It was a noise she had trained herself to hear while living in the forest.

She glanced to the side, tensing, readying herself to react to what she saw, whether it was a kangaroo or a marine with a musket.

A slightly darker patch of night was moving to the edge of the trees, resolving into a shape. Instead of sprinting away, Jenny moved towards it. Charlotte trailed after her, opening her mouth to call out a greeting before remembering the sea dragons.

'You took a risk, coming here,' Jenny muttered.

'One worth taking,' whispered Bea. 'Are you nearly away?'

'Yes, just us to load now.'

'Good. You need to hurry. Elenor thinks she knows something. She's not sure what, but Bruton tends to make a bit of noise whenever he sneaks away from the men's huts late at night, and Joe has seen him heading towards your hut a few times.'

Jenny glanced behind Bea. 'Has she told anyone? Is she coming?'

'I don't think so. Not yet, anyway. She was making noises about paying you a visit tonight. I stole Suse's rum, making sure Elenor saw me. So of course she took it from me and drank it down before Suse could wake up. Elenor's sleeping now but snoring loudly enough to wake the governor. You might have more time, but you might not.'

'You know, Bea, you are far better than her. Be careful, though.'

'I will, and I hope my caution has earned me a last embrace from this one,' Bea said, kneeling and smiling at Charlotte, holding a finger to her lips. Bea took care not to hug the girl tightly enough to draw out any noise. She stood, wordlessly embraced Jenny, then pushed her towards the boat before she walked away.

The cutter had been brought in close enough to be boarded. Dan and Yarramundi had swum out to retrieve it, hauling it back in as they had guided it to the inlet last month.

Yarramundi stood there now, his hand on the point of the bow, holding the boat steady as the men climbed in. He smiled when he saw Charlotte, who smiled back and waved, but then held her finger to her lips and stared at him sternly. Yarramundi, looking suitably chastened, reached out his arms for the little girl and deposited her gently in the boat.

When he reached out for Emanuel, Jenny handed the boy over. 'You are risking a lot for us,' she said.

'Help was needed with a boat, and help is what I gave,' he said. 'I do not recognise any law which prohibits that.'

Jenny climbed in next to Charlotte. As she took Emanuel from Yarramundi, he leaned forward and Jenny did likewise, so that their foreheads touched. She suddenly seemed to feel a sadness heavier than that which saying goodbye to Bea had called forth. *This is the last time*, she thought, *that I will meet someone like this.*

In the stern, with his hand on the tiller, sat Dan. Each of the men took an oar. Vincent, the keeper of the chart, was stymied for now by the lack of light.

They floated there, for a moment. Yarramundi nodded to Dan and let go of the bow after aligning it with the outgoing tide. Dan said, 'Row.' The oars lifted and fell, forced through the water, and the noise seemed to echo off the cliffs and around the settlement.

But no one came running down to the shore. None of the nightwatchmen raced with torches to the headlands or went to wake the governor. And if any of the convicts heard them, they were not disposed to disturb the rest of the authorities.

The cutter was, very quickly, far enough from the shore that anyone chasing them would have trouble gaining on them. Especially in one of the few small fishing boats that were now the only vessels in this whole land aside from the native canoes.

The lookouts on the headland, though – they had muskets. They were supposed to be pacing around as they scanned the water for the merest disturbance.

There was enough light, just, for Jenny to make out the glowering shape of South Head. Even had there not been, she would have known they were leaving the harbour. The seas became rougher; the nose of the boat rose and then fell, sending spray onto those in the front. But she would never know if that night lookout was asleep, or daydreaming, or unable to see far enough in the darkness. She would never know if the sound of their passage, which seemed to cry out like a horn, was loud enough to echo up the cliff into his ears.

No musket was fired, no signal fire was lit, and no shouted warnings floated across the bay.

Although there was enough wind now to allow them to proceed under sail, the pale patch of cloth, glimmering out of the darkness, might alert the lookout. They were out of musket range, and certainly beyond immediate pursuit, but what if the *Supply* returned in the next few days, or another ship? They didn't want to reveal their direction to anyone.

'Can I talk now, Ma?' Charlotte asked.

'Yes, duckling. Very quietly, though.'

'Have you seen any sea dragons?'

'They're all tucked up beneath the waves, by the look of it. Maybe they'll come out in the morning. You should sleep now, and I promise I'll wake you if they lift their scaly old heads above the water.'

Charlotte leaned into her mother, claiming the opposing arm to the one that held her brother, and with the ease of which only small children seemed capable, she shut her eyes and fell asleep. Jenny gently lay Emanuel on her lap and tethered his leg to her wrist with a thin length of rope.

The oars continued to splash, and the usually full-throated, roaring men made no sound. Charlotte dreamed on through the pitching of the boat and the occasional spray of salt water, and her mother eventually joined her, her chin knocking up and down on her chest as the sky slowly lightened, and the settlement behind them woke to find itself depleted.

CHAPTER 22

Jenny had never paid more attention to the wind. The roaring gales, the impossibly thick rain, had not come yet. But they could. Most in the governor's cutter knew how quickly the weather could change. They tried to divine a meaning from the smallest breezes, from a ripple or a rising peak, from a distant whitecap.

So far, though, their luck had held.

But Thomas Harrigan, the farmer, clearly wasn't feeling particularly fortunate. A son of the earth rather than the ocean, he did not approve of the sea's mercurial nature. At first light they had allowed themselves a small amount of pork, and Harrigan's had been regurgitated into the ocean almost immediately, as had every meal since.

'Put a line in, Dan,' Bruton said after one of Harrigan's noisy evacuations. 'You might get some interest.'

Dan laughed, but not unkindly, and Jenny glared at Bruton. 'I'll enjoy seeing you planting and hoeing when the time comes,' she said.

He held up his hand in surrender, still smirking at the unfortunate Harrigan, who was surely feeling too miserable to care. He would care, though, if everything he ate reappeared over the gunwales. He would care if some of the others decided it wasn't worth feeding him as much, as it would only be wasted. He would care if Bruton's taunting emboldened the others, made them decide that Harrigan would be the scapegoat for everything that annoyed, frustrated or terrified them on this journey.

Jenny was certain there were annoyances, frustrations and terrors ahead, in great number. She would not allow Bruton to sneer at anyone else, to try so quickly to divide their little floating commonwealth. Divisions, she knew, could be fatal.

Really, she didn't feel like playing nursemaid to two grown men, breaking up squabbles in which those involved displayed less maturity than the boat's youngest passengers.

Because one of the boat's youngest passengers was getting very, very cranky. Emanuel wriggled and squirmed sometimes but was otherwise content to lie in his mother's lap, or be hoisted onto her shoulders so he could look back towards his father at the tiller. Dan would make faces at him for the joy of hearing the little boy's abandoned chortle.

Charlotte, however, was far less happy with the situation. The sea dragons had failed to come, for which she blamed her father, mother, and the men at the oars. 'They're noisy,' she said. 'They're scaring the dragons away.'

'You can't scare dragons, duckling. Perhaps they went in the other direction.'

Charlotte gave her mother a glare that would have felled the governor. She was fidgety and restless, and more than once Jenny had to reach quickly to stop her climbing over the edge of the boat. She had tried to tether Charlotte to herself, as she had Emanuel, but the girl would not submit to it, so Jenny contented herself with vigilance for now. If the weather worsened, though, Charlotte would not be given a choice.

'We'll need to land soon,' Jenny said.

'I'm not putting in simply to stop her grizzling,' said Dan.

'No more am I asking you to. Finding some water, though – that's a good reason to put in, isn't it?'

They had been travelling for two days in a boat barely longer than three men laid end to end, and barely wider than one. They slumped on the benches or lay in the hull to rest. For the most part, they'd been able to use the boat's new flax sail, as the winds had been blowing from the south, not roaring along the coast as they sometimes did, at least not strongly enough to cause the boat significant trouble. Most of the time, those at the oars had been able to rest their arms.

Carney and Bruton had discovered a shared love of gambling. Neither, though, had thought to bring any dice, so they bet on how many trees they would see on the next headland, or how long it would take before Harrigan was sick again. Bruton didn't like losing, and when he did he usually accused Carney of foul play; Carney, who viewed himself as a man of honour, would take great offence. The two of them would pull their shoulders back and face each other, animals preparing to charge, until Jenny talked one or the other into turning away.

She couldn't do it forever, though. They all needed to land. Not to stop Charlotte grizzling, but to stop the men from killing each other. And to refill their water flagons, although they were not yet running dangerously low.

When Charlotte slept, and when the men did not require her intervention, Jenny would scan the coast for a landing place. They were probably the first of their kind to slide so close to these cliffs and points and outcrops. Certainly, those who had been on deck when the fleet made its way into Sydney Cove would not have seen this stretch of land, as they had come from the south.

Jenny looked, too, for faces. For the amused eyes of a man like Yarramundi, or the cautious curiosity in the face of another Mawberry. She occasionally saw natives on the cliffs who did not shake their spears and yell as they apparently had when the first fleet had arrived. They watched, then perhaps sent word northwards, rumours of a strange vessel full of ghosts.

The word may have travelled as quickly as the boat, for when the little party did make land, a group of natives was waiting on the shore.

It was a small beach fringed with thick bush, and a little stream ran alongside. Sheltered, with fresh water and even a chance for them to put the net out.

The natives seemed watchful but unconcerned. They were casually holding their spears, and did not bother to point them or give any indication that they intended to threaten the newcomers.

Dan, Carney and Bruton vaulted from the boat when it was still in the shallows, beginning to drag it to the shore as Harrigan and Langham got out.

'Stay there,' Dan told Jenny. She'd been intending to do exactly that, as she could hardly see herself splashing into the water with a baby on her shoulder and a little girl under her arm.

'Give them something,' she told him.

'What?'

'Remember what Corbett told us – the governor had a box of trinkets with him, to give to the natives. We have to give them something.'

'We didn't happen to load a box of trinkets,' said Dan.

Jenny reached under the bench. There was a small wooden crate housing those items that she had hoped to keep dry. If they were unfortunate enough to hit a storm, anything in the box would get as soaked as everything else on board; but for now, the timbers had shielded the contents from the worst of the water. She pulled out a shirt – she thought one of Dan's, but she couldn't be sure – and a bonnet, and handed them to him. 'Give the natives these.'

'Jenny, we can't go giving things away every time we land! We'll have nothing left.'

'You'll have no use for a shirt with a spear in you. Give them these. If you don't, I'll throw them overboard.'

'I'll throw you in after them,' he said, with a grin that took the latent violence out of the words. The man who hadn't yet been flogged had grinned like that. The man who'd felt he had a measure of control over his destiny. Perhaps that man might reappear.

Dan shrugged and walked over to the group slowly, holding the shirt and bonnet on flat, upturned palms. One of the men stepped forward, looking at these offerings. He glanced up, nodded, and took the clothes. Dan made a circle with his fingers, held it to his lips and tilted his head back. The man nodded again and pointed to the thin stream that snaked around one side of the inlet. Then he turned, together with the others, and walked into the trees.

The water was sweet enough, and they filled their flagons and drank as much as they could stomach. A small net, when they put it out, returned with enough fish to feed them.

Harrigan seemed a lot more comfortable, now he was on land, and was examining the fringes of the bush for anything that might be edible.

'Dan!' he called out.

He hadn't found food. He had, however, found the means of cooking the fish. Jutting out here and there were rocks that had little in common with the pale sandstone of which the entire country seemed to be made. These rocks were black and shiny; they looked, if anything, like coal. When Dan broke some off with an axe, they burned like coal too.

The group stayed for a few days, and Carney started referring to the place as Fortunate Bay.

Charlotte, in particular, seemed delighted; she had found that the night-time trees contained tribes of possums. She assumed that this was where they were going to live, that the long and boring boat journey was over.

Harrigan also would have liked nothing better. The soil was poor, he said, but he had managed to bring some vegetables to maturity at Sydney Cove, and surely it could be no worse here.

Jenny found it comforting to think of their party laying claim to this inlet, of their building huts like those of the natives – which they could see a bit further down the bay – and fishing and farming. But they were barely two days from Sydney Cove – less, for a ship like the *Supply*. They would, with near certainty, be discovered here. And Jenny did not care for a life as the sole grown female among this group.

So Harrigan grudgingly accepted the fact that the voyage would continue, cheered somewhat by Dan's promise that they would put in every few days.

CHAPTER 23

By now there would be searchers. No one felt like leaving, but everyone understood the necessity. A wind from the south pushed them along after they launched the boat, freeing Bruton and Carney from the necessity of rowing and enabling them to win and lose each other's possessions in a never-ending cycle.

'Are we going home?' asked Charlotte.

'Yes,' Jenny said, 'but not to our old home. To our new home.'

'Will other children be there?'

'Oh yes, certainly. But no one to tell Ma or Pa what to do.'

'Will there be food?'

Charlotte was asking a question that consumed all of the adults. Vorst had praised Coepang: its markets and broad streets and hospitality. The Dutch were traders, he'd said. All the delicacies of the world flowed through their hands.

Whether any of those delicacies would find their way into the bellies of the convicts, none of them knew. None of them knew if they even existed, come to that. Vorst had his own reasons for helping them, and chief among them was to annoy the governor. He could just as easily achieve that goal with talk of an island of plenty that didn't exist.

But there was a more immediate concern. The bottom of the boat was slowly filling up with water. Whenever it reached their ankles it was bailed out, to be replenished almost immediately.

The bays here did not announce themselves. There was no shadow in the coastline ahead, nothing to warn of an indentation. Just league after league of striated rock with jutting edges that might hide a small beach, the entry to a magnificent harbour, or nothing. The convicts' eyes were always roaming over the sandstone, out of fear of missing a haven and sailing on into thirst and hunger.

Still, they nearly missed it – the small opening, the narrow gate. Not until they had started to pass its entrance did they realise that they were sailing past a harbour.

Carney saw it first. 'Dan! About, about! Port, hard aport!'

Dan rammed the tiller to the side as far as it would go, and Carney quickly pulled in the sail, tying it close to the mast so that the wind wouldn't push them too far. Bruton, Langham and Harrigan rowed for all they were worth.

A larger harbour lay beyond the first one, through a narrow point between one cliff and another, a small island choking the entryway. They rowed to a flat beach, sheltered with the gentle slope that would enable them to easily pull the boat ashore.

Straightaway Carney and Dan had it upturned, attacking the seams with what little resin they had. The nets came out, too, and Jenny stood with her skirts tied up as she had as a child in Penmor, nearly waist deep in the water, telling Bruton and Langham when to haul. By late afternoon, their catch was equal to a reasonable day's fishing in Sydney Cove.

'The land is getting better as we go north,' said Harrigan. 'Why not stay here, or somewhere like it? They may give chase, but you heard them after Tallow escaped – they gave him up for dead, did not even try. And we, low in the water and close into the shore, nearly missed this bay. Who's to say they wouldn't do likewise, even if they did come after us?'

'This place is not what we need,' said Dan.

'It seems to have exactly what we need: fresh water, lots of fish, cabbage trees. Secrecy.'

'No money,' said Dan. 'No taverns, no docks. No means of earning a living.'

'We could live for a living,' said Harrigan.

'If you can call it that. I'd prefer a dock, and an inn nearby, and a deal to be made.'

They might have argued about it through the night, around the fire that they were about to set with some black rocks they had taken from Fortunate Bay.

The decision, though, was made for them.

Jenny had unrolled a length of canvas for Charlotte and Emanuel to sleep on, with her beside them, the three of them making indentations on a beach that may never have seen such creatures.

As it happened, though, the beach was no stranger to humanity. Some of that humanity appeared with the dying light in the trees. It was hard to see how many there were, at first. One or two only, Jenny thought. As her eyes adjusted, she picked out more white teeth, more eyes. It seemed that all of the spaces between all of the trees were clogged with them.

This time, there were no women or children. Every hand was holding a spear.

Jenny cried out, calling to Dan to come, as the natives advanced on an unknown signal. Others emerged until several dozen stood between their group and the woods.

Dan scrambled to his feet and knocked over a pot in which Jenny was boiling water for sweet tea, scalding himself and cursing. He walked slowly towards the natives, moving his hands up and down in a gesture of calmness, peace.

It didn't seem to have any effect. If the natives knew what Dan was trying to tell them, they gave no sign. He hurried back to the boat, running sideways so he could keep one eye on the men near the forest. Jenny scooped up Emanuel and dragged Charlotte back towards the water's edge, the only avenue now open to them. Still watching the natives, and with the other men seemingly paralysed, Dan reached into the boat and scrabbled around for something, anything that could be given to the tribe as a sign of peace.

His hand closed on the quadrant, and as he held it up Vincent Langham broke out of his staring stupor. 'Are you mad, man? How am I to get us there without that?'

'How are you to get us there if you're dead?' asked Dan, advancing slowly and holding the quadrant in his upturned palms.

The man who seemed to be the leader looked back at him and raised his spear.

Then this place, used to the presence of man, heard a new sound.

Bruton had worked his way slowly back to the boat, pulled out a musket, raised it in the air and fired.

All of them had seen, or at least heard of, the effect that a shot fired into the air had on the natives of Sydney Cove when the colonisers first arrived. Mr Corbett had told them of the fear the noise engendered in those who were losing their land. They did not turn and run. But they did back away, they did use caution. They did, most importantly, leave the settlers alone to get on with things.

These ones, though, did not move, flinch or blink. The one to whom Dan had offered the quadrant raised his palm in the air, said something, and stepped forward. Every man behind him stepped forward too, and kept stepping. There was no time to shuffle sideways now, no time to pick their way cautiously to the boat. They stumbled backwards, turned and ran for it, the men vaulting in, Jenny shoving Emanuel at Dan and scooping up Charlotte.

Eventually they reached a small island in the middle of the bay. They wondered among themselves if the natives had canoes. Bruton thought not – surely, if they did, they would be rowing over?

But Jenny saw, as night fell, the fires lit in the canoes, small flames on blackness that she knew to be water. The natives, it seemed, had no objection to the strange intruders camping on the little island. Once they had been ejected from the tribe's territory, they were free to live or die as they chose.

Charlotte slept on the canvas next to her mother, and in the morning paddled in the water, gently slapping its surface with her palm, trying to call forth whichever creatures might be lying there. Emanuel fed and slept and gurgled; his pale skin was suited to the land in which Jenny had been born, and she had erected a lean-to out of canvas and twigs to stop his reddening as hers had.

She and the men gambled and ate and quarrelled and slept through that night and the next, with no attempt by Harrigan to convince them to settle here.

They rowed out of the bay after two nights on the speck of land, watched as they went by faces here and there among the trees or on the beaches that fringed the bay. Jenny thought, at one point, that she saw a woman. Pregnant, as Mawberry had been. She raised her hand and waved – a ridiculous gesture, but an irresistible one. It was not returned.

She turned to Harrigan, smiling to reassure him though he did not yet know he needed reassurance. She had noticed what he had not: here, behind two sandstone gates that had given them a calm entry, the wind was penetrating and plucking the water's surface up into waves that slapped against the boat's newly caulked hull.

Conditions were worse once they reached the gap where the bay gave way to the ocean. The winds seemed unable to decide on a direction, filling the sail one moment and leaving it slack and empty the next, before snapping at it from the opposite direction. The blank-faced sandstone cliffs hurled the waves that assaulted them back at the sea, churning the water so that one moment the boat was pitching forward, and the next tilting sideways. Sea spray was fanning up the sides of the boat, curving inwards and landing on everyone, and Harrigan's composure deserted him along with his breakfast.

The only way for them to avoid it was to go further out. But there they met flat-faced waves that would rise under them, lifting them up before disappearing so that the boat slammed down into the water from a distance of several feet, as though picked up and dropped.

Under the noise of the water Jenny couldn't hear if the timbers were creaking, complaining at this insult, but she would bet they were. Charlotte, she could see, was crying and picking at the rope Jenny had tied around her waist while they were still in the bay, tethering her to her mother and the vessel.

Each time the boat was lifted and dropped, it settled into the water much lower than they would have liked. Bruton was kept busy continually bailing while Harrigan was continually sick, needing more water than two of the others put together.

'Why did you come, if you haven't the stomach for it?' Bruton yelled, deliberately splashing the farmer with the water he was bailing.

Harrigan shrugged, perhaps asking himself the same question.

'You want to eat when we get there, don't you?' Jenny yelled at Bruton. 'You've met Vorst. Do you think the Dutch are in the habit of giving away food for no consideration? What have we to offer but some dirty clothes? If we need to farm, we will need a farmer. That's why he's here, and I'll thank you to try not to kill him.'

Harrigan turned around and tried to smile at her, although his expression told her that he felt murder at Bruton's hand might not be the worst of all possible fates.

Jenny was distracted by her desperate worry about Charlotte. The little girl had been complaining incessantly for the first few days, when the storm was in the business of driving them out to sea. Now that they were here, and facing the constant battering, she had gone silent. She sat next to her mother, cradled in Jenny's free arm. She slept in starts, took a little water and a mouthful of rice, and slept again. She had lost the will to complain, lost the will to allow her mother to spin stories about sea dragons. If this was what sea dragons could wreak, Charlotte was no longer interested in meeting them.

Emanuel was fretful too. Born on land, he had never experienced such elemental violence. He was, though, too young for the deadening mixture of terror and boredom that was afflicting his sister. He cried and occasionally emitted whimpers that only Jenny, holding him close into her side, could hear.

The noise of the wind died down after a few days, but the seas didn't. They still had to bail; they still had to brace themselves every time another shelf of water obscured half of the sky. The only new thing they were able to do, now that they could hear each other, was quarrel.

Harrigan seemed, finally, to be getting used to the ocean. At least he had stopped dropping the contents of his stomach overboard. He was sufficiently recovered to object when Bruton reached out and casually took his portion of salt pork from him.

'You've dumped more into the sea than I've eaten on this whole trip,' Bruton said. 'It's owed, is what it is. Make no objection and I will consider the debt paid.'

Harrigan looked up, and his shoulders hunched slightly. They were, Jenny remembered, the shoulders of a man who could lightly walk away from a farm with a pig under each arm. He may not have Bruton's strength, or his viciousness, but he was robust enough, even after all the privations of the past week. He was also, Jenny suspected, smarter than Bruton, and he was getting very, very angry.

'I'll make no objection,' he said, 'if you're too weak to survive without my food well as your own.'

Bruton stopped eating the stolen food, looked up and narrowed his eyes. 'It's this weakness that kept you above water,' he said. 'Bailing the boat out while you were leaning over the side with your mouth open, drooling into the waves.'

'What will you do when we land?' asked Harrigan. 'Perhaps they have need of oxen.'

Bruton was impressively quick for a man of his bulk standing on a moving surface. He was on his feet, picking up Harrigan under the arms and turning his torso, in order to get the momentum to hurl him into the water.

'For God's sake, John, stop them!' yelled Dan, who was

holding the tiller – letting go could have fatal consequences. Everything depended on Dan keeping the nose of the boat aimed into the highest waves. If the boat turned, and one of those waves caught them broadside, they would almost certainly capsize.

Carney darted forward but seemed at a loss. There wasn't enough room to separate two fighting men by force, not without one or more of them ending up in the sea. In these conditions, once they were in the water, they would likely remain there.

Jenny was sitting in her usual space, just in front of Dan. She had been stroking the hair of a glassy-eyed Charlotte with one hand and clamping onto Emanuel with the other.

The possibility of a capsize visited her in nightmares. Although she could swim and had been teaching Charlotte, the girl had only paddled around in the shallows of Sydney Cove on a calm day. If the boat capsized, even if Jenny could untie them all quickly enough, Charlotte would have no hope of keeping afloat in these seas. The image of Emanuel, his limbs flailing, his mouth open in new surprise, sinking into the darkness would not leave her.

These two idiots were bringing them perilously close to making her nightmare real.

She had no free hands, engaged as they were in keeping her children on the deck and alive. So she stuck out a foot – unshod, as there was no point protecting them from getting wet – and jabbed her heel into the back of Bruton's leg.

He did not lose his footing, but he did let go of Harrigan, who fell to the deck where the rough edge of a seat opened a gash in his forehead.

'Sit down, Bruton,' Jenny said. 'Here, near me. I have something to tell you.'

Bruton, who rarely followed commands, did as he was told and sat on a plank facing her.

'Now,' said Jenny, 'lean forward.'

He did his best, in this world where forward could become backward in an instant.

'Are you really, truly so delicate that an insult from someone like Harrigan can goad you into risking everything?'

'He called me an ox,' Bruton said.

'So you are. An ox who no longer has to work at the government farm, or on the kilns. An ox on his way to making his own decisions again, to deciding which tavern to walk into, which woman to take. You're an ox who will not starve to death in Sydney Cove. But you very nearly became a drowned ox, and you very nearly took us with you.'

He scowled, but said nothing

'Now,' Jenny said, 'lean a little bit further forward.' When he did, she drew back the arm that had been around Charlotte and slapped his cheek so hard it forced his head to the side.

He did not cry out, just sat there, rubbing his cheek and looking at her. Had they been on land, with Dan nowhere nearby, she would have had significant fears for her safety. But once she had called on bluster and bravado for assistance, they would not let go of her. *Once you decide to make them your allies*, she thought, *they will not be abandoned.*

'Will you now squall about being slapped by a woman?' she asked Bruton.

He said nothing, still. He had stopped rubbing his cheek, and now he sat there as still as possible, his hands on his knees, staring.

'I will, I promise, slap you again,' she said, 'if you try to throw anyone over the sides of this boat. If you try to take anyone else's food. Do you know, Bruton, of the crime for which I was transported?'

Still just the glare, no words.

'Highway robbery,' she said. 'I tended to use a knife. I still have it with me.' Bruton didn't need to know that it was old, rusty and barely capable of cutting into a fish. 'If you ever do anything again to endanger my children, I will slit you from your chin downwards, until we need to bail out your blood.'

CHAPTER 24

When Jenny first woke from the fractured chin-on-chest sleep that had become her only rest, she couldn't decide what had changed. She felt for the children as she always did on waking, resting her hand on each little chest to make sure it continued to rise and fall. She rubbed her eyes, and found them dry.

The sea was no longer slapping her in the face, no longer peppering her cheeks with spray. The winds, which she had half believed would never die, were beginning to fade. But they had driven the little boat far out to sea.

For the past three weeks, only an occasional glimpse of a smudge of land told them that they hadn't drifted fatally, irrevocably.

It was still there, that dark line. Such things could be imagined, Jenny knew, by a hopeful mind or a desperate one. But if the low darkness of the land was a fantasy, it was shared by them all. Finally, the waves were settling back into the sea, no longer called out by the wind, and the small boat turned towards shore.

No one had perished in the storm, but Harrigan lay across one of the benches, his eyes open but unfixed as though they had given up the task of holding on to anything in this constantly moving world. The skin was flaking off his face, and a row of blisters had formed on his forehead. None of the men paid him any attention. He was unable to bail, or reef the sail in, or throw out the sea drogue, or row, so he was not worth their attention.

Bruton suggested throwing him overboard. 'There's little enough as it is,' he said. 'We should not be wasting the water.'

'Yes, why not?' said Jenny. 'Of course, you won't mind if we apply the same rules to you, if you're ever unable to row.'

Bruton grunted, and returned to his oar. Jenny resumed her practice – a thrice daily ritual – of trickling enough water in through Harrigan's broken lips to keep him alive.

'You know I don't like Bruton, nor trust him,' Dan whispered to her that night. When the wind was low, it was impossible to have a private conversation in any but the quietest tones.

'Yet he is here at your urging,' she said.

She still suspected that Bruton had threatened Dan and Carney in order to come on the journey. Whether the threat had taken the form of physical violence, or an intention to inform on the party and its plans, she didn't know. But here he was, with his need for continual bullying, continual threats to prevent him drowning those he held in contempt.

'Still, I can understand him,' Dan said. 'If Harrigan cannot help us ... Has it occurred to you, Jenny, that you might be giving him water that you'll need to keep the children alive?'

'So you would like to dispense with some ballast as well? Roll him over into the sea?'

'No! No, I'm not Bruton. Perhaps, though ... perhaps we might reduce the amount of water you're giving him, bit by bit. Then allow things to happen as they will.'

'A quick death by drowning, or a slow death from thirst,' said Jenny.

'A chance,' said Dan. 'If we're all to have a chance, perhaps I am being too generous.'

'We are not holding water back from him, and we are not throwing him overboard. Once we do that, it will not stop, I promise you. Bruton will be wondering what the point of having two children on the journey is. He will start looking at the water Charlotte drinks, wondering if it could be put to better use in his mouth.'

Dan jutted out his lower jaw, as he often did when she disagreed with him. He didn't argue, though, and when Jenny next raised water to Charlotte's lips, extracted from rain-soaked clothes she had wrung out, he kept his eyes on Bruton.

Charlotte was not in much better condition than Harrigan. She hadn't spoken for a week. She sat up to drink the water her mother gave her, and sometimes ate the food. But she had the same unfocused stare as Harrigan. Jenny was no longer being called on to spin stories out of the sea mist, or asked about the possibility of a sea dragon finally breaking the surface. Charlotte had sunk into herself so deeply that boredom could no longer touch her.

Jenny held a shawl over her daughter's head during the day to save her skin from the worst of the sun. It had reddened and flaked, and the skin around her nose had peeled so many times it was covered in a hard armour of damaged tissue.

Emanuel was shaded as well, and drank from his mother rather than from a cup. But he, too, had gone quiet. He rarely cried, and when he did there was a hoarseness to it, and it seemed to cost more effort than it was worth.

Jenny's world had shrunk to the length of the bench she sat on, and the two children tied to it. She turned sometimes, hoping to catch Dan's eye, perhaps smile. He would glance at her, then stare ahead in clench-jawed concentration. Her hand, when she placed it on his knee, was usually ignored, as was Charlotte.

As the spray receded and the waves dropped and they turned towards shore, Jenny wanted to take an oar herself. She was desperate to sleep on ground. The fear had been growing in her, these past weeks, that she would doze and wake to find one of the children gone. To sleep properly, without fear of the sea claiming them, became one of her most fervent wishes.

They managed to find a beach and hauled the boat ashore on land that looked much like Sydney Cove – so much so that Jenny was gripped by an irrational fear that the wind had forced them backwards, and that Mr Corbett would walk onto the beach at any moment with a party of marines to arrest them.

Corbett, though, did not come. Instead, while they were filling their water flagons, two native women and a few children appeared on the beach. They stared, surprised, at the newcomers. They did not turn and flee. But immediately, and piercingly, they started to wail.

Jenny approached them – better her than any of the men, especially Bruton. She made signs to calm them, both palms facing the ground as she moved her hands up and down, but they continued to stand their ground, and they continued to wail. There was only one reason why a frightened, wailing woman would stand her ground when faced with intruders. When she was not wailing out of fear: when she was sending a signal.

Jenny walked back to Dan. 'Others are being called, and they will be here.'

He looked over at the women, nodded and called everyone back to the boat. They rowed away from shore as a dozen tribesmen arrived. Although Jenny saw canoes on some of the beaches they passed, no one took to them. The natives seemed to be satisfied that the intruders were going; they did not care where to.

The convicts sailed on, then, staying close to shore.

Jenny had been watching Charlotte as she slept. Wondering, as she often did now, if in trying to save her children she had condemned them to a slow progress towards deaths which might not have claimed them in Sydney.

Charlotte's nose twitched. Perhaps she was dreaming, or perhaps it was a response to the strand of hair that had just been blown across her face.

Then a thick lock of Jenny's own hair, matted and brittle and studded with white flecks of salt, was thrown across her face by the wind.

When she removed it, she looked up. The clouds, which had been hanging in the sky like white outcrops, were now being scraped across it, melded together and spread too thinly to hold their shape. Sea dragons might be fantasies, but cloud dragons clearly still existed, and were ruffling the surface that, less than an hour ago, had been smooth.

The ocean responded very quickly, and the boat was marched on by ever-increasing hillocks of water, until half the time they couldn't see the sky without craning their necks.

Jenny had been right to think this coast looked like Sydney Cove. Because it certainly had the same rains: the kind that came on suddenly as though a hatch had been opened, almost thick enough to grasp. Certainly thick enough to add to the water that was filling the boat.

She didn't realise she was gripping the children so tightly until Charlotte whimpered, waking briefly before slumping again. Langham was the only one bailing. Carney was doing his best to reef the sail while Dan gripped the tiller, looking grimly ahead so that he could steer the boat into the face of each wave. 'What happens tonight?' he hissed at Jenny. 'A new moon. What happens when I can't see what's coming?'

Jenny didn't know. But she knew what would happen if Dan, robbed of sight, allowed the boat to drift side-on to a wave. They were so high that the boat had to travel two, three times its length to reach their peak. If they were caught side-on, with that much water crashing onto them, the boat would not hold together.

Then a wave *did* break on them, curling over on top as they climbed it. When it passed, the boat contained so much water that the top of the gunwales were inches above the surface.

'Bruton!' Jenny yelled. 'Get the crate – underneath the bench – hurry!'

The crate contained all of their belongings that weren't immediately needed. Langham had tucked the quadrant into the shirt he wore, together with the chart. But apart from food, everything else they owned lay inside the wooden box. Bruton turned, and she saw an expression on his face she had never thought to see: uncomprehending fear.

'Bruton, the crate! Do you want to drown?'

He responded this time, reaching under the bench on which she sat gripping the children. He dragged the crate out by one of its rope handles, put it onto the bench in front of him, and then looked at her. He was waiting, she realised, for an instruction.

'Throw it overboard!' she yelled.

'Are you bloody mad, Jenny?' Dan yelled. 'We will have nothing. How are we to trade for food when we get there?'

'How are we to trade for food when we're dead?' she yelled back. 'Bruton, over the side with it! Now!'

Standing up, he kept his legs wide and bent so he didn't get hurled overboard. He twisted his torso and threw.

Langham cried out when he saw the box sinking, and Carney must have noticed its splash near the bow but was surely too distracted to remark on it.

If ditching the box had made any difference, it was only a fraction.

Bruton sat again silently, not flinching when sprays of water blasted his face.

'Sitting there with your mouth open, are you hoping a fish will jump in?' Jenny yelled. 'Bail! We will founder soon enough. You need to start bailing, and keep bailing!'

'Nothing to bail with,' said Bruton, and turned away.

'There's the privy bucket! It's not doing any good.' Its contents had been spilled over the deck so many times, they had stopped bothering with it.

Even with Langham and Carney bailing, the water was replenished with such speed that it was still, for a while, rising faster than they could get rid of it.

Then the rain stopped, and the water level in the boat slowly lowered, although streams of spray continued to replace it. Bruton and Langham resumed their vacant expressions, as they settled into a rhythm of bailing, propelled more by momentum than by conscious will. Jenny watched them as she held painfully on to her children, willing herself not to fall into a sleep that might loosen her grip.

CHAPTER 25

This place didn't look like Sydney Cove. Not anymore.

On the other side of the storm, the water was so calm and glassy that Jenny couldn't believe it was the same substance that had battered the boat for so long. The land was different, too. The sandstone cliffs, which Jenny had assumed the country was ringed with, had gone. So, for the moment, had the mainland itself.

They were drifting between small sandy islands, some barely bigger than Jenny and Dan's hut, some surrounded by sharp and vicious rocks, while others were little more than sand. The convicts were unlikely to find fresh water here, but they needed to land somewhere, and soon. They were out of resin, and their only means of repairing the hull was the soap they had brought with them. It would have to do, though, because the boat was desperately in need of repair. The battering from the heavy seas meant that at least one of them, usually two, had to bail constantly even in calm conditions, and the boat would not survive another storm.

They passed several beaches and inlets, and then a somewhat larger island. One with green on it, and a little crescent of beach.

The little slice of sand, innocent of human footsteps, was gouged by the hull as the boat was dragged ashore.

Emanuel was still, floppy, as Jenny laid him on a bed of leaves she had made. She draped her sodden shawl over two upright sticks to shade him. He gazed at her with eyes which seemed not to belong to him, which did not question but just accepted that misery was normal.

Charlotte, on the other hand, was making a lot of noise. Not what Jenny wanted to hear, though – not shouting and laughing, or even grizzling. The noise was coming from deep inside her chest as she shook with wet coughs, trying to expel the sea water that she had inhaled during the storm.

Charlotte was in pain, as they all were, from the sores opened up by salt-sodden clothes rubbing against skin. The rope that Jenny had used to secure her had left an indentation on her wrist, deep and with an angry permanence like the marks from the irons Jenny had last worn in England.

She held Charlotte on her lap, rubbing her back as the girl coughed out gobbets of salt water-infused phlegm, then laid her down next to her brother where she slept, exhausted from the effort. Jenny lay beside them, leaving them to the shade of her shawl, fully exposed to the sun but no longer caring; she could feel the itch of the blisters on her face and doubted any worse damage could be done.

She had slept on the boat, after a fashion. Slept through short snatches of the storm, through longer periods of the calm before it. She had not, though, allowed herself to surrender fully to unconsciousness. The ropes tethering her children to her could snap, or Bruton could decide they were a drain on resources and attempt to rectify the situation. The boat could keel over. She knew, even in her sleeping mind, that she could not afford the seconds it would take to struggle to full consciousness.

So now, for the first time in weeks, she closed her eyes and welcomed sleep.

Jenny was woken by the sound of Charlotte laughing.

It was a sound she had not heard since the first day or two of the voyage, and then infrequently. It had once been a sound as common as birdsong. But birdsong had been in short supply since they'd taken to the sea, except for the flat and rasping voices of the gulls, and childish laughter had become almost non-existent.

As Jenny sat up she felt her clothes stiff around her, salt inhabiting every available space between the threads, making the fabric as abrasive as bark. She glanced over at the men, who were sleeping further down the beach. Then at Emanuel, who was still sleeping, and she fixed her eyes on his fragile chest to make sure it was rising and falling, before seeking the source of the laughter.

Charlotte had risen. She was still coughing, still thin, not dancing about the shore as though trying to make as little contact as possible with the earth. She was walking slowly and occasionally crawling, following something up the beach.

The tide was coming in, and Jenny sprinted down to her daughter in case it began to lap at her, tried to claim her. And she saw what Charlotte was chasing. The girl was not, as Jenny had feared, crawling out of weakness. She was crawling because that was what the small turtle was doing.

Charlotte had seen creatures that girls of her age in England would consider monsters, and that their parents would dismiss as fantasies. But Charlotte had never seen a turtle. Had never seen a drawing of one, had never been told of them.

She looked up at her mother. 'Is it a sea dragon?' she said.

Jenny laughed, a chuckle that ended in cough. 'No, duckling. It's a turtle.'

'I will name him Corbett,' Charlotte announced.

Jenny did not want her daughter bestowing a name on the turtle, and an identity that came with it. She knew the fate she intended for the creature. But she was seeing her daughter smile, a smile that had disappeared under the weight of tons of water.

This turtle, Jenny decided, would be saved.

'Hello, Corbett,' she said to it, curtsying as she and Charlotte had done at Sydney Cove.

And Charlotte was off again, crawling close to the water's edge to keep pace with James, who was clearly seeking a way back into the ocean that Jenny had been happy to leave.

'I think Corbett wants to go home,' said Jenny. 'Shall we help him?'

She and Charlotte nudged the turtle out into the water, watching him as he moved far more quickly, gracefully than he had on the sand.

'Has he gone home?' asked Charlotte.

'Yes, duckling. I believe he has.'

'Can we go home?'

Jenny sat on the sand, crossing her legs and dragging Charlotte onto her lap. 'We're finding a new home, now. One where there is plenty of food and no mean people. Where we can do what we like.'

'And we will be there soon?'

'I hope so. We might need to be in the boat for a bit longer, but we are on our way.'

Charlotte frowned, nodded and coughed again. Jenny brought

her back to the makeshift lean-to, the shawl now dry and warm. She settled Charlotte next to Emanuel, rubbed her back and hummed until she drifted off to sleep, and then went to tell Dan and Carney about the turtles and to insist that they be slaughtered out of sight of her daughter.

Jenny didn't tell her daughter what she was eating that night, nor did the little girl ask. All of them would have eaten anything given to them, their hunger obliterating curiosity.

There was a broad, flat rock a few paces from the water's edge, where strips of turtle meat were laid out each day to dry. They had hopes of finding more turtles, and other food besides, but they knew to prepare for scarcity.

They soon discovered that the fat of the creatures, boiled down, helped in sealing the seams of the boat, together with soap.

Jenny took Charlotte with her sometimes underneath the upturned boat, elevated on some small rocks, and taught her to look for the chinks of light, the betrayals of gaps. Charlotte yelled to Dan, and they would get out of the way while soap and fat was drizzled, closing up the small openings that would otherwise, over time, admit enough of the ocean to drag the boat down.

There must have been fresh water somewhere to feed the trees that sprouted the strange fruits they ate. The water, though, must be buried underneath the ground where it was doing them no good. Had there been springs or streams, and had Harrigan suggested it, they would have had trouble resisting his usual entreaty to stay where they were. The place felt insubstantial, dangling off the edge of a mainland they could no longer see, beyond the blank face of the ocean and the horrors the wind sculpted from it. Jenny didn't know how far they would have to sail, in the other direction from the mainland, before they hit another landing place. Perhaps they never would.

If they did, though, they would need to explain themselves.

Jenny had not allowed herself to imagine their journey ending, to hope for a life beyond the waves. But they had come impossibly far already, and might yet get further. She had accepted the possibility that their journey might end at the bottom of the sea, but she would not have it end in a gaol cell – a certainty if they were known to be convicts.

Dan and Carney had the chart, brittle from being salt-soaked and then dried, spread on the upturned hull when Jenny approached them. 'Vorst told me of this place. The small islands stretch a long way to the north. One of them, surely, is bound to have some water.'

'Vorst told you a lot of things,' said Jenny. 'And what will you do if he was wrong, or if he lied? Will you sail to Batavia and ask for your money?'

Dan scowled at her and turned back to the chart.

'Dan, whalers let crew bring their family aboard, sometimes, don't they?' she asked.

'I suppose. Why?'

'Because wherever we sail, we will need to explain what five men, one woman and two children are doing on an open boat.'

Carney looked up. 'The crew of a wrecked whaler?'

'We will not be the crew of anything if you do not leave me in peace with this chart,' Dan said.

'It makes sense, though,' said Carney.

'And names,' said Jenny. 'We will need names. Keep our Christian names, perhaps. Easier to remember, harder to get caught out. But change our last names. John, your mother's maiden name?'

'Larkin,' said John.

'So you are John Larkin. Tell the rest to start thinking of themselves by their mothers' maiden names. We should stay with what we know as much as we can. Dan – your last name could be Trelawney.'

Dan stared at her for a moment, gaping.

'You want me to take your maiden name?' he said after a moment.

'You know it. So do the others. It will be safest.'

Dan pounded his fist on the upturned hull, and it creaked alarmingly.

'That fat hasn't set yet,' said Jenny. 'If water starts seeping in, I'll know why.'

He opened his palm and showed it to her. A red, suppurating gash ran along its length, fringed with blisters. His fingers were dotted all over with red where splinters had wormed their way in.

'I held that tiller,' he said. 'I've held it for weeks now, weeks and weeks. I've used it to steer into waves taller than any building I've seen. And you've tied yourself to your bench and slept. And now you want to foist your name on me.'

'You didn't hold it all the time,' she said. 'Carney had a go too, when you slept.'

Dan spat on the ground and walked off towards the water, wading in to his ankles, his shoulders tense. He looked out to sea as if some other islands might have appeared during their argument. She should not, she thought, have goaded him. She should let him have his moment, praise him for destroying his hand in service of their escape. She would have, perhaps, had he not insisted on holding himself forth as the unquestioned leader, the one who had conceived the plan and brought it into being without assistance, king of their small floating colony.

She thought of walking down to him, of agreeing with him,

giving him the praise and thanks he always seemed to be after. This would, though, make him more demanding, embolden him to go further in imposing his will on the rest of those in the boat.

Carney would take it, had always been Dan's lieutenant. Langham was used to Dan's authority going back to the *Charlotte*. Harrigan had occasional moments of lucidity but was in no condition to object to anything. Jenny thought that the farmer might become a little overbearing himself once he was recovered and given something to farm, and his skills became more important to their survival than those of the mariners. For now he was in a constantly moving, unfamiliar country and would place his trust in whoever yelled the loudest. But Bruton had come because he did not want to be shouted down, did not want to submit. He would be even less likely to submit to another convict than an officer. Yet another argument, on yet another mountainous sea, was something Jenny wanted to avoid.

But in the end, there was only one real impediment to her walking down, squeezing Dan's tense shoulder, looking at a shredded hand and exclaiming over the bravery of its owner. She had not, for the most part, been sleeping when she had tied herself to the bench. She had been bullying, cajoling, encouraging, yelling, doing everything to keep them focused, to keep them from killing each other while Dan at the tiller kept the ocean from killing everyone.

She had been, all that time, keeping the children alive.

But he had not, in all the talk of water and islands, once mentioned Charlotte and Emanuel. He had not, once, expressed happiness at the idea that they were still alive. He had not, once, mentioned Jenny's role in keeping them that way.

CHAPTER 26

Six days of eating fresh turtle meat, six days of searching for water in places that they had searched many times, and collecting as much as they could from the afternoon rains, Jenny using broad leaves to trickle it into Charlotte's mouth. Six days of melting turtle fat, sealing the boat, drying meat for the onward journey. Resting, sleeping without fear of being cast straight from a dream into the sea.

Dan, of course, got his way. They would weave through the islands he was sure lay just to the north, outcrops which Vorst had told him were surrounded by water too shallow for a brig, or a snow like the *Waaksamheyd*. But plenty of depth for a small cutter, and plenty of protection from the worst of the winds.

Charlotte leaned over the gunwale, trailing her hand in the clear water.

Jenny had never been able to see the bottom of Penmor Harbour. In Sydney Cove, there were days when she could see the dark shadows beneath the surface, kelp beds that often disappeared from view when the water had been churned up by a storm or heavy seas. But she had never been able to see the bottom of the ocean from a boat. This water, though, was miraculous. On the sea floor she could see the shadow of the boat moving along, distorted as it travelled over brightly coloured trees and domes. And she was grateful to it, so grateful, this element that had nearly drowned them. It kept Charlotte in a state of still wonder, leaning over and focusing on coral hillocks studded with small fish.

Unfortunately the fish were a little too small for the convicts to eat. They tried island after island, looking for water and more turtles. They found enough water to keep them going, but never again saw small dark smudges moving along a beach. The best they were able to manage was shellfish, small and tough, the kind anyone with a choice would reject.

Every few hours Vincent would get out the chart, spread it on the bench in front of him – which was now blessedly dry – and make calculations with his quadrant. 'Gulf of Carpentaria,' he said one afternoon. 'If we can get across here, perhaps get water, we've then got a straight line all the way to Coepang.'

A statement like that might have excited Jenny, earlier in the voyage. She had stopped believing that they would ever finish sailing. A large part of her had accepted the fact that she would continue to live on the ocean, scavenging for water and turtles and shellfish, until she was old and covered in salt sores and had forgotten what it was like to walk on land.

So she was happy, at first, when another island appeared. This one had well-built huts on the shore, tall enough for a tall man to stand in, made out of bark and leaves. There seemed, at a quick glance, to be enough space under those roofs to house at least a hundred people.

There would definitely be water.

Dan nudged the tiller across – he had recently wrapped his hands in fabric from the hem of her skirt, and brown blotches were seeping through. 'Just two of us will go out this time,' he said. 'Two is enough to get the breakers filled quickly, and if they turn out to be unfriendly it will be easier to get away.'

No one on the shore was unfriendly, because no one was there, so John and Bruton dragged the flagons over to a small spring behind the huts and filled them with enough water for several days. They were so weak from the lack of it they had trouble getting the flagons back into the boat.

There was a reason, though, that no one was at the huts.

As the convicts soon discovered, they were all on the next beach around, preparing to launch an attack.

Jenny, with nothing to do but hang on to the children, was constantly looking about her. She saw them first. Two long, sturdy canoes with matted sails, each holding around twenty men.

A man stood in the bow of the first canoe, shell adornments draped over his shoulders, and behind him more men were standing. The second boat was just behind them, and Jenny could see more massing on the shore.

'Dan!' she yelled. 'Dan, look! They are coming!'

The men had been resting, a light and favourable wind filling the sails and pushing the boat along in a desultory fashion – now snapping the sheet tight, now letting it lie limp – but moving fast enough so that it hadn't been necessary to row in the midday heat.

At Jenny's shout, Dan looked around. 'Row!' he called to the others. 'Row, row!'

Really, they were in no state to. Harrigan, with his copper hair, seemed to have suffered worse than any of them from exposure to the sun. His face was covered in blisters, and he had returned to the bottom of the boat, staring and occasionally raving, talking to an unknown woman who, he said, had rejected him for a far worse prospect. Bruton leaned over and slapped him on the side of the head, hauling him upright onto a bench and putting an oar in his hand, where he ineffectually moved it backwards and forwards, his cracked lips slightly parted as he gazed ahead.

The rest of them, though weak, still held their wits and could see as well as Jenny what was coming. They needed no further urging. As she looked back again, she saw that these natives did not have large spears, sharp and thick with a limited range. They had bows and arrows, and some were standing on platforms in their boats, taking aim.

'What do they want with us?' she yelled at Dan. 'We're leaving – can't they see we are leaving? Why are they chasing us?'

'Seems to me they want to kill us,' he said. 'I've heard tales, true or not, that some tribes around here are headhunters.'

Had she not needed to protect Charlotte and Emanuel, Jenny would have vaulted forward and taken an oar herself. As it was, all she could do was hunch over the children as arrows began to land in the water nearby.

John Carney, handling the sail, reached in and scooped one out, throwing it into the bottom of the boat where Harrigan had lain until just a few seconds ago.

The men were rowing, but not in a coordinated fashion. They seemed to have forgotten how to time their strokes with those of their neighbours, so that the boat lurched forward a little to the left and then to the right, zigzagging across the ocean at a pace that was far, far too slow.

'Row on my call,' Jenny yelled out.

'I'll take no orders from a woman,' Bruton yelled back.

'Then by tonight you'll be a trophy in that village over there, probably the ugliest one they've ever taken,' she called. 'Now, ready – stroke! Stroke!'

The coordinated movement pulled them ahead a little more quickly. It also helped that their sail was more flexible than the large mat sails of the canoes, which weren't able to catch the wind quite as efficiently. With John Carney manipulating their sail, and the men finally rowing in unison, they were able to gain some distance.

Still their pursuers kept coming.

'Why aren't they giving up?' Jenny asked.

'I imagine they don't get much opportunity to capture a boat,' said Dan. 'They'll give up when they can't see us any longer.'

She nodded and hoped he was right.

They crept forward, dragging themselves by the oars and harnessing as much wind as they could, until the chasing boats began to recede. Eventually, after over an hour's chase, their pursuers were out of sight.

Bruton made to haul in his oar.

'They could still be coming, you fool!' yelled Jenny. 'They'll know we might slow down when we can't see them anymore. They could still be just back there, waiting.'

So Bruton picked up his oar and rowed along with the rest of them, and another two hours passed before everyone felt secure enough to haul in the oars and let the wind push them onwards.

It was, actually, a decent wind. One which, if it held, and if the chart was correct, would take them straight to Coepang.

They used the last of the light to spread out the chart again and see if its lines had resolved into a somehow more promising shape.

'This is our best chance,' said Jenny. 'If you're right – yes, yes, I know you are, I did not mean to question your skill. It seems we're as close to Coepang as we can get without turning.'

'We should cross the Gulf,' said Langham 'A straight line, then. No wasted movement. And it will give us a chance to get more water.'

'And a chance to be attacked again,' said Bruton.

'We don't have enough water to last us, though,' Dan said.

'Do the winds always blow from this direction up here, or is this a lucky one?' asked John. 'What if it turns, blows in our faces?'

'That's true,' said Langham. 'I don't know what the winds do up here. Nor does anyone else. For all I know, this could be the first southerly that ever blew over these waters.'

'If the wind turns, we'll float until we are picked off, or we die,' said Jenny. 'We will just have more time to run into bad luck. And do any of you really believe this boat will *survive* another storm? If we go, we might die. If we don't, we *will* die.'

Dan clapped his hand on Langham's shoulder, an affectionate gesture and the first she had seen him employ for many weeks. It was hard to forgive him for making such an effort with Langham but not with her or the children. Although Langham, she supposed, was far more important to their survival at the moment.

'If the wind holds,' Dan said, 'and if we're lucky, how long will the crossing take?'

'Two days, maybe? Perhaps a little less.'

Dan turned to Carney and asked, 'Will the water last two days?'

'Barely,' he said. 'If we are on half-measures.'

Dan looked at Jenny, raising his eyebrows. 'What do you think?'

She almost forgave him, in that moment, for the weeks of petulant silence, and the way he now held back affection from the children as though it was a commodity to be hoarded.

'We have kept moving, up to now,' Jenny said. 'If we stop, we may never start again.'

He nodded. 'We will go then. We will go.' And he turned the tiller, and John moved the sail, and the boat turned, slowly, to point out into the featureless blue of the Arafura Sea.

CHAPTER 27

Another night, and another day. Then darkness again, and Jenny wasn't sure if there had been two nights, or three, or a hundred.

The wind held, more or less, and did not strengthen to the point where the boat was endangered. Occasionally a small amount of spray splashed onto the convicts, who welcomed it. The air was getting hotter, and it had a smothering heaviness that made Jenny's skin slick and wet.

She dozed from time to time, dipping in and out of the world made up entirely of ocean. In her dreams she visited a grotesque Penmor where her mother had starved for want of assistance, where her sister cursed her name.

Now that it was no longer possible to see the underwater forest, Charlotte had retreated back into herself. Leaning against her mother, she took the occasional mouthful of rice or sip of water but otherwise was still and silent.

Emanuel lay far more still than a baby should, far more still than any baby Jenny had ever seen.

Dan shoved her shoulder. She was shallowly unconscious, and the push bumped her chin against her chest and brought down her teeth on her tongue, so that she was turning as she sat up, thinking

271

of which curse to use on him. He wasn't sneering, though, or tight-faced. He was pointing – pointing ahead.

She turned and saw it. The dark line on the horizon. The seabirds, in the distance. It was not until she felt the wetness on her cheeks that she realised she was crying.

There was a man standing on the dock, dressed in breeches and a shirt with a neckerchief, looking as though he could be on the sea wall at Penmor Harbour. When he saw them, though, he yelled in a foreign language. After not getting a response, he turned and ran, pushing aside a man carrying a basket of fruit and dodging a group of women, skimming the paving stones towards the town and the squat tower above it.

Soon enough he was back, as they were approaching the dock. He'd brought more men like him, wearing the strong and rough clothes of dock workers, and other people wrapped in coloured strips of cloth or in smocks with small caps on their heads. All of them crowded towards the end of the dock, waiting for the boat to close the last few dozen feet.

The man who'd first seen them reached down and handed a rope to Carney, who tied it to the bow. The man ran to the back then, leaned over and gripped Charlotte beneath her arms, lifting her until he stopped with a jerk. The girl was still tethered to the boat and her mother.

It hadn't occurred to Jenny to untie them. It hadn't occurred to her that they might reach a place where such a precaution was no longer necessary.

The man vaulted into the boat, a movement only possible for the well fed. He untied Emanuel and handed him up to a woman standing on the dock. She smiled and tickled him, then frowned when she got no answering gurgle.

Charlotte was hoisted up to one of the bystanders who wore a colourful cloth in place of breeches. The little girl reached out to Jenny and whimpered, but it was a small sound, rasping and lost in the noise.

Jenny didn't know how many languages were being spoken, but she didn't understand any of them. People shouted to one another and more came down to the dock while the man who had first seen them kept shouting a command over his shoulder. He seemed not to aim it at anyone in particular, perhaps just hoping somebody would catch it.

Jenny, untied now, tried to stand. She had never been unable to get herself out of a boat – had as a child reached up to the dock and pushed herself up with her arms at low tide, doing it far more smoothly than many of the boys. But now her legs would not support her. They buckled, and she crashed painfully back down to the bench. Her tears were still clearing a passage through the grime on her face, and the thought that she had arrived only to be unable to clamber onto the wharf, forced her into great, gulping sobs.

The man lifted her as easily as he had the children, but she noticed that some of the men on the dock, those with black caps, stepped back, reluctant to receive her. She lay on the wooden planks, staring at the frantic shadows around her.

The woman who'd taken Emanuel had also accepted Charlotte as a charge, and she came over saying words of comfort which Jenny could not understand. Their tone, though, left no doubt as to her meaning, when she laid Emanuel on Jenny's chest and moved her arm around him.

Dan pulled himself up from the boat, repeating again and again a phrase that Vorst had taught him. 'Ik heb uw hulp nodig. Ik heb uw hulp nodig.' *I need your help.*

Jenny started to giggle with a sound she had heard from some of the women in the hulk, those who had been there longest, who cackled at the nonsensical. She thought that if it wasn't evident from their condition that they needed help, no amount of repetition of the rote-learned phrase would convey the message.

Jenny limped to the end of the dock with an arm around one of the wharf men, the other holding Emanuel. The woman walked next to her with Charlotte, still saying unknown words in her comforting voice.

Dan was able to hobble by himself, making slow progress, as was Carney, and Bruton refused any help, walking more strongly than any of them. Harrigan's eyes were open, but he made no attempt to move as he was hauled by three men onto the dock and then carried by them, arms under his shoulders and one sun-spotted hand on each ankle.

They were all loaded into a horse-drawn cart, and Jenny nearly screamed in protest – she hated carts. Experience had taught her that such journeys rarely ended well. This one, though, drew to a stop outside a handsome stone house with wide windows to catch what breeze there was. A man stood waiting, well fed and with sharp, darting eyes, dressed in what seemed to be the clothes of an administrator: a plain, neat brown coat over an impeccable shirt.

When Dan saw him, he repeated the phrase that now seemed to be all he was capable of saying.

The man nodded, frowning. 'I would say you all do,' he said in accented English.

'We were wrecked,' said Dan. 'Wrecked off …' He was breathing heavily. The exertion of hauling himself along, on legs that had not stood in weeks, was beginning to tell, and the words of his story were already jumbling in his mouth. Jenny worried that they would become unintelligible or, worse, implausible.

But the man held up his hand to silence Dan. 'There will be time to hear your story, and I will listen with great interest. But a dead man cannot speak, and you will be one soon unless we give you the help you are asking for.'

So each member of the group limped, or was dragged or carried through the door by which the man stood. They made their way into a flagstone courtyard with a tree in its centre that produced flowers of an almost violent purple.

The men were taken into a room at the end of the courtyard, and Jenny and the children into a side room, in the company of the friendly woman. She guided Jenny – who was still clutching Emanuel – to a couch, then lifted Charlotte up beside her. She left and came back a few minutes later with a plate bearing slices of a strange white fruit. When she lifted a piece to Charlotte's lips, the girl just stared at it. Jenny picked up a slice and began to eat, slowly and then with more urgency, unable to stop, unwilling even to delay the strange fruit's arrival in her stomach by chewing it.

The woman quietly took a small bowl from a nearby table and carried it over. She handed it to Jenny when her stomach revolted at the forgotten feeling of fullness, ejecting the fruit. Then the woman gently cleaned her, clicking her tongue and muttering. She cleaned the children, too, and brought Charlotte a plain muslin smock, the cleanest and brightest garment Jenny had seen for some time.

Charlotte had been able to keep down a small amount of fruit, and Emanuel had been given a water-soaked cloth to suck on. Both were still barely moving, the skin on their faces supported by no fat at all, so that it drew back and emphasised the hollows of their eye sockets, their eyes seeming to protrude as though in permanent surprise.

The woman picked Charlotte up and carried her into the next room, then returned to pick up Emanuel in one arm while helping Jenny to her feet with the other.

The next room contained the most valuable treasure Jenny had seen.

It was a bed of plain and meticulously sanded wood, and a mattress stuffed with more feathers than on all of the fowl Jenny had seen during her time at Sydney Cove.

Charlotte was already tucked in and drowsing. The woman pulled back the covers and gestured, and Jenny sank into the mattress, tugging the light cotton sheet up to her chin despite the heat. She cradled Emanuel and found sleep even before she reached out for it.

Dan was lying there beside them, stroking Charlotte's hair, when Jenny woke. He was on top of the covers and dressed in rough but clean clothes of the type the dock workers had worn.

This was the first time, Jenny realised, that they had lain together in a bed with legs, on a mattress that was raised off the floor.

When she moved to get up, he placed his hand gently on her shoulder, pressing her down. 'No need to move. No need to get up, no need to bail, no need to look for water.'

She smiled, feeling one or two of her teeth move as she did so. She pressed them gingerly with her tongue, not wanting to lose them but unable to resist seeing how far they would go.

After a minute she gave up and focused back on Dan and the sleeping Charlotte. Jenny kissed Emanuel's head and squeezed a small hand that should have been padded with far more flesh than it was.

When she woke again the corners of the room were dark, the light slowly backing away through the window. Dan was still there, still awake, but frowning now. 'We are to dine with the governor,' he said.

She sat upright before a sudden dizziness dragged her back to the pillow. How had Governor Lockhart made it here? Had he led a group himself to recover the escapees? And why on earth, if they were found out, would he wish to dine with them?

Dan smiled. 'Not that governor,' he said. 'The Dutch governor of this island, Van Dalen. The man who spoke English to us. He wishes to hear our story.'

'And you will tell the story?'

'Yes. We are the crew of a whaler,' Dan told her. 'We were wrecked, somewhere near Batavia. We got away in the cutter, and our captain and some others managed to clamber aboard another small boat. We will warn the Dutch to keep watch in case other survivors arrive.'

'Is it not cruel, ungrateful, to ask them to stand on the dock waiting for phantoms?'

'It is what's needed,' he said.

'And this whaler – we did not agree on a name.'

'The *Janus*.'

'Dan, don't be stupid. Don't amuse yourself with a little joke that could get us found out.'

He smiled, even winked. Clearly delighted. Jenny wanted to hit him. 'I'm not responsible for what the ship is named,' he said.

'You are if you're the one naming it! Why on earth call the ship a name that makes educated people think of liars?'

'Well, *Janus* it is. I've already spoken to all of the lads – even Harrigan, who will be too weak for dinner tonight but is conscious now. Thanks to you, I must say. He says it too, and will say it in person when he's well enough.'

'That is wonderful – at times I thought he was already dead.'

'All he needs is food and sleep,' Dan said with a smile. 'So, as for the finer details of our tale – when we were wrecked, I helped get you into the cutter before the rest of us. We collected everyone we could, and then we saw the other boat with the captain and a few men rolling in the opposite direction. We tried to call to them, but they didn't hear us. We hope, pray, that they will find land, perhaps even this land if God is with us.'

Jenny shook her head. 'How do you explain the presence of a farmer on a whaler?'

'We will think of something. Harrigan isn't well enough to be quizzed tonight. Perhaps he was paying for passage, and we brought him with us for the same reason we *actually* brought him with us – his experience may be useful.'

'And our revered captain? His name is ...'

Dan swore. 'We forgot to name the bastard, didn't we. I'd better go back to the lads. Let's call him Captain ... Captain Spikerman.'

'And do we like Captain Spikerman?'

'Well enough. He can be a hard bugger at times, but generally fair, and nice to the children.'

Jenny sighed. 'All right. Oh – and how long have we been floating around for, if they ask?'

'Close to a month,' Dan said quickly when the governor asked. 'As near as we can reckon, at least. It's very easy to lose track.'

'Yes, that's what Captain Halifax found too,' said Mattias Van Dalen from the head of a long table, covered in candles. Other local worthies were studded around it, interspersed with the convicts. Everyone else's attention was focused on them, the strange visitors. 'Extraordinary to have two such parties arriving within the space of a few years. His voyage was much longer than yours, though, of course.'

'Oh, yes. It must've been.'

'Mrs Trelawney,' said the governor, turning to her and smiling.

She smiled back. Dan, in the end, had introduced himself by her name, had even smiled at her while doing so.

Van Dalen nodded to one of the servants, a man wearing a smock tied with a piece of cloth around his waist. He set in front of her a dish of the same white fruit she'd been served on arrival, this time soaking in a bowl of milk.

The governor addressed her again. 'Your shipmates, my dear, have praised your courage, your tenacity. Mr Larkin, I believe, told me there were times when your urging was the only thing driving you all forward.'

Carney, at the other end of the table, smiled and raised a cup in her direction. She did not turn to look at Dan, but could feel him tense beside her.

'I don't believe any one of us was responsible for the happy end to our voyage, sir,' she said. 'Of course, without my husband's direction, we would have been in a far worse state. And we would have very possibly been lying dead now had it not been for your kindness.'

The governor smiled again and inclined his head.

'My wife was our saviour, at times,' Dan said. 'I was very clever to marry her.'

This, even delivered as a fleeting compliment, delighted Jenny. It was not the talk of a man who believed he wasn't really married.

'I must remark,' Van Dalen said, 'that I was surprised by the state of you all. You were in no better condition than Captain Halifax and his crew, and they had been sailing for at least twice as long. You looked as though you had endured a voyage of two, three months, not one.'

'Well, we had some bad luck with the weather,' said Dan. 'I can't be sure it was a month. We did drift around a bit, having no way of knowing where we were headed.'

'Yet your navigator is, I am told, in possession of a quadrant,' said the governor.

'Oh, yes,' said Dan. 'But not in possession of the wit to use it.'

Langham, next to Carney, narrowed his eyes.

'Well,' said Van Dalen, 'I rejoice that you found us, and that we were in a position to assist. You may stay here in Coepang for as long as you wish. You may find the climate a little warm, but the people are congenial enough. Men such as yourselves, when your strength returns, will have no trouble finding work on the docks, and I will recommend you for it. Of course, we will also understand if you wish to seek passage onward.'

'You're kind,' said Dan. 'I fear we must eventually leave you. If we can stay for a short while, though, we'd be very grateful.'

'Of course,' said the governor. 'Of course. I look forward to getting to know all there is about all of you.'

Jenny didn't know whether they were watched. But she often ran into the governor or waved to him in the streets of Coepang.

Otherwise Jenny seemed free to explore on her own. She enjoyed walking through the markets, where people would bring a potatoes for sale, or a few strips of turtle meat, and after making their transactions would sit in the market square chewing betel, which blackened their teeth. They were friendly and relaxed, and as Charlotte grew in strength she would drop little curtsies to them as she walked, holding her mother's hand, through the square.

Within the week Dan had begun working at the docks, as had Carney, Bruton and Langham, and employment would be found for Harrigan when he was well enough.

For the first time since leaving England, Dan was being paid for his labour, and it suited him. If he did spend a considerable amount of time in the tavern, at least he now returned with fruit that had caught his eye in the market, or a bright flower that he would, kneeling, present to Charlotte.

'I will miss those flowers,' Jenny said as she watched on.

'You don't need to miss them,' he said. 'I found that one on the road from the market.'

'Dan, we can't stay. Not for long. There will be word, eventually, of escaped convicts in a stolen boat.'

He sighed. 'I know. But we have time, still. We can't steal another boat and sail to England. I need time to earn the coins to pay for passage.'

'Perhaps you should stop giving them to the tavern keeper.'

He scowled. She reached out for his hand and kissed his ruined palm.

For the first week, Jenny stayed as far as she could from the ocean, trying to pretend it wasn't there. But it was incessantly whispering, rasping against the rocks, sending its scent to her on the wind. Eventually she found that she no longer wanted to stay away. She was ready to resume a tentative acquaintance.

She would take Charlotte down to the shore or the docks, with Emanuel supported in a sling on her front, made of a matted plant fibre. He was slowly filling out but still lacked the sense of barely restrained outrage that Charlotte had specialised in at his age.

Jenny's daughter was becoming more her own person with each passing day. She resisted bedtime, and washing, and all of those natural enemies of children.

Jenny had bought a few fishhooks and strung them to poles, using thread from the tattered clothes in which she had made the journey here. She and Charlotte would sit on the dock, dangling their lines in the water. Occasionally they would catch something. Most of the time, they talked about what they wanted to catch. If they hooked a sea dragon, he might be so outraged that he'd consume the entire dock.

One day a shadow, terminating in well-used but polished boots, fell over them.

Jenny stood and smoothed the simple gown which she wore at the sufferance of this man, who had given orders that everything they needed should be provided without cost. 'Your Excellency,' she said.

Charlotte, perhaps sensing unaccustomed deference in her mother, dipped in a curtsy that made Van Dalen smile.

'You come to this dock a lot, I think,' he said. 'It has been – what? – a fortnight since you joined us, and I'm told that you have been a daily presence here for the past week.'

'I hope I am not in anyone's way,' she said.

'Not a bit of it. I presume you are watching for your captain.'

'Watching ... Yes, I am. It would be a blessing were he to suddenly arrive. And his crew, of course. The chances, though ... Given the weather we had on our voyage, I would say they are not good.'

'Perhaps not. Still, it is good to know you will be here, should I need to find you. I will leave you to your vigil, and please do not lose heart. It would be foolish to try to predict where the sea will bring any of us.'

Jenny turned a little as he walked away, then she and Charlotte sat back down, dangling their legs over the edge of the wooden tongue that pierced the ocean's flank.

'Yes,' she said, 'it would.'

PART THREE

CHAPTER 28

Afterwards, Jenny tried to pinpoint the moment when things changed. The look or word that beckoned something dark to slither out and wrap itself around Dan's mind, to blot out everything except his need to stand in front of her and intercept her unsought glory. It probably, though, wasn't a look or a word. Perhaps it was the cheers, the congratulatory hoots.

Two months, they had been here. Two months, during which Jenny had watched the boats come in, bringing unimaginable spices, and fabrics in colours that she had never known. Boats had carried her through her childhood, but she felt no urge now to climb aboard them. And she would be surprised if Charlotte could ever be coaxed onto one again.

Two months of sunshine and fresh fruit and fussing from Gert, the Dutch woman who had helped them ashore that first day, had seen Charlotte's face round out. The plumpness that belonged by right to every child had returned to her arms and legs. The same two months had made Emanuel the kind of baby who cried and gurgled and laughed, rather than lying in his mother's arms, staring at nothing.

This, surely, must be their life from now on. They had earned it by surviving the sea.

But the caution of a forest dweller had never left Jenny. She had never been given a reason to set it aside. She still kept the clothes she had travelled in, rough as they were. She had added a lock of Emanuel's hair to the knife and tea leaves sewn into the hem, along with a ribbon that Charlotte had pulled out of her hair in a temper. Mrs Trelawney did not want to put Jenny Gwyn's clothes on again, but she would at least have some treasures if she had to.

And every time she saw a boat being unloaded, she wondered if a ship with a cargo of soldiers was just on the other side of the horizon.

She would do anything to avoid those soldiers. Including buying a chicken.

Usually they ate fish for dinner, at the scrubbed, wooden table in the house given to them by the governor. It was the same house they had been taken to when they arrived, with its courtyard tree sprouting impossibly vibrant flowers. It had a comfortable sitting room with cushioned chairs positioned to catch the breeze when the door to the courtyard was open. But they always ended up eating in the large, simple kitchen, with bare wooden benches lining each side of the table.

Dan would go to a small beach, dangle a line in, and usually have reasonable luck. And often, all of the men who'd been crowded together in the cutter would crowd around the Gwyns' table and assume a right to anything on it, one they felt had been conferred on them by months of forced intimacy.

They were all used to fish, so Jenny thought a chicken might have better luck opening their ears as they stuffed their mouths.

She had bought the bird in the marketplace and wrung its neck herself after dropping some small silver discs into the hand of the smiling, elderly man who sold it to her. He had a languidness to him and, had she shared his language, she suspected he might have told her that he didn't particularly mind whether he sold the chicken or not. He was deferential to her, though – an odd mix of friendliness and shyness, common to most of those she had met here. She was surely strange to the islanders, a woman who shouldn't have survived, one who might have one foot in the world beyond all waves, who was known to be a favourite of the governor, of course. Such a creature was to be smiled on from a distance, not embraced like a friend.

The chicken had taken her the better part of an hour to pluck, with Charlotte's help. The little girl couldn't resist reaching out an increasingly pudgy arm to grip a feather and pull ineffectually, then take the ones her mother was withdrawing from the bird's skin and weave them through her hair.

Langham arrived with Bruton, who had found work on the docks with Dan and Carney. His shoulders and back were valuable commodities; he now used them in the service of getting paid, rather than to avoid a flogging for idleness. He had not become any less taciturn, but he had been keeping the worst of his latent violence in check. Until, apparently, last night.

'Sweet Jesus,' Jenny said, 'what happened to your eye?'

'They tried to swindle me,' Bruton said, sitting down uninvited. 'At the tavern. Think that because I don't speak like them, I'm stupid.' He looked at the table with disappointment as nothing had, as yet, been placed on it.

'He's not allowed back,' said Langham cheerfully. 'The tavern keeper's son has a broken nose. And you don't need language to know what he was about when he threw Bruton onto the street. Quite a nasty sword hanging there above the bar. He keeps it sharp.'

'Will you ever, just once, look to your own survival, never mind ours?' asked Jenny. This, after all, was the man who had sat staring at her, a pail between his knees, refusing to use it to empty out a boat that was filling with water. 'If we get a reputation for lawbreaking – well, we do not want to give anyone here any reason to question our character.'

'And if we give them reason to question our wits, we will wind up with a knife through the shoulderblades one dark night,' said Bruton.

Dan and John Carney came in then, Dan cradling some potatoes. He had traded a fish for them, an act for which he could no longer be flogged. He took in Bruton's mashed face with an approving grin.

'You're all as stupid as each other,' said Jenny.

Dan frowned, turning towards her. 'I do beg your pardon. We are, of course, in the presence of the heroine of the seas.'

It was a phrase the governor had applied to Jenny several times in public, so that anyone able to understand English repeated it in her hearing – and often in Dan's.

'I did not ask for that title,' she said.

'Yet it rests around your shoulders like a shawl,' said Dan. He handed her the potatoes then reached for a jug on the shelf, sloppily pouring sharp-smelling liquor into earthenware cups.

By the time the chicken bones had been picked clean, the men seemed calmer. Dan had smiled at her, thanked her. That was as good an invitation as she was going to get.

'This place,' she said, 'it has been good to us.'

'Aye,' said Harrigan. On occasion he was unable to resist

scratching at the flakes of skin on his cheeks, condemned by his red-headed complexion to a more fierce beating from the sun than the rest of them. But he had been restored to life by exposure to the earth. He was fascinated by the farming practices of both the natives and the Dutch, shooting broken questions about crops and rain at anyone willing to entertain them.

'And its people have been good to us, particularly the governor,' said Jenny.

'Particularly to you,' said Bruton, grinning until he caught a glare from Dan.

'And how would they treat us, do you think, if they knew?' she asked.

'Well, I imagine they'd lock us up,' said Carney. 'But they don't know, Jenny. Nor will they.'

'Working on the docks, you lads have all seen the ships that come here. More foreigners than we ever saw in Penmor. I think enough time has passed that they might bring word. And you've all earned enough to pay for our passage out.'

'Where would we go, though?' asked Langham. 'I've seen the charts – not much of note between here and Batavia, and that place ...' He shivered involuntarily. 'People die in Batavia. The air itself is poison.'

'Not Batavia, nor any other big port,' said Jenny. 'Somewhere quiet. Even inland, maybe, where word of escaped convicts is less likely to reach.'

'And we would stand out there like balls on a bull,' said Dan. 'We're safe enough here.'

'We are not safe,' Jenny insisted. 'They'll be keeping an ear out for us, if they're not searching. Lockhart and the rest – we've embarrassed them. Worse, in their eyes, than any amount of theft from the stores. We can't stay.'

'Well, we're not going!' Dan said. 'We've food, money. More than we thought we'd ever have again. You want to trade it for ... what? An uncertain fate in the jungle? Another bout with the ocean? No, Jenny. No, this time you will not sway me.'

He rose unsteadily, looked at the lads and jerked his head towards the door.

Carney raised his eyebrows at Jenny. Langham and Harrigan pressed her hand and thanked her for the meal. Bruton said nothing. Then all of them stood and went out, leaving her alone with the chicken carcass on the table.

It would be the most appalling cruelty for them to be discovered, to be dragged back down into the darkness. Cruelty, though, was one of the few commodities Jenny had seen in any significant quantity.

The danger, she thought, lay in the mouths of sailors. Dreadful gossips, most of them. And this news would fly: the woman who had offered herself and her children up to the ocean. If a sailor from Batavia brought, with weevil-ridden wheat and sour butter, news of a bedraggled group washing up at Coepang, that snippet of information could be fatal.

But the men's faith that all would be well was seductive. The torpor brought by a full belly, the joy of Emanuel's wails and Charlotte's laughs, made Jenny want to believe that this could be their home forever, that Charlotte and Emanuel would grow up knowing nothing of their birthplaces.

Disconcertingly, though, Jenny found herself at the centre of a growing fascination.

She would walk to the market, enjoying the movement of clean, salt-free fabric against her thighs, letting Charlotte run a little ahead in pursuit of a chicken or another child. When the jungle pathway that led from their house gave way to the broader streets, feeding into the market square, she could feel the scrutiny. The looks were not unkind, but nor were they restrained. Her story was the property of anyone who cared to pass the afternoon discussing it. And surely a great many did.

The men, she imagined them saying, *to be sure they did well to survive. But, well, surviving is what men do. The woman, though! And the children! And people say the whole party would have died without her.*

Jenny took to exploring the jungle, carrying Emanuel in his sling, Charlotte by her side. She didn't know if there were snakes. If there were, would their fangs carry sufficient venom to be a danger? But Charlotte's thick leather shoes, one of many gifts from the governor, would protect her. And the girl knew not to pick up anything from the forest floor, even if it looked like a branch – the ground snakes of Sydney Cove had taught her that.

She would have stayed in the jungle if she could, where there was no one to gawk, point, whisper. Whenever she was in a public space with Dan and became aware she was attracting curious stares or smiles, she would drop behind him, and he would smile and nod and take all the glory for both of them.

From time to time, Van Dalen would appear at the cottage unannounced, often when Dan was at his work. The governor would offer Jenny a stroll along the edge of the jungle or through the market. 'To let everyone know you're under my protection,' he'd said the first time. 'So that they don't charge you for three potatoes and give you one.' It had occurred to Jenny that Van Dalen might have more interest in her than Dan would like. If that was true, though, he made no move to act on it, save for frequently seeking her company.

Until the night of the governor's party.

One afternoon Jenny opened the door to Detmer, the governor's secretary. A thin man, he always wore meticulous woollen clothing far more suited to Holland than Coepang. Constantly mopping his brow, but not made irascible by the heat, Detmer would wave to Charlotte whenever he saw her, just as he did to the native children.

This afternoon he did not wave, but bowed deeply in Jenny's doorway, as though she was a visiting princess. 'I have the honour to invite you – all of you – to a dinner at the castle,' he said.

'Oh ... thank you,' said Jenny, trying to effect the air of one who was used to such invitations. 'What time would His Excellency like us to arrive?'

'Oh, not tonight. No, no, you must not think this is one of the normal dinners. Tuesday next. Seven o'clock. Gert will sit with the children, I have already asked her.'

'Tuesday next. Very well.'

'There will be a new gown for you as well,' he said. 'It's the governor's birthday, you see. And he does like things to be just ... just so, is that the expression? So your muslin, lovely as it is, will be replaced by silk!' He clapped his hands and looked at her expectantly.

She had never worn silk, and did not know whether it was worth such excitement. But Detmer clearly expected a response to mirror his own, so she dragged her mouth into a wide smile. 'Very generous of His Excellency,' she said.

'Exactly so, yes,' said Detmer. 'And make sure those men of yours present themselves neatly, no? We don't want them bringing the smell of the docks with them.'

On Tuesday next, it took her at least half an hour to convince Dan to shave.

'Don't insult the governor, for God's sake,' said Jenny. 'We will have to look our best.'

'Had I the money for the clothes Detmer wears, I might be able to look presentable,' grumbled Dan. But eventually he took a blade to his cheeks until they were red, nicked in places but clear of all growth.

The birthday guests dined at a long table especially set up in the entrance hall of the governor's residence. His staff were there, along with prominent merchants, leaders of the local tribes. Jenny, in her yellow silk dress, her scalp still stinging from Gert's brush, was seated opposite the man himself.

It amazed her that all speeches were the same. She had heard Governor Lockhart often enough, at Christmas or on the King's birthday, or his own, talking about how humbled he was, how they were all part of the one endeavour. She hadn't believed him then – hard to feel part of an endeavour that emptied your belly and refused to refill it – and she had trouble believing the sentiments now. If humility was part of Van Dalen's thinking, he surely would not have invited the rich traders whom he normally preferred to avoid.

One thing she'd never heard during one of Lockhart's speeches, though, was her own name.

'All of you know Mrs Trelawney,' Van Dalen said, nodding to her. 'All of you know how she and her family got here. And here she is tonight, bearing little resemblance to the half-dead woman from the sea. But she, my friends, is the reason that everyone in that boat was not wholly dead. She is here to remind us all of the need to meet adversity with bravery, no matter our station. I thank you for the toasts you have raised to me, and now I propose another. To the brave woman of the ocean.'

He raised his glass and drank. Some did likewise, but others cheered, thumping the table with their fists. Everyone was looking at her – and the yellow gown was like a beacon – so she could not look in the one direction she wanted to. She had to meet all of the eyes that were on her, while smiling at their owners. She could not afford to glance at Dan.

And by the time the attention ebbed, and she was able to turn towards him at the end of the table, she saw his seat was empty.

Later that night Jenny found Dan in their bedroom, sitting with his hands on his knees and head bent. She saw the wounded pride in him, knew she should tread carefully if she wanted to avoid confrontation, perhaps even a crack across the face with the back of his hand.

There could be a price to his petulance. Van Dalen had followed her gaze to the empty seat. He'd frowned, and Jenny had too. Offending the governor would put them at far greater risk.

But Dan's slumped shoulders angered her most. They were free shoulders now, and he received money when he used them in someone else's service. That could not continue if his petulance did.

'You know, don't you, Dan, that the man whose table you walked away from could put us in gaol, with a nod to Detmer?'

Dan looked up, staring at her through the red web of veins in his eyes. 'Ah, but he wouldn't, would he? Not the brave woman of the ocean. How many people did you need to speak to, Jenny? To start the rumour spreading, that you were the one who saved us all?'

'I never claimed credit for our survival, although at least some of it belongs to me.'

'Did you nearly cut your hand in half gripping the tiller?' Dan shouted. 'Did you restore the boat month by month?'

'I've never denied you the honour of your part in it. But you wouldn't have gone if it wasn't for me.'

'I wouldn't have needed to!' he yelled. 'My sentence was expired! I could have signed on as a mate on a ship without having to drag you and the –' He stopped himself.

That's something, she thought. He was unwilling, as yet, to malign the children. If that changed, their world would become even less secure.

'You got many benefits from marrying me, Dan Gwyn. The trust of the governor, of Mr Corbett. Command of the fishing fleet. The hut.'

'I could have gotten those on my own,' he said. 'And I would not have suffered the shame of losing them, either, nor of a hundred cuts to my back, not if I hadn't had to trade the fish to feed you and ... to feed those who needed feeding.'

'And now all those who need feeding are being fed! Don't think for a moment that you would have escaped the famine had you stayed – and don't think, either, that the authorities would have let you sail off on a merchant ship, even if your sentence expired, not with you the only trained fisherman. Having a wife and children means people trust you more. We need everyone to trust us, Dan, now more than ever.'

'Do I have a wife, though?' he said, standing and moving slowly towards her, scaring her far more than a headlong rush would have. 'Married in a place not even God has heard of. Who's to say it's valid? What's to keep me tied to you?'

'The governor is not the kind to approve of that sort of thing.

An upstanding man, him. Don't think he would look well on a man who abandoned a woman and children.'

'No,' said Dan, 'he wouldn't. Especially when that woman is his sea goddess, someone he clothes in silk.' He glared at her, reached out, grabbed the neckline of her dress and tore it open down the front.

This shocked her far more than any blow would have. The silk was likely worth more than her parents' home in Penmor. Dan would know it, too; when he worked as a smuggler, fine fabrics must have passed through his fingers.

She knew him well enough to know that any sign of distress from her would outrage him further. So she forced herself to stand still, feeling the humid air paint moisture on her exposed breasts. Perhaps he would try to take her, valid marriage or not.

He looked at her, assessing. Then shrugged, turned, and left the house.

Jenny changed into a nightdress, the yellow silk folded on the bed, its front facing downwards. She heard footsteps approaching and looked up, seeing Gert walking down the corridor and into the bedroom. The slam of the front door must have woken her.

Gert and Jenny had been teaching each other their words by small degrees, almost hesitantly. Jenny felt that their easy coexistence, the warmth that had been established between them, might be dismantled by too much understanding. She sensed that Gert felt the same.

Gert frowned, gesturing with her head towards the front door. 'Hij is boos,' she said. 'He is angry. Why?'

'Ik weet het niet,' Jenny said. 'I don't know. It doesn't matter. Thank you for minding the children.'

Gert smiled and spoke another quick sentence in Dutch. Jenny couldn't understand all of it, but she thought she heard the word for 'play'. Dan was very probably seeking his own fun in the tavern by the docks.

For most of the lads, the novelty of having money for ale and rum, and the freedom to drink it as long as that money lasted, was almost as intoxicating as the drinks themselves. Carney was the only one who seemed immune. Jenny didn't know what he did with his money, but it wouldn't have surprised her to find it in a hole in the floor of his cottage, like the one that possibly still gaped in the Gwyn hut. Carney took a lot of teasing from the men, particularly Bruton, about his lack of head for drink. Jenny, though, was grateful. At least someone would get the rest of them home.

Women in Coepang didn't go to the tavern. Not the wives of merchants or those of the ranking natives, and certainly not those of the governor's staff.

'Believe me, my dear, you're lucky to avoid it,' Van Dalen had said to her. 'Full of sailors, deckhands and the like, that tavern. Rough men, Mrs Trelawney. Your husband, I dare say, could hold his own. But they would eat you alive.'

Jenny smiled and thanked him. She doubted the place would be any worse than the Plymouth taverns in which she'd fenced stolen trinkets, but of course she had no intention of acquainting the governor with this particular part of her history.

Dan, though, loved the tavern. Not just the rum, although that was welcome.

'He sits there, and the Coepang men stare at him,' Carney had told her. 'He smiles, nods, and buys some ale for those who seem most curious. Some of them speak English, and he tells them about the voyage, about the times he stopped the boat capsizing.' Jenny had been pleased to hear Dan had some praise coming to him, until Carney had said, 'All the time they tell him he was lucky to have such a companion.'

'Ah. He won't like that.'

'No. Those who say so do not receive any more ale from him.'

The last time Jenny had heard pounding on the door, it had been Howard Tippett bearing the body of her father. A few nights after the governor's party, it was Carney bearing the intoxicated form of the man who might or might not be her husband.

This was by no means the first time Dan had come home drunk. More nights than not, he would stumble in and breathe rum stink over her.

At the sound of a fist on wood, she rolled over to face the wall, throwing off a sheet that had become soaked with her sleeping sweat. She had never gotten out of bed when Dan came home drunk, and saw no reason to start now.

But the hammering continued – hammering in this house with no locks, hammering even though Dan and Carney would have had no trouble getting through the front door.

The hammering, she realised, was at the door to their bedroom.

'Jenny! Jenny, you have to get up!'

Not Dan's voice. Carney's.

'Would you stop it, John! You'll wake the children!'

This, in her view, was a great sin. She sat with them as they slept for an hour or more each night, listening to the little noises they made, loving the absence of pain and fear on their faces as sleep slowly brought them to health.

As she opened the door, she realised she had forgotten to put a robe over her nightdress. Not that this was really a concern for her – after more than two months in a small boat with Carney and the others, she had no modesty left to preserve.

Carney's teeth were clenched. Dan was draped over his shoulder, muttering and unsteady on his feet, but Carney had the clear eyes of a sober man. 'You'll have to get them up anyway, bring them into the kitchen,' he said. 'Wait till you hear what the idiot's done!'

He pushed past Jenny, half dragging Dan to the kitchen, where Dan tumbled into a chair, his upper body slumping across the table. Carney looked up sharply. 'I wasn't jesting, Jenny. You need to get the children.'

Dan had enough wits left to look up at Jenny through red-threaded eyes. 'Only said the truth.'

'Jenny, he's told them,' said Carney. 'Told them all. About us.'

CHAPTER 29

Their last escape had been planned. She'd had time to soak her mind in it, to follow threads of probabilities, to snip the ones that led to unacceptable destinations.

This escape would need to be headlong, frantic and silent – and immediate.

'Go!' she said to Carney. 'Get the others, bring them … to the jungle, I think. Yes, these trees just behind us. I'll meet you there. Don't stop to get food, clothes, anything. The jungle will give us what we need, but we have to go now.'

Carney nodded, then ran.

Dan had propped himself up on his elbows, staring at her.

'Get up,' she said, in a voice she did not own. The voice of somebody calm, measured.

'Don't have to, *my* house,' he said, and put his head back down.

She stalked over to him, grabbed his hair, pulled his head back and slapped his face. 'Get! Up!'

That got him to his feet, rubbing both the back of his head and his cheek where her hand had connected. 'Going to bed,' he said.

'Don't you understand? They will come for us! Somebody will be going to the governor right now, if they haven't already.'

'I'm going to bed,' Dan repeated.

'Go, then,' she called over her shoulder as she raced towards the children, who were mewling at the noise. 'You wake up in gaol, but I won't. I can't.'

She scooped Emanuel out of his bed. He was beginning to cry. Charlotte, though, was sitting up and looking at Jenny, saucer-eyed but not crying or questioning.

Charlotte had done this before.

'You've seen the monkeys,' Jenny said. 'The ones in the jungle, the ones who scurry through the trees, sometimes steal food in the market.'

Charlotte nodded.

'You're going to be a monkey now. Climb on my back, and we'll run like monkeys into the jungle.' Jenny turned, holding Emanuel, and Charlotte clambered onto her mother's back, the little arms around Jenny's neck nearly choking her.

She ran out of the house as fast as she could without the risk of falling and smashing Emanuel onto the flagstones. She didn't close the front door, and this time her daughter didn't ask her to.

As she turned towards the jungle she could see lights on the road. Coming closer.

She thought, or hoped, she and the children would be safe among the trees. She didn't want to go in deeper, not until daylight would help her pick a safe path. For now she would stay just inside the boundaries of the jungle, watching the lights march up to her front door.

She heard the yelling from inside the house, saw dark shapes drag someone out, heard her husband's cursing. And Detmer's voice, calling in a Dutch she was only beginning to understand. She heard a word that she thought meant close, or nearby.

There was no sign of Carney and the others, and probably just as well – the more of them crashing through the undergrowth, the greater their chance of being caught. But she couldn't stay just within the shelter of the trees. She would need to commit herself and her children to them.

She was familiar with this part of the jungle, knew the small paths which had been worn by generations of feet. She could afford, she thought, to go further in.

Emanuel, who had been quietened by her movement, was beginning to fidget and whimper as fern fronds scratched at his cheeks and unfamiliar noises sounded in the dark.

Jenny came to a small clearing, one she had been to before. Lowering herself down carefully onto a rock, she let Charlotte off her back as she pulled down the neck of her nightdress, giving Emanuel the only solace she knew would quiet him.

As she was feeding him, Charlotte quiet beside her, a hand clamped down onto her shoulder, and Detmer's voice said, 'I know the forest paths too, Mrs Trelawney.'

And then more dark. The kind that did not lift with the sun.

The others had been captured on the way to meet her in the jungle. It was their trajectory that had told Detmer where to look.

Sunlight dribbled in through slits in the walls of the cells beneath the castle, almost directly under the hall where the governor's party had been held. Enough light for Jenny to see Dan sitting on the floor in the corner, hugging his legs with his head on his knees. She and the children were on a bench nearby.

The other men lay, leaned or sat, moving only when necessary. They had exhausted themselves during the first hours in the cell, roaring at Dan, asking him why, calling him the murderer of them all. Bruton had walked over to Dan's corner and begun kicking him. No one tried to stop it, including Jenny, until Charlotte began to wail at the violence to her father. Perhaps she was too young, Jenny thought, to remember seeing him flogged. But perhaps the image was always there, shuttered behind the girl's eyes, maliciously popping out whenever her father groaned.

'You have put your children in a gaol,' Jenny said to him now. 'One they have done nothing to earn.'

He looked up at her, blank-faced, and returned his forehead to his knees.

Carney was leaning against the opposite wall.

'What happened?' she asked him.

He shook his head and sighed. 'This one fellow in the tavern – an English sailor, crew on a merchant ship I think, haven't seen him before – he said to Dan, "Must be nice to have a woman to save you."'

Dan groaned. Carney glared at him, and Bruton started across the cell towards him again. Langham managed to haul him back – another fight would win them no favours, if there were still favours to be had.

'And then Dan turned to this fellow,' said Carney, 'and asked if he'd ever had the courage to escape. If he'd brought everyone else through seas the size of houses, of hills. If he'd been quicker, brighter than the governor of an entire colony. And ... I'm sorry, Jenny ... if he'd done it all shackled to a woman he'd married in a sham ceremony.'

'I see. And did Dan enjoy his moment? The surprise on the man's face just before he got up to tell the guards? Or is this all truly for nothing?'

'I ... I couldn't say, Jenny. He went back to his drinking.'

Jenny, who had once seen Dan as a saviour, now looked on him as her executioner. She just hoped there might be some leniency for her children from the governor.

Van Dalen visited the cell a few hours later. He was holding a handkerchief to his nose. Charlotte sat up, smiled and waved. But when Van Dalen ignored her, walked over to Dan and cuffed him, the girl started to wail again. Dan grunted and keeled over sideways, making no attempt to break his fall.

'Please, Your Excellency,' Jenny said, as Charlotte clung to her, whimpering. 'My children –'

He looked at her with apparent indifference. 'Will stay where they are. As will you all, until the next English ship arrives. I will hand you to the captain.'

'Don't punish them!' said Jenny.

'Why not, for the sins of their mother?' he yelled. 'I offered you friendship, offered you clothes, offered you food and housing. Thinking you were a singular woman, a strong one. An honest one. And now! Laughter, laughter on the seas as the story spreads about the dupe of a governor. So you will look at these walls, and then you will look at the inside of the hull of the ship, but you will never look at me again.'

He turned to the door, nodding to the guard who opened it for him and closed it pointedly afterwards.

After Charlotte stopped crying, she lay on the bench with her head in her mother's lap. Jenny tried to feed Emanuel, but the milk suddenly would hardly come, so he alternated between listlessness and a wail that echoed off the walls.

Perhaps, Jenny thought, the next British ship to come into port would be a blessing. Perhaps its captain might take pity on her children, at least. Allow them fresh air, fresh food. No decent person would treat them as criminals.

The walk to the dock after two months in the cell, even under heavy guard, was almost transcendent. Jenny enjoyed being able to move freely and to inhale, without effort, the scents of flowers and cooking instead of shit. While she could, she drew in great gulps of air until she thought her ribs would crack. She knew what the inside of a hull smelled like, could see none of the hatches open on the ship that waited at the end of the dock.

The hold of the *Rembang* was worse than the *Charlotte* had been. That ship, at least, had been washed with quick lime on occasion, and the surgeon had shown an interest in keeping the convicts alive. *This* hold was damp and fetid, and so thick that it required an effort to breathe.

She had assumed the men would be chained. Perhaps she would be as well. But a sailor came over with small irons and bent towards Charlotte's ankles.

'She is a child!' said Jenny. 'For God's sake, what are you doing?'

'Captain's orders,' mumbled the sailor, refusing to look at the little girl as he fastened the irons.

And then the captain was there, tall and dark-haired and long-nosed and imperious and immaculate, his boots the only items in the hold with any shine. He was followed by another man, also in the dress of a captain, but scuttling, uncommanding, without hauteur.

'Captain!' said Jenny to the imposing man. 'You can't chain a child! Surely!'

He refused to look at her – not with the same discomfort that the sailor evidently felt, but with a clear indifference. He turned to the sailor. 'Half rations. No time on deck. No water for washing.'

'Andrews,' said the other captain, 'surely a cabin for the woman and children!'

'No,' said Andrews, 'no, Tennant, I think not. Punishment must be painful, otherwise it is not worthy of the name. And the creature clearly has little regard for the safety of her children, or she would not have taken them on such a journey.'

'I remind you, Andrews, that the *Rembang* is my vessel.'

'And I remind you that I have the authority to commandeer it, and have done so. If you object, take it up with the King.' Andrews turned and left, and Tennant hurried after him, leaving Jenny, chained to the ship beside her daughter, holding a quieter Emanuel.

The hold was shuttered and had clearly been thoroughly gone over with pitch, so no light came in. Over the past fortnight, Emanuel had gone silent and floppy. A fever had broken out on the *Rembang* and was afflicting even the paying passengers in their airy cabins. If it touched Emanuel, Jenny doubted he would survive.

Charlotte had cried for the first day. Big, desperate gulps. Jenny wanted to tell her to stop, please stop taking in this poisonous air. But it was the only air they had.

Now Charlotte only cried during storms. There had been one some time ago – a few days? A week? It had pushed the vessel onto one side and then the other, and Jenny had thought it might capsize them. She did not think anyone would come for them if the boat sank.

She'd had hope, at first. Hope that the captain was simply showing his strength; that she and the children would be lifted out of the dark. The guard must have seen this expectation in the way she lifted her head whenever he opened the cell door. He would shake his head. Occasionally, he snuck her more food or water than the captain would approve of.

'You need to know who you're dealing with,' he told her once. 'The navy's worst monster.'

Captain Andrews, the guard said, had been sent to round up those who had mutinied aboard the *Bounty* – the mutiny that Vorst had told Jenny and Dan about. No one had expected these men to be dealt with leniently. But no one had expected Captain Andrews, either.

He had a cage installed on the deck of his ship, the *Pandora*.

'We called it Pandora's box,' the guard told Jenny. 'We got some of the mutineers at Otaheite, dragged them from their new Polynesian wives and put them in the box, poor bastards.'

Andrews didn't like wasting time. He even sailed at night. So it was inevitable that he would eventually sail into a reef.

'We begged him to unlock the box,' the guard said. 'The prisoners were howling, rattling the bars. The water got to their ankles, their knees, and we thought he'd let them out then, that he was teaching them a lesson. But he forbade us to help them. Just before the cage went under, they were pressing their faces to its ceiling, screaming and begging and gulping air. He just watched until the screams stopped, until the cage was gone.'

The guard was silent for a moment.

'I'll do what I can for you,' he said. 'But do not expect mercy from the captain.'

Jenny spent her days in suspension, allowing her mind to lightly skim the reality in front of her, to sample it briefly before recoiling. Everything softened around the edges, fading in and out of relevance. The only sounds that could call her to full consciousness were those made by her children.

Then Dan started coughing. Not the occasional bark – they all did that, but violent wet convulsions.

She hadn't addressed a word to him since their first day in the hold. 'Do you feel you have the credit you deserve now?' she had asked.

She'd wanted, desperately, to lash out, to throttle him with the chains between her manacles. But she knew her energy might yet be needed in some other service.

Dan hadn't said anything, simply glanced at her and returned his forehead to his knees.

'You have credit now,' she'd said. 'Credit for our deaths, when they come.'

He was the man she had latched on to as a shield from the other men. The man she had grown to care for. Someone with a seamanship she could respect, and a strength to go with it. Someone who had treated Charlotte with kindness, never once letting her believe she was any less precious to him than his own legitimate child.

Someone Jenny now wanted to kill.

She gradually trained herself to stop noticing him. He was meat in the hold's corner. To look at him and think that this sack of flesh contained remnants of Dan Gwyn, to think that a fragment of him remained, was more than she could bear.

But the coughs that threatened to turn his lungs inside out were making it impossible for her to ignore him – and for her to ignore what might yet be there inside him.

'I can ask for water,' she said eventually. 'More food.'

'Will do you no good,' said a rasping voice from the darkness, perhaps Carney's. 'If they'll not give it for the little ones, they'll not give it to Dan.'

'I can ask,' she said, though she knew it was futile.

A few hours later, she was woken by a jab to her upper arm. Her eyes opened to the same blackness that they saw when closed.

Dan had managed to wriggle close enough to reach out a manacled hand and poke her. He was breathing heavily. Each gulp of air was filtered through the mess in his lungs. She had heard that kind of breathing before, and it never went on very long.

His hand felt down her side, along her lap, and rested on Emanuel's head. It had been a long time since the little boy had emitted anything more than a mewl.

'I'm sorry,' Dan said, and Jenny did not know whether he was speaking to her or his son.

He removed his hand, and she felt a weak squeeze on her shoulder.

'I'm sorry,' he said again.

She might, then, have fallen back to sleep. In the absence of light, and of anything resembling hope, the boundaries between consciousness and oblivion were disappearing.

Jenny was next brought to awareness by the rattle of the door as the guard brought in their tiny rations.

After she touched Emanuel's chest, which was rising and falling slowly, she felt around Charlotte's head until her hand was in front of the girl's mouth, feeling the light breath.

Jenny was blinking in the dim greyness that the guard had allowed to follow him in. That light, the hard bread and the trickle of water were her only proof that they weren't already in hell.

The guard placed a bowl into her hand, then moved to the side. He turned back after a moment, handing her another bowl. 'I'll not tell the captain,' he said. 'Not until the little ones have a chance to eat this. If he knew it wasn't needed, he'd have me take it back.'

She stared at him, picking out the blurred features in the small ration of light, tracing with her eyes the hard face which nevertheless bore something that looked like concern.

He remained standing there, perhaps waiting for her to say something.

When she didn't, he sighed. 'Get it into them, quick as you can. Lest they join him.' And he nodded in Dan's direction. 'I'll be back for him in an hour or two.'

Then Jenny understood. The bread and the water, desperately needed by everyone here, was no longer required by the one for whom it was destined.

A short time later, Emanuel's coughs began to mimic those that had taken his father.

Jenny was not allowed on deck for either burial. She did not know if her husband and son now occupied the same stretch of ocean, or if they were leagues apart.

Emanuel hadn't outlived his father by long. Less than a day, perhaps. His coughs had become stronger as he grew weaker, and she'd faded out of consciousness to their sound. She was next aware of holding a small, stiff bundle and feeling a wetness on her face.

She was not told if a man of God had said words over the dead. Had they been wrapped in shrouds and slid off a plank, or just thrown overboard like buckets of fish innards?

She didn't suppose it mattered to either of them. But she was distressed at the thought they might have been sent into the ocean separately, and desperately hoped that they had entered it together. She did not want Emanuel to be lonely.

CHAPTER 30

Jenny knew they must be in port. Out at sea, the usual sounds were the creaking of waves against wood, and ocean birds glorying in sunlight or being drenched by a storm – all inches from her head through a veil of wood, while she knew nothing of sunshine or storms.

She'd still heard coughing, too, though that was less common than it had been. Bruton and Harrigan and Langham had all been taken away. She had wept for them. Particularly Harrigan, a man of the earth who would never rest in it. She had even grieved for Bruton; this malaise, too small to be seen, had taken down one of the biggest men she knew.

Just her and Carney were left. And Charlotte, who occasionally cried for her father or her brother, but was mostly silent apart from coughs that were beginning to build. Sometimes Carney would sing her a rasping song. Jenny had no songs.

Now, there were other sounds. Shouts too distant to come from aboard the vessel. The faraway hooves of horses striking a ground Jenny had forgotten existed. Hatches being opened. And then the door of their cell rattling. Hands on the manacles. Carney was dragged to his feet, but the seaman who had come for them was far gentler with Jenny, and even more so with Charlotte. He glanced at the manacles on the little girl, shaking his head.

'Are we going home now?' asked Charlotte.

'I don't know where home is for you, lass,' the seaman said. 'But I hope you'll find kinder treatment here than you have had so far.'

Even outside, Jenny didn't know where they were. The sun punished her for her long absence from its grace by taking away her sight, leaving her blinking and shuffling and clanking. Urged along by a hand at her back, she reached down to Charlotte's hand and didn't find it.

'I have her,' the seaman said, and he grasped Jenny's hand and moved it up so that it rested on what felt like her daughter's head.

When Jenny's sight did return, she saw a child in the sailor's arms who was thinner than the one who had left Sydney Cove. The night they had fled, the night Charlotte had climbed onto Jenny's back, she had been wearing her embroidered white nightdress. She was wearing it still, but it was dark grey and torn. Her skin was covered with sores, and she had marks on her face where she'd scratched herself. Large clumps of her hair were missing. But she was still far more beautiful than any creature her mother had seen, and Jenny smiled.

Charlotte smiled back, showing fewer teeth than had been there before. Then her mouth contracted, opened, and let out a wet cough.

The seaman paused for a moment, and Jenny leaned in to her daughter. 'Not you, too,' she whispered. 'I promise, not you too.'

The sunlight was not theirs to keep. There was another hold, in a ship called the *Gorgon*. Jenny didn't see the captain before she left the light again, but he seemed a better sort than Andrews, as she and Charlotte were not shackled. They had more food, too. Narrow rods of light struck the floor from the partly open hatches, and she was given a dish of water and a cloth to bathe Charlotte's face.

Jenny did not look to her own appearance. Saw no point in washing. So the man who pulled open the cell door next morning gaped at her. He looked as though he was trying to convince himself that he was truly looking at a woman.

'Good God, Jenny. What have they done?'

She ran her eyes slowly up the man's legs, which were wrapped in almost impossibly white breeches, his torso a frame for the ubiquitous red coat. His face, though, was unique.

'You are not here,' she said.

The man knelt and ran his hand gently over what was left of Charlotte's hair, frowning as he had when they'd stood in the shallows together, hauling in lighter and lighter nets. As he had when Dan was flogged. Perhaps he had worn the same expression when he'd discovered their escape.

'I assure you, I am – although you barely are,' said Corbett. 'We will see what's to be done about that.'

Mr Corbett interceded with the captain to arrange a cabin where Jenny could care for Charlotte.

They were, she learned, in Cape Town. The port near which Charlotte had been born. And a staging place between England and its furthest satellite in Sydney Cove. All marines heading to the new colony stopped here; all those returning did likewise.

Jenny wasn't the only woman aboard. The *Gorgon* was taking a detachment of marines home, and it carried several paying passengers and their wives. A few of them would come up to Jenny while she was walking Charlotte around the deck to see the sun. They would put out a hand, perhaps to stroke the little girl, and then withdraw it. Jenny could only assume that she owed one of them for the plain, clean dress she now wore, and perhaps for Charlotte's clean nightdress. Jenny would smile at them, but would not speak. All of her words belonged to Charlotte.

Soon after they came on board, Corbett sat with Jenny as she spooned dribbles of soup between Charlotte's cracked lips.

'Governor Lockhart was furious,' he said. 'The last time I saw him like that was when he argued with the Dutch sea captain – who had a hand in your plot, I am presuming?'

'I'm not to say,' said Jenny. Corbett was speaking as though they were old friends. She knew, though, that she was a prisoner, as was her daughter, in a confinement that had taken her husband and her son.

'The judge advocate thought Dan had planned it all – that you had found out about it and blackmailed him to take you.'

Jenny chuckled, a rustling without any joy in it.

He was silent for a moment, then asked, 'You are not going to tell me the how of it, are you?'

'I will be facing a court on my return, Mr Corbett. And a noose, in all probability. I would not wish to put you in a position where you had to testify in the case for ending my life.'

He nodded, then stood. 'I cannot come again, you know. Cannot be seen talking with you. But I wanted to ...' He cleared his throat. 'Wanted you to know how extraordinary you are. All of you.'

'We failed,' said Jenny, 'and the most innocent among us now lies under the water somewhere south of here.'

'Yes, and officially I must celebrate your failure,' Corbett said. 'But you have done what few could. The captain of the *Bounty* made a shorter journey to Coepang, but he was a highly trained mariner. To do what you did – well, you have miscarried, but it was in an heroic struggle for liberty.'

He stood, saluted her, and left.

Mr Corbett kept his distance after that, though she suspected she had his intercession to thank for the continued use of her cabin.

She would lie in her bunk, cuddling her daughter's thin body. It felt like a collection of sticks that shuddered and moaned through night after night, as the small brow grew hotter, sweated and then stopped sweating.

Charlotte's whisper, amplified by the night, reached Jenny over the creaking timbers. 'Ma, I want to see the sea dragons.'

'You will, duckling.'

'Will you take me?'

'I might be … somewhere else. Someone would take you, though, I promise. You have family where we are going. They are waiting to take you on sea dragon rides.'

'Emanuel is across the seas, then,' said Charlotte.

'He is across another sea, duckling. One we can't travel on, not yet.'

Jenny stroked her daughter's cheek in the darkness, felt wetness there, then withdrew her hand as waves of coughs came back and made words impossible. The tide went out, and Charlotte was left wheezing. Jenny held her and rocked her until she descended into a gurgling sleep.

When sunlight drizzling through the hatch woke Jenny the

next morning, a stiffness was in her arms, and Charlotte had gone to Emanuel's sea without her.

The tears would not come. The wails were so insistent they'd bunched in Jenny's throat, but never emerged into the air.

The other women on board stood in a knot behind her, taking care not to get too close in case her despair became theirs.

She didn't listen to the words the ship's reverend said over the small shrouded form. Nor did she wish to. Entreaties to a god who would allow this were worthless.

The plank was tipped, there was a splash, and Jenny watched the small white form sink slowly out of view.

Then there were whispers. 'She's not crying,' one of the merchant's wives said to another. 'She must be a hard woman.'

Jenny turned. She wanted the woman to know she had been heard.

She was young, this lady, little more than a girl. She held a baby tightly to herself as if to prevent it sliding off the same plank that Charlotte had just travelled down.

'Keep holding him,' Jenny said. 'It will do no good, if it's not fated to – he will be taken from your grasp anyway. But while you can, keep holding him.' She turned to the captain. 'As I no longer have a sick child to care for, you'll be putting me back below, I think.'

'You may remain in the cabin for a time,' he said in a thick voice.

'I do not want to.'

Jenny turned, walked to the hatch that led down to the hold and waited until it was opened for her, as she knew it would be.

CHAPTER 31
London, July 1792

This courtroom was far less grand than the hall in which she had been sentenced to death. A functional wooden room with no arched windows, no aisles to accommodate a procession of judges.

The outcome, though, might yet be the same.

'Have a care for your immortal soul, madam.' He was the second judge to invoke her soul, which seemed to have far more value to the authorities than her body.

'You think I might lie to avoid the noose?' Jenny said. 'I welcome it. I beg you to hang me.'

The murmur of voices behind her crested, then ebbed.

'We are not speaking of hanging,' the stipendiary magistrate said. 'Not at this stage.'

Jenny nodded. She knew they weren't. And she knew why.

At the moment, the name Jenny Gwyn was being passed in whispers among washerwomen at their cauldrons, lords on their hunt, and just about everyone else. Her escape, her capture, all that she had lost. It was bundled up and brushed down and flattened onto the pages of newspapers which used her children's deaths to turn a profit, while their souls were currency in coffee house gossip.

In Penmor's church, the reverend read the *Western Flyer* to anyone who cared to hear and could not read for themselves, while the wet stones of the nave were still digesting the whispered gossip from the last service. She knew that newspapers usually thundered against people like her, calling for their excision from the civic body. But not now. Now, they had found someone of exactly the right shape around which to build a scaffold of martyrdom and heroism. Someone to be pitied and admired all at once. Someone who could bring people close to danger, without them actually having to smell it.

Several of the papers had taken to calling for mercy for this woman who had risked so much, gained so much and lost so much.

The problem was, Jenny didn't want mercy. And in any case, she doubted she would get it from the expressionless magistrate who'd been sent to interview her, and from there to decide what on earth was to be done with a woman suddenly too popular to hang.

'Do you know, Mrs Gwyn, that you would have been free soon, had you stayed in Sydney Cove.'

'Freedom is not possible in Sydney Cove, sir,' Jenny said.

'Well, whatever your beliefs, why take such a risk with your life? Your children's lives?'

Jenny had, over the years, practised bringing a blankness to her features, smoothing away all emotion when confronted with insults from magistrates, or the horror of their decisions. This talent, though, had deserted her. The muscles in her face clenched and contorted at the mention of her children.

This must have been apparent to the magistrate. He looked over her shoulder, over the heads of those who had crowded into the courtroom, to a functionary standing near the door. 'A chair for Mrs Gwyn,' the magistrate called, 'if you please.'

Jenny turned briefly, getting the impression of a tall, thin man in a black coat and white breeches. 'Sir,' said the man, 'it is not customary for prisoners to …'

'Kindly do not lecture me on what is customary and what isn't, Mr Binder. A chair for the prisoner.'

So one was brought, held aloft by the disgruntled Binder over the heads of the voyeuristic mass. It was rickety and probably the worst one the clerk could find.

'You must not consider me insensible to everything you have suffered,' the magistrate said. 'I am simply endeavouring to arrive at the facts. To understand why you left as you did. You are, I apprehend, familiar with boats, with the ocean?'

Jenny nodded.

'So you knew the dangers, yet you chose to face them. Why?'

'Because to stay, sir, would have been more dangerous than to go. And before that place took our bodies, it would have taken our souls.'

The gaolers, she noticed, handled her gently for the most part. They seemed to be treating John Carney well too. He had been waiting outside the courtroom as she left, and they had nodded to each other. It seemed a ridiculously impersonal greeting for two people who had been mashed together on a small boat for so long.

'You may find a bit more comfort when you get back,' one of the guards said, as he helped to lift her manacled feet into the cart that would return her to Newgate Prison.

'Oh? Had I not comfort enough?'

He chuckled. 'Your story has brought a fever upon people. Some of them, see, have taken up a collection. There's a packet of money been delivered this morning to the warden. Has your name on it, to be used to buy whatever comforts you wish. Food, bedding. You might find things more bearable.'

'Very kind,' she said. She doubted, though, that the money would make any difference one way or the other. She had been scoured from the inside. Feeling joy at the prospect of more food, more comfort, would have required the capacity to feel.

The journey up the Thames in an open boat, from the *Gorgon* to Newgate, had been the longest period Jenny had sat outside in several months. The boat wasn't slow enough for her liking, but it made a sedate progress along the river. It was the first time she had seen London. Sydney Cove, she had thought, was crowded: certainly it had more people than it could support. And Coepang was less densely packed, though she hadn't yet seen every face twice by the time she was arrested.

She had never seen as many people as those lining the Thames – hadn't known so many existed. Navvies and ladies and sailors and clerks and whores, calling out to one another or lifting their noses to avoid the worst of the river's stench, laughing in small knots or walking alone. And none of them paid the slightest heed to the woman in the little boat.

They paid more attention once she was locked away. The gilded theatres and the gilded actors, the parks and promenades, clearly weren't providing enough entertainment. Because when they got bored, some of the more idle in the city decided to go to Newgate. They would look at the prisoners, exclaim over their degradation, openly discuss why this person or that had committed their crime, remark that a particular man had the face of a murderer, while another the demeanour of a brawler.

There would often be a coin or two for Mr Arum, the gaoler, who also took money from the prisoners to remove manacles, provide soap, increase rations.

Since Jenny had been in Newgate, the coins collected by the gaoler had increased.

The spectators were waiting when she was brought back from the court, and she heard a collective intake of breath, then a gasp as she was led back into her cell. Some of those who had read her story had been shocked or thrilled by it, deciding that they must see this woman. See if she looked lucky or heroic, see if the journey had left marks on her face, on her body. See, perhaps, if she was even human.

So Jenny would sit in her cell in the Female Quarter, looking at the floor as fine shoe leather and the hems of skirts moved in and out of view. Ladies clutched the arms of gentlemen and held handkerchiefs to their faces, staring without remorse or apology. Jenny found it tiring to see their incomprehension at the small, dirty, sallow woman with matted hair where they had expected an Amazon. She rarely looked at their faces. When she did, she would choose one person at random and stare, silently daring them to find an answering spark in the large grey eyes that punctuated the grimy face, challenging them to reconcile their vision of the now famous adventuress with the woman in front of them.

For the most part, though, she ignored them. The wardens were making money off her notoriety; she would not assist them by acknowledging the existence of those who paid so that they could breathlessly tell friends, *I saw her, yes, a wild creature, clearly depraved.*

For Jenny, it didn't end when the paying customers left. The other women crammed into her cell were equally fascinated, and saw the departure of the voyeurs as their signal to pepper her with questions. But instead of staring, they asked – and asked and asked, questions that gave Jenny more information about them than she ever gave back.

The tarts, for example, asked about the size of the natives' members, and how many of the marines had been fucking the convict women. Jenny tried, at first, to answer them flatly, factually. 'Haven't seen that many male members, but the natives look to be around the same as everyone else.' 'There were a few affairs here and there, it happens at the end of the world.' 'Me? I had a husband. And family. I had no wish to look anywhere else.'

And they would cackle, and ask her to confess to profaning affairs with the governor, or his second-in-command, or one of the natives. When they asked about her family, she turned and faced the wall and would not say anything more.

For some of them, she suspected, it didn't matter what she said. Those who earned their living on their backs would say to their customers, as a sweetener, that they had heard from the famous Cornish woman that the natives of Sydney Cove were three times the size of any Englishman, and voracious.

One girl never asked about affairs and male members. Helen was in Newgate for taking a shawl from her mistress. She was, possibly, a little simple: she had a tendency to view her fellow humans as genial, kind beings who were sometimes forced into unkind acts by circumstances.

Jenny found it soothing, restful, to talk to somebody who didn't see sex as the most interesting aspect of the colony on the other side of the world. Helen asked about the animals and the birds in the trees, who Jenny's friends had been, what she had eaten, what her favourite time of day was.

When the gaoler shooed paying customers out before he delivered the rations, Helen said it was because he wanted the women to have privacy. 'It's just so we can eat in peace,' she explained earnestly to Jenny.

One of the other women said, 'He cares about our privacy so much he is going to get rid of people with money in their pockets, but at the same time he's got us all crammed into this one cell. You're a daft bitch, you are.'

Jenny had stood, walked over to the woman, and slapped her across the face. 'Plenty of others to call us names,' she said. 'Don't need you doing it.'

There was a more prosaic reason for the gaolers to clear out gawkers before the rations were brought in. Since Jenny's arrival, there had been so many of them that the gaoler would have had to turn himself sideways and hold food above his head to get through.

And now, back in the cell after her hearing, after the starers had goggled and had their fill, he did the same.

She didn't immediately notice the male visitor who remained. Not until he spoke.

'You might not care if you hang,' he said, 'but personally I think it would be a terrible pity.'

She looked up. He had been fetched a chair that looked far more sturdy than the one which had been brought for her that day. Perhaps he had trouble standing – a silver-topped cane rested between his legs. His waistcoat was made of white silk embroidered with gold thread, and perhaps it cost even more than the cane, given the amount of fabric that was required to cover his paunch.

Jenny had almost forgotten what jowls looked like, but this stranger had them in abundance.

He was the kind of person whose death stood politely behind the door like a servant with a tray. Present out of necessity, but easy to ignore. When it eventually did step into the drawing room, its arrival would be marked by a genteel funeral with restrained mourners.

Jenny's death sat with her in prison, whispering promises of public putrefaction. It had walked in shrunken skin beside her at Sydney Cove. It sat with her on the boat, eyeless and bloated. And it had crouched just behind the horizon in Coepang.

'You can come and keen at my grave, then,' Jenny said to the man, 'but if they've a mind to hang me there is nothing you can do about it.'

'Dear girl, I'm quite sure you didn't get all this way, overcome what you have, by making assumptions. Please don't start now – they are very tiresome things.'

Jenny was transfixed by the movement of his jowls as he spoke. They seemed to add depth to a voice that was low and soft: the voice of a man who did not have to yell to be heard. The voice of a man whom others stopped speaking for.

'I'm not forcing you to stay here and listen to my assumptions or anything else,' she said. 'You are at liberty to go, God rot you.'

'As shall you be,' said the man. 'If you trust me.'

'I have encountered, sir, a great many people since leaving England. I might not have letters, but I'm not a stupid woman, and one thing I have noticed – people who ask you to trust them are the least trustworthy.'

The man threw back his head and laughed so that his belly shook in its skein of silk and gold, and the timbers of the chair supporting him creaked.

Jenny had been chained and starved and paraded before the

court and jammed into a cell and used as entertainment. She would not be laughed at. She turned her back, sat down, and bent all her effort towards ignoring him.

The chair timbers creaked again as his laughter subsided. He was getting up, then. So he was capable of it.

She heard the clink of metal against the bars of the cell, perhaps the buttons of his waistcoat or the top of his cane.

And she heard something else. Whispering. She looked to the side and saw Helen and some of the other women huddled together, looking at the visitor, looking at her, and whispering. She raised her eyebrows at Helen, a silent request for information.

The girl sidled over to her, moving slowly as though it was an offence for them to speak together, as though she might be caught and have her rations halved.

'You don't know who he is,' said Helen.

'Of course I don't,' said Jenny.

Helen smiled. 'It's all right, I didn't either. But Harriet over there' – she inclined her head towards a spindly girl with fading freckles, red hair and a chin that had never reached its full potential; a girl who had been parlour maid until a brooch went missing – 'he used to visit the house of Harriet's master, you see. Quite famous, he is. A writer. And a lawyer.'

'Then I'm sure he won't have any trouble finding something other than us to entertain him,' whispered Jenny.

The man had been silent during their quiet conversation. He could not have heard what they were saying, but she had the odd feeling he was giving them the chance to say it.

'I am sorry,' he said when she turned around. 'I was not laughing at you, dear lady. It's simply that what you're saying is utterly true.'

'You find the truth amusing?'

'I find it sublime. I laugh with joy when I encounter it.'

'Now that you have encountered it, I presume you will be off.'

'Oh no, not yet. We have a transaction to discuss, you and I.'

'I am not yet that desperate, sir. And you strike me as the type who would be able to afford somebody who didn't come with a lice colony.'

The man blushed, making the thin red veins in his cheeks less visible. She had the impression it wasn't something he did frequently. 'I did not mean – oh my dear, no, I must be more careful, not that sort of transaction. Do forgive me.'

Jenny would be damned if she would forgive him, despite his blushes. She continued staring, returning to him the looks she had been given by others over the past few weeks.

He cleared his throat, perhaps still a little wrongfooted by the misunderstanding. Good.

'My name, by the way, is Richard Aldred,' he said.

'Told you,' Harriet hissed to Helen.

'And now we've established what I don't want,' he said, 'perhaps I should tell you what I do want.'

'If you like,' she said. 'I doubt I'll be in a position to give it to you, though.'

'We shall see. I am, you understand, a lawyer. Among other things.'

'I have no money for lawyers. There was a collection, I was told, but all the money is gone to the gaolers.'

'I do not seek payment from you. What I seek is your freedom.'

It was the cruellest statement he could have made. Freedom to live in a world without her children. Freedom to desperately seek her sister, her family, perhaps to find they no longer wanted anything to do with her.

'As do I, along with the fairies which are said to dwell in the corner of the cell.'

'It is not, Mrs Gwyn, such an impossibility as you might assume,' he said. 'Your freedom, that is. Not the fairies. I do believe – given the prevailing sentiment – that a strong case might be made for clemency. Even for a pardon. By one with the right contacts, of course.'

'And you would be such a one, I suppose?'

'I would, as a matter of fact. Went to school with the home secretary, for a start. Didn't get along with him – dreadfully boring man, but that doesn't matter. He will see me, and he will hear me. And he might even listen to me, when I say that you have been punished more than sufficiently to atone for your crimes. If your treatment at the hands of that blasted Andrews was not enough, there is your family –'

Jenny wailed, and threw herself at the bars harder than she had seen anyone else do, in a place where desperation often forced flesh to hurl itself into metal.

'You will not use my family,' she said, putting her face close to his through the metal, noticing absently that a drop of spittle had landed on his cheek. 'You will not refer to them, think about them, or talk about them. You will not take the death of my children and make it into a tool to unlock my bars, so you can boast about how you were the clever man who freed me. There!'

Aldred frowned. 'I am sorry, truly. It was not my intention … But of course, I will do as you wish. I do beg you, though, to consider my request.'

'I'm still not entirely sure, Mr Aldred, what your request is.'

'Simply this – allow me to represent you. Plead for you. Try for clemency.'

She turned her back and walked as far as she could into the cell's corner. 'It is a cruelty you do me, sir. You give me hope where none exists. I have already seen everything I had hoped to preserve taken. And you think I still wish to preserve my life?'

'I hope you do.'

'It's easy to hope on a full belly. It is easy to hope in a feather bed. It is something, though, in which I no longer have any interest. Please leave me.'

'But Mrs Gwyn –'

'I will not buy whatever it is that you are selling. I have yet to see a man of your position act from pure charity. You profess some concern for my circumstances – if you do not wish to cause me further pain, you will leave, now.'

He opened his mouth, closed it again, nodded and left. She heard the gaoler call him 'my lord' on the way out.

'Not the shrewdest thing you could have done,' said Harriet.

'I am finished doing shrewd things,' said Jenny. 'They led my children under the waves, and they led me here.'

CHAPTER 32

The courtroom was even more crowded than it had been the previous day. Court officers had to go ahead of Jenny as she was led in, to make a path for her to reach the dock.

The same chair on which Jenny had sat yesterday was waiting for her today, and the magistrate gestured her to it.

'All rise,' Mr Binder said in a high, reedy voice. He visibly straightened as he said it – this was probably the best part of his day.

The magistrate gestured for everyone to sit, at least those who had seats. Many were leaning against the courtroom walls or crouching in the aisle.

Jenny stayed standing. The magistrate looked over at her, and nodded.

'I prefer to stand, sir,' she said. 'If you approve, of course.'

Binder gave her an even more poisonous glare: he had carried a chair for nothing.

'As you wish,' said the magistrate. 'You will be aware,' he said, turning towards the throng, 'that Jenny Gwyn, also known as Trelawney, is charged with escaping transportation, an offence which carries the penalty of death by hanging. We are here to determine whether she should be committed for trial. In my view, that requires determining whether the punishment she has received has already exceeded the severity of her crime.'

He asked her about the seaworthiness of the boat, and she told him of pitch and turtle fat. He asked her about food, and she spoke of palm hearts and rice. He asked how her children had stayed aboard, and she told him about ropes and crushing hugs.

She did not speak of boredom and terror holding hands with each other, of the madness that nibbled at the edge of the boat. She did not tell him about the bickering and the salt sores, or of her mistrust of her own eyes when Coepang came into view.

She tried to avoid mentioning Charlotte and Emanuel as much as possible. She did not want to share them, and was fearful that mentioning their names would lead the magistrate to question her further about them. But eventually it couldn't be avoided any longer.

'I'm afraid, Mrs Gwyn, that I must ask you about the circumstances of the death of your family.'

The crowd was all held breath and tension. This is what they had come for. Tales of turtle fat and ropes were nice appetisers, but the crowd fed best on loss and horror.

Jenny looked at a few of them, one by one, staring just long enough to let them know she had seen their avidity: a pinch-faced matron, a balding merchant, a young, rich scrap of swagger and stupidity. *Why should you still grow?* she thought. *Why should you still be breathing?*

Then she did sit down.

'They died, sir,' she said. 'Surely that is all the court needs to know.'

'Perhaps it is,' the magistrate said. 'But we will not know that with any certainty, I'm afraid, until you are able to speak of the details.'

'There is one detail I will gladly share with you,' she said, standing again and leaning forward in the dock. 'You treat children as though they had committed their parents' crimes. That is why my children died. They had the misfortune to be born to me.'

'Perhaps you should have thought of that before you robbed someone.'

An anonymous voice from near the back of the room. She looked towards it and saw Richard Aldred raising himself on his cane from his chair, craning to see if he could identify the man who had spoken.

She would later think back on the interjection with gratitude. Because at that moment, the shell in which she had crammed herself cracked open. It spilled out and consumed her – the pain at the loss of her children. And the anger.

'You, then, would have had them chained below decks?' she yelled to the back of the room, hoping the words found their mark. 'Denied them food and water, kept them in darkness for months? When the fever came, there was no hope. They were not strong enough. Because they had been treated like murderers, like thieves, when their only crime was not to have been born to a rich woman.'

She stopped talking, feeling dizzy, aware of the rise and fall of her chest as it accommodated the air she was suddenly ravenous for.

'Ask yourself,' she said, 'whoever you are – a brave soul who is content to yell from the back and not show anyone their face – ask yourself if you would have done the same. And if you would, I will most certainly meet you when we are both in hell.'

Binder was glaring, now, shaking his head. The magistrate was gaping.

Jenny lowered her head. It would come now, she thought. The reprimand from the magistrate, followed by his order that she be committed for trial. There was no question of her innocence. Her crime, escaping from transportation, was as public as a crime could be.

She half hoped he would hang her.

He banged his gavel and cleared his throat. 'It is my direction that Jane Gwyn do not stand trial for escaping from transportation, that she instead be returned to Newgate to serve an appropriate sentence to be determined.'

He banged the gavel again, and sat down, as more in the crowd – those who hadn't already been standing – rose to their feet and cheered the substitution of almost certain hanging with almost indefinite imprisonment.

When she was brought back to Newgate, and guided back into the cell with the other women, Aldred was already waiting for her. He was sitting in the same chair, holding the same cane, although he clearly had more than one waistcoat – this one was blue.

'Pardon me, my lord?' said the gaoler as he squeezed past Aldred's knees to open the cell.

'Oh, my lord, is it?' Jenny said, dropping a mock curtsy.

'Yes, as it happens, not that it's relevant.'

'Yes, riches and shelter and food are only irrelevant to those who have them. Why do you even work, lawyering or anything else, when you're a lord?'

'Not much money in it these days, I'm afraid,' said Aldred.

'Even less in fishing.'

'Yes, I imagine so. And none at all in being a prisoner. Which is why I'm here. You did well today. Wonderful performance.'

'It was not a performance.'

'I did not mean to imply … never mind. I hope you recon-
sidered, that you will allow me to represent you.'

'In exchange for?'

'In exchange for nothing.'

'You asked me to trust you, Mr Aldred. I do not trust anyone
who asks for nothing.'

The joviality had drained out of the spiderwebbed cheeks, the
darting blue eyes.

'Understandable, and entirely wise,' he said. 'And you're right,
of course. I will get something out of such an arrangement.'

Harriet and some of the other girls snickered. They were
enjoying being watchers for a change.

Aldred glanced at them, looked away immediately and squared
his shoulders. 'You will probably dismiss what I'm about to say –
however, I assure you it's the truth. I will get the satisfaction of
knowing justice has been done.'

She turned away. 'I'm sorry, Mr Aldred, but you're too pompous
to be believed.'

'You are a maddening woman, you know. And you're not the
first to make that observation. Very well then, complete honesty.'

'Has your honesty been incomplete, up to now?'

'Very possibly, yes, actually, although I wouldn't have characterised it as such if you'd asked me even a few short minutes ago.
But what will I get out of it? It was true, what I just told you:
satisfaction. But also, and I will deny this if you ever tell anyone,
I do quite enjoy a certain amount of notoriety, and my ability to
obtain mercy for you – I do assure you that ability exists, by the
way – will do no harm to my reputation.'

Jenny turned around slowly. 'You seek fame.'

'Already have it, dear girl. But it drains away if you don't
continually replenish it.'

'I can trust that,' she said. 'I can trust an exchange.'

'If you insist on seeing this as a transaction, I am satisfied.'

'And if you fail?'

'I will come in there with you and look for the fairies in the corner myself.'

'There are conditions, of course,' Jenny said.

'Of course.'

'One, actually,' Jenny said. 'What you do for me, you also do for John Carney.'

'Easily done. Already done, in fact. I came to see him before I saw you. Wanted to get the measure of things, you see. Asked him what you were like.'

'And what did he tell you?'

'That you are braver, stronger and more resolute than the men in that boat combined. That you were the most remarkable woman he had ever met. And I had no reason to doubt him, but I can see that he did not go nearly far enough.'

'Watch him,' said Harriet, after he'd left. 'He is one for the ladies. Propositioned me in my master's house. Did it as easily as breathing, and with as little thought.'

'Very little he can do in here,' said Jenny. 'And I doubt he'd appreciate you watching and commenting on his performance.'

Harriet's face twisted in disgust. 'I'd appreciate it even less,' she said. 'If he means to free you, though, there's a good chance of it. He knows people. And is known.'

'Known as what?'

'A writer. A drinker and a gambler and a womaniser. And a taker of hopeless cases.'

But Aldred didn't seem to believe that Jenny's case was hopeless. He visited almost daily, telling her about what he'd been doing on her behalf. He spoke in the same tone she imagined he would use while sitting in his club, a port in his hand, conversing with a colonel about his tour of duty in Madras.

'Wrote to the home secretary,' Aldred said to her one day. 'Made the point – he'd be aware of it anyway, but it doesn't hurt to remind people – that the magistrate decided not to commit for trial because he felt that due punishment had already been exacted. Under that logic, there is no point in keeping you here.'

'There is, though, isn't there?' said Jenny. 'People know who I am. That's why I'm not standing trial, not being hanged.'

'Highly likely,' he said.

'So I would think it would suit them very well to have me here. Until they forget. Until I become easier to hang.'

Aldred shook his head. 'You are the most extraordinary ... but we are not going to let them forget, are we? Believe me, Mrs Gwyn, they are already singing songs about you. No, it's true! Some of the songs, it has to be said, are a bit indelicate. But they are sung in taverns in drunken voices and on street corners, perhaps even in wealthy homes, although the owners of those homes would never admit it. The people are calling you the Girl from Botany Bay.'

'The Girl from Botany Bay. Is nothing to be trusted anymore?'

'Nothing ever was. Why do you object to it?'

'I never set foot on the shores of Botany Bay.'

She had heard the water lapping against those shores, had heard the shouts of Dan and the others as they went ashore and tried to make the place yield something more than rocks. She felt a sudden astonishment that she had travelled to the other end of the world and back again, and lived for three years in a cove from which she could have walked, with some difficulty, to Botany Bay, yet never been there.

'None of it matters, Mrs Gwyn,' Aldred said. 'Few people here will care about the distance between Sydney Cove and Botany Bay, and whether you left a footprint on the shore of one or the other. What matters is that they now have a name for you. One which is exotic, one people will remember. One we will make them remember.'

'Fame drains away if it's not replenished, you told me,' she said. 'They will forget, in time.'

'Not for a time yet. I will be bending all my efforts to reminding those who have power over your fate that it doesn't do to hang a brave heroine, or to leave her mouldering in gaol.'

Moulder, though, she did. When other visitors came in, very occasionally she would turn, sometimes even smile if somebody looked particularly friendly. For the most part, though, she faced the wall.

Until the gaoler said, 'They came to see your face, my lovely. Thems the ones that pay for fresh bedding and better food. If they stop coming, and stopped paying – well, you'd be back to sleeping on a wooden board.'

So she would face the crowd, but she would not perform for them.

'I had an appointment with the home secretary this morning,' Aldred told her.

He was such a regular presence, now, that a chair was kept permanently for him, and he'd reached an arrangement with the gaoler to come and go as he pleased.

'Yes. Probably at the same time as my appointment with the Queen,' Jenny said.

He looked at her sharply. 'Do not mock me. Question me, by all means. But do not insult me by doubting that I'm doing everything I can.'

She felt oddly chastened. He was, after all, bending a lot of his efforts towards gaining her freedom, without asking for payment.

'And your appointment with the home secretary,' she said, 'how did it go?'

'It didn't, as matter of fact. I waited for an hour – no sign of the man. He was like that at Oxford as well, unreliable. I did, actually, leave a rather sternly worded letter expressing my disappointment, for all the good that will do.'

'Will you try to see him again?'

Aldred nodded. 'I even went to his wife, you know. Used to be a lively girl, gone a bit sour now. I asked her to plead your case with him, and she told me she makes it a policy not to discuss such things. You should have seen the mouth on her. She looked as though she was trying to prevent a bee from escaping.' He stared at Jenny expectantly.

He wants me to laugh, she thought. *To shake my head and say he's a dreadful rogue, but at least he tells a good story.* 'I could not care less, Mr Aldred, about the home secretary's wife and whether she has a bee imprisoned in her mouth.'

The gaoler, ever near, walked over. 'You will refer to his lordship as "my lord",' he snapped.

'I will refer to him as I please,' said Jenny. 'Do not forget who I am. And do not think that a lecture in manners from you is the most frightening thing I face.'

The gaoler was looking at her quietly, probably weighing up

whether a visible, swift punishment would win him favour with the illustrious visitor.

'Please don't worry about it, Francis,' said Aldred. 'I don't stand on ceremony, as you know – I find all of that lordship stuff rather irritating, if I'm honest.'

Of course, Jenny thought. *He's found out the man's name and will use it at every opportunity.*

'No one will forget you, Jenny,' said Aldred, after the gaoler had walked away. 'If we are going to dispense with the ceremony, I would feel better using your given name, as we are embarked on this adventure together. Have you any objection?'

'None. Assuming of course you'll allow me to call you by your first name.'

He laughed. 'Seems fair. You may call me Richard. Try to avoid it in front of the gaoler, though. The man seems a little sensitive about rank. Often the way with those who have a small measure of power over the powerless. But you are not powerless, Jenny. You are simply resting, preparing for the next escape.'

CHAPTER 33

Jenny did not feel as though she was resting. She felt as though she was rotting.

Aldred went away for a few weeks to visit his ailing wife. Without his constant presence, she noticed her ration slowly dwindling.

'The money's running out, you see,' Mr Arum said. 'Not as many coming.'

She had, actually, noticed a reduction in visitors. The fewer who came, the less frequently her bedding was changed. Sores appeared on her skin. More than once she heard people asking the gaoler for their money back, refusing to believe this scrap had defeated the ocean.

'What would his lordship say?' she asked Mr Arum as the bread got staler and smaller.

'His lordship isn't here.'

The next morning, when the dwindling crowd was let in, they found the women lying on their bedding, facing the walls and moaning. No amount of yelling from Mr Arum would make them move, and he was chastised by a few of the visitors for cruelty.

That night, the rations improved again. Even before they arrived, though, the women seemed miraculously recovered.

'Your doing, I'll wager,' Mr Arum said to Jenny.

'Me? No. I will say, though, if you're selling something, best to make sure your wares are in good order.'

Aldred opened the door casually, as if he had last visited yesterday, and looked around for the chair that had long since been removed.

Jenny ran to the bars, so that some of those who'd come to look at the women stumbled back, perhaps thinking she intended to attack them.

Even with the reduced crowd, Aldred had trouble reaching her. She had assumed he had been exaggerating his fame, even when Harriet had said he was well known. Now, though, she could see he may have played it down. As he politely asked people to excuse him, and then pushed his way past them without giving them a chance to get out of the way, she heard an intake of breath from one young lady, a gasp from an older man standing near her.

'Aldred! Extraordinary,' one man said to the young woman on his arm. 'I had heard ... But there are so many rumours, you know. I didn't think there was anything in them.'

Mr Arum came in after Aldred, stuffing something into his pocket. 'All right, all right, we need everyone to leave,' he said. 'We have a legal representative in consultation here. Very private.' And he began to usher people towards the door.

'Should we clear out as well?' yelled Harriet.

Aldred stood by the bars, bouncing on the balls of his feet. She had seen Dan do that, when he was waiting to tell of a particularly good catch.

'I did, as I promised, bombard the poor home secretary with letters pleading for your pardon. The secretary to the colonies, too, and every lord and member of the House of Commons I could think of who might have some influence over the man.'

'I congratulate you.'

'You will, when you hear about the letter I received this morning.'

He lifted a piece of paper, cleared his throat, and took a ridiculous amount of time adjusting his spectacles. 'There are some niceties,' he said. 'And then it says: "whereas some favourable circumstances had been humbly presented to us on Jane Gwyn's behalf" – I need not tell you who presented those favourable circumstances, need I?'

'No, and I'll welcome hearing about it as soon as I know what the letter says.'

'Very well, very well. The letter says that these favourable circumstances have "induced us" – that's the King, although it's really the home secretary, of course – "to extend our grace and mercy unto her" – that's you – "and to grant her our free pardon for her crime. Our will and pleasure therefore is that you cause Jane Gwyn to be forthwith discharged out of custody and that she be inserted for her crime in our first and next general pardon that shall come out for the poor convicts of Newgate without any condition whatsoever."' He lowered the letter, clapped his hands and asked, 'What do you say to that?'

'I ...' Jenny backed against the cell wall and slowly slid down onto her haunches. His voice became muffled, along with the footsteps of her cellmates who were rushing to her.

She looked at him, and the satisfied grin on his face faded. He turned to Harriet. 'See to her, if you please,' he said. 'Don't let her hit her head on the stones.'

'I wish I knew,' she whispered. 'Wish I knew how long it was since I was last free. Properly free, without having to pretend.'

'Ah, that I can tell you,' Aldred said, clearly relieved to have been given a task. He pulled a few papers out of the leather wallet he habitually carried with him. 'Let's see – over seven years. I can work it out to the day. If you like.'

She shook her head. 'No need.'

'I must say, dear girl, you don't seem as delighted as I had anticipated.'

'Are you absolutely certain? Am I to walk out of here, now, in my gaol clothes? And where am I to go?'

'Well, as to the first – a few bureaucratic wrinkles to be dealt with, but you'll walk out before too long. As to where you will walk to … I have taken the liberty of arranging accommodation for you.' He looked at the ground, hands clasped behind his back, tracing the floor with the toe of his shoe. 'I hope you don't consider that too presumptuous.'

'No, I don't – thank you,' she said absently, frowning and looking at the cell wall as though it could explain to her what it meant to be free.

She felt the skin on her lips cracking, a droplet of blood running down her chin. And she knew why. For the first time since their capture in Coepang, she was genuinely smiling.

Jenny woke up cold, as she usually did. The muted throb in her lower back was there, as it always was, the product of sleeping on a rough board or the floor.

A thin stream of light was coming in through the cell's small window this morning, speaking of indecently bright sunshine outside. It might, then, be a blessedly quiet day. Those who might have come and stared at the Girl from Botany Bay might instead take a turn around the gardens.

She was disappointed when the door opened – she hadn't thought herself to be such an alluring prospect that people would even shun sunlight for her. She turned towards the wall, trying to guess from the heaviness of the footsteps whether it was a man or woman.

The person entering now, walking up to the bars, was heavy, had expensive shoes, and walked with a cane.

'Not feeling social today, I see,' Aldred said.

She said nothing.

'Well, I can't force you to greet me,' he said. 'You are, after all, a free woman.'

Harriet called her a lucky cow. Aldred nodded to Mr Arum, who came forward and unlocked the cell door.

The shawl Aldred had brought with him, which he now draped over Jenny's shoulders, was of the softest wool she could remember feeling. She had never even stolen such a garment. They walked towards the door at the end of the corridor, through which she had passed months ago for her hearings before the magistrate, and not since. The gaoler walked slightly ahead of them and stood aside when they got there, handing Aldred a package.

Aldred drew back his shoulders, straightened, and adopted the accent and tone she'd heard from those issuing commands in Sydney Cove. 'Mr Arum. Kindly open the door for the lady.'

The gaoler gaped at her for a moment, seemingly wondering how anyone could refer to such a creature as a lady.

'We are waiting, Mr Arum,' Aldred said.

Arum gave a shallow bow. 'As your lordship pleases,' he said, and opened the door.

Jenny walked past him without a glance, her chin raised as she imagined a lady's would be, with the air of somebody who was smelling something slightly unpleasant but trying not to make a fuss.

Once the door had closed, and they were standing in a courtyard she only vaguely remembered, she looked down. 'And where am I to go, though?' she said.

He smiled, took her hand and squeezed it. 'You're not to worry for a moment about that. I told you I have everything organised. Now, this bonnet ...' He handed her the bundle that the gaoler had given him. 'A little small, wouldn't you say? Understandably so, of course, but we'll see what's to be done about that when we get home. For now, though, I want you to pull that shawl about yourself, tight as you can. Anyone looking at your skirts will know where you've just come from. But we want their eyes to slide over you.'

A guard stood by the main door, leading onto the street. Aldred nodded to him, and he opened the gate with no hesitation.

Jenny stepped out into a river of people, more than she had seen in one place since trying to offload stolen clothes on the crowded streets of Plymouth. She almost expected them to stop, to point. Nudge the people they were walking with, nod in her direction, raise eyebrows at the presence of Richard Aldred at her elbow. Instead, they parted around her as though she was a rock in a stream, a momentary and quickly forgotten disturbance in the flow of their journey. Those who did glance at her, quickly glanced away again. Aldred had been right: she looked, barely, respectable from the waist up, and they were all far too busy to probe any further.

He led her down the road a little way, where a carriage was waiting. 'This will take us home.'

'Home – your home?'

'No, yours.'

And now we come to it, thought Jenny. *The business of payment*.

She had, she realised, been looking at him with some affection. His fat-bound frame could not be more different from Dan's wiry strength – but he was the first man, at least since Mr Corbett, to assume that she was worth something without having to be shown proof first. In the cell late at night, she had almost been able to see herself with him.

He would probably assume he had a right to her, given the service he had done her. And most men of his standing would see her as a whore anyhow.

He saw her frowning and must have guessed. 'Your home, my dear,' he said quickly, slightly annoyed. 'I will then go on to my own. I assure you, they are two different places. And I can assist you, if you like, in finding your real home – in getting you back to Penmor.'

In Newgate, Jenny had imagined a weeping welcome from her sister, an enfolding embrace from her mother. Now, nothing except money – of which her companion had plenty – was stopping her from going to Penmor, and the prospect terrified her. She couldn't bear replacing her fantasies with a turned back, a slammed door, a disavowal.

'Perhaps – perhaps I need to get used to freedom first,' she said.

'Very well. It won't be the last time I mention it, though.'

She noticed that the coachman had put down a small box for her to step on. Once in the coach, she would happily have lived in it. The dark red upholstery, trimmed in gold braid, was the softest she had felt. And she had never before seen curtains on such a tiny window, when the windows in her childhood home had been bricked up to avoid tax.

She moved the curtain slightly to the side, peering out with

one eye, and he laughed. 'You are perfectly welcome to pull it all
the way back. You're perfectly welcome to open the window and
shout, if you want, although it might excite a bit of talk. But if
you want to see outside, can't say I blame you, having been deprived
of any view except my beauty.'

So she hauled back the curtain, drinking in the land-bound
version of the scene that had greeted her on the way up the Thames:
the carts and children and dogs in puddles and rotting food and
fine ladies with feathered hats and tarts against walls, some of
whom waved at the coach as though they recognised it.

The coach pulled up, after a while, in front of a white cottage
with broad windows and a tidy path.

'Quite small,' said Aldred, 'for which I'm sorry, but certainly, I
hope you'll agree, more than adequate for now. Until we can find
you something better. Oh, and Mrs Titchfield comes with it.'

Why he considered the cottage's size inadequate, what
something better might look like, who Mrs Titchfield was – none
of these were subjects that he felt needed any further elaboration.

As they got out of the coach, he fished into one of the small
pockets on his waistcoat – red, today – and drew out a small key.
He was about to apply it to the lock when the door opened, and
a thin, plainly dressed woman emerged.

'Ah, Mrs Titchfield, remarkable woman that you are! Here
already! Marvellous. I presume everything is in order?'

The woman half knelt in a curtsy. 'Yes, your lordship,' she said.
She looked, then, at Jenny, taking in the incongruously fine shawl
and the tattered bonnet, her eyes snagging on the state of Jenny's
skirts. She made no move to issue a greeting.

'Mrs Titchfield,' said Aldred, 'may I present your charge, Mrs
Gwyn. She will be in need of your excellent roast beef, as well as
a change of clothes.'

'Quite,' said Mrs Titchfield, clearly feeling Jenny wasn't worthy of a curtsy. She turned and entered the cottage, expecting to be followed.

Aldred urged Jenny forward, bending to whisper in her ear. 'A dragon, that woman. Was my governess, if you can imagine me ever having such a thing. I'm quite ungovernable, I assure you. But not a bad sort, once you get to know her.' The warmth of his bulk against Jenny's back, the whisper in her ear, produced in her an involuntary shudder.

They reached a parlour, small but with window seats and panes against which heavy drapes were pulled back, and a polished table hemmed in by beautifully brocaded chairs.

Aldred pulled one out for Jenny. 'Sit, please,' he said. 'You must need to, after your journey.'

Mrs Titchfield again looked at Jenny's skirts, then at the seat of the chair, clearly fearing the light blue silk would be eternally marred by contact with such a posterior.

'And quite a journey it was, I understand,' she said. 'Will you be joining us for supper, your lordship? Roast beef.'

'I thank you – however, I have a … well, an appointment.'

'And the name of your appointment, my lord?'

Aldred chuckled. 'Only you would venture such a question, Mrs T. I suppose you've earned the right to it, having cleaned up after the worst of my escapades. Her name, however, will remain unsaid. But she does not appreciate waiting.'

'And how is her ladyship, my lord?' Mrs Titchfield asked, widening her eyes in feigned innocence.

He frowned. 'Perhaps not as well as one would hope. She remains resting in Scotland. She has never been one for London.'

After he had left, Mrs Titchfield stood in silence, staring unashamedly at Jenny.

'Perhaps you would feel more comfortable eating supper in the kitchen,' she said eventually.

'As you wish, missus,' said Jenny. The deference stabbed at her – this woman would not have been able to survive what Jenny had. But the mention of roast beef hadn't escaped her, and she would happily have eaten it on the street.

She sat at the kitchen table, itself larger than the table in her childhood home, and Mrs Titchfield put a plate of roast beef and potatoes in front of her. She picked up the beef and bit into it, the juices running down her chin. As delicious as it was, she would have time to taste things later; for now, she just wanted to get them into her stomach.

'I presume,' said Mrs Titchfield, 'that before your … adventures … you came from a home where people did not eat like animals.'

The anger began to return, slowly at first, running warmly through Jenny, collecting in her fingertips, piling up, suddenly demanding release.

'You know of me, of what I've done, of where I've come from,' she said. Her voice sounded strangled, choked, and she feared to open her entire throat to it. She suspected that if she did, it would come out in a howl.

'It is difficult to avoid mention of you at present, Mrs Gwyn. Surely you have seen the newspapers.'

'No, I –'

'Not much opportunity in your … former lodgings, I suppose.'

'No, and anyhow, I cannot read.'

The smallest of smiles appeared on Mrs Titchfield's face, barely a quirk at one corner, but Jenny saw it – and in it all the small smiles to come, those that would contort the edges of the mouths of all who met her. They would view her as a wild curiosity, with animal manners as well as animal cunning, and no more literate than an animal either.

Not that it mattered. She suspected Mrs Titchfield would sneer even if her new charge had the manners of a duchess. No point in trying to win the woman's approval. Might as well revel in the sneers.

'Do I amuse you, Mrs Titchfield?' she asked.

'I can assure you, Mrs Gwyn, this entire situation presents me with nothing to laugh at.'

'Wise of you. After all, you're alone with a criminal. A twice over criminal, whose first crime drew blood. Very few people who found themselves in such a forest would pause to chuckle.'

Mrs Titchfield drew herself up. 'Good Lord, you seem almost proud!'

'I simply did what needed to be done, as I will continue to. And I am no threat to you, unless you are a threat to me. Are you?'

'I am an old woman, Mrs Gwyn, what possible threat could I be? No, I'll take you at your word that you will not assault me, any more than you are doing at the moment from the odour coming off your dress. We shall see what we can do about that, at least. We might find each other's company more pleasant when neither of us is thickening the air.'

CHAPTER 34

All evening, Jenny had dispensed tight smiles and said 'hello, pleased to meet you', extended her gloved hand to be shaken and kissed, and pretended not to notice the stares.

The play was miraculous, she thought. Fairies had interfered in human affairs for their own amusement, as she'd always suspected they did. Changing one man's head to that of an ass – she could think of a few who deserved similar treatment.

Sitting in the box, looking down on the balding heads of the aristocrats below her, she was unable to resist constantly running her hands along the skirt of her dress. Silk, and of almost the same yellow as the dress Governor Van Dalen had given her, but far more elaborate, and far less comfortable thanks to the whalebones that stuck into the flesh beneath her breasts.

The dress that had encased her from Sydney Cove to Coepang to Newgate was now ashes. But she had snatched it after her first bath, as Mrs Titchfield was about to throw it on the fire, and unpicked the hem to extract the packet of tea leaves, together with Charlotte's ribbon and Emanuel's wispy hair.

Every so often, her hand would move to the brooch at the neck of her gown. It was a jewelled fairy with filigree wings and had arrived with the dress, and a note Mrs Titchfield grudgingly read to her: 'I found this in the corner of a Newgate cell, and was hoping you could give it a home.'

'Does your wife enjoy the theatre?' Jenny whispered to Aldred before the performance.

She did not know what he was to her, or what she wanted him to be. The first was a decision that may well be out of her hands; the second was one she could not make without knowing more about this presence in the north.

Aldred cleared his throat – a trick she knew he used when he wanted a few extra seconds to think. 'My wife has a rather delicate constitution,' he said. 'She would find all this rather tiring.'

'Should you not be with her, then, if she is delicate?'

'Jenny,' said Aldred, 'this is not your concern. I will say, though, that I am fond of her, and I am receiving regular word of her condition. But London is where my work is, and a marriage for, well, for someone like me is not like a convict union.'

'And how would you know what a convict union is like?' she said.

He frowned. 'Shall we attend to the stage? The actors are waiting for us to finish so they can get a word in.'

This was the third such performance she had attended in the past month. Each arrangement had followed the same pattern. A footman would arrive in the morning, handing her a note to inform her she would be collected at a particular time. While the invitation was couched in the form of a request, Jenny was under no illusion her attendance was assumed.

It wasn't as though she would have refused, given a choice. She had nowhere else to be in the evenings; knew no one in London apart from Richard Aldred, Mrs Titchfield and the women whose incarceration she had shared.

Mrs Titchfield would make her sit straight-backed, her hands folded daintily in her lap, for an hour without moving. 'If his lordship intends to take you to the theatre, you will need to sit for longer like this,' she said. 'I will not have him embarrassed.'

Jenny had no intention of embarrassing Aldred. But the one attribute of a lady that Mrs Titchfield refused to teach her was the only one in which she was really interested.

'But surely,' Jenny said, 'his lordship would be happier if I could read about the places he takes me to and converse with him about the books he reads?'

'There is no requirement that you to learn your letters,' said Mrs Titchfield. 'You'll be going into service eventually, I expect. Kitchen maids don't need to read.'

'Are the grand houses of London in the habit of employing former convicts?' Jenny asked.

'On his Lordship's recommendation, some would employ the devil himself.'

It was the same every evening. Mrs Titchfield would fill a bath with scorching hot water, have Jenny lie in it, and scrub her roughly as the water wrote grooves into her skin. A clean nightdress would hang over a chair near the fire, and when Jenny was pronounced clean and dry, she would lift her arms as Mrs Titchfield pulled it over her head, as though she were a child in need of dressing.

Every time, she saw Charlotte's arms raised towards her, demanding that she be carried. The face that emerged from the neck of the nightgown was sadder than the one that went in.

Jenny would lie in her soft bed and reach under her pillow for a small packet of leaves, a ribbon, and a lock of hair. Often, she would wake the next morning with the ribbon in one hand and the hair in the other.

It was warm on these nights, so as soon as Mrs Titchfield bade her goodnight, as soon as Jenny heard the tumblers of the lock click shut, she would throw off the covers and open the window, and then lie back against the pillows holding her relics.

She was drifting off to sleep one night when she felt the thump at the end of the bed.

The candles were out, and because of the heat no fire was set. There was just enough moonlight, though, to make out a dark shape at the end of the bed.

She sat still for a moment, following the law of the forest – wait, and watch.

The shape was darker than the blackness surrounding it, and seemed to be pulling the tiny ration of light into itself. It pulsated, stretching and contracting and circling.

Then it meowed, and Jenny laughed.

'You stupid thing, you scared me,' she said. 'I thought you were a ghost. Don't believe in them, but always hope never to see one.'

She sat forward in bed, reached out a hand and the cat padded towards it, sniffing as it went.

It stretched out its chin and demanded a tickle, which Jenny provided. Then it turned around and lay down next to her.

'Oh, you think you get to share a bed with me?' she said.

The cat – almost completely black in this low light – did not respond.

'If you must. Better be off before dawn, though. Otherwise Mrs Titchfield will have you for breakfast.'

'Get out, useless animal!'

Jenny had awoken to worse curses, but she hadn't thought even the disapproving Mrs Titchfield would refer to her as an animal. The woman was looming above the bed, with a broom alarmingly raised, and Jenny instinctively put an arm up to protect herself.

When the broom came down, though, it became apparent Mrs Titchfield was aiming towards the end of the bed. She did get Jenny's shins, but Jenny chose to assume that was an accident.

The cat, on the other hand, did not seem inclined to give Mrs Titchfield the benefit of the doubt. It hissed and jumped off the bed, tail suddenly twice its former size, galloping for the windowsill. Then it paused and looked around for just a moment, and Jenny could see a white belly and two small white paws amid all the black. It launched itself at the window frame, hovered on the sill, and was gone.

Mrs Titchfield turned towards Jenny, who feared that she might now be the target of the broom.

'Really, Mrs Gwyn, we have discussed this! You must always leave your windows shut, otherwise pests like this can get in. And on your bed! I do hope there are no fleas now. It might have eaten a rat.'

'I imagine it eats rats because that's all that is available,' Jenny said. 'We would all eat roast beef, if we could get it.'

'Thankfully for you, you can, due to the generosity of his lordship,' Mrs Titchfield said.

'Anyway, I knew it was in here,' said Jenny. 'It came in late last night, walked around in circles about fifteen times – why do they do that, I've always wondered – and went to sleep. It was nice, actually, to have another heart beating in here.'

Mrs Titchfield was gaping in a most unladylike way. 'You mean to tell me,' she said after a moment, 'that you allowed that thing to sleep in the same bed as you? Well. I knew standards were different in the colony, and for people of a certain ... a certain class, but that – that is quite extraordinary!' She moved towards the head of the bed, running her hands along the sheets, perhaps hunting for fleas. Then she clicked her tongue against the roof of her mouth. 'Ah, look here, you see? That thing's already brought in some refuse.' And she picked up the ribbon on the lock of hair, tied in a tatty sprig, and made to fling them out the window.

Before she could draw her arm all the way back, her wrist was encircled in a grip that made it clear Jenny didn't care about how much pain she inflicted.

Mrs Titchfield became still, standing straight: her instinctive response to anything unknown or disconcerting. Jenny had sprung up from the bed more quickly than she'd thought possible to grab the woman's wrist. Still gripping it, she moved so that she was facing the governess.

'I want to make something very clear,' Jenny said, surprised at the steadiness of her voice, the enunciation – the result, perhaps, of the elocution lessons Mrs Titchfield had been giving her. 'Any possessions I have are those which Richard has bought for me.' She saw Mrs Titchfield flinch at the familiarity, and was glad, even though his name felt strange in her mouth. 'Apart from those pieces of refuse, as you call them, that you hold in your hand. They were not, I assure you, brought in by the cat – which, might I add, will be allowed to come and go as it pleases.'

'That, actually, is probably worse,' said Mrs Titchfield, rotating her wrist in a futile attempt to free it. 'You are willing to sleep in detritus.'

'My son's hair, and my daughter's ribbon. The heads from which they came now lie underneath different oceans.'

Mrs Titchfield paled slightly. 'I ... yes, the newspapers mentioned. I see.'

'You cannot possibly see. Not unless you have held your child as they died.'

Mrs Titchfield said something under her breath.

Jenny inhaled, gathering the words to throw at the woman, words with which she had been peppered during every lesson and every conversation since she arrived.

'Kindly raise your voice,' she said. 'Mumbling is the height of rudeness.'

'I said, I have – held my child, as she was dying.'

Jenny slowly let go of her wrist, and Mrs Titchfield exhaled, suddenly looking pale.

'You should sit,' Jenny said.

And Mrs Titchfield did, on the unmade bed, possibly the first time her posterior had connected with such a messy surface.

'My daughter, Elizabeth,' Mrs Titchfield said. 'Consumption. She had just turned two. She would be forty-three now. Perhaps I would be a great-grandmother.'

Jenny sat down beside her, and Mrs Titchfield handed her Emanuel's hair and Charlotte's ribbon, closing Jenny's fingers around them and covering Jenny's fist with her hand.

'One forgets, sometimes,' she said. 'Or tries to. And then it jumps out at you, like a thief from an alleyway.'

'You seem to have been practically a mother to ... to his lordship,' Jenny said. If Mrs Titchfield preferred her to use formal titles, this was a concession she was more than willing to make for someone who had held her child and found herself suddenly holding a mere object, one incapable of laughing or wailing or returning her embrace.

The older woman looked as though she was about to cry. Then

she inhaled, slowly, pushed herself off the bed, and rubbed her hands together. 'Well, Mrs Gwyn. We had best start our day. Please ensure, as much as you can, that the feline and I never cross paths.'

Whenever Richard Aldred took her to the theatre, she drew more attention than the actors on the stage.

Aldred had been a feature of newspapers and gossip since Jenny had been released. Just when readers had begun to tire of the Girl from Botany Bay, the aristocratic lawyer, celebrated for his writing, entered the public imagination and snatched her from the gallows. And to see them together, Jenny imagined them thinking – to speak to the creature, look at her arms and try to see the sinews that had dragged a boat across oceans – what an opening gambit for the next time one ran into one's old schoolmate at the club.

These people would come up behind Aldred and clap him on the back, laughing heartily when he turned in surprise. They would approach obliquely, seeming to bump into him by accident. Or they would barrel right up, a full-frontal attack aimed at claiming the high ground of his attention. They would ask, uselessly, who his charming companion was, and he would introduce her politely and quite simply as Mrs Gwyn. Some of them would pretend not to know of her; some would easily ask her how she was. A few would express admiration for what she had done. No one expressed regret over the death of her family, but she fancied she could see it sometimes, the shadow behind their conversation. There would, frequently, be invitations to house parties in which she wasn't included. It would not have occurred to most of them to invite the curio along with the collector.

She sometimes heard them, as they walked away, discussing her.

'Doesn't look up to much, does she?' an older gentleman once whispered to his wife. Perhaps he was hard of hearing and didn't realise how loudly he had spoken, because his wife swatted him on the arm with her fan.

'You mustn't mind them,' Aldred said in the coach on the way home. 'You have survived what they never could. You mustn't think they view you as less than human. Perhaps they view you as more.'

'Or perhaps I am simply a better dressed, better washed version of the person they came to gawk at in Newgate,' Jenny said, turning to look out the window of the coach. Hard to see much except splashes of yellow light underneath the lamps they passed, the occasional dark scurrying shape.

'I am sorry,' said Aldred. 'You must not think that your attendance at these performances is the price you have to pay for living in the house.'

'Is it not?' said Jenny. 'Why do you bring me, then?'

He put his head down. Then looked up at her. 'Do you know, you are one of the most honest people I have ever met?'

She laughed. 'I am a thief and an escapee, and I lived under a false name for months.'

'All this is true. And those with money and influence have done worse, I assure you. They are simply better positioned to navigate around the system. And they will praise you to your face, and turn around and deride you five minutes later. At least with you, Jenny, if you think I'm an ass, you will tell me.'

'Very well then, you're an ass. A kind one, and an intelligent one.'

He smiled, staring at her until the coach hit a rut and he bumped his head on the window.

'You're right, I am an ass. Part of the reason I bring you to these things is that I know people are interested. Because I want to show you off, to remind everyone of why you are in a theatre instead of a cell.'

'Your great mind, your love of justice.'

'Not to put too fine a point on it, yes,' he said. 'That is not, however, the main reason I bring you. I am, I must say, your most devoted admirer.'

Jenny found herself blushing in the carriage's darkness. Was this, she wondered, when he finally asked of her what she had been expecting him to ask?

'I don't want you to think, though, that you must come with me to go on living in the house, enjoying the tender affections of Mrs Titchfield. I wonder – have you given any more thought to finding your family?'

'No, Richard. They'll not want me.'

'You can't know that!'

'I don't want to know it. Ever.'

He sighed. 'Jenny, the house is yours to inhabit for as long as you wish it. Consider me the one paying this country's debt to you. But you belong in Penmor, and I won't necessarily be seeking your approval if I decide to try to get you there.'

CHAPTER 35

The carriage rolled up in front of the cottage in the middle of the day, an unusual occurrence. Jenny went to the door as she always did when she heard the hoofs and wheels; she nodded and smiled at Arthur, the coachman with whom she had become familiar.

She could hear, even several feet away, Richard's rumbling laugh emerging from the carriage. Unless he had lost his wits, he was not alone.

Arthur hopped down from his seat with a practised smoothness, grabbed his little box, put it in front of the carriage door for those inside to step down, and pulled the door open.

Richard emerged as he always did, stooping to squeeze his large frame through the carriage door and blinking a little.

The man who followed him out was blinking too, and had more of a reason to, having been deprived of sunlight for months. Richard, though, seemed at least to have arranged for fresh clothes and washing water, because his charge was plainly but respectably dressed, and clean.

This man, thin and less muscular than Jenny remembered, ignored the step and slid down from the carriage onto the road.

He looked up at Jenny and smiled, and she saw he had mislaid a tooth or two in the past few months.

Jenny ran to him, nearly knocking him over with her embrace – John Carney had always been a creature of the sea, and never planted his feet too firmly on the ground.

Mrs Titchfield tried to settle them in the parlour, but Richard refused. 'No, my dear lady, we will be perfectly at home in the kitchen. I'll be down to the manor in a week, and I will have my fill of parlours then.'

He hadn't told Jenny he was planning a trip to his country estate, and she found herself oddly annoyed. Of course, he was under no obligation to inform her of his movements. She had, though, grown used to his presence, his open curiosity, his unquestioning assumption that her mind was as fine as his.

'Will you be gone long?' she asked.

A pinched, anxious look crossed his face. 'My wife – her illness, it seems, has worsened.'

'I am sorry.'

'I do hope her ladyship recovers swiftly,' said Mrs Titchfield, placing tea things in front of them.

John stared rapt at the daintily painted teacups with gold leaf around the rim, inhaled the fragrance coming off the infusions. He wasn't able to fit his index finger through the cup's handle; he picked it up in both hands like an offering. 'This brew is the finest stuff tasted since ... matter of fact, can't remember having tasted anything this lovely.'

Mrs Titchfield gave him a smile that stayed on her face for more than a second. 'I am glad you're enjoying it, Mr Carney. If it can help dull the memory of some of the horrors you have seen, I will be delighted.'

Carney beamed at her, his teeth more absence than presence.

'I am afraid Mr Carney had to spend a little more time in Newgate than you did, Jenny,' said Aldred, drinking his tea with a delicacy that seemed odd on such a large man.

'Not quite as famous as you, you see,' said Carney, grinning.

'And what will you do, now?' Jenny asked him.

'It's an odd thing – all of these years, wishing for freedom, and now that I have it, I'm scared of it. Decisions – you get out of the habit of them. But I'm fairly certain I've made one.'

'I should think so,' said Richard. 'We already booked the passage.'

'I'm back to Antrim,' said Carney. 'For a time, anyway. Until I … Well, I just need to discover a few things.' He paused.

'Discover …?' Jenny asked.

'Whether my parents are alive, for a start. I'm not sure they know where I've been, these past years. They can't read the newspaper, and word travels slowly. When I tell them I've been to the other side of the world and back again, I'll probably get a clip from Da for telling lies.'

'And you're not worried they might reject you?' Richard asked, looking at Jenny.

'Yes, but they've suffered on my account. They at least deserve to know what became of me.'

Jenny had hoped Carney would be staying with them for a time. He had, though, been booked onto a ship leaving London for Ireland that night. Everything he owned was encased in a rough grey bag that sat, while its owner drank from a china cup, on the seat of the carriage.

And now that he was gone, Jenny felt insubstantial, ghostly. The last person she knew from her convict life, the last person who had stood on the shores of Sydney Cove with her, would soon be at an impossible remove, and would likely never appear again.

Richard must have noticed some change in her demeanour, a slumping of the shoulders or a lowering of the head, because he said, 'That play you like …'

'I'm not sure I know any, apart from those you've taken me to.'

'What about the Shakespeare that marine once read to you?'

'Oh! Yes, something involving taming, I think. And I did like it, until the end.'

'Ah, you feel Katherine should have continued in her resistance. And maybe you're right. She was, though, discovering that society punishes those who have within them the divine spark of independence. It is a lesson, I am sure, that is not lost on you, my dear.'

'So we make sure that spark dies with the embers from last night's fire, do we?' said Jenny. 'You wish me to imbibe this lesson, and you are letting our old playwright do the work.'

'I wish no such thing,' Aldred said. 'Society frowning on something has never been, for me, a compelling enough reason not to do it. I simply thought you might like to see it performed. Given the circumstances under which you last heard the words, sitting in a theatre box in a fine dress with a full belly might be welcome. So I thought, anyway.'

'But your wife?'

'Is gravely ill, and will have me by her bedside.'

This fragile, faceless creature. Someone who would never have survived in Sydney Cove. Someone who would never be asked to. The woman had one foot in this world and one in the next. Jenny didn't know what manner of woman she was, and it did not matter.

Many of those who did not know *her* had wished her dead. She did not intend to do the same to another.

'I hope your wife recovers,' she said.

Richard frowned. 'Thank you, my dear. A good woman, certainly. She has been ill for some time, and I would not have her die, if indeed she is on her way to the next world, without my being present. To do otherwise would shame her. I'll be going back more frequently.'

'That is very ... kind of you,' Jenny said. Actually, she thought it was the least he could do.

But Richard clearly agreed. 'The woman has an ocean of patience,' he said. 'I can assure you, I would hate to be married to me. I've tried to take care never to embarrass her. Sometimes, though, I have failed.'

'You are not the worst of men, Richard.'

'But I am a long way from the best of them. When I return, we might go to that play. Yes?'

'Yes,' said Jenny. 'I believe that would be quite ... suitable.'

The day Richard was expected back from Scotland, Jenny found a bag near the cottage's front door. She felt a stab of panic. *He has tired of me*, she thought. There would never be a dreadful, wonderful proposition from him. She was being evicted, to somehow make her own way through London, perhaps working in a tavern where she could listen to tuneless renditions of the bawdy songs being sung about her throughout the city.

Then Mrs Titchfield came down the corridor dressed for travel. 'His lordship has decided that my sister in Bath needs to see me,' she said. 'How he could possibly know is beyond me, but I am not going to miss the opportunity.' She leaned over and patted Jenny's shoulder. 'You are not the worst of them, Mrs Gwyn. A long way from it. That is why I say, guard yourself. His lordship is known, shall we say, for certain appetites ...'

Certainly, Richard – nearly twice her age, and probably closer to three times her girth – was not the sort of man Jenny could ever have seen herself yearning for. But his open, uncomplicated nature could not be further removed from the scheming and hiding and double-dealing of the penal colony, the hulk and the *Charlotte*. His admiration of her, she had to admit, was pleasing, and she thoroughly enjoyed his company. She appreciated the earnestness with which he asked her questions, the avidity with which he listened to the answers, so that during their talks, she was almost able to allow the ghosts of Charlotte and Emanuel to rest.

Struggling into the yellow silk dress was difficult without Mrs Titchfield's help. The thing was constructed better than the sails of many of the ships she had been on, and she had to twist the bodice strings around the bedpost and walk forward to tighten it.

When she looked in the mirror, she thought that she had done a reasonable job – certainly better than she'd known how to do until Mrs Titchfield got a hold of her.

So when the carriage rolled up, and Jenny walked outside at the sound of the wheels, she was gratified by Richard's open-mouthed admiration. 'It is no thanks to you,' she said. 'Despite the fact that you were kind enough to give me this dress, you then went and robbed me of my dresser.'

She paused for a moment, and then laughed at the sheer ridiculousness of someone like her making such a comment. And Richard laughed with her.

'Do you know, dear girl, I might come in for a snifter. If you have no objection, of course.'

That night at the theatre, there had been the usual parade of voyeurs, whiskery men kissing her glove, women nodding to her briefly, some unashamedly staring. She always stared back.

'Well, Richard, it is your house,' she said.

'But with Mrs Titchfield not there, you see, it might feel ...'

She smiled at him, patting his hand. 'Before I answer that, Richard, perhaps you'd better tell me what a snifter is.'

When they got down from the carriage, Richard told the coachman he could go, and she caught a sidelong look from the man. He, clearly, was not going to assist Mrs Titchfield in preserving her reputation.

'I assure you, Jenny, this isn't as bad as it looks,' said Richard, opening the door for her. 'My lodgings are a few short streets away, but I was enjoying your company so much that I did not want to curtail the evening, especially as we had hardly a chance to talk.'

So they went inside, where she learned that a snifter was a strangely shaped glass for the consumption of brandy, some of which happened to be hidden in a compartment beneath the window seat cushions.

'Mrs T would probably throw it out if she found it,' he said. 'Terrible waste.'

He offered Jenny some, but she declined. She had seen more than enough drunk women to know that once they got far enough, those who saw themselves as witty or attractive or alluring actually just looked messy. She shook her head to dislodge the image of Elenor exposing her breasts to the marines.

'Now, madam,' Richard said, slapping his palms on his thighs, a habit of his when the conversation was about to change course. 'What are we to do with you?'

The question could have meant anything. Probably it was deliberately ambiguous – Richard Aldred chose his words with care. If his meaning wasn't clear, it was because he intended this. Perhaps he was opening a door through which she could choose to walk, or not.

But his ill wife still hung in the air. And from what she had heard of Richard's proclivities, she was reasonably certain the door would open again.

'Well … I was hoping, Richard, for a rather large favour from you. In addition to the favours you've already done for me.'

'If it is in my power …'

'I was hoping, actually, that you could teach me to read.'

He raised his eyebrows. 'A fine ambition, dear girl. I am, however, not the most patient of teachers, I fear. Perhaps we shall arrange a tutor for you?'

'That would be wonderful, thank you,' she said – a bit shocked, as she always was, when she heard herself speaking as Mrs Titchfield would, expressing gratitude or regret or concern in the voice of an officer's wife rather than a felon. 'I might,' Jenny added, 'be able to get a position that would support me, if I could read.'

'Yes, although you don't need letters to go into service.'

'I'm not made for service, Richard.'

'No, I suppose not,' he said. 'I'm sure you didn't endure everything that you did to empty someone's chamber pot. And of course, as I've told you, you're welcome to stay in this cottage for as long as you wish. But I must confess, I have detected a certain … restlessness.'

'You must think me terribly ungrateful,' Jenny said. He was right, though. She had experienced a vast prison and a constricted freedom; she was desperate to find the unequivocal liberty that, so far, she had only found at sea. But the sea was closed to her. If she was a man, she could do as John Carney had done: sign on to a merchant ship or purchase a fishing vessel. As things stood, she needed to find another means of supporting herself.

It was odd being back on the same slice of land as her mother, her sister. Being within a feasible journey of them. But would they welcome her? The thief. The convict, the bereaved mother, the famous fixture of newspapers that occasionally printed poems about her which would have made Helen blush. Jenny would rather imagine Constance and Dolly pining for her than face a reality in which they wished she had stayed lost.

'I suppose,' she told Richard, 'if I could read, I might find work as a governess.'

She would have responsibility for somebody else's progeny. Children who would never have to die in stinking wet blackness. Uncomplicated, unsullied little beings. She felt suddenly desperate to be around them.

But Richard gave a short bark of a laugh. 'Very few women need to read. And to be honest, dear girl, no one would have you.'

She felt anger starting to stir. 'You must know some families. Surely you would be willing to tell them I'm not going to teach their children how to pickpocket.'

'Of course you're not. But, my dear, you are a felon, or have been. Nobody would employ you. Nobody would let you have charge of their children.'

'So I am fit for nothing,' she said, standing and beginning to pace. 'Except to adorn your arm and help polish your image at the theatre. And to provide inspiration for songs in taverns.'

'It's not a question of what you're fit for,' Aldred said, sounding frustrated. 'It's a question of how people see you. And the reality is, seven years' transportation for a violent crime is going to colour

people's views. Not to mention the fact that half of London believes ... well, you did mention those songs.'

'You could do something about that, at least. You could deny it.
Make it clear that we're not ... acquainted in that way.'

'I don't see much point in it, though,' Richard said. 'I've never
been much of a denier, even of my worst excesses. If I started now,
people might wonder why.'

'So your reputation remains intact, while mine keeps me
imprisoned.'

Richard stood a little unsteadily, as several snifters had passed
his lips. 'You are upset, and that's understandable. It's probably best
if I wander off home now, leave you to rest.'

'I have had enough rest to last me a lifetime! I want to be free.
And you sit there, tipping drinks down your throat and lecturing
me on my reputation!' She swept a hand in an arc, knocking the
glass out of his hand so that it shattered on the floor.

He looked at his empty hand. When he spoke his voice was
calm, and flatter than she'd ever heard it. 'And you are free. But
you will never be free of your past, Jenny, never. You need to make
peace with that – and with your family – or you will never have
any peace at all.'

He took his cane, his coat and his hat, bowed stiffly and formally,
and made for the door.

CHAPTER 36

It was, as far as Jenny could remember, the first night she had ever spent by herself. She wandered up the stairs into her room, wondering if she should lock the door – indeed, where the key was, for Mrs Titchfield had never entrusted her with one.

Jenny hunted half-heartedly in the parlour sideboard and in the kitchen for a key, but gave up. She was tired, and she felt slightly nauseated at the fact that the man she thought was her friend, the man who had been her saviour, felt she wasn't good enough to be a governess, and that she had knocked the drink out of his hand. It seemed ridiculous to quibble, now that she had a full belly, that this wasn't the sort of freedom she had been looking for.

In the end, she just went to bed. If somebody was going to break into the house, she thought, let them. In her current mood, she would have liked to see them try. But she did take the poker upstairs and put it in the bed beside her.

Someone did break in: the cat, perhaps sensing Mrs Titchfield's absence. Jenny was dimly aware of him as she drifted off – jumping up on the window ledge, walking slowly over to the bed, turning round three times in a ritual only he understood.

When Jenny next woke, there was a heavier weight on the bed. A man's weight.

She sat straight up, grasping at the poker, hoisting it back so it would have a decent amount of heft when it connected with the head of whoever had joined her.

'For God's sake, dear girl. Once in a night is quite enough.'

She couldn't see Richard clearly, but she could hear him slurring. Even when drunk, staggeringly so, he never slurred.

She put the poker down, leaned forward and squinted in the low moonlight.

Something black glistened down the side of his face. She knew, though, that it wasn't really black. The substance – trickling down from his forehead, coating his cheek and dripping onto his pearl-coloured waistcoat – would be bright red in daylight.

'Jesus Christ,' she said, 'what happened to you?'

'Well, He had nothing to do with it, certainly,' said Richard. And, when she didn't react: 'Do forgive me. Bad humour is something I only resort to in extremis.'

She hauled herself from under the covers and crawled towards where he was sitting. The cat, curled up as far from these noisome creatures as he could possibly get, looked up quickly, then decided it was none of his business.

'For the love of God,' she said as she got closer. 'That's a deep gash, that is.'

'I must say, I'm feeling slightly unwell.'

'Do you want me to bathe it, there?'

'If you like. Yes, that would be nice. Always surprises me, how sticky blood gets. Dreadful feeling. Cloying.'

She raced to the pump in the backyard, not bothering with her robe, flying as her white nightdress billowed behind her. By the time she got back, Richard had lain down next to the poker. She picked it up, stirred the embers in the fireplace, before starting to clean his wound.

He had, he told her, been walking back to his lodgings. There had, as she knew, been brandy and sherry and whiskey, and before that, at the theatre, uncountable glasses of champagne. So perhaps he'd been somewhat unsteady. Unsteady enough to tempt two thieves. One of them knocked him to the ground and slashed him with a stick; the other yanked at his pocket watch. He swung his cane, and they ran off.

'We will look for them tomorrow,' Jenny said. 'Get your watch back. I know how these things work. It's time that my expertise was of use to you, rather than the other way around.'

'No, I won't have you involved in all that again, not even for a good cause. They may or may not be caught – and if they are, they may end up in Botany Bay. But you and I, we will not be the ones doing the catching. We don't know their circumstances. They could be thugs, louts, ignorant boys out for what they can get. Or they could be starving, or have a sick family.'

'Every lag says they have a sick family, or that they are starving,' said Jenny.

'More often than not I'm sure they are. You were, were you not? No, I won't punish someone for doing what they need to do to avoid dying.'

He hauled himself upwards as she finished cleaning his wound and began dabbing it dry.

'I don't know if Mrs Titchfield has any bandages,' she said.

'Not needed, the bleeding stopped – I left a fair bit of it on the cobblestones. I was thinking, you know, as I was walking.'

'Always good to be able to do both at once.'

'Now, don't be cheeky, dear girl, I'm not quite in the mood for it. But I was, as it happens, thinking about you. You are not happy here, yet you won't go to Cornwall.'

'I don't know what I would find. Whether my mother is there, alive. Whether my sister is married, has children. Whether they would want to see me. Being in London – you are right, it doesn't suit me. But I have lost a husband and two children, and I would rather hold my family safe and alive in my mind than find out my losses have doubled. Or that my family no longer consider me one of their number.'

Richard nodded slowly. 'But, as it happens, I know people.'

'Yes, you paraded me in front of half of them.'

'Oh, at least half. Some of them, you see, might make inquiries. Find out how your family is faring. Perhaps even find out whether they would be delighted to find you at their doorstep.'

The enormity of it was crushing: the possibility of finding her family and losing them in a single exhalation. The alternative, though … Being suspended in a grey sameness punctuated by occasional outings. Being stared at, examined. Almost worse, the inevitable day when people would no longer stare.

'Yes, all right. Yes.'

'Good girl. Now, if you have no objection, I would rather like to lie down again.'

'Of course.' She got up and made for the door, wondering if she could clean Mrs Titchfield's room well enough that the woman wouldn't notice it had been slept in.

'I didn't, Jenny, say anything about lying down alone.'

The slur had gone from his voice, now. It was thick, heavy with intent.

This man who listened to her, who had spoken for her. Who had secured her freedom – not his fault that this particular brand of freedom wasn't for her – and who seemed to be on the verge of securing it again.

An ugly man with beautiful eyes capable of seeing past a violent robbery, an elaborate deception, an escape.

It felt, actually, almost inevitable. As though by bringing the act into existence, she was redressing the imbalance in the world.

Yes, she thought. *I have no objection to lying down with you. None at all.*

Richard lived at the cottage for three days, only leaving on the day Mrs Titchfield was expected back. He continued to drop in to the cottage over the next few days. He was very correct with Jenny, far more than he had been. He would, loudly and in Mrs Titchfield's hearing, claim the reason for his visits was to update Jenny on his search for news of Penmor.

In the event, though, news of Penmor found him.

It came in the shape of Alan Nance, a glazier who had trailed Richard to his club, and who paced in the street outside the cottage as Richard spoke to Jenny about him.

'I've never heard the name,' she said.

'Yes, Mr Nance said you wouldn't know him. He lives in Penmor now, but he was in Menabilly during your childhood. Nevertheless, he claims to know your mother, your sister, your neighbours – and a great deal about you.'

'Do you think he is genuine?' she asked. 'Everyone knows each other in Penmor, and each other's business.'

'It is odd, then, that you have not heard of him, even if he lived in a neighbouring town. I think, my dear, we had best keep our guards up while we hear what he has to say.'

'But if he's a fraud, what could he want?'

'Who knows. Payment, perhaps, to carry messages to his supposed contacts in Penmor. We shall find that out, too. I have a nose for such things. I wanted to prepare you, though. You must not show him too much encouragement. And if it turns out that he is indeed an imposter, you must try not to be too disappointed.'

The man was ushered in by a frowning Mrs Titchfield, and Richard offered him a seat at the parlour table with the barest minimum of flourish that courtesy required. 'Mr Nance,' he said. 'May I present Mrs Gwyn. Jenny Trelawney, as she was.'

Nance looked to be between Jenny and Richard in age, perhaps forty or so. Clean, plainly dressed, with the callused hands of most of the men Jenny knew. He smiled at her with what seemed to be genuine warmth. Jenny, though, had seen much that appeared to be genuine and wasn't. *It will take more than a smile*, she thought, *I promise you that.*

She inclined her head as she had seen Mrs Titchfield do. 'Mr Nance,' she said.

'Mrs Gwyn! What a pleasure. I have read about you, as has most of London. It was a joy to find out you had survived and were back with us.'

'Thank you. As you say, though, most of London has read about me. I am sure you understand, I would very much like to hear of Penmor, including details with which most of London is not familiar.'

Nance frowned for a moment, and Jenny resolved to apologise to him later if he was indeed what he claimed to be.

'I've seen you before, you know,' he said. 'At church, sitting near your neighbours.'

'Oh. Howard and his son John?'

'John? No, Stephen. I didn't know there was a John.'

And there wasn't. Jenny caught Richard's eye, nodding slightly.

'Young Stephen,' said Nance, 'he isn't the lad he used to be. Married. Lost a babe to the fever.'

The disease Jenny had fled from. It had straddled the world. In failing to take her, had it taken one of her family instead?

'There ... there was a fever,' she said.

'Yes. Winter of 1790.'

'And how many ...?'

Nance suddenly seemed to realise what she was asking. 'No one dear to you, as far as I know. Your mother, she is well. Mrs Tippett now. Grieved for you, for a long time.'

'And my sister?'

'Dolly is in service here, in London, as it happens,' he said. 'It was she, actually, who set me the task of finding you!'

'And she has been in the same city, this whole time?'

'Not just in the same city – less than a mile away!'

'Why, though, did she send you? I mean no disrespect, but why did she not come herself?'

'Well, two things,' said Nance. 'First of all, she knew it would take a bit of asking around. She is a little shy like that, is Dolly.'

Jenny nodded. 'And the other reason?'

'She was not sure, you see, if you would welcome her,' Nance said.

'She was not sure ...'

Jenny shook her head, to clear it. The knowledge that she and her sister had probably walked the same paths within hours of each other. That they might have passed each other without recognition. It was almost too much for her to bear.

'I can assure you, Mr Nance, I would welcome Dolly very much indeed,' she said, and did not realise until she saw droplets darkening her napkin that she was crying.

CHAPTER 37

After agreeing to arrange a meeting between Jenny and Dolly, Nance came back that afternoon with news. Dolly had each Sunday free from her position as a cook. Sunday was the next day.

'She wants to see you, not your dresses,' Richard said. He now unashamedly walked into her room at will. 'Mrs Titchfield has seen worse, poor woman,' he'd assured Jenny when she objected on the grounds of propriety.

On this visit, Richard was greeted by a bed covered with every day gown he had bought her.

'She will have decided about me, though,' said Jenny. 'It has been seven years. She will have decided on a picture of me, and there has been more than enough time for it to replace any soft memories she might have. I need to supplant it. One of these dresses will help me. I just need to decide which one.'

'You're expecting her to disapprove of you?'

'Why would she not, Richard? A thief, a convict, the rumoured mistress of a known philanderer – oh don't frown, you know what people say, and I suspect you enjoy it.'

'As long as the gossip doesn't board a coach and visit Scotland,' he said.

'It's a little late to be concerned about that. Didn't you come back from a trip to Paris once with a French noblewoman?'

He smiled. 'Ah yes. Well. I do take your point. And you must take mine. Whatever her view of you – and I do doubt it is as negative as you fear – it's unlikely to be swayed one way or the other by what you are wearing.'

'But should I dress richly, or plainly? Should I look like a penitent?'

'Dress as yourself Jenny. You are what you are. The woman who sailed over those uncountable leagues did not manage it by worrying about clothes.'

In the end she chose the blue muslin she used for walks in the gardens with Mrs Titchfield.

Richard wasn't there to distract her – he had gone with Nance to fetch Dolly and bring her to the cottage. Jenny had never learned the significance of the filigree metal hands on the clock face in the parlour; she had always measured time in tides and shoals. Now, though, she couldn't stop glancing at it each time she reached the end of a transit around the room.

Turning away from the clock for what must have been the twentieth time, Jenny found Mrs Titchfield standing a foot away. The woman reached out and took Jenny's shoulders in a disconcertingly strong grip, turned her around and propelled her towards a chair at the polished table, which had been set with tea things and little cakes. When they got there, Mrs Titchfield pressed down firmly until Jenny found herself sitting.

'You simply must calm down, Mrs Gwyn,' Mrs Titchfield said.

'What will she think if she walks in and finds you pacing like a caged animal?'

'I was a caged animal.'

'Well, precisely! Why remind her?'

They heard the door opening, and Richard's rumbling voice say, 'Right this way, my dear.'

And then Dolly was in the doorway, dressed in grey wool, her hair far neater than Jenny had ever seen it and scraped back under a servant's cap, but otherwise unchanged, suspended for the course of Jenny's absence.

Jenny stood slowly, opened her mouth, closed it.

Dolly stared at her, her eyes shining. Took a step. Did not take a second one. She stood there for precious seconds, attaching them onto the tally of Jenny's absence.

Then, very suddenly, Dolly started to cry, great gulping sobs that pulled Jenny to her with a speed she hadn't thought herself capable of. Jenny was taller, and she drew her sister's head down onto her shoulder and stroked her immaculate hair, while tears and mucus darkened the shoulder of her dress. She heard, dimly, Mrs Titchfield withdrawing to the kitchen, and Richard ushering Mr Nance towards the street.

After a while, Jenny kissed Dolly's forehead, turned her around – as Mrs Titchfield had turned Jenny earlier – and led her towards the table. 'You should eat something, Dolly. You look too thin.'

'But you!' said Dolly, and her voice was still as soft as it had been in Penmor. 'You nearly starved! Starved, drowned – nearly eaten by natives, if what the papers say is true!'

'Not the last, no. But I very much hope that God has tired of trying to find ways to kill me.'

Dolly let out a laugh at the same time that she was inhaling for another cry, the result a most unladylike snort. 'At least he's paying you some attention,' she said. 'We … we thought you were dead, or so lost to us that you might as well be.'

Jenny reached out and touched Dolly's cheek. It was smooth, pale. Her own face, she was constantly told by the mirror in her room, had been roughened by a fiercer sun than a London cook could imagine.

'Dolly,' she said, and her throat convulsed at the need to speak the next words. 'You had a niece. A nephew.'

Dolly looked as though she would start crying again, and Jenny was dimly aware of moisture on her own cheeks, of the sudden heaving of her chest.

'Yes, I know. The papers said that, too. Were they wonderful?'

'Yes,' said Jenny. 'More than wonderful. And brave.'

'That awful man. Who would be cruel enough to put them in a hold like that? I read he is going to be court-martialled.'

'You read it yourself?'

'Yes. My mistress taught me to read so I could use her old cook's recipes. And I remember the first time I read about you. That you had come back. That we were on the same piece of land, that there was no ocean between our two pairs of feet.'

'I'm sorry,' said Jenny, barely able to talk now. 'For everything. The going away. The way I came back. For the way you found out about it.'

Dolly was smiling, shaking her head. 'But it was wonderful! And I was able to write to Mother, to tell her! She would have had the reverend read it to her, of course. He wrote back for her – the letter arrived so quickly, he must've done it on the same day he read it to her.'

'She must … must hate me. Or be ashamed, at least. Perhaps it would have been better if I had stayed dead, at least in her mind. I couldn't have caused any more trouble, then.'

Dolly shook her head so vigorously that strands of hair came loose from her servant's cap. 'Ma sent me a message to give to you, when I found you. She can't read, can't write. But she had the reverend write it on a piece of paper, so she could copy it onto another. She wanted it to come from her hand.'

Dolly reached into her pocket, then handed Jenny a slip of paper.

Jenny opened it, saw jagged, crooked letters spelling out two words that she was no more capable of deciphering than her mother was. 'Dolly, I … I'm sorry, I can't read either.'

'I will teach you, if you like. But I don't think I shall wait for you to learn these words. Shall I read them for you?'

Jenny forced herself to nod. Truthfully, she was terrified of the meaning that those marks on the page might convey, fearful they were an admonition, a rejection.

But Dolly was smiling as she took the paper and laid it flat on the table, pointing to the first word. 'This here, you see, says "come".' She moved her finger to the second word. 'And this one, Jenny, says "home".'

Richard must have been listening at the door. He returned that evening with the news he had booked a passage for her: one that would take her down the river and around the coast of Cornwall. One that would end at the dock in Penmor Harbour.

'I am sorry, I won't be able to come,' he said. 'Perhaps, though, you might consider dining with me tonight?'

Mrs Titchfield served them herself, squeezing Jenny's shoulder as she put the last course of summer berries down in front of them, then filling Richard's sherry glass. The old woman cleared her throat. 'I do suddenly feel rather tired,' she said. 'I do hope you'll forgive me, your lordship, if I take to my bed now.'

Richard beamed at her, nodded, and told her to take all the rest that she needed.

He was far more urgent that night than usual, losing the gentleness that came from fear of hurting a much smaller creature.

'You do not expect to see me again, do you?' Jenny said later, as he came back to the bed, having placed the invading cat on the sill and closed the window.

He was silent for a moment, then said, 'You are welcome here, at any time.'

'That is not what I asked, Richard.'

'Look, you're a creature of the sea. You're not at home in London. The crush of so many people must be disconcerting, even to somebody who's been jammed up against so many others in the hold of a ship.' He lay down next to her, propped himself up on one elbow and ran a hand across her cheek. 'I am a town mouse, Jenny. Always will be.' He rolled over onto his back. 'I will, though, make sure you are taken care of. There will be a monthly stipend.'

'And what if I don't want that? What if I don't need it?'

'Take it, Jenny, with my love. You know better than I do that money can cushion against horrors.'

'So you have finished with me?'

'No, my dear, but I rather think you have finished with me.'

And when the sloop sailed out at the mouth of the Thames, when the first foamy wave slapped it for its temerity to stick its nose into the ocean, she knew he was right.

This was her first time on the ocean since the *Gorgon*. She stared at the walls of a pleasant cabin, finding no meaning or comfort in them, or in the language of the seabirds and the insistence of the waves. But the tilt of the boat felt natural, comfortable, far more so than a stilted walk through the park with Mrs Titchfield; Jenny's legs instinctively bent and stretched to compensate for the boat's movement. She felt sorry for those others on board who couldn't read the intentions of a wave and position themselves to meet it.

She would, too, have felt sorry for the passengers, women and men, who responded to the ocean's heaving by splattering the rails with their stomach contents. She didn't have the time for sympathy, though, when she was doing the same.

She had never been sick on a boat – except once, on the journey to Australia. Then, the sea had not been the cause.

The sea calmed, and Jenny saw the squat towers that sprang like warts from the arms of Penmor Harbour. The ship cut through the water to the dock where only one passenger would disembark before the rest travelled on to Plymouth, a place she did not wish to visit.

She hid in the shadows towards the back of the deck and watched the dock approaching, and the woman on it. A woman who was more thickset than she had been, and better dressed, too, in plain fabric that was faded but undecorated by oil or fish innards. Her eyes were not vacant, sitting uselessly in a head that never turned; they were raking the bay, then the deck of the ship. Their brows knitted together when they found no sign of an answering gaze.

This wasn't the face of a woman who would turn at the sight

of Jenny, who would glance back up the hill, who would say she was no daughter anymore.

Jenny stepped out of the shadows, and those flickering eyes found her and began to spout tears.

She'd had visions of walking, straight-backed, down the gangplank to the dock, of greeting her mother with the best possible manners. Of showing her that her daughter had finally learned how to leave a dress unstained for more than a day.

She had never, though, walked sedately off a boat, and her legs seemed to know that, because now they were carrying her at a run to the dock, and her hands were pressing down on it so she could push herself up as her father had taught her to, ending up on her backside at her mother's feet, with her dress collecting splinters and stains along the way, scissoring into a sitting position and pressing her body against her mother's now comfortable curves, as Constance's hand came around the back of her head, with fingers threading through her hair, pushing until Jenny's cheek was on her mother's shoulder, and the grip at the back of her head told her she would never be released again.

EPILOGUE
Somewhere in the English Channel, off Penmor, Cornwall,
1845

'This might have to be the last time, Will. I feel the waves more than I used to.'

Her grandson frowned as he struggled to keep the boat's nose turned into the waves. 'I have never heard you worry about it before. Shall I go in?'

'Perhaps. Are the wind dragons stirring?' Will Gwyn shielded his eyes, staring at the clouds that jostled for position on the horizon. 'Maybe. Yes, we'll turn back. And then straight home with you.'

'Not a bit of it!' Mrs Gwyn said. 'They'll be expecting a story. I'd face any danger before a gang of disappointed children.'

'No one ever believed her wilder stories – they enjoyed listening to them, though.

'Have you noticed,' said Maisie Lowe, a pert madam who enjoyed holding court at the side of the church after service, 'that the less she goes to sea, the wilder the stories get? Bloodthirsty natives, sea dragons –'

'But it keeps the children entertained,' said Sarah Parkey.

'Not mine, I assure you,' said Maisie. 'I don't let them anywhere near her. You've seen her, you must've. With her own grandchildren lashed to the bench of a boat before they could walk.'

'Keeps them safe, I suppose, while they learn the business,' said Sarah.

'Fish are not a business!' said Maisie, looking more petulant than any child lashed to a bench. She didn't mention that she had grown up eating the fish Mrs Gwyn's fleet brought in, or that her husband rented their cottage, one of a row owned by the old woman.

Mrs Gwyn didn't get out on the ocean as much as she used to. But she still tried to go out once a week on one of the fifteen fishing boats she owned. Preferably piloted by her grandson, who had learned to sail almost before he could walk, and who was now in command of the Gwyn fishing fleet.

Her expeditions had become even less frequent since she had convinced Richard to move back to Penmor. She had showed her son off at church on his return from London, where his life had clearly been comfortable enough to earn him something of a paunch.

Mrs Gwyn, they said, could read the wind like a book, even though words on a page were still a mystery to her. Will had the same talent, honed by his grandmother during frequent childhood trips on summer oceans. Perhaps that was why, when his mother fell to a fever, he had stayed with his grandmother rather than moving to London with his father.

The seamanship seemed to have skipped a generation: Richard had fallen out of most boats he had ever been in. His talents lay elsewhere.

'We need lawyers in Penmor too,' Mrs Gwyn had said while she gripped his arm after the service, as though afraid he might go back to London. 'You don't have to like the sea to live near it.'

No one knew where the money had come from for his education. Mrs Gwyn was one of the most successful boat owners on the coast, but even she would have struggled to find the funds needed for top-drawer legal training. There were whispers of a mysterious benefactor – but then, there were whispers about a lot of things.

Including the identity of Richard's father. There had been a half-remembered scandal when she'd sailed into Penmor Harbour with Richard in her womb and no chance that her deceased husband was the father, and there were still whispered stories of a less-than-upright past.

No one, though, could imagine Penmor without her, especially as a significant number of the village's young men worked for her in the summer months. She paid them fairly and treated them well. She even let them keep a small share of the catch. But if one more fish than their allotted ration went home with them, they never got work from her again.

There were plenty of lads to replace them, and the men in her employ cheered and whistled whenever she appeared at the dock.

'We haven't seen you in a week,' said Sarah's husband, Jack, when Mrs Gwyn came to see off the fleet on one of the last trips of the summer. 'We thought you'd forgotten about us!'

'Such a handsome flotilla?' she said. 'I'd never.'

Jack vaulted up to the dock from the boat he'd been standing in, and drew close to her. 'Should we worry about you, Mrs Gwyn? Have you need of anything?'

'You're sweet, Jack. No, please only worry about the fish. There's nothing wrong with me save the occasional creak. To be expected

I suppose. Do you know, since Enid Luttrell died I'm the oldest person in the village.'

'And the most creative. You have my boy believing in otters with duckbills, and giant jumping rats. And sea dragons, of course. I haven't the heart to tell him it's make-believe.'

'Oh, you must never do that,' said Mrs Gwyn. 'If they don't listen to the fantasies, they will never hear the truth.'

AUTHOR'S NOTE

This novel is based on the life of Mary Bryant, the woman behind one of history's most daring escapes. Many of the major elements are based on events which actually occurred and people who actually lived. It is, however, a work of fiction, and some elements of the story have been changed or invented.

Jenny versus Mary

Mary was illiterate, so there's no record of her thoughts and feelings, and the only record of her words is in court transcripts. We can only guess, based on her actions, at her personality and what she felt. It seemed wrong to ascribe thoughts, emotions and beliefs to her when I had no idea whether they were actually hers; it felt better to have a fictional character who could fully own all of this.

A few characters have been named after their real-life counterparts: Charlotte, Emanuel, Dolly, Will and Mary's victim Agnes Lakeman. All of the ships are named after those of the First and Second Fleets, and others that visited the colony.

Mary's early life

Mary Broad (or Braund, as she is in some official documents) was born on or around 1 May 1765 to Will and Grace Broad of Fowey, Cornwall. She had a sister, Dolly, who went into service, and a brother who died in infancy.

There's no evidence her father was a smuggler, although it can't be ruled out. He was certainly a mariner, and like others in Fowey would have been hit hard by the combination of the disappearance of the pilchards and steep taxes on the salt needed to preserve them.

The death of Will Broad's fictional counterpart, Will Trelawney, is the first of a number of departures from historical fact.

We don't know an awful lot about the circumstances surrounding Mary's descent into crime, and Mr Black is a complete fiction. However, court documents list her as a forest dweller, and she was convicted of robbing Agnes Lakeman. Two other women – Mary Haydon and Catherine Fryer – were also convicted in relation to the crime, and were also transported. There is no way of knowing if Mary's relationship with them mirrored that of Jenny with Elenor and Bea. The courtroom scenes throughout the novel are fabricated.

Transportation and the colony

Jenny meets her future husband Dan Gwyn (and sympathetic officer Captain James Corbett) aboard the hulk *Dunkirk* and makes the journey to Australia with them on the *Charlotte*. Mary met her husband Will Bryant (transported for resisting a revenue officer) under the same circumstances, and also seems to have had a good relationship with Watkin Tench, the inspiration for Corbett.

We don't know the identity of another important man in Mary's life: Charlotte's father. The name Mary gave for her child's father was Spence, but no one of that name appears on the *Dunkirk's* manifest – and given the date of Charlotte's birth, the *Dunkirk* would certainly have been where Mary conceived.

Dan's flogging, the reasons behind it, and his insistence that his marriage wasn't valid are all based on fact, as is the edict preventing convicts with dependents from leaving the colony; however, Joe and Elenor's role in the flogging and in Jenny and Dan's dispossession are invented.

Pietr Vorst is based on Dutch captain Detmer Smit, who did have a vicious argument with Governor Arthur Phillip over supplies and the cost of passage from their colony. He sold Mary and Will a chart, quadrant and two muskets.

The Bryants also appear to have had a friendship with Bennelong and Barangaroo, on whom Yarramundi and Mawberry are based. Jenny's interactions with Mawberry are fictional (and it's unlikely she was the one to introduce native sarsaparilla to the colonists), but the help Dan receives when his boat capsizes is broadly based on an actual incident. We will never know whether Bennelong farewelled the Bryants as Yarramundi does the Gwyns.

The escape

The journey to Kupang, West Timor (or Coepang, as it was known in the late eighteenth century) took sixty-nine days for both Jenny and Mary; however, Mary made more stops, including a likely visit to Moreton Bay in Queensland. We know this because James Martin, one of Mary's fellow escapees, left a bare-bones description that is the only existing personal account of the voyage. It has been wonderfully interpreted by Tim Causer of University College London. Will Bryant apparently also wrote an account, but this has been lost.

On the subject of the escapees, I have greatly reduced the

number of people in the boat. Mary and Will escaped with nine other convicts in addition to their two children.

In *The Girl from Botany Bay*, Carolly Erickson suggests Mary tied her children to the bench or to herself, and I have adopted this as it's hard to see how the children could have survived otherwise.

It does seem as though Will was to blame for the group's recapture after two months in Kupang. Martin says that Will argued with Mary and betrayed everyone. In *To Brave Every Danger*, Judith Cook suggests it is unlikely Will would have done so in a premeditated way, as such a betrayal would probably result in his own death. I agree, and have used a combination of drunkenness and pride as the cause of their recapture.

Captain Edward Edwards was every bit as vile as his fictional counterpart, Andrews, and did indeed have a cage known as Pandora's box in which he kept the *Bounty* mutineers captured at Otaheite (Tahiti). His treatment of the convicts probably cost Will Bryant and little Emanuel their lives. They died in Batavia (Indonesia), not aboard ship as they do in the book.

Shortly afterwards, aboard the *Gorgon*, Mary saw Watkin Tench again, as Jenny sees Corbett. Reflecting on the meeting, Tench wrote: 'I confess that I never looked at these people without pity and astonishment. They had miscarried in a heroic struggle for liberty, having combated every hardship and conquered every difficulty.' As Jenny's daughter does, little Charlotte Bryant died aboard the *Gorgon* and was buried at sea.

Mary's hearings before the stipendiary magistrate would have taken place in an office rather than a courtroom, and there is no evidence that people visited her cell in Newgate for entertainment (though the practice wasn't unknown).

As for the other significant man in Mary's life, James Boswell did put her up in a house and then sent her a stipend after she returned to Cornwall, until his death. The nature of their relationship remains uncertain, although there was at least one risqué poem about them that did the rounds of London.

And that is the last we know of Mary for certain. Another Mary Bryant married in a different part of Cornwall many years later, but as Judith Cook points out, the girl from Botany Bay (as she was dubbed by writer Frederick Pottle) would have been in her late forties at a time when female life expectancy was forty.

So the epilogue is a complete fabrication: I wrote for Jenny the ending I feel Mary deserves.

The books and documents I relied on in writing this story include:

- *A Complete Account of the Settlement at Port Jackson in New South Wales*, Watkin Tench
- *An Account of the English Colony in New South Wales*, David Collins
- *The Voyage of Arthur Phillip to Botany Bay*, Arthur Phillip
- *Memorandoms by James Martin*, ed. Tim Causer, University College London
- *The Transportation, Escape and Pardoning of Mary Bryant*, C.H. Currey
- *Boswell and the Girl from Botany Bay*, Frederick A. Pottle
- *To Brave Every Danger*, Judith Cook
- *The Girl from Botany Bay*, Carolly Erickson
- *Mary Bryant – Her Life and Escape from Botany Bay*, Jonathan King
- *1788: The Brutal Truth of the First Fleet*, David Hill
- *The Colony*, Grace Karskens

ACKNOWLEDGEMENTS

I owe more than I can say to Tom and Judy Keneally, both generally and in relation to this book. Tom is the one who first told me the story of Mary Bryant, and he and Judy were massively generous with their time in reading early drafts and giving feedback.

I'm also indebted to Jonathan King for his advice, Tony Curtis for sharing his maritime expertise, Gay Hendrickson for her friendship and historical nous, and Aunty Edna Watson for reading the book from an Aboriginal perspective.

Of course there's no book without a publisher, and I'm so grateful to Angela Meyer of Bonnier Publishing Australia for her unflagging passion and commitment to the project.

I'm also indebted to my agent, Fiona Inglis, for believing in this book from the beginning.

Finally, to Craig, Rory and Alex, for putting up with the strange creature tapping away in the corner. I love you all.